PAINTED
RED

Painted Red

ALINA HARPER

<h1 style="text-align:center">Tropes & Content Warnings</h1>

Dear Reader,

This book contains scenes and themes that some may find distressing so please read the contents below before continuing.

Tropes

Set in the Pacific Northwest, instalove, why-choose turned throuple relationship, childhood enemies-to-lovers, one bed, grumpy x sunshine, opposites attract, forced proximity, strong FMC, hurt/comfort (lots of it)

Content Warnings

Explicit language, mature sexual content, talk of loss of a parent through illness, stalking, blood and gore depiction, talk of domestic violence, murder, abduction, gassing, graphic depiction of a cat having a seizure, mention of animal death, anxiety, depression

Book Playlist

Perfect — Anne-Marie
Red — Taylor Swift
Golden (feat. Sia) — Travie McCoy
18 — One Direction
Feel so Close (Radio Edit) — Calvin Harris
What About Us — P!NK
Midnight Rain — Taylor Swift
Close to Me — Ellie Goulding, Diplo & Swae Lee
Hide and Seek — Lizz Robinett
that way — Tate McRae
Stay With Me — Sam Smith
8 Letters — Why Don't We
White Walls (feat. ScHoolboy Q & Hollis) — Macklemore &
Ryan Lewis
Hold On — Chord Overstreet
Afterglow — Taylor Swift
Are You With Me — nilu
Dollhouse — Melanie Martinez
Lover — Taylor Swift
One Day — Matisyahu
Dark Red — Steve Lacy

Whispering — Alex Clare
You Can Run — Adam Jones
Where the Watermelons Rot — Madelynne Whitt
Unsteady (Erich Lee Gravity Remix) — X Ambassadors
Rescue — Lauren Daigle
I'd Come for You — Nickelback

Dedication

To women everywhere.
Never forget your strength.

Chapter One

TATUM

"He got bailed out of jail today," my best friend, Maya, reminds me. Even through my phone's speaker, I can sense she's rolling her eyes. "Mommy's money is coming in handy once again."

"Yeah, I know. My sister told me what happened earlier."

My ex-boyfriend getting arrested for domestic violence is the reason why the view I'm looking at right now is water-logged pine branches instead of skyscrapers. Not that I mind the change, though. As someone who was born and raised in Dallas, Texas, I eventually found the city to be exhausting. Dallas is just a handful of minutes away from my parents' estate and many people moved into the city in search of an opportunity. It was time for me to move out of it, though, for the very same reason. That's how I landed in Maple Crest. It's a small city that's nestled at the base of a mountain with giant maple trees that line the main street. Many of the old homes feature historical plaques beside their front doors. Due to the almost always overcast weather here, it sometimes feels like time has stopped in the middle of Fall. That's one of the reasons why I moved to this particular town in the Pacific Northwest in the first place. I've always loved the weather most people hated; a strong wind that shakes the treetops, lightning that lights up the night sky, and above all else, rain. Standing by the window with a warm mug of cocoa, I soak in the sight. The sky is dark gray today and it's starting to rain. To me, rain means comfort, and there's plenty of that here.

Thinking back to what Maya and I are discussing, I know I got lucky regarding what my ex did to me. The first time he raised his hands to me was the only time. I made sure of that. He attacked me, and once the shock wore off, I wasn't afraid to hit him back when he tried to take things even further. Once I managed to subdue him, I called the cops. Because there was physical evidence of what he did marking my body, he got arrested, and I remained free on the terms of self-defense. Unfortunately, however, there's hardly any real justice when the wealthy are involved. Both of our families have money. His just has more.

"I was seriously hoping that someone was going to shiv that motherf—"

"Maya," I interrupt, then let out a breathy chuckle. "Jesus."

"What? You wished for it too. I know you did."

There's a pause in our conversation because we both know that she's right. People like Lucas are dangerous and are likely going to snap any day. He didn't show signs of violence before we got together; otherwise, I wouldn't have committed myself to him. But before I kicked his ass, I could see in his eyes that he enjoyed the pain he inflicted on me. Lucas is not only capable of, but will do worse in the not-too-distant future. It's just a matter of time before he lowers himself to that level again.

"I wish all this shit didn't make you have to move away. You've only been gone for three months, but I miss you like crazy," she admits.

"What happened with him wasn't what made me want to move. It was my decision and something I was already considering before that happened." I let my hand fall away from my neck where I swear I can still feel the bruise Lucas left. "I miss you too, though."

She sighs, "As soon as I can, I'm taking a trip down there. Got it?"

"Got it," I affirm. "Hey, I've got to get going, but I'll call you later."

"Okay, fine. Be safe, Tatum. Love you."

"Love you too."

Feeling something rub against my legs as I hang up, I look down to see my cat's emerald-green eyes staring back at me. Coincidentally, they are the same shade and color as my own. He's a pain in the ass and was the kitten nobody else wanted from a stray litter Maya had found a few years ago. Lenny was dumped on me out of the blue once she got too busy to take care of him. I was less than thrilled about it at first, but he's my pain in the ass and has become my little shadow ever since.

"The move was worth it, don't you think, Lenny?" He meows his response and rubs against my leg again. Moving here vastly differs from the big city I grew up in. Still, after my uncle died earlier this year and left his small, cabin-like home to his next of kin, my dad, the decision to move here was a no-brainer. My dad was going to sell the place if I didn't take up residence so there was no point in letting the opportunity go to waste.

Like me, my uncle chose to live a different life than the rest of the family. Because of that decision, though, we never had much of a relationship with him. His relationship with the rest of the family fizzled out at some point, so he never came to see us, and we never came here to see him. I wonder what he'd think about me doing the same thing he did. In the same house even.

My parents fit in well with big city life. Mom is a well known surgeon, and Dad is the CEO of a bank. Together, they wouldn't be caught dead in a home like this. Not if it meant leaving their huge estate with an inside pool, a chandelier in the foyer, too many bedrooms that never get used, and hired staff.

As I pull my sandy blonde hair into a braid and throw on a

coat, I can't help but think of how vastly different the last home that I shared with Lucas was compared to this one. He'd moved in with me, then complained constantly about the apartment since it wasn't as lavish as what we were both used to. My parents had offered to pay my rent for a much nicer place, but I liked the satisfaction of independence. That little apartment was all I could afford from selling my artwork at the time. However, *I* didn't like that every time I left my door, there were always too many people. Seclusion was a rare delicacy before I came here. Now, on the other hand, pretty much the only way I run into someone is if it's on purpose.

The town is a five-minute drive from my new home, and running into hikers on the trail behind my house isn't too common. That's not because there's a lack of outdoor enthusiasts, though. In fact, the town thrives on the citizens' love for the outdoors. It's just rare to run into someone since the amount of public land is so vast. In a more populated area, being alone would probably be intimidating. But from what research tells me, there's hardly any crime in Maple Crest.

Stepping outside, I walk across my backyard to where my property line ends, and the public land starts. I love that aspect of this place. My land seems never-ending, with a whole pine-filled forest at my feet. Today, it'll serve as the perfect distraction to clear my mind of Lucas' release back into an unsuspecting society.

Both sides of the drenched wooden walkway are lined with thick, dark green vegetation from the abundance of moisture caused by rain and lingering humidity. Some places resemble a rainforest so closely I have to remind myself I live here, as unreal as that is, with its incredible beauty.

I've walked along this path several times during the last two months, and although the view could never get old, I want to see what other sights this place is hiding behind its branches. Taking a chance, I step off the boarded path and venture into unexplored territory to find something new. As I walk, wet leaves sway against my black leggings. I can feel the coldness through the material, so I make a mental note to wear thicker pants the next time I leave the main trail.

For a while, time escapes me as I walk. I become so engulfed in thought that I hardly even notice when there's a large, dark shape up ahead of me on the trail, though it's difficult to tell what it is through the swaying branches. Curiosity gets the best of me, and I take a couple of cautious footsteps forward, trying to get a better look at the moving object ahead. When I get closer, my heart tinges with fear as the shape bounds through the foliage into a clearing. That's when I'm able to see its full image. Standing a short distance away from me is a black bear, its hide glistening with rain as it stares back at me. Knowing that black bears are usually timid and scared of people helps shift my fear to excitement at this experience. This is the closest I've ever been to a wild mammal, especially one of this size.

I want to paint this moment.

The whole scene is ethereal. We stare at each other for a minute longer before it turns and runs into the pine trees and into the thick fog that's rapidly making its way down the mountain, coming my way. Deciding it would be in my best interest to turn around, I start to make my way back home, but my surroundings become harder to see with each passing second due to the settling fog. Maple Crest doesn't have a lot of crime, but there isn't a shortage of hikers who get lost, sometimes for good, in the surrounding mountains. Often, it's hikers who have a hell of a lot more experience than I do since Dallas isn't exactly known for its abundance of mountainous trails.

As I move along a narrow path next to a slope, the rock I step on comes loose, sending me tumbling recklessly down the steep hill. After landing roughly at the bottom, I cry in pain as I try to stand, only for my ankle to give out underneath me.

"Damn it," I curse through gritted teeth. Pulling my cell phone from my coat pocket, I hold it high, trying to get cell service with no luck. "Hello?" I yell from my spot on the ground. "Can anybody hear me? I need help!" My only response is the echo of my voice. I curse again. Thinking of the bear I saw mere minutes ago; my mind can't help but wander to the thought of dying down here. I'm going to end up as bear scat after it uses my dead body to fill its stomach.

Pulling on the plants around me to act as a pulley, I try hobbling and climbing back to the top, but the rain has made the ground beneath me too soft to support my weight. Pulling on one of the bushes, its roots rip from the soil, and I'm sent falling to the bottom of the hill all over again. My leggings are streaked with more mud now, and the skin on my hands is marred with thin lines of blood.

"What the *hell* are you doing down there?" a low, slightly English-accented voice calls down to me. My head shoots up, and through the faint haze of the fog, I see a man who appears to be in their mid-twenties, same as me, in a dark jean jacket, black jeans, and black hiking boots staring down at me.

"Thank God. Please help me get out of here. I think my ankle is broken. I can't walk."

The man starts to side-step down the hill making his way towards me. "Silly girl, why on earth did you go hiking in the rain?"

"If I waited for it to stop raining before leaving the house, I would be shut in for months. Plus, you're doing the same thing, so...."

"I suppose you're right." He squats down in front of me. "May I?" he asks, gesturing towards the injured ankle. I nod, and he unlaces my boot. I wince as he pulls it off and slides my sock almost entirely off my foot, then shudder at the sudden coldness. *I'm so glad I had clean socks today.* "Oh, darling, it doesn't seem to be broken, but you've got a pretty gnarly sprain." The stranger carefully places the sock back on my foot but hands me the boot. He stands up and extends a hand to help me balance on my good foot, then turns around, showing me his back with a slight squat.

"Hop on," he tells me. As awkward as it will be to jump onto the stranger's back, I don't have any other choice, so with some assistance, I do.

There's a slight struggle getting back to the top of the steep hill, but he does it with much more ease than my failed attempt and holds on to my thighs to keep me secure as he starts the walk back to my house. *Maya is going to love this story.* While he follows my instructions on where to take me, I introduce myself.

"I'm Tatum Davis, by the way. And you are?"

"Anthony Kensington,"

"Wow, sounds prestigious."

He laughs lightly, and I find that it's a charming sound. "That word works. Though many people may consider having that family name is to be anathematized."

My brows lift behind his back. "Huh. That doesn't make me nervous about being injured and literally in your arms, seeing as to how we just met."

Anthony chuckles again, then sighs, "I suppose it wouldn't. I'm sorry. Let me try that again. My last name might hold high status, but having admiration and respect are other stories. In some instances, that is."

"From where I'm currently sitting, I'd say you have both of those, and I am *very* happy to have met you, Anthony. You could've left me to be someone else's problem or bear poop, but you didn't. I'm not sure what I would have done if you hadn't come along."

"Oh please, a strong girl like yourself? You would have figured it out. I simply sped up the process. I've seen grown men in tears from an injury like yours, yet all you did was curse at the universe."

Once we return to the house, he sets me down on my back porch and turns to face me where I stand on one foot in front of the door.

"I know I've said it already but thank you again." I look

around, trying to think of something I can do to make it up to him. "Can I get you a drink or something to warm you up?"

"No, I better be going, but thank you," Anthony declines. He asks if I need further help to get inside, but I shake my head with a smile, telling him I'll manage. "I'll see you around, Miss Davis." With that, he turns and walks away right back into the forest.

Getting settled inside the house proves to be a more difficult task than I'd expected with my freshly sprained ankle, but after I get into some pajamas and curl up on my lounge chair, I decide to call the only friend I have in this town and ask her to come over. While I wait for her arrival, I almost look up Lucas' social media accounts, but I decide to look up my handsome rescuer's name instead. Despite his profile being relatively empty and made up mostly of scenery pictures with only the occasional photo of himself, he has thousands of followers. Pulling up the first picture of him I see, I feel my face flush and I swear the temperature went up ten degrees. The man is super-hot. Like an age-appropriate, fan-fiction version of Draco Malfoy which, as a fervent member of AO3, I really appreciate. He'd been wearing a beanie when we met so I couldn't see his light blonde hair before. Now that I can, I see it perfectly matches his gray eyes. In the picture, he's wearing an all-black suit while at the bar of a diner, pouring syrup over a stack of pancakes and giving a playful, yet scolding look to whoever was taking his picture. The fancy clothes make him look out of place, yet the scene seems to work together perfectly anyway.

I'm looking at the picture, admiring it, and considering sketching it for practice since I'm an artist, and he'd be a beautiful subject when Lenny jumps onto the arm of the chair. He knocks the phone out of my hand, making it fall flat onto my blanket-covered lap as he gives me an envious stare, wanting to be the center of my attention.

"Don't worry, buddy. I'm only looking. You know you're still my number one guy," I soothe as I scratch behind his ear. Satisfied with the affection he's receiving, Lenny lifts his tail and steps off the arm of the chair and onto my lap so he can lie down. In doing so, he also steps on the phone screen. He manages to push multiple things, including the 'like' button to Anthony's photo. "No, no, no, no, no." I panic as I lift the screen in front of my face, hoping the illuminated red heart I saw was a trick caused by the angle I was looking at it from. But nope. It looks the same, the red heart filled in, even as I twist and turn the phone and find no trick at all. The year-old photo has officially been 'liked.'

"Lenny!" I exclaim though I could never really be mad at him. A loud groan leaves me as I bounce the now-locked device off my forehead. That's when I hear my friend walk through the front door.

"Clearly, I missed something," she acknowledges.

"Hey, Nyasia, you didn't miss much. Just the reason why I'm going to hide away for the rest of my life." I lower the phone so I can look at my newest friend. Her long, curly black hair is pulled back and she's still wearing her work shirt. She must have come straight from the café. Though she complains about the diner almost daily and always tells me she's going to quit, she's constantly picking up extra shifts to save money. Her biggest goal is to save up enough to get out of town. She says Maple Crest holds no opportunities, only a depressing future. After high school, the options are apparently limited; you either end up a logger, changing sheets at the motel, or as a waitress. She's good at her job, but she doesn't bother to hide her displeasure of being stuck in a small town where most people never leave. Even to the patrons she serves. That's how she and I met. On my third day after the move, I stopped by TreeCutter café for breakfast. We connected instantly over the feeling of not belonging somewhere. The difference between us, of course, is that I was able to leave for somewhere that's better suited for what I currently need in life, and she isn't.

After Nyasia sits in the cushioned chair opposite mine, I explain everything to her, starting with the bear and ending at Lenny accidentally announcing to Anthony that I'm a stalker. I reject a blunt from her, though she claims it would take the pain away, and then she makes a fire in the fireplace. Once the flame is lit, we start a movie night to get my mind off the pain of my incredibly swollen joint. As if we're still teenagers in high school, we stay up too late and eat too much junk food before passing out in the living room in front of the glowing TV screen and the dimming light of a dying flame.

Chapter Two

TATUM

It's been two weeks since I sprained my ankle. The first week I spent limping around on crutches Nyasia had packed away from the time she tore her ACL. Now, I can walk around without their assistance. So as long as I don't spend too much time on the joint without taking a break.

My hopeful eyes scan the faces around me whenever I go into town. Each time, I look for a particular blonde-haired someone, but I'm never there long, and I haven't seen Anthony again. By the time week two since the injury came around and I could ditch the crutches, I'd given up on seeing him again. I chalked him up to be a passerby on the move. From what I've been told, that's not unusual for Maple Crest. People always pass through, but no one seems to stay. If they do, then it's not for long. Usually only a single night or two.

Walking into the coffee shop this morning, I'm greeted by Nick, the sociable barista I'd become friends with after the first few times he'd taken my order. He gives an excited shout of my name and a wave. Multiple sets of eyes turn to stare at me, but I pay no attention to them. Walking through that front door is like walking through the door to my own little utopia every day. I'd gotten so used to being overlooked in the big city, even when family surrounded me, that something as simple as the barista taking the time to get to know me is part of the reason why I pay for overpriced coffee every day rather than making my own.

"You getting your usual?" he asks, but he already knows the answer. He's seen me come in nearly every day for months now. I always order the same thing; a large, iced coffee with three pumps of vanilla, two pumps of hazelnut, heavy cream, and extra caramel drizzle. I know the drink is more of a dessert than it is coffee, but there's nothing wrong with treating yourself. And I don't care how cold it is outside; my drink will *always* be iced.

"You know it," I wink in reply. Nick's teeth look impossibly white as he gives me another handsome smile. At the same time, he finishes the order he was working on before coming to the register to ring up my treat for the day. Nick is beautiful with his light blue eyes, rich brown skin, perfectly styled dark hair, and the right amount of stubble he clearly takes the time to manicure. Unfortunately for everyone in the world, though, he's already in a committed long-distance relationship. One which he's very happy in otherwise, I'd have taken a shot at being with him myself weeks ago. Maybe I would have even tried to set him up with Maya, telling them to work through her packed schedule because I know they'd be perfect together.

As if I could forget, Nick reminds me of the price, when a smooth, accented voice behind me leaves goosebumps on my skin.

"I'll pay for it."

Turning around, I'm met with the sight of a tall, platinum-blonde man dressed in an all-black suit. *Anthony*.

"Oh, you don't have to do that." My cheeks start blushing the moment I lock eyes with his vibrant gray irises, and I hope a smile will cover up my awkwardness. I feel almost positive that there's a neon sign saying *I THINK YOU'RE SUPER HOT!* shining brightly all over my face. Subtlety has never been a strong suit of mine.

"Please, it would be my pleasure," he smiles, clearly having read the invisible sign loud and clear. He orders a tea for himself, then hands Nick some cash, telling him to keep the change. Anthony turns to face me once he's finished paying and asks if I'd like to share a table. We walk towards a table for two by the window, and each take a seat. Rather than look at him, I gaze around the room at everything else the cozy space has to offer, even though I already have the interior of this place memorized. But doing so doesn't take much effort since there are only three double seated tables along the large windows, a couple of cushioned chairs off to one side, and a booth in the corner. Meanwhile, I can feel Anthony staring straight at me. "I see your ankle is feeling better," he finally breaks the silence between us.

"Yeah, I mean, it still hurts a little bit if I spend too much time on my feet, but I don't have to ride on any more strangers' backs to get around." I laugh along with him as he chuckles, but I'm cringing at my response the second he leaves to grab our drinks.

"Now that you're doing better," he starts again as he pushes my cup along the table before me, "I was wondering if you'd like to get some pancakes. After all, you do seem to fancy them." I choke a little bit on the sip I'd just taken, and I'm sure my face turns some dark shade of red. It's mortifying that he brought up liking his picture, let alone remembers that it happened at all. Surely, he's regretting his last statement thanks to my less-than-flattering reaction, but when I look at him, he's holding a smug smile. "Do you not like pancakes?" he teases, clearly amused by seeing me caught off guard like this.

"What? No, pancakes are great! I— I love pancakes, actually," I hurry for an explanation. "I just— I didn't mean to like that picture. In fact, I didn't. My cat liked it by accident when he stepped on my phone." He raises his brows. "Not that I didn't think your picture was great, because it was, just, no buttons were meant to be pressed, and he pressed one."

Anthony clicks his tongue. "Well, that's a shame," he laughs at my still-reddening cheeks. They must be trying to set a new record or something for how dark of a shade my face can get. *I wonder what shade I am right now since I can't see my reflection anywhere and can only feel the heat from my face. Am I a cute 'Santa's rosy cheeks' kind of red, or am I more of a 'Santa's hat' kind of red?* "I was hoping to take you to get a stack, but it looks like I'll be taking your cat instead."

I laugh. "I'd love to get pancakes with you." The bell above the door chimes, and Anthony's whole demeanor changes when he sees the group of two men and one woman that walk in. Like Anthony, they're all dressed in rich clothes that seem out of place given their current location. The man in front exposes a mature and stern face as he looks around the room. He meets Anthony's stare for a moment, then looks away.

"Tomorrow morning at TreeCutter Cafe, 9 o'clock. It was lovely to see you again, Miss Davis. I'm glad to see your ankle is better." Anthony hurriedly leaves and meets up with the small group who sit at a table in the corner. Based on their expressions, they appear to be discussing something important as I walk out of the building.

The first thing I see when I get outside are the three cars that look like they cost more than every single penny that every citizen of Maple Crest makes in a year, combined two times over. Having wealthy parents who like to show off their money, as do their friends, I learned to be able to identify expensive vehicles. In the lot of the small town are a matte black Audi R8 with tinted windows and electric blue accents, a cherry red Draco GTE, and a black Kawasaki Ninja 1000 with electric green accents. *I wonder if one of these is Anthony's or if they belong to the three people he met up with.*

And then there's my car. A gray Mercedes C Class that currently has Nyasia leaning against it. It's still nicer than most people's cars here, but not on the same level as theirs.

"Was that Anthony Kensington you were talking to in there?"

"Yeah, that's the guy who helped me back to my house when I sprained my ankle." Once the car is turned on, I blast the heater. Although I love this dreary weather, that doesn't mean I enjoy its coldness. Because I don't. At all. I only like looking at it while covered in comfy layers through a window where I'm nice and warm on the other side. "I told you his name, remember?"

"Only his first name," Nyasia states while 'fixing' her makeup in the mirror in my passenger seat. Both of us are artists. But where I use paint and a flat canvas, she uses makeup, and her canvas is her face. She's incredibly talented, and I'm waiting for the day the right person will see the makeup videos she makes on YouTube and TikTok. She's got the talent to make it amongst all the big names of makeup. My friend just doesn't have the time to sit and record videos constantly to prove it. "Besides, I was a little bit faded when you told me. One of those flashy vehicles that scream *look at me; I'm an asshole who likes to show off all the money I have to you poor folks* is his." Guess that answers my question.

I choose to ignore her passive aggression. "So, you know him, then?"

"Mmm," Nyasia bites her plump, freshly glossed lip in thought. "I mean, not personally. But by reputation, I guess. I saw that Clay walked in. That's Anthony's dad and another proud owner of one of the douche mobiles. He's a real piece of work. That's what some of the people around town say anyways. You'd have to go to one of the other cities around us to find anyone that likes him. But yeah, they moved back here like three years ago, I guess? They moved from London when Anthony was a little kid, spent a few years here, then moved back. He was a couple of grades ahead of me. I don't know what they find so fascinating about this place, though." If he was a couple of grades ahead of her, then that must mean he's twenty-five. Only one year older than I am, since Nyasia is a single year younger than me.

"And Anthony? Is he like his dad, reputation-wise?"

"Sort of. Anthony's not as bad, but he's not the nicest guy out there. What were you two talking about anyway?"

I tell her about our date tomorrow morning, but Nyasia makes a face of disapproval.

"I don't know. I'd be careful with that one, Tatum."

Though I'm grateful for her input, I've always preferred to make my own judgments on things rather than listen to what everyone else has to say. I'm more considering when it comes to people, of course, but I still barely know Nyasia. I only met her three months ago so I'm still getting to know her. She's a take-no-bullshit, open, and honest sort of person. That makes it pretty easy to know where and with who she stands for the most part, but still. I prefer coming to my own conclusions about things because you never know what you might miss out on if you don't take the chance. *But then again, no one told me to be careful around Lucas...*

Would I have even listened then if they had?

I take Nyasia home and watch her pretend to hang herself as she walks up the driveway to the side door of her parent's house, which she rents the bottom half of, then go home to add to the painting I've been working on. I've been selling my art for about two years now and it still blows my mind that people spend their money on something I created. I'm not a big name, yet, and I don't feel like a professional yet either, but like Nyasia, I'll get there. Someday.

MY EYES SHOOT open in the dark after a nightmare gets a little too intense. Feeling uneasy, I slip my feet into the slippers I left on the side of my bed and put a kettle of water on the stove. Lenny followed me into the kitchen and meows now at my feet.

"What is it, buddy?" I ask him. I know that technically it isn't logical to ask your cat questions, but it helps the occasional feelings of loneliness one gets when living alone. Lenny meows again and rubs against my leg so I bend down to pick him up, groaning a little on the way back up since he's a 15-pound tom cat. In the orange light from the bulb above the stove, we sway back and forth, two-stepping to no music until the water is hot enough for a mug of hot chocolate. It's my current hyper-fixation drink, so I've been drinking it like crazy.

Since the clock reads 5:47, I decide to stay awake rather than go back to bed. I turn on the lamp in the living room and pick a book off the shelf, reading until sunlight is pouring through the windows, and the clock now reads 8:00. That is, as much sunlight as your average gloomy day in Maple Crest allows.

Deciding it's time to start getting ready for my breakfast with Anthony, I flip through everything in my closet five times. No matter how many times I push the hangers from one side of my closet to the other, I don't see any date-worthy clothes. I gave a lot of my stuff to my sister before moving to make things easier and because a lot of it wouldn't match the weather here. But to be honest, part of me regrets doing that every time I see a picture of her wearing something that used to be mine. I especially regret it now that I don't have a lot of cute date outfits to choose from.

After things went down with Lucas several months ago, I wasn't looking, or even ready, for a new relationship. But I'm starting over here and I think I'm ready if the right person comes around. I won't let what happened in the past keep me from new opportunities.

Picking out a burnt orange sweater dress that compliments my body, some tights to help mask the paleness of my legs, and black high-heeled ankle boots, I touch up my curls from the day before and am out the door. Reaching the diner, a little earlier than we planned, I'm not worried Anthony isn't here yet, so I take the initiative of getting us a table while I wait for him.

By 9:05, I start to wonder about his tardiness but blame it on traffic. Even though traffic is something nearly nonexistent in this town. The only traffic occurs at the coffee shop and the diner, which is where I am, and he is not.

By 9:15, the crowds of people coming in for a weekend breakfast is hard to ignore. I try not to feel guilty occupying a perfectly good table while couples and families wait in line for one by the door. I shoot the rest of my water back like it's a shot of liquor and regret not getting his number yesterday so that I could call him. Or actually, *he* should be calling *me* since he's the one that's running late. That's just common courtesy.

By 9:30, I can longer deal with the pitiful looks from people who no doubt know I'm being stood up. Before getting up to leave, I put a $20 bill on the table for Nyasia who's working this section today even though all I had was a cup of water. It's my apology for taking up space. Walking across the street to the coffee shop, I'm greeted again by Nick who whistles at my appearance.

I give him a small smile and a twirl so he can see the whole outfit, even though I'm not in the best of moods anymore. "How's it going this morning?" I ask after I approach the counter.

"It's another beautiful day," he chimes as he starts making my drink and gestures to me with one hand. "Speaking of beautiful, you look great. Is there any particular reason?"

"Thank you!" My smile spreads a little wider as my coffee shop utopia quickly begins to brighten my gloomy start to the day. "I had a date."

Nick looks at the watch on his wrist. "And it's over by 9:35 in the morning?" A look of realization crosses over his handsome face. "Or is it only now ending from last night?"

I let out a quiet scoff. "It never even started, actually. The guy never showed." My shoulders bounce up and down in a shrug that I hope comes off as careless. I'm not crushed by being stood up, but it wasn't the best feeling in the world.

Nick frowns while he places the coffee cup in front of me. "He didn't show? Who was your date supposed to be with?"

"Anthony Kensington." I pull my wallet from my purse, but Nick waves me off.

"Don't worry about it. It's on me today," he smiles. I urge him to let me pay, but he declines so I drop the cash in the tip jar when he briefly turns around to answer another employee's question before he faces me again. "I was worried about Anthony getting to you when I saw him talking to you yesterday. Look, I know we only know each other within these walls, but would you allow me to give you some advice?" I agree before taking a sip from my cup. "Anthony is...a difficult person. His family isn't the kind of people you want to be associated with. They have a reputation for being cruel at times."

"Cruel how?" I question.

"His dad, Clay, has put a lot of people out of business by buying their companies and kicking them out of it, leaving them broke. That family believes that anyone below their status isn't worth their time or respect. So, that being said, I'd like to set you up with a friend of mine. He's a good guy, and I promise he won't stand you up."

I think about the offer momentarily then grab a napkin and a pen, writing my name and number down, having learned my lesson. "Sure, why not?" I smile. "Tell him to give me a call sometime.

We say goodbye, and I head back to my car to go home and finish a particular painting I've been working on. It's a 24x36" oil painting of the bear I saw in the forest. Before I paint, I connect my phone to my Bluetooth speaker so I can start singing along to Anne-Marie. I let myself forget about my public humiliation of waiting for someone who never showed up by drowning myself in the confidence the song '*Perfect*' never fails to give me. Then, I get lost in my work for hours. Only when the sky is dark, and my back feels like it's been stomped on by elephants due to my horrible posture do I realize I haven't even eaten yet. Stretching my arms over my head first, then stretching out the rest of my body, I groan out loud as I get my muscles to loosen up and then check the time. The diner will be open for another hour, so I hurry and call to place a to-go order since I don't feel like cooking tonight.

One more day, and I'll have this project done. It's been a massive pain in the ass — or rather, pain in the back — but I love how it's been coming along. Part of me wants to keep it, like I usually want to keep every project I accomplish. But I'm also excited to list it on my website for that little rush of making a sale. That might take a little while, though. With the move, and getting set up here, I took a little bit of time to myself. Now my sales are struggling a little bit. Maybe I should get more social media apps to promote my work. The problem with that is that I've never been very good at social media.

Since Nyasia was working this morning, she wasn't there for the closing shift tonight meaning I'm in and out of the diner in two minutes. As I'm pulling back into my driveway, my phone screen lights up with a call and it starts to vibrate. 'Unknown' is all it says, and I find myself hoping it's Anthony calling to apologize for standing me up.

A little too eagerly, I answer. "Hello?"

"Hi, Tatum?"

My lips twist in disappointment at the lack of an English accent on the other line. "This is her."

"My name is Hayden, I'm Nick's friend. I hope I'm not calling too late, but he talked you up so much that I couldn't wait to call you and ask if you'd like to go out with me."

I stay seated in my parked car and grin a little. "I'd love to. When were you thinking?"

"Is tomorrow afternoon too soon?" Hayden asks if I'd be interested in going to the grand opening of an art gallery a few towns over in a city called Ragsburrow. We work out the details of when and where to meet, then hang up for the night. I can't tell you anything about famous artists or explain the history behind their work since I never paid attention to those details during mandatory art classes in grade school. Still, the subject excites me now regardless.

I text Nyasia and let her know what happened. She replies immediately.

Nyasia:

Whoo! Date talk from 2 guys in 2 days.
Look at you go, you little seductress!

I chuckle a little, but then she sends another one.

Nyasia:
Are you worried about being forever alone?
Because I can tell you right now that that is
NOT something YOU will ever have to worry
about.

I'm not desperate to be in a relationship. I won't feel incomplete if I'm not going on dates because I'm comfortable being by myself. These two just happened to line up one after the other. Before I moved, there wasn't a shortage of men who would want to take out a cute girl from a wealthy family. What there wasn't a lot of, however, was men who would take a woman who wanted to pursue being an artist seriously. I'd be busting my ass, racking up hours on projects just to hear the words *cute* and *hobby* as if it didn't count as real work like any other job. Then when I did find a man who would take what I did seriously, he got intimidated by the thought of my success. He essentially told me to give up my dream so that I didn't outshine *him* and *his* career. I mean, seriously? Who still even thinks like that these days? Damn patriarchy.

And especially now that Lucas is out and about again, I'm also ready to be. No hiding, no holding myself back. When he attacked me in a fit of rage that I still don't understand, it didn't terrify me or ruin all men for me. Again, I got lucky regarding how bad it could have been. I completely understand women who *are* afraid after something like that happens to them. I would never judge them for that reaction. But one of the significant feelings I felt that day was refusal. Refusal to feel afraid of him and refusal to let his actions ruin my life. I choose to believe that he's a single, sick-minded man and that the rest of the world is good.

So, no, I'm not worried about being forever alone. If anything, I'd be more concerned about being stuck with someone who didn't take me and my goals seriously. I'm ready to replace the memories of the last man who entered my life. Out with the old and in with the new, as they say.

Chapter Three

TATUM

The nearest mall is a forty-five-minute drive on a clear day, but it goes by quickly after I start my private concert for one. Once there, it's not long before I have a stack of clothes that I'm excited to try on and find my way to the dressing room. If my sister, Grace, was here, we'd try on outlandish designs of linen and lace that count as style these days. The outfits remind me of stuff people in the capital would wear in The Hunger Games, though. Then, Grace would give me her honest opinions about *not that dress; it does nothing for your boobs, that dress makes you look like a hooker,* or *yes, that's the one! Your boobs look amazing!*

In case it's hard to tell based on the three reactions I'd have received from her, the universe was a little too generous in the breast department when creating me. I know, *but Tatum, people pay money to have boobs like that, and you got yours for free.* Well, that works both ways, itty bitty titty people. People pay to have boobs like that, too, so if I have to count my blessings, so do you.

Without having Grace around, I have to guess what looks good on me and hope for the best. By the time I pick out an outfit, I must've sent her about thirty different pictures trying to get her opinion from afar. In the end, I finally settle on a black, fitted, turtleneck long-sleeve shirt, a black skirt that hugs my legs and ends mid-thigh, and a black overcoat. I have some sheer black, patterned tights, black boots that end below my knees, and a simple silver chain necklace back at home that will pair nicely with the outfit. Since I'm already here, I buy some things for another day, then start the drive home to prepare for the date.

With Nick being the common link between my blind date and I, we decide to meet at the coffee shop. Recalling the events from yesterday morning of being publicly stood up in a town I'm still trying to make an impression on, I take my time getting ready. Then, I only show up five minutes early rather than my usual fifteen. What can I say? My anxiety keeps me very punctual.

Breathing in one last breath of courage before I walk through the doors, I look at my phone and the text message that just came in from Nyasia.

Nyasia:
Saw your car pull up! Good
luck hottie!

I smile, then throw my phone into my bag, waving across the street to the diner at Nyasia before going through The Brewed Bean's front door. The first thing I see is Nick leaning across the counter talking to whom I assume is my date based on his gallery-worthy attire. The stranger is wearing taupe dress pants with a dark brown belt, a light gray shirt, and a dark blue tie to match the jacket he has draped over his arm. I immediately start giving mental kudos to Nick for picking a handsome one as I walk up to the two men.

"Ah! Tatum! This is Hayden Williams. Hayden, this is Tatum...I don't know your last name, actually." The handsome man straightens and greets me with a brilliant smile that shows deep dimples on his smooth face. He's much taller than my 5'4" frame by at least eight inches, and he has shaggy brown hair that has my hands practically begging to run through it.

"It's Davis," I inform them both.

"Wow," the man, Hayden, speaks while still smiling, "you are *stunning*. I brought you something." Grabbing an object I can't quite see yet from the counter, Hayden exceeds my expectations by doing something I didn't think men did anymore. He extends his hand and gifts me a single orange rose. The three of us chat for a few more minutes before Hayden and I make our way out the door. "So, Nick says you moved here a few months ago? I'm kind of surprised I've never seen you around," Hayden states after we're both seated in his vehicle. It's a beat-up old Chevrolet with faded orange paint and the occasional chip in the metal. But by the looks of the inside, it's clear he values the things he owns, no matter how old they may be.

"Well, to be fair, I don't spend much time in town." I tend to get enough groceries to last me about a month. Plus, Nyasia always comes over to my place since she doesn't like spending much time living in the basement apartment of a toxic home, so there really isn't much need for me to leave my house.

"What do you do for work?"

"I'm an artist. Painter, mostly. How about you?" Hayden goes on to explain how he's a logger alongside his dad. I can't help but think of Nyasia's comment about no one ever leaving Maple Crest and how the majority of the more physically fit workers are destined for a life in the woods removing trees. Though from the way he talks about it, Hayden doesn't seem to mind the job. Being a logger is the family business, and he's happy to be a part of it.

By the time we reach the gallery, I feel like I've known him for years. Conversation flows effortlessly between us, and his warm personality makes me forget about this rainstorm we're stuck in. With our heads hunkered down, we hurry across the sidewalk that's flooded from the rain we're rushing to get out of. Stepping inside the gallery, we shake the water from our coats, chuckling under our breaths while Hayden hands someone the tickets he secured. Then, we each accept a complimentary glass of wine before joining the crowd.

All the other guests are already gathered in the front room of the building ahead of us. There's a speaker on a temporary stage dedicating the new gallery, thanking its sponsors, and whatever else, before he officially opens the doors to the exhibits. Since we are the last people to arrive, Hayden and I stand in the back cracking jokes about how we're late, and both forgot umbrellas.

"I'm still freezing," I whisper to him with a quiet laugh after sipping some of the complimentary red wine.

"Well, we can't have that," he whispers back, his face twisted in mock seriousness. Wrapping an arm around my shoulders, he rubs up and down rapidly to warm me up with friction. We continue to laugh with each other, not paying any attention to the speaker, and gain rude stares from a couple of other guests as another speaker takes the platform. When I look back at the stage, I'm met with the sight of combed back, light blonde hair, and a man in an all-black suit. Anthony speaks to the crowd about how it's an honor to have the privilege of opening Ragsburrow's newest gallery. But as he speaks, I can't help but think of what his reason is for missing a date he seemed to have been genuinely interested in.

That is, until the reason walks on stage next to him. She's tall and beautiful in the silk, emerald-green gown she's wearing. Her long black hair is curled, and she has a smile that lights up the room. As she glides over the temporary stage with each step forward, I realize I've seen her before. She was with the two men Anthony met up with in the coffee shop as we were setting up our date. *I wonder if she knew what he'd been up to seconds before she walked in.*

Anthony kisses her hand.

"But of course, we wouldn't all be standing here today if it wasn't for the tireless efforts of this wonderful woman. Zara, I couldn't have done it without you. Literally," he emphasizes, "she saved my skin on this project more times than my pride would allow me to admit." The gathered guests laugh as he looks around the room with a content look until his crystal gray eyes meet mine and falter. Looking from me to Hayden, I think I glimpse confusion on his face, but he's back to smiling and talking to the crowd again so fast that I'm not sure it was ever really there.

Finally, the doors to the gallery open, and the art displayed was well worth the wait. Pieces from every sort of medium available are featured, giving a tasteful variety of work to be seen. When Hayden had first asked me if I wanted to come to the gallery, I thought he was simply asking because he thought this was something I, as a girl, would be interested in. After all, he didn't know what I do for work before this evening. But seeing the way his eyes light up when he sees a particularly interesting piece, I now know that he's genuinely sharing with me something he's interested in. We spend nearly four hours going through the multiple levels of the building, taking our sweet time at each display. Anthony and the girl from the stage picked these pieces well.

We're almost at the end of the gallery when I spot Anthony and Zara, along with a small group of important-looking people, ahead of us. Zara's hand is on Anthony's shoulder when his eyes flick in our direction, clearly noticing how my arm is linked through Hayden's. Excusing himself from the group, Anthony begins to make his way toward us. I straighten my back, preparing myself for an altercation, but no such situation comes. He continues past us, close enough for me to smell his rich cologne, without even looking at me again.

Okay...first, he stands me up. Now he acts like he's never even met me. What a dick.

"Aw crap," Hayden groans after he opens the gallery doors on our way out of the building. The freezing rain is coming down much harder now than when we arrived. "Wait here. I'll go grab the truck so you don't get wet." Hayden runs down the sidewalk, not realizing that the rain is one of the reasons I moved to Maple Crest.

Now that I don't have to worry about my makeup looking perfect, I step out from the shelter of the balcony above me to feel the cold water on my face. Heavy raindrops only attack me for a couple of seconds before they suddenly stop, now hitting an umbrella that's being held above my head.

"What are you doing out here?" an accented voice asks.

Knowing it's Anthony since I can't think of another Englishman who'd be asking me that, I don't turn to look at him. "Are you always going to greet me by asking why I'm in the rain?"

"Perhaps, if I keep finding you like this."

"So you're talking to me now?"

"Yes." I roll my eyes at his stupid answer and lack of an explanation. "Did you like the gallery?" Anthony questions when I don't reply.

Sighing and deciding to be the bigger person, I finally turn to face him. Besides, it was one failed date with a man I'd barely met. There's no point in being petty. "Yes. Those pieces were stunning. You and your girlfriend have a real eye for that kind of thing. Now I understand why you were too busy for breakfast yesterday." Okay. Maybe I'm not quite ready to let bygones be bygones yet.

"Girlfriend?" His face contorts like he has the sour taste of a lemon in his mouth.

"Yes. The girl you had on stage with you."

Anthony starts laughing, "Do you mean Zara?" he stops. "Don't be ridiculous. That was my sister. Besides, you showed up here to rub your new date in my face, so clearly, you're not that upset I didn't show."

That makes me scoff. "That is *not* what I was doing. I had no idea you were even going to be here. Don't forget that I've only seen you twice and know nothing about you. Don't go around thinking I got my heart broken over a stack of pancakes. I'm irritated by your lack of basic respect, but believe me, I am just fine."

Hayden pulls up then and stops directly in front of where Anthony and I are standing. He leans over the seat and opens the truck door for me, and I catch the two men eyeing each other with tension filling the space between them.

"Goodbye, Anthony." Stepping out from the cover of his umbrella has me drenched in the seconds it takes to get into the seat of Hayden's truck. Hayden already has the heater cranked as high as it can go as we pull back into the street.

"What did Anthony want?" he asks.

"You know him?"

"Yeah, we used to go to school together for a little while," he explains. Judging by the look on his face, it's clear they hadn't been friends.

"Oh, he was asking how I liked the gallery, that's all."

"And?"

"And what?" I ask.

"How did you like the gallery? The horse sculpture made of all those pieces of locally collected driftwood was my favorite. I mean, seriously, you've got to have an incredible eye if you can look at a thick stick and say, 'I think this looks like a horse's cheek.'"

That makes me erupt with laughter. "I did like that one a lot. But there was something about that hall of black and white abstract paintings that got my attention. I heard someone say they were all too scary for her taste, but that's not how I saw them."

Hayden takes a moment to recall which hall I'm referring to. "How did you see them, then?"

I look out the window at drops of rain that shatter against the glass. "Sad."

Hayden glances at me, considers something, then returns his eyes to the road. "Black and white paintings with faceless figures and ghostly hands are enough to make most people uneasy. But not you. You're sympathetic with the subjects in the paintings, explaining that to you, they simply seem misunderstood by most of the people who see them. That's why it's sad to you, am I right?"

He'd guessed my thoughts exactly. "I'm impressed. How did you know that?"

"I spent a semester away at Stanford in an art history class before I had to come back home and help support my family. But because of that, I know you can tell a lot about a person based on how they interpret art. It's refreshing to have met someone who appreciates it as much as I do. You don't find that too often in Maple Crest." Who would've thought that the tall, muscled logger who works with an ax all day has a soft spot for artwork?

Perhaps Hayden does mind the way Maple Crest affects the people who live there, especially if he had to leave college behind to help his family. I ask more about his parents, and what college had been like and the conversation doesn't stop until we make it back to town. Pulling into The Brewed Bean's parking lot, Hayden parks beside my car, bringing the night to a close far too soon.

As Hayden gets out of the truck, I pick up my rose as he comes around to get my door. My car is the only one left in the parking lot and the rain didn't reach our town, so we take our sweet time walking the short distance from his vehicle to mine. When he opens up my door, I'm not sure what to expect. Hayden is kind and respectful, but I'm not sure if he's the kind of guy who will kiss me goodnight and leave, or expect to follow me home for a little late-night fun before going our separate ways. Honestly, I wouldn't object to the latter. He's extremely attractive and packed full of exceptional qualities. Plus, he definitely gives off the energy that he knows how to treat a woman. In more ways than one.

"Would it be too cliché of me to tell you I had an amazing time tonight? Because I don't want to sound unoriginal but, I really did have an amazing time. As far as first dates go, I think this one is my favorite."

Hayden smiles so widely his perfect teeth show. "It might be a little cliché, but in the best way. It's cute. Besides, I had an amazing time tonight too. You are..." he lets out a breath through pursed lips, "you are something special, Tatum. Goodnight." He takes my hand and kisses it. *I guess that answers my question.* But I'm not upset that he wants to end things here. It actually kind of makes me like him more.

"Goodnight, Hayden." I can feel my cheeks blushing over such a PG moment, but I don't even care. He gives me a final smile before he walks back to his truck and he only drives away once I'm safely leaving the darkened parking lot.

Once I'm home and otherwise ready for bed, I fill a small jar from my art room with water. After inhaling the rose's sweet aroma again, I plop the stem in the water I placed on my bedside table and fall asleep wearing the smile he gave me.

POUNDING on my front door wakes me up while it's still dark outside, making my heart jump to my throat. Checking my phone, I see it's nearly three in the morning. A look out my bedroom window isn't helpful at all, since the only thing I can see is the shine of headlights broken up from the trees in my front yard.

I know that whoever is at my door right now isn't Nyasia. Plus, with being this close to the forest on the outskirts of a town I've only lived in for a few months...I'm not going to take any chances, so I unlock my phone and dial 911. Right as I'm about to press the green call symbol, the pounding starts again, but the accented voice that accompanies it this time halts my finger from connecting with the screen.

"Tatum! Are you in there? Open the door!" More pounding. "Tatum, open up!"

Against my better judgment, I rush to do just that.

"*What is the matter with you?*" I hiss at him as I finish securing my robe around myself. Anthony, still dressed in his suit from the gallery, looks me over then hastily looks over my shoulder, scanning the room behind me. "Excuse you." Stepping outside and pulling the door mostly shut behind me, I widen my eyes at him in a way that demands an explanation.

"Are you alone?"

"Am I— what kind of question is that to ask a girl?" *Especially this late at night and especially when I am alone.* I'm seriously starting to question why I opened my door because now I'm getting kidnapper vibes.

Anthony sighs and looks everywhere but at me as if this situation is making *him* uncomfortable. "Did Hayden Williams stay after he dropped you off tonight, or did he immediately leave?"

Oh. I get what's happening now.

I narrow my eyes on him. "Are you trying to ask if we had sex?" He doesn't reply. He only swallows and clenches his jaw. *Unreal.* "Not that it's any of your business at all, but oh yeah, we had lots and lots of hot sex. For hours, actually. In fact, he just left because we ran out of condoms, so he'll be back soon with more so we can—" I gasp as he presses me against the wall of the house. One of his hands is on my waist, and the other cups my cheek tenderly. His skin is so warm in contrast to the chilly night air surrounding us. Weirdly, thinking about his warmth gives me goosebumps. It doesn't help that the alluring scent of his cologne mixed with the combination of his touch is muddling my head with all sorts of thoughts I shouldn't be having right now.

"Are you lying to me right now, Tatum?" It takes several seconds for my mind to clear enough to form coherent thoughts and even then, I still don't know if I'm more scared or turned on right now. Or pissed off by his audacity and the fact I'm even questioning whether or not this situation is hot. It should be a no-brainer that it's not but, well, here I am.

"Maybe. Maybe not." I definitely am. *Why am I egging this situation on further? Remember, you hardly know the man, Tatum! And right now he has you pushed against a wall in the dark with no one else around.*

Anthony squints his eyes as he tries to read me, his thumb

starting to rub gently against my cheek. With each rotation of his finger against my skin, all rational thought gets swept away. His gray eyes drop to my lips, linger there, then work their way back up. I think he's going to kiss me. I think I want him to, even, but then he pulls his hand away and puts space between us. I don't move from the spot against the wall, already missing his scent filling my nose and the touch of his hands.

"Why did you go out with *him*?" His nose scrunches with disgust as he finishes his sentence, and I barely stop myself from rolling my eyes at this man's dramatics. Just like that, my momentary trance has been broken.

"He actually showed up." Anthony's face instantly softens.

"I am so sorry, Tatum. Something really important came up and I couldn't. Plus, I had no way of letting you know that I couldn't show."

Ugh, please. "You clearly remembered where I live. Would it have been so difficult for you to show up after you were done doing whatever it was that kept you from showing up to at least tell me we'd have to reschedule? Or at least tell me sorry for not being there?"

"Yes!" Okay, I was expecting to put him in his place. Maybe even make him feel a little bit bad. I wasn't expecting him to get so upset and honest while saying 'yes' like that. "Tatum, I shouldn't even be here right now."

I want to ask why that is but I'm starting to get upset with the way he thinks he can show up at my house in the middle of the night like this and get uptight when he thinks I'm having sex with someone. What really pushes me over the edge is him saying that it was too hard for him to show me common courtesy after he stood me up.

"Then leave. I don't want you here, anyway." He takes a deep inhale and stares at me. Anthony looks like he has so many things he wants to say to me, but he doesn't say a single one. Instead, he turns around and walks off my porch, right up to his car which costs more than my house and car combined, and drives off without saying another word. Guess the Audi from the parking lot was his.

I growl in frustration, then walk back inside, slamming the door behind me.

It feels like my eyes have only been closed for five more minutes before there's knocking on my door again, except this time it's much more gentle. Opening my eyes, I see that at least the sun is up this time and when I check my phone, it's precisely 8 o'clock.

"One minute," I shout. Rolling out of bed, I look in the mirror and try to adjust my hair as much as I can, then wipe underneath my eyes. Quickly rubbing some chapstick on my lips, I hurry to the door and stand on my toes so I can peek out the window. Seeing who it is, I drop back flat on my feet and sigh. Anthony is standing on the other side, holding a large brown paper bag and a *gorgeous* bouquet of flowers. "What do you want, Anthony?" I call through the door blandly.

"Open up and I'll tell you, I'm not going to hold a conversation through a closed door." I do and he immediately walks past me, inviting himself into my house, and goes straight for the kitchen.

"Um, excuse me? What do you think you're doing?"

He sets the bag on the counter, then turns to face me. This frustrating man looks way too handsome this early in the morning. His blonde hair is styled back, his face is clean-shaven, and I can see the collar of a black shirt underneath his equally dark, buttoned-up overcoat. After coming to a stop in front of me, Anthony hands me the large bouquet which consists of burgundy and blush pink flowers with beautiful dark greenery that fills in the spaces.

"Let's have a second try at that first date. I brought everything that's needed to make pancakes and I would love nothing more than to be your personal chef this morning if you'll allow it. Please."

"Um," I place a considering finger on my chin and pretend to think things over for a second. "No."

He blinks in surprise. "No?"

"No," I confirm. "The last thing you said to me last night, at three in the morning, might I add, was that you shouldn't even be here. Now you want to make me pancakes? That's weird."

He sighs and sets the flowers down lightly on the counter before looking back up at me again. "I am sorry. Really." He shakes his head at himself. "I've already made multiple mistakes with you and we've only just met. To be completely honest, it's been a tough week. You have no reason to give me another second of your time, but if you do, I would love the chance to show you I'm not a complete wanker."

My arms are still folded, but I let my gaze soften. I can understand not acting like your usual self when you're having a bad week. I've had plenty of those. "It was a little crazy, you showing up here. You know that, right?"

"I know that," he admits, "and I swear to you that if you let me stay, I will be nothing but the perfect gentleman to you from this moment on. But if you tell me to leave, I will leave without another word."

Alright, I have to give him some credit because this is all kind of romantic and a single glance at my bookshelves will tell you I'm a bit of a sucker for romance.

"Mind if I change out of my pajamas first?" I relent. I'm wearing a navy blue, satin pajama short set and a pair of cabin socks I threw on before I answered the door. It'd be nice to look a little more put together if we're indeed having our first date, even if it is in my very own kitchen.

"I'd rather you didn't," he responds, surprising me further. "I like seeing the version of yourself when you're not trying to impress anyone. When you're simply you." Looks like I'm having my first date in my pajamas.

"Fine, but you're not talking me out of brushing my teeth, so I'll be right back." When I get to the bathroom, I do more than brush my teeth. I can't help it because he can't show up looking like *that* and expect me to be fine with having rolled out of my bed myself. It's morning, meaning I don't have the breath of an angel, and the thin material of my pj's doesn't do much to hide my double d's so I throw on a bra, comb through my hair, put on some deodorant, and add a little bit of mascara.

When I walk back into the kitchen, I find Lenny wasted no time trying to get to know our company, who ditched his overcoat on a chair and has started mixing ingredients he pulled from the bag he brought. Anthony doesn't appear to be a big fan of Lenny, though. Despite being repeatedly nudged away, Lenny, being the clueless and needy little bastard he is, keeps coming back to rub against Anthony's legs.

"You're not allergic to cats, are you? I think I have some Claritin in the medicine cabinet if you need it."

He turns and eyes me up and down again, his lips curving up into a small smile before he replies. "I'm alright, thank you. Is this the pancake lover?"

I chuckle. "Yep, this is him. His name is Lenny. So if you're not allergic, what's the problem? You don't like cats?"

His lips form a straight line. "It's not that I don't like them. It's that I've never really been around any. My father never had any pets growing up."

When Lenny jumps up on the counter, I pick him up and drop him back on the floor. "Did you want any pets?"

Anthony sprays the pan on the stove and starts to pour the first pancake-to-be on the hot surface. "For a little while. But once I got older, I realized it was probably for the best that we never had any."

"Why's that?" I take a seat on one of the bar stools I have in front of the small counter space and prop my head on my hand, enjoying the view in my kitchen right now. If anyone else suddenly found themselves in a situation where a handsome man with an accent started making food for them, they'd be doing the same thing.

Anthony appears to be in great shape. He's not big and bulky like his entire personality consists of being at the gym, though. He just looks like someone who cares about his body being healthy and strong.

"We've always been too busy. I realized that there was never any time to show something the love and attention it deserved."

"And now? Still too busy?"

He looks from one of my green eyes to the other. "Now, if I want something, I'm not going to stop putting in the work to get it." The way he's looking at me makes me think he's not talking about a pet anymore, but about *me.*

I pause, unsure of what to say when there is another knock on my freaking door. My eyes widen slightly and I let out an exasperated huff.

"What the hell is going on?" I ask myself out loud as I hop off the chair and walk to my door. With Anthony here and Nyasia at work, now I *really* have no idea who's waiting for me on the other side. Opening the door, I find Hayden holding...oh my God. He's holding a bouquet of flowers.

Note to self: start waking up earlier than the ungodly hour of 8 am, and always wear cute pajamas because evidently, phone calls are an afterthought in this town.

Chapter Four

TATUM

"Hayden, hi!" His smile falters a little. Probably because Anthony and the flowers *he'd* brought — which look substantially more expensive — are visible as he flips a pancake in my kitchen. *I hope he isn't comparing what he brought to what Anthony did.* The price tag doesn't matter to me. The thought behind the act does.

Like Anthony, he's wearing a black shirt, but that's where their similarities end. Hayden's wearing a thick red, orange, and black flannel over his t-shirt, jeans, and heavy work boots. His shaggy hair is brushed, but not exactly styled. In a way entirely separate from Anthony, he looks really cute right now.

"Hey," he starts a little apprehensively before shaking himself from the surprise and flashing his full smile at me again. "I'm on my way to work and wanted to stop by to give you these and ask if you'd like to go on another date?"

"Breakfast is ready!" Anthony shouts with unnecessary volume.

Universe, can you hear me? Could you please open up a sinkhole right where I'm standing and swallow me whole so I may escape this situation entirely?

I step outside and close the door behind me, accepting the flowers from Hayden and bringing them to my nose so I can smell them. Where the other bouquet is made up mostly of dark blooms, this one is bursting with bright orange. I elect not to acknowledge the man in my kitchen; the man Hayden clearly isn't the biggest fan of and vice versa.

"These are beautiful. And I can't believe you stopped by before work. That's so sweet, thank you." I smell them again, taking a peek at him as I do. A faint blush flashes across his cheekbones as he grins.

"Well, to be honest, I don't think I could have gone my whole day without talking to you, so I figured I might as well do it in person."

"Hayden, this is so—" The door opens behind me, and I feel Anthony practically towering over me, leaving very little space between my back and his chest.

"The food is getting cold," he states simply.

I highly doubt that. It's been 2 seconds.

My eyes roll before I invite Hayden in to grab some breakfast before he goes to work.

Anthony interjects again before Hayden has the chance to reply. "There's only enough for two."

Part of me wants to elbow him in the stomach for being so rude but I manage to contain my temper. For now.

Hayden, though he's still smiling, has a wistful look in his eye and I feel my heart tinge with guilt from it. "That's alright. I've got an order waiting for me and some of the other workers over at TreeCutter. Thank you though, maybe another time. You have my number, feel free to use it anytime and we can set up that date when you don't have company."

"I will," I assure him eagerly.

He nods his goodbye at me and then the smile drops when he dips his chin again, this time at the man behind me.

"Anthony."

"Williams," Anthony replies. I remain on the porch while Hayden walks back to his old, orange pickup truck. It's so at odds parked behind Anthony's perfect-condition Audi.

I wonder what he's thinking about after finding Anthony here so early. Will he still want to go on another date if I text him, or will he delete my number instead? I haven't done anything wrong and I know that, but for some reason, I feel like I just got caught with my hand in the cookie jar. Only once he's driven off do I turn and glare at Anthony.

"Not exactly the best start to our date, *Kensington*."

"What?" he shrugs innocently. "I only wanted to ensure you were able to enjoy warm pancakes."

"Uh-huh," I deadpan, not believing him for a second. His wide eyes and that damn accent makes him nearly too cute to be mad at, so I force myself not to get sucked into them and walk past him instead. He follows me inside and I see that he's already found the plates and utensils. I set the new flowers beside the... fifteen minutes *not so new* bouquet and sit back down on the stool. "What do you have against Hayden? He's so nice."

Anthony stacks a couple of pancakes that look so perfect they almost look fake onto my plate. "Any chance we can enjoy *our* date first and talk about yesterday's date later?"

"Nope." I drag out the *n* and pop the *p*. I wish I could save the pancakes for after the conversation too, but they smell freaking amazing and I'm starving. So, I lather them in butter that starts to melt the moment it makes contact with the warm golden surface, then drown them in syrup. "Give me a reason first, then you can have my full attention."

"I don't have anything against *him*."

"So what's the problem, then?" I take a bite and, wow, how the guy managed to make something as simple as pancakes taste this good seems supernatural. I nearly sigh with satisfaction.

Anthony smirks at me as if he knows exactly what I think of his cooking. When my tongue darts out to lick syrup from my lips, I note his eyes watching the movement and lingering there before he pulls his gaze away to the plate in front of him.

"He had something I wanted. It was stupid, and we were kids. I didn't know how to act any other way when it came to dealing with that, so I resorted to being a bit of a bully. Then it carried into adult life. Among other petty things, now here we are. It's too late for change, even if I wanted it." What could Hayden possibly have that Anthony would want? Anthony has a better car, more money, and more opportunities. It doesn't make any sense to me, but I told him we could get back to our date if he answered my question and he did. It's my turn to keep up my end of the deal.

"Speaking of being here, what brought you from London to Maple Crest, back to London, just to come here again of all places? You and your family kind of stick out like sore thumbs in this town."

"My mom keeps bringing us back. She was a tourist in London on a trip with her friends when she and my dad met. They fell in love at first sight and not long after, she dropped everything to move there to be with him. She got homesick after a few years, though, so my dad dropped everything to move here for her."

I imagine the love they must have for each other in my head. "Why'd you move back to London again if this is where your mom wanted to be?"

His eyes are fixed on his plate as he pushes a piece of pancake through syrup but doesn't lift it from his plate. "She actually got sick while we were in the states. When she died, my dad couldn't stand to be here without her. It took him years to want to come back without my mom, and we only decided to move our business here again 3 years ago. That man hardly loves anything, but I never had any doubt that he loved her more than he loved his own breath. That's why he eventually wanted to be back in the place she loved, even if she wasn't here with him anymore."

"Anthony...I'm so sorry."

He shrugs his shoulders. "It is what it is. So, what brings you here, then? I would've noticed if you were a local here before." It feels wrong to start talking about myself after he just told me that his mom died, but it's easy to see that his mom is a sensitive subject for him, so I take the bait for a subject change.

"I felt like I was suffocating in Texas. I needed to get away for a little bit and focus more on my work."

"Which is?"

"Art. I've grown to have quite the passion for it. A passion that kind of came out of nowhere, to be honest. So I have no real knowledge about what I'm doing, but I've been enjoying myself a lot."

"Art, huh? I thought you must be an artist of some sort judging by your expressions at the gallery."

I give him a befuddled look. "What do you mean 'judging by your expressions at the gallery?' You were watching me?"

"Not intentionally, at first, but it's nearly impossible for my eyes not to be drawn to you. Especially when you're all dressed up the way you were last night. In a room full of pieces of art that cost thousands of dollars each, you have no idea how many sets of eyes were set on *you* last night, Tatum. Mine included, and I'm not the least bit ashamed to admit that." I'm blushing again. Not only that, but it feels like dozens of butterflies have been released in my gut. "Can I see some of your work?" he asks.

"Sure. I'll show you my studio when I finish my plate." I'm not the kind of person to brag about what I do, but I don't shy away from it either when asked. I fall somewhere right in the middle of the modesty scale.

We start having typical first-date kind of talk while we finish eating and manage to steer away from the heavy topics we started with. After breakfast I lead Anthony to my art room. I like to work with a lot of natural light, so I picked the room with the biggest windows to work in. The space is furnished with a loveseat, a desk, a corkboard with pins and clips, a supplies dresser, and canvases that I have scattered *everywhere*. There are several finished projects, the ones I decided to keep, hanging all around the room with no particular system in mind. Other pieces are propped against various surfaces to dry since the drying rack is overflowing. Anthony takes a second to look around then goes straight for the easel my current work in progress, my canvas of the bear in the rain, is on.

He seems to be thinking of what to say and I suddenly find myself self-conscious in the presence of his silence.

I lean my weight against the doorframe.

"Tatum, this is incredible. You truly just picked up a brush one day out of the blue?"

I shrug a single shoulder. "Yeah. I've spent many hours honing the skill since then, though." I started selling my work two years ago, but it's been about six years since I first picked up a brush. Anthony can't seem to take his eyes off the painting, so I elaborate. "That's a real scene, you know. The day I met you, actually. Before I fell down the hill, I saw that bear and the scene looked exactly like this. It was one of the most beautiful sights I'd ever seen."

When Anthony turns from the painting to face me, I can see his interest in something I had said written clearly on his face. "This is from the day we met?"

"Mmhm."

"How much are you selling it for?"

"Probably about $1,000 once I finish it."

"Add a zero and let me buy it." I choke on absolutely nothing but the air leaving my lungs.

"I'm sorry. What did you just say?"

"You're selling yourself short by only charging $1,000 for this. Your talent is well beyond that and I could think of plenty of buyers that would want this even with the new price. But I don't intend to let any of them have it, which is why I want you to sell it to me."

I'm a little stunned by pretty much everything that came out of his mouth. "You want my bear." Even I don't know if that was a question or a statement.

"You said it's the day we met?"

"Well...yeah," I say a little slowly.

His response, however, remains haste, "Yes. I want your bear."

"For...$10,000?"

Anthony eyes me with a hint of confusion twisting his brow. Maybe even a little worry.

"Yes, Tatum. For $10,000. Are you feeling okay?" *No, actually. I'm pretty sure I'm going to pass out, or throw up or something!* I come from money, yeah, but not as much money as he appears to have. Plus, for the past two years, I've been living mainly off of the earnings from my small art business. I haven't seen that much money for myself since I first moved out of my parents house.

Half an hour later after he washes the dishes, Anthony leaves. He made sure to grab my number this time and tells me to let him know when I'm finished with the painting. When I close my front door again, my head is reeling with the way my morning has gone. Turning around to press my back against the door, I see not one, but two bouquets. These boys couldn't be more opposite from each other.

Finally changing out of my pajamas, I shoot Hayden a quick text.

Me:
*How's the tree cutting going?
Have you had a Lorax scream
in your face yet about how
you're ruining the
environment?*

He responds almost immediately.

Hayden:
Just one so far. Although his name

*was Richard and his face was more
red than yellow. But he made sure to
let me know* exactly *what he thought
about what I do. Other than that, it's
going pretty well, actually. It's always
nice when Maple Crest has one of its
rare, sunny days. You must be good
luck. I should stop by more often to
keep this weather!*

I open one of the windows to my art room because I too am
enjoying the rare bit of sun.

> ***Me:***
> *Oh no! Like a real person?
> On a side note, sorry, but I can't
> take credit for the sun. I've been
> thinking about today's forecast
> since I first noticed it on the
> weather app two days ago.
> You can still totally keep
> stopping by though ;)*

Hayden:
*Yep, like a real person. It's alright
though. It wouldn't be a normal day
without someone letting you know
that you're the reason the world is
dying. I didn't see the forecast, so
I'm still going to think of you as a
good luck charm.
Break's over. I've got to go. I'll talk
to you later!*

"Poor guy," I mutter to myself as I connect my phone to Bluetooth again. If everything goes according to plan, today's the day I finish the painting. *And then sell it for freaking $10,000.* Part of me doesn't want to sell it, especially for that much, to the man I'm going on dates with. But I've been struggling to sell anything since the move, and the money would be too nice to pass on. And I say 'dates' because Anthony is taking me out again in a couple of days. I'm not sure what his plan is yet. All I know is that I'll need to dress in something classy.

When my phone rings a few hours later I see Nyasia's name on my screen so I hastily throw my paintbrush handle in my hair and answer the call.

"Hey!" I greet her. I'm thankful for the excuse to stretch my back.

"Hey. What are you doing?" Her car door shuts and I hear a muffled thud, presumably her bag as it hits the passenger seat.

"Painting, how about you?"

"I just got off work. Would it be okay if I came over to your place for dinner?" My friend sounds utterly exhausted and I already know why. Early this morning, she'd told me via text that her parents were fighting on the floor above her, keeping her up for most of the night. In the short amount of time I've known her, I've come to realize that her asking to come over for dinner is simply because she's not ready to go home yet. She'll probably end up sleeping here tonight as a temporary escape as she's done several times before.

"Sure." I glance at the large clock on my wall. "I'll probably be finishing up in my art room by the time you get here. Just walk in. My door has seen enough action today."

"What's that supposed to mean? And speaking of action, did you get any after your date last night?"

"I'll give you the details to both of those questions when you get here."

"Sounds good. Bye!"

"B— and she hung up. That's nice." I don't think she means to be rude, it just sort of comes off that way sometimes. I shrug it off and go back to adding the finishing touches of the painting to my canvas. Sure enough, I hear my front door open and close about ten minutes later, followed by her footsteps as Nyasia works her way to my art room. She whistles from the doorway.

"Damn girl, that turned out pretty good."

"$10,000 good apparently," I mutter quietly, more to the canvas than to her since I'm still coming to terms with it. Lucas would never have supported this.

Lucas wouldn't have supported a lot of things and I shouldn't waste any more time thinking about someone from the past. Move. Forward.

I clean my paintbrush and turn around. When I see her, my mouth opens involuntarily. "Shut the fuck up."

Her perfect brows pull together. "I didn't say anything."

"You literally just got off of, like, a 12-hour shift. How do you look like that?" Her wavy black hair is resting over her shoulder and is volumized by having been recently pulled from the ponytail it was in all day. As always, her makeup is flawless.

She rolls her eyes, but I can see her fighting a smile. "You're dumb. What's for dinner?"

Nyasia follows me to the kitchen where I open up the fridge to see what I can make. "What are you in the mood for?"

She examines the contents of the fridge over my shoulder. "Pizza?" I chuckle, then we order two personal pizzas before plopping down on the couch with wine coolers while we wait for the food to arrive. "So tell me everything. Don't skip out on the dirty details."

I'm barely over halfway done telling her everything by the time our food arrives.

"And neither of them has kissed me yet!"

Nyasia's highlighted cheeks are full of pizza when she speaks up. "Which one did you want to kiss you?"

"Both? I don't know." I groan and take another bite of the large slice in my hand.

"Hayden Williams...he's like, Maple Crest's most eligible

bachelor and you've already got him wrapped around your finger. He's not the kind of guy to kiss on the first date, though. His parents gave him a butt load of manners and all that. But it is surprising that Anthony didn't kiss you. Maybe you need to take the initiative and kiss one of them yourself. Or both. Or you know, take things further than kissing since you're not in junior high anymore."

"Trust me, I wouldn't mind going further with either of them. I'll see how it pans out, I guess." My phone dings with a message.

Hayden:
So about that second date.
Are you free Wednesday?

Of course he wants to go out on the same day I already have plans with Anthony.

Me:
Actually, I'm not.
What are you doing
tomorrow?

Hayden:
I wish I could say I was
seeing you. But unfortunately,
we have some important stuff
going on at work I can't miss.
Thursday?

Me:
Thursday works!
But I want to plan it (:

Hayden:
Deal!

"Sooo, which one is it?" Nyasia asks. I set my phone down and drag my pizza through the blob of ranch on my plate before I take a bite.

"Hayden. He was setting up our next date."

Nyasia makes some sort of noise that sounds like something that would come from an animal. "You seriously have the jackpot of all lives, you know that? It's so hard to get a date around here because I already know all the boys after going to school with them. Do you know what that means?" I shake my head. "It means I know how annoying and obnoxious they are. Plus, I saw too many of them eat their boogers when they were kids. I will *not* kiss the mouth of a known booger eater, I don't care how long ago it happened."

I cringe because I wouldn't want to either. "Hayden didn't...did he?"

She waves the question away. "No, you're good. He's safe. Anthony too, as far as I know, but I don't know for sure about his England years."

It occurs to me that she mentions going to school with Anthony even though he's a couple of years older than herself, but hasn't mentioned his sister once.

"Is Anthony's sister older than him or something? You never mention going to school with her."

"She's younger. My age, I think. We were in the same class for a while, but then she disappeared. I think her dad sent her away to a boarding school after their mom died. Hey, would you want to go to a bar this weekend?"

"Maple Crest has a bar?"

"No, but there's a nightclub about an hour away in Ragsburrow."

Chapter Five

TATUM

I've been staring at my phone for the past eight minutes straight. I'm not even sure I've blinked. Plus, I'm chewing the hell out of my thumbnail. The cause for my current anxiety? The painting is ready to be sold.

So sell it.

I can't think of anyone else who would have such a hard time accepting so much money and I don't know why I'm having a problem with it, either.

"Will you call him already?" Nyasia is still here since she doesn't have to be at the diner until a little later today.

"I will. I'm just...you know what? There are still a couple of things that need to be added to the painting. It's not done yet, so there's no point in calling."

"Oh, there is?"

"Yep. Lots to do. Lots and lots to do," I lie.

"Fine. My phone is dead, can I borrow yours for a sec?"

"Sure!" I hand her my phone and she presses one button before holding it to her ear. My mouth drops open with the shock of betrayal.

"Anthony? Nope, not Tatum. Nyasia. Remember me? Whatever. Your painting is ready." There's another pause on her end as he speaks, and I mouth the words *I hate you* to her when she looks at me. "Uh-huh. Hmm. She'll drop it off. Okay. Yep. Have the cash ready." She hangs up.

"You're a bitch," I tell her as I snatch my phone back.

"No, I'm helping you with your anxiety. You'd be stressing over that damn call for who knows how long, and I handled it for you."

My phone dings with a text and I see it's an address sent from Anthony. "Thanks for volunteering me to drop off the painting. That's just awesome." My voice is dripping with sarcasm.

"With you dropping it off, you'll be able to know where he lives and see what his house looks like. You know, level the playing field a little bit since he's already been here. So you're welcome *twice*."

We make breakfast burritos and then she helps me wrap the painting and move it to my car before she leaves for work. I shoot Anthony a text letting him know I'm on my way, then put the address into my GPS. A short while later, I'm turning into his long driveway. Like myself, he doesn't have neighbors immediately beside him, mostly trees that provide him with plenty of privacy. Driving past the stone wall where the gate is currently open for me, I find a black, modern-styled luxury home and his Audi at the end of the driveway.

I'm taking the painting out of the back of my car when I hear his front door open and close, then steps descending the few stairs that lead to the door.

"It's not hard to guess your favorite color," I tell him when he reaches me. He hasn't said anything yet, but he's been giving me a close-lipped smile since he started down the stairs.

"Is that so? What do you suppose it is, then?"

I gesture first to the house, then his car, then his clothes. "Call it a crazy guess, but I'd say it's black."

"If you told me to make it black, then that's what it would be. Otherwise, my favorite color is blue."

"Then why not make everything you own blue?"

He shrugs and puts his hands in his pockets. Who would've thought that something so normal could look so attractive?

"Black looks better on houses, cars, and me. Black is my second favorite color, though, so I'm not suffering through dealing with it for the sake of appearances. What's yours?"

"I don't know," I tell him honestly.

"How do you not know?"

"I can't pick." I always think I have the answer to that question figured out, but the second I put any thought into it, it becomes too hard to settle on only one.

"Between which colors?"

"Green, red, black, gold, blue. But very specific shades of each. I like dark green like the moss and ferns in the forest. I like deep reds, but not quite cranberry. Black and gold are easier, although I don't know if I like rose gold or regular gold the best. And blue... well, I guess I like most shades of blue."

Anthony smiles widely. "It sounds like we found something in common. Would you like to come inside and be present for the unveiling?" I agree, and he takes the covered canvas from me as we go in.

His modern taste extends from the exterior of the house to the interior as well. Everything has sharp corners with lots of space so as not to look cluttered. The ceiling is higher than what you'll find in most homes, and there are no fancy light fixtures hanging down. Instead, the lights are embedded into where the walls and ceiling meet, creating a glowing line of light that softly illuminates the space. The house smells clean. Not like fresh linen and lemons, but crisp like eucalyptus and cypress. Every surface is spotless, not a single thing is out of place. In fact, with nothing to show for his hobbies, everything made of darker shades of gray, and not even a fingerprint on any of his stainless steel surfaces or massive windows, I would almost think of the place as being uninhabited.

"You're a gallerist, right?" There's no denying the man has crazy money. That much was obvious from the moment I saw what he drives.

"Software engineer," he corrects.

I stop gazing around his house in order to look at him, surprise. "But what about the gallery you and your sister opened? Is that just a side hustle, or what?

"My dad made sure Zara and I were well rounded in many things, so although my main skill is in computers, my family and the people in my father's company have many talents. That gallery was one of my father's latest investments. Since he had business to attend to elsewhere, it was mine and my sister's responsibility to open."

I want to ask him if he's aware of his and his family's reputation in town, especially since it doesn't seem fitting if he's simply a software engineer, but I decide not to. Besides, I'm sure they're pointless rumors, anyway. Nothing I've seen so far supports that he's cruel in any way. Perhaps a little rude, and lacks some boundaries, but not cruel.

When we reach the living room, he stops and unveils the finished painting. His mouth opens a little in awe as he stares at it. It's hardly changed since the last time he saw it, but he's staring at it painting as if this were the very first time he's seen it.

"Anthony? Why are you buying this? You may like art enough to open a gallery for other people to buy, but you don't have a single thing hanging on your walls."

Everything Anthony needs to hang the painting is already waiting for him nearby so he moves to do so.

"This painting is not only made with extreme talent, but it represents the day both of our lives changed for good."

My brows fly up. "And why's that?" I'm sure I already know what he's implying, but I want to see if I'm right or not.

As he begins to hang the painting above his stone fireplace, he glances over his shoulder at me. "It's the day we met. You said it yourself."

I let out a surprised laugh. "Awfully presumptuous, don't you think? We still hardly know each other. You never know, we could end up getting infuriated with one another and one of us could cut the other person off."

"What reasons do you have that would lead you to think of that happening?" He smirks as he folds his arms, settling into the conversation now that the picture is hung.

One of my shoulders lifts in a shrug. "I don't know. I talk. A lot."

"I'm a great listener."

"I spend a *lot* of time painting."

"I spend a lot of time reading."

"I'm horrible at singing, but that never stops me. I'm constantly singing along to my music."

"I'm actually quite good at it. Our voices will complement each other, then."

I huff a little, and now I'm folding my arms too. Anthony's smirk only grows.

"I have a cat. And he doesn't know what personal space is, so you wouldn't have much of it."

"I'm growing quite fond of Lenny. I wouldn't mind being around him more. Look, Tatum, I can do this all day if you want. I know I'm not the only man you're currently sharing your time with right now and that's fine. As long as you keep in mind that I intend to win you over and be the only one you end up with. You're right, we do hardly know each other still, but I want to know everything there is to know about you and I think we're off to a fairly good start. Don't you?"

He's a little presumptuous since he stood me up for what was supposed to be our first date. But he's also confident, and if I only consider our redo date, then yes, I do think we're off to a fairly good start.

I search his gray eyes for...*something*, though I'm not sure what I'm hoping to find. Everything in the house nearly replicates their shade and emphasizes the color of his eyes. *I wonder if that was intentional or not.*

"You're not afraid of hiding your feelings at all, are you?"

"From you? I never will be. Honesty is key in a relationship."

I throw my hands up a little. "Now, hold on, we're not in a relationship. We're dating, as in going on dates, but we're not a couple. As you said, you're not the only person I'm talking to. I like spending time with you, but I like spending time with Hayden, too. And I'm not ready to commit to either of you yet. I've only had one date with each of you."

Anthony makes a slight face when I mention Hayden, but he rids himself of the irritated look quickly. "Honesty is important for any type of relationship, darling. I know you're not ready to pick between us yet, but I'm both patient and confident." He checks his watch, which, no surprise, is all black. "I've got somewhere I need to be. Allow me to walk you out."

I take another look at the painting and where it's now hanging up, and feel a spark of pride in my chest. Even though everything in Anthony's house is made of shades of gray without any sort of pattern or design, the painting doesn't look out of place here. It attracts attention without demanding it. The painting has a mix of greens from the trees and other plants depicted, but still matches with the rest of the room's surroundings thanks to the gray of the fog, the dark shadows that are featured, and the black bear itself.

"It looks good in here," I tell him. "I'm glad that you were the one that bought it." When I twist to look at him, I get the feeling he's been looking at me for longer than when I first started speaking to him.

"Yes, it does. Ready?" On our way out of the house, he hands me a thick manila envelope that contains my payment and it makes me feel like some sort of dealer with ties to the mafia. How could I not while carrying money like this in a luxury home, with a handsome man in all black escorting me? All I'd need to complete the feeling is a gun, and I'd be set. When we reach my car, he opens the door for me. "Are you afraid of heights?"

"Nope."

"Perfect. I just wanted to make sure everything is all set for dinner tomorrow. I'll pick you up at six. Goodbye, Tatum." Once he closes the door to my car, he gets in his own vehicle and follows me down the driveway. Where I make a left to go back to town, he takes a right on the main road heading further away. As I start down the curved road, I find myself wishing for the hours to go by faster so it'll be 6 p.m. tomorrow already.

Chapter Six

TATUM

"**Y**ou look like a stripper holding that much money," Grace quips over FaceTime.

"If I were a stripper, these would all be single dollar bills, not stacks of hundreds, Grace." I've been sitting on the rug in my room leaning against the bedframe for a while now, staring at all the money. We were never short of it growing up, and I've always been surrounded by nice things thanks to my parent's money. But this is all mine, earned entirely by me.

"Alright then, you look like a very high-class stripper. What are you going to do with it? Spending spree?"

"No, I'll probably just store it in Uncle James' wall safe. I'm twenty-four, Grace. I told Mom and Dad I didn't want their allowance a few years ago. I need to make what I have last." Grace's mouth falls open, and her doe eyes widen. She's a couple of years younger than me and still relies heavily on their money.

"Why would you tell them you don't want their money? You don't have to do anything to get it. They literally just hand it to you, are you crazy?"

"That's exactly the reason why. I wouldn't earn it. That's fine if you want to keep being supported by them, I'm not judging you one way or another, but I hated that feeling. I want to have my own success. Not live off of theirs my whole life."

Independence. That's what I came to Maple Crest for. To know I can do things on my own and make a sustainable life for myself *by* myself. I came here for the opportunity to take my art somewhere it might be appreciated. Sure, I didn't get this house all on my own, but it was exactly what I needed for a fresh start. Besides, it didn't come from my parents. It came from my uncle who came here for the same reason I did. Now, looking at the thousands of dollars that came from a single sale of my work, it's a life-changing moment that truly solidifies this was the right decision.

Grace doesn't seem to get it though, so I decide to play along with her.

"Or, fuck it, maybe I'll treat myself with a private plane to Paris and a shopping spree. Or maybe a yacht. Remember that time we went with Mom and Dad, like, eight years ago?"

That sets Grace off with excited chatter, recalling the memories of that trip and their upcoming one to Italy. She's their princess and will likely live off their money and in their guest home beside the main house forever without ever getting a job, or doing anything for herself.

Finally standing, I grab the manilla envelope of what I've been referring to as my *mafia money* and take it to the living room. When this house belonged to my uncle, he installed a hidden safe on the wall. I stuff the cash inside, then take my phone into the art room so I can get started on another project. After propping my phone up somewhere so I can still see Grace, I twist my thick hair into a bun and step into my painting overalls which are stained with various colors.

As we talk, laugh, and poke fun at one another, I fill my palette with black and white. When I think of the black and white abstract hall at the gallery with Hayden, I let my mind take over from there. It's raining heavily today, so I let the dreary weather affect the mood of my painting. My brush slashes across the large canvas with no order, the paint at the tip alternating between dark and light until I'm satisfied with the background. In many spots, the strokes of my brush mixed the colors to form shades of gray, but many slashes remained purely white or black. I love those spots the best because I like being able to see the texture of the bristles. It's chaotic, yet smooth. Complex, but simple at the same time, and I love it.

Since I'm painting with acrylic rather than oil paints for this project, I use my hair dryer to help dry the background now that Grace hung up. That way, I can move forward with the rest of the painting faster than normal. I slather dark paint around to depict someone's body and use white to highlight parts of a face in the darkness. When everything else is finished, it's time for the final part. The part I've been looking forward to the most. Throwing the handle of my brush in my hair, I put one of my palms directly on top of the pile of white. When it's adequately saturated, I rub my hands together to ensure every crease on both of my hands is evenly coated with paint. After one more dip to be sure there's enough, I hover my hands over the canvas until I decide on placement, then press them firmly against the abstract portrait. When I lift my palms, there are two perfect imprints of my hands.

Taking a few steps back, I take a sip from my drink and stare at my latest piece before deciding it needs one more detail before I can consider it finished. So I add a frame to give it the illusion that someone is peering in through a window. Now it's finished, and only a couple of hours after I started.

The more I stare at it, the more I love it. I don't think this one will get listed on my website. Setting my wineglass down, I pick up my phone and take a picture of my project to send to Hayden. He replies a few minutes later.

Hayden:
Is that one of yours??
It looks great! Let me

guess; it's not spooky,
it's misunderstood.
Right?

Me:
Right. They're looking in
from their abstract world
into ours, and it's actually
kind of sad because it will
only ever be perceived as
something it's not. Which is
scary and threatening. Not
misunderstood or longing.

Hayden:
I love the way your mind
works.

I send the picture to my family's group chat too, though I'm unsure why. They've always been fairly supportive, but they don't always understand the things I create. Maybe I was encouraged by Hayden's positive response.

The responses I get from my family support everything I said about the way it would be perceived. One of my parents even goes as far as to say that hanging it in my house would be like inviting in a demon. That makes me roll my eyes.

That's a little dramatic, don't you think?

Maybe it's a good thing this piece isn't being listed for others to see. Either way, I'm happy with it, and it looks good where it now hangs on the wall.

IT'S DATE DAY, so I invite Nyasia to get her nails done with me in one of the neighboring cities since I bit mine down to the skin. She gets round, all-white nails, and I get almond-shaped, matte red ones to match what I'll be wearing tonight.

A couple of hours later, at exactly 6:00, there's a knock on my door. On the other side of it, Anthony gives me a handsome, close-lipped smile the second he sees me and takes in my appearance. Tonight, I'm wearing a red, square neck, long-sleeved dress that ends mid-thigh and some sheer black tights.

Anthony looks handsome as ever. His face is smooth, showing off its sharp edges. Every strand of hair on his head is brushed back and sits perfectly in place. There isn't even a speck of lint on his all black clothing, which is truly an impressive feat. With the way he holds himself and that delicious accent of his, I could easily see someone mistaking him for a prince.

It takes a couple seconds of me admiring his appearance before I notice the small gift bag in his hand.

"What's that?" I ask him.

He looks at the bag like he forgot he had it. "I got something for Lenny, actually. I don't know much about cats but, well, I thought he might like this."

After being handed the bag, I open it and find a stainless steel cat fountain inside. My answering smile is immediate.

"You got Lenny a drinking fountain?"

Anthony gives me an uneasy shrug that he tries to play off as casual. "I noticed the other day that he kept drinking from the faucet in the kitchen. I know you have a bowl for him to drink from already, but I thought he might like this. According to articles I found online, these aren't only preferred by cats but it's good for their health too." It feels like my heart did a flip so impressive it would make an Olympic gymnast jealous. I wonder if hearts are showing in my eyes right now, just like the emoji. Whether he brought this solely for Lenny or as a way to impress me, I can't be sure, but there's no denying the thought behind the act.

"I don't know what to say. This is perfect, thank you. I'm going to get it started for him real quick." Regardless of whether he meant to impress me, consider me thoroughly impressed.

'According to articles I found online....'

Imagining this man looking up articles on cats is one of the cutest things I can imagine. He definitely earned some brownie points with that move.

I know I should probably wait until after the date to mess with this kitty fountain, but I can't help myself. Luckily, Anthony doesn't seem to mind since he's petting Lenny while I fill up the device. I barely finish pushing it up against the wall when Lenny rushes over with immediate curiosity.

"Ready?" Anthony asks as he attempts to brush cat hair off his nice clothes with little success. He pulls a few hairs off before giving up and taking my hand to walk me outside and get me seated in his car. Aside from a couple of small accents on the outside of the vehicle, the spotless interior appears to be one of the only things he owns that has any color. Blue, of course.

"Where are we going?" We're headed away from everything in town and we're not going towards Ragsburrow either, which is where everyone else who lives here likes to temporarily escape.

"To the airport." My mental question about Maple Crest having an airport must be evident on my face even in the dark, because he chuckles. "It's a private airport."

When we get there, he drives right up to a helicopter and parks beside it. We get out of the vehicle, and he hands the car keys to someone standing nearby before escorting me to the helicopter's other side. I expect that we'll be sitting in the back with someone else piloting, but Anthony sits me in the cockpit before moving back around to sit in front of the controls.

"You're seriously taking me flying as a date? I mean, being in the air is incredible all by itself, but *you're* going to be the one piloting?" I gape.

"As I said, I have many talents. I'd be more than excited to share them all with you." He winks at me, and an excited, nervous chuckle leaves me. I've been flying several times before but never in a helicopter. This seems intimate. And *seriously* romantic. I'm sure we've all read books and seen movies where some lucky girl gets taken out on a date like this, but I never expected myself to have this experience.

"Where are we going?" I ask him as I watch his car get driven off to a nearby hangar.

"To dinner." He hands me a set of headphones and I put them on as he starts to push buttons and flip switches to get the helicopter started. He puts his own set of headphones on, and once the rotor blades have picked up enough speed, we begin lifting off the ground. I squeal a little from excitement and I see his teeth show with a smile, but he doesn't take his attention off the controls. Meanwhile, I can't drag my attention away from the windows.

After a few minutes in the air, there are lights everywhere on the ground below us. They're a little spread out at first and then become more and more clustered together as small towns become more populated cities. Quaint homes slowly become apartment buildings, and family-owned businesses become skyscrapers.

Nearly an hour later, the helicopter is landing on a helipad attached to a tall building in a city I'm not sure I know the name of. As the spinning of the rotor blades dies down, Anthony takes my hand and helps me out of the helicopter. After linking my arm through his, we walk across a small runway that leads from the platform to the building's rooftop entrance. Standing beside the door, waiting for us, are a couple of men in suits. The shorter of the two shakes Anthony's hand.

"Good evening, Mr. Kensington. Did you have a good flight, sir?"

"I did, Kenneth. The skies are perfect tonight."

"Very glad to hear that, sir." The man, Kenneth, looks at me and nods his head. "Follow me, miss. Your table is this way." Kenneth and the other man guide us inside, down a hall, and into an elegant restaurant.

We have almost every eye in the place on us right now. Everyone wants to see who the people who rode in on a helicopter are, but the thing is, I don't even care. Anthony has all of my attention. When we reach our table, he takes my coat from me and pulls out my chair. Every minute spent here with him adds up to truly become a night to remember. Anthony is charming and a shameless flirt. Not at all the man everyone back home made him out to be.

Walking out hand in hand to the helipad after our meal, it's just the two of us, no escorts this time. Anthony continues for the helicopter, but my feet stop when we're a short distance from it, jerking him to a halt.

"What's wrong? Is everything okay?" He looks confused, perhaps even a little worried.

"I'm not ready for the night to end," I tell him honestly. It's getting late and even though city lights are illuminated all around us, things are winding down. Anthony steps back beside me, still gripping my hand in his. When he stops in front of me, he rubs tender little circles on my skin with his thumb.

"Who said it has to end? Just say the word and I'll stop time for you." He starts to lift my hand to his mouth so he can place a kiss on my fingers, staring directly into my eyes as he does it. Right before my hand connects with his lips, though, everything stops. Our gazes are still locked with his mouth an inch from my hand, but there's no more movement. We're sucked into this current moment with each other so intensely that I almost begin to think he really did manage to stop time for me. But that's before I realize the reason my hand came to a stop is because I pulled my hand back enough to stop him at the last second.

"Please don't kiss only my hand. Kiss *me*," I whisper. Or beg. Whatever. I don't care whether I sound desperate because all I care about right now is that he didn't have to be asked twice. Anthony springs forward so quickly it's as if he were a suffocating man and my kiss is a breath of fresh air. My hand dives to cup his face and I lean into him to deepen our kiss. One of his hands slides to my lower back and the other holds onto my arm.

Kissing Anthony is passionate, hot, exciting, and— and interrupted.

"Well, well," a man chuckles as he emerges clapping from somewhere behind us. Our lips break apart, but I stay close to Anthony as he looks at the man I don't recognize. His previously lust-filled expression immediately turns stony.

"What are you doing here?" he asks in a near growl. The stranger's entire aura is unsettling and his grin seems more like a snarl than anything else. His face is made up of sharp edges, hollow cheeks, and cold eyes that send a slight chill down my spine.

"I'm here for dinner, same as you. But then I saw you walk out here and I thought I'd follow you out for a friendly hello." This man's voice sounds anything but friendly and from the way Anthony's body tenses, I get the feeling he's thinking the same thing. The brown-haired stranger shifts his attention to me. "And who's this? Care to give me an introduction?"

Not knowing what's happening between them and not wanting to be rude, I extend my hand to him.

"I'm—"

"Her name is Evaline. Evie, this is Benjamin. There. Now you've said hello and had your introduction. Time to go," Anthony's tone is as hard as his expression. I barely catch myself before I make a face at his lie, but surely he has a reason for what he did so I go along with it and stay quiet. For now. I'll make him explain himself once we're alone again.

"Evaline." Benjamin tests my name on his tongue. *Evie*. Do you have a last name, Evie?" The way he talks almost makes me convinced he knows Anthony gave him a false name on my behalf.

"Ben," Anthony's voice is stern and full of warning, "it's time for you to go." Benjamin is still holding onto my hand, and he begins to rub the back of my hand like Anthony had done right before we kissed. He makes it difficult, but I manage to pull my hand out of his grasp. Anthony's hand tightens on my waist.

"You are such a beautiful little thing. I mean, *wow*, if you were mine, I'd have to lock you away to keep you safe from the prying eyes of the public. Can't be too careful with a treasure like you."

"It's a good thing I'm not yours then and will never have to worry about that."

"Never say never, honey. You don't know what the future may hold."

Anthony takes a step toward him, bringing them mere inches apart. They're nearly the same height, with Anthony being only an inch or two taller.

"Careful," Anthony warns him. "You're stepping into dangerous territory."

"No, Anthony. I'm not. You are."

Anthony glares at him for a few moments before turning away and helping me into the helicopter. He shoves past Benjamin on the way to his seat.

"Get the fuck out of the way if you want to keep your head," he snaps at him before closing the door to the helicopter and doesn't wait for Benjamin to move before he starts turning everything on.

"Who was that? And why did you give him a fake name?"

"Give me a minute. Let me get us out of here first, okay?" He looks at me earnestly and I nod. As the helicopter begins to lift, Benjamin smiles that unsettling smile and waves at us until we turn from view. When we're in the air with our headphones on, Anthony speaks again. "I'm so sorry, Tatum. And I'm sorry we can't have a normal date."

"Who was he?" I ask again.

"He's one of my dad's former employees. They had an ugly falling out, and he's been making things difficult for months."

"Is he dangerous? Why didn't you tell him my real name?"

Anthony grabs my hand and gives it a gentle squeeze. "No,

he's not dangerous. But I care about you, Tatum, and I don't want to take any chances. I'm really, truly sorry."

"For what? For protecting me? Call me biased, but I don't think that's something you should ever be sorry for." I consider something for a second, then speak again. "I can think of something else you can apologize for."

Anthony's shoulders drop a little. "What's that?"

"For ending our kiss looooong before I was ready."

I catch him pinching his bottom lip with his teeth as he smiles. "Is that right?"

"Mmhmm."

"Well then, let me land this damn thing and I'll give you a proper apology once we make it back."

Chapter Seven

TATUM

I don't think I've ever ached more for an apology in my life. I'm not sure what he'll consider a 'proper apology,' but I hope he and I have the same thing in mind. Seeing the tense set of his body as he drives the car back to my place makes me think we do. I've also noticed he's subtly adjusted himself in his seat several times since we left the airport, making me think that perhaps his pants are getting a little too tight in all the right places.

Parking rather abruptly along the curb in front of my house, he's quick to come around the car and take my hand as we walk toward the door. When we get to the porch, it's hard to tell which of us moves first, but our mouths reconnect and I nearly sigh from satisfaction.

That nighttime helicopter ride was amazing and beyond gorgeous. But I was a little distracted all the way home, thinking about this moment. His hands are in my hair, and I'm running my arms up the length of his. Even though I don't want to stop what we're doing for a second, I pull away enough so I can talk.

"You're coming inside, right?" He answers me by kissing me firmly and mumbling his response against my lips. It's hard, but I manage to pull away and turn around so I can get the front door open. As I insert the key in the lock, he runs one hand along my waist and uses the other to brush my hair to one side so he can kiss the skin where my neck and shoulders meet. My eyes flutter closed and if he keeps doing that, I don't think we'll be able to make it inside.

By some miracle though, we make it in the house and close the door behind us before I spin around and reconnect our mouths. With Anthony's hands now in my hair, he walks me backward until my back connects with the wall. My hand slides over his chest and comes to a stop. Beneath my fingers, I can feel the pounding of his heart. It's in sync with mine, which is beating just as hard and fast.

Running my other hand up the back of his neck and into his hair, I gently pull on his blonde strands to tilt his head back. When the muscles of his throat are exposed, I press my lips to the tender flesh. As I kiss him, I look up through my lashes at his face and find his eyes clenched tightly as a satisfied breath leaves his mouth. He leans down then to grab my thighs and secures my legs around his middle.

"Bedroom?" he asks, his voice husky.

I jerk my head behind him. "Over there. It's the first door on the right."

He kisses me as he finds his way there, then lays me on the bed. Anthony shrugs off his coat and my fingers undo the buttons of his shirt. When his shirt is off, I take in the delectable sight of his bare chest while he begins to remove my shoes. But where he was quick with his actions before, he's taking his time now as if he's soaking up every second of this.

Anthony's warm hands run reverently up my legs, then underneath the hem of my dress. Our eyes stay connected even as, underneath the red fabric, his hands travel to my hips and grab hold of the edge of my tights. His brows raise in quiet question. I nod, all words lost to me right now.

Still staring into my eyes, he slowly pulls the tights down my legs until he's able to toss them on the chair across the room. With my legs pressed together, I drag my heels towards me along the bed until my knees are in the air. Then, I leisurely let them fall apart so he has a good view of my black thong.

Anthony's gray eyes fall to my center. "Christ," he whispers, thoroughly taking in the sight. Removing his knee off the bed, he lowers his body until his arms are propping him up in between my legs, his face lowering to kiss each of my thighs.

"Didn't you owe me an apology?" I ask.

A lustful grin spreads along his face. "Indeed, I do. It's going to be a lengthy one. Think you can handle it?" Anthony hooks a finger into my underwear and slides it aside. When his hot breath brushes over my newly exposed skin, a shiver wracks throughout my body. Then when he latches onto my clit, my back arches and I throw my head back with a moan. Anthony works his tongue with obvious talent from my slit to my clit, paying attention to all the right places and making my body shake with an impending orgasm.

When he inserts his middle finger into me and crooks it to rub against my g-spot while still licking, sucking, and nibbling at my clit, I'm practically done for. It's when he adds a second finger that I'm sent over the glorious edge with a shout. He rubs me and pumps his fingers, all while still licking me so he can drag out my pleasure for as long as possible, adequately taking care of my body. Once the orgasm ends, Anthony kisses my thigh again before climbing up my body and kissing my lips deep and slow.

My center already misses the attention he was giving me and my hips rise off the bed to meet his.

"Is that apology enough or do you want more?" he asks, his tone teasing. We both know we're far from done. I can feel his hard length trapped behind his pants and I *definitely* want more of his unnecessary apology.

"I think you can do better." That's a lie. He already brought me to a height I'd never been to before with only his tongue and two fingers. We still have more pleasure to experience and from what I've felt through his pants, I know I'm going to be satisfied beyond measure tonight.

With the two fingers that were inside me mere moments ago, he gestures for me to stand up. "How do you normally like it?" When I'm standing, he turns me around and brushes my hair aside so he can grab the zipper of my dress. He pulls it down with unnecessary slowness in order to drag out the moment. Whether he knows he's also prolonging my torture, I can't be sure, but I'm aching to feel him inside me fully.

My dress slides to the floor and his hand snakes up my neck, into my hair. I must take too long to answer, too lost in thought, because Anthony's fingers clench. My head is brought back to his shoulder as he takes a small step forward, closing the distance between us. Excitement swells in my chest.

"Tell me how you want me, Tatum. You like this, huh? Do you want more of this?" Despite the strong hold he has on my hair, his voice is soft and light. Caring.

"Yes, now stop stalling and take your pants off already, Anthony." His grip on my hair tightens, but I hear him chuckle behind me. His mouth rests against my ear and I can feel the shape of his smile on my skin.

"I like it when you say my name. Now I'm going to make you scream it."

And he did. Anthony Kensington fucks like a god and his dick is like a drug. The euphoria he brings to my body is unlike anything I've experienced before. Tonight won't be our only night together. There's so much chemistry between us — chemistry I know he feels too — that we'll both need another hit.

LOUD YOWLING and the crash of glass in the morning have me jolting up in bed, Anthony doing the same beside me since he stayed the night. For a second, we both stay frozen, straining our ears to see if we can decipher what just happened. When another terrible cry fills the air, I jolt from my bed wearing only an oversized PJ shirt and race around the house to find out what's happening.

"Tatum! Tatum, wait!" Anthony catches up to me and pulls me behind him. He didn't stop to put on clothes because he's still only in the black boxer briefs he fell asleep in. He did, however, stop long enough to grab his gun from the holster he placed on my dresser last night when he removed his pants. Raising the weapon, he continues in front of me. When we reach the main room seconds later, he cusses and runs to the far wall of the kitchen. When I see what's happening, my mouth drops with shock, and tears instantly flood my eyes.

"Oh my God, oh my God. Lenny!" His body is jolting violently on the floor with a seizure and Anthony is holding his head off the floor. Lenny's nose is bleeding, suggesting that his face was bouncing off the wood before we found him. I can't do anything to help him until the seizure stops, so I stay kneeled beside him, sobbing with fear for his life.

Too many long seconds later, it ends. I cry out Lenny's name and take over holding his head while Anthony stands to do... something, I ignore what. All my focus is on my cat who's lying in a puddle of his urine and breathing heavily on his side. I'm terrified to touch him in case I'll somehow end up hurting him, but I also can't stop stroking his fur as tears stream down my cheeks. I repeatedly whisper that he's okay, but the truth is, I don't know if he will be or not.

Anthony comes back with a towel and wraps Lenny's listless body in it before handing him to me.

"Come on," he urges, helping me stand on unsteady feet. I hug Lenny close to my chest and press my face into his fur. He's conscious but too exhausted to move.

Anthony kneels in front of me, holding out a pair of loose

shorts for me to step into. Then he puts on my socks and shoes for me so that I don't have to set Lenny down for a single second before throwing his own clothes on. As soon as he's dressed, he grabs his keys and guides me toward the door.

"Where are we going?"

"To the vet." He holds onto my elbow gently as we walk outside and opens the door to his Audi so I can get inside. The pungent scent of cat urine fills the spotless vehicle. Maybe I should feel guilty for sitting on the clean seats when I know my legs are soaked from the puddle I was kneeling in, but I don't. I don't care about anything except for how fast we can get to the vet. Anthony calls them to let them know we're coming, then puts his hand on my knee in an attempt to comfort me once he hangs up.

Although Maple Crest's veterinary clinic is on the other side of town, Anthony parks in front of it fairly quickly. Since my arms are full, he first opens the car door for me, then the door to the building and I rush to the front desk.

"This is Lenny, we called not too long ago about his seizure." My words are hurried and full of panic.

The girl working the front rushes around the desk. "Over here. We'll put you guys in this room. Tell me what happened." I recount the story, every detail, while she examines Lenny. When she's done, she leaves to get the vet. I cradle Lenny in my lap, still crying, while Anthony sits beside me with his arm wrapped around my shoulders, holding me against his side. When the vet comes in, I tell the story again while she too examines my little shadow before taking him to draw blood.

My body is shaking with nerves. I know many people wouldn't understand why I'm reacting the way I am and tell me *it's just a cat*, but I love him as if he were a child.

Nearly two hours later, Lenny is ready to be taken home. I keep him in my arms while Anthony takes the bottles of medication and a small stack of papers from the vet tech.

"Oh no, I— I forgot my wallet at the house. I wasn't thinking, I didn't grab it," I stress.

"Don't worry about it, I'll take care of it," Anthony assures me as he opens the exam room door for us to walk out. His brows scrunch as he stares at something on the other side. He doesn't move or say anything for a moment before stepping aside and opening the door wider, giving me space to walk out. When I do, I see Hayden sitting in the lobby dressed in jeans and a dark gray hoodie.

His concern is clear as day on his face when he sees me and stands up, pushing his shaggy hair out of his eyes. "Hey, is everything okay? What happened?"

"What are you doing here?" I ask, confused by his presence.

"My sister works here. I was dropping something off when I saw you walk in. You were in such a hurry you didn't see me and I didn't want to go into the room and invade your privacy, but I couldn't leave without knowing you were okay." Anthony steps around us to go pay the bill, leaving Hayden and me to talk.

"Oh. You waited this whole time?" Lenny squirms a little in my arms and I pet his fur. Hayden reaches over and carefully scratches behind his ear.

"Of course. You were hysterical. I was worried."

I tell him what happened and that the doctor is unsure what caused the seizure yet since we have to wait for the results of some of her tests. Plus, I still have to travel to the vet in Ragsburrow for others since this clinic doesn't have the necessary equipment.

"Jesus. I'm so sorry, Tatum. That must have been terrifying." I hug Lenny closer to me as I remember the screams of pain he made right before his seizure started. The doctor guesses he has epilepsy and that the commotion which woke us was a pre-ictal headache; a sort of warning of what was to come.

Anthony comes back and lightly puts his hand on my waist, leaning close to my ear to speak quietly. "Are you ready?"

I nod. "Thank you for waiting to make sure I'm alright. I really appreciate that."

Hayden nods, but he still looks worried. "Of course. Do you need anything?"

"No, I'm fine. Thank you, though. I'll text you later, okay?" Anthony and I start for the door and I'm halfway out of it when I turn around. "Oh my God, we were supposed to have a date today! Hayden, I'm so sorry, but—"

He lifts his hand to stop me with a reassuring smile. "Don't worry about it. We'll reschedule. I was planning on it the second I saw you run in here. Just take care of your cat and give me a call when you're up for it."

"Okay. Okay. Goodbye." My mind is all over the place and it's hard to focus on anything for longer than a few seconds even though Lenny is alive and safe in my arms.

Anthony drives me home and walks inside with me when we get there. I wipe Lenny down with a washcloth to clean the urine off him, then get him set up on the bed. Although he perked up at the vet, his energy is depleted from the whole ordeal.

"I cleaned the floor where we found him earlier. If you want to take a shower, I can watch him until you're done," Anthony offers. I take in his appearance now for the first time this morning. I've only seen him a few times, but every time I have, he's been well put together. I get the impression that's how he always is; not a wrinkle in his fine clothes or a hair out of place. But right now, his clothes are ruffled and his hair is messy.

I take him up on his offer so I can shower. While I wait for the water to heat up, I notice my own appearance in the mirror. My hair is sex and sleep-tousled. I'm wearing an oversized shirt that's mine but could pass as a mans. There's a good reason for that too, since it came from the men's section of a store. To top it all off, I was very lazy while removing my makeup last night, so there's mascara smudged underneath my eyes. I cringe at the fact that I went into public looking like a hot mess. Not only that, but the other man I'm dating saw me like this with another man. He's not stupid. I'm sure he was able to put two and two together to conclude that I spent the night with Anthony.

Way to go, Tatum. Hayden was cool with the whole Anthony surprise once. I doubt he will be again.

I scrub my face out of frustration before stepping into the shower to rinse the cat urine and dried sweat from the night before off my skin. When I open the bathroom door in my fuzzy robe and with towel-dried hair I find Anthony seated on my bed, which he made. Lenny is purring and rubbing against Anthony's chest as he stands on his lap. Anthony's once black shirt is now covered with cat hair, but he continues to scratch his fur anyway.

"Thank you for all your help today," I say from the bathroom doorway, bringing his attention to me.

"You don't have to thank me for anything."

"Yes, I do," I tell him as I take up the space beside him on the bed. "I know he's just a cat, but I was...that was awful, Anthony. Seeing him like that was awful, and I don't know what I would've done if I was alone this morning."

A considering look fills his features as he tilts his head to see me better. "That's the second time you've underestimated your-self around me. I guarantee you're stronger than you think. I know you are. You could've handled yourself with your sprain, and you could've handled this. I'm glad I was present, and I hope I will continue to be around if or when tragedy strikes again, but you don't *need* anyone but yourself. And Lenny is a cat, yes, but he's not *just* a cat. It's obvious he means the world to you, and that's what matters." I continue to pet Lenny rather than say something back because I don't know what I'd say.

"Do you want to stay for a while longer?" I ask instead.

Anthony checks his watch and frowns. "I wish I could, but I have to go." I'm unsure how to handle him walking out now. Do I wave goodbye? Do I kiss him? Do I kiss his cheek instead? Maybe a handshake? No, definitely not a handshake. Last night was far from my first time having sex, but it was my first time having sex while not in a relationship.

Anthony must see the indecision on my face because when we reach the front door, he smiles and bends down to kiss me.

But the moment the kiss ends, I remember he paid for the vet visit today.

"Wait, how much do I owe you for the appointment today? Let me grab some cash to pay you back before you leave."

"Don't worry about it. The little fur ball has grown on me. I'm happy to do something to help him out."

"Anthony," I scold softly. "You're not even my boyfriend. I'm not letting you pay for his bill."

"Not your boyfriend *yet,* but I will be." He winks at me, and my heart beats a little harder.

"Anthony," I press, rolling my eyes while also fighting a smile.

"Fine, if you're so intent on it, I'll let you pay me back the next time I see you. I'll tell you what the cost was then. That's my insurance for another date."

Despite the way our day started, he manages to make me smile. "Fine. But just so you know, I wanted to see you again even before you pulled that move."

"Good." He pulls me into a hug and kisses the top of my head. "Take it easy today, darling."

"I will," I assure him.

Anthony starts to walk out the door, but stops himself and turns around halfway through. "Oh, before I forget, adjust the prices on your website if you can this morning."

My brows scrunch. "My...prices? Why? What's wrong with them?"

"Know your worth, love. Aim for the stars and you'll reach them. Trust me, the right audience will find you. Just adjust your prices more towards what I paid. And do it soon. I'll see you later." He leaves with a smile on his face.

Right, I'm going to find multiple *people willing to pay several thousand dollars for my work. I highly doubt that.*

After locking the door behind Anthony, I grab my laptop and bring it to my bedroom, opening it on my bed. Pulling up my website, I'm disappointed to see I've made only one other sale aside from Anthony's in the past couple of days. I used to have more interest in my work than this, but it's my fault things are slow now since I slowed down on marketing after the move.

Willing to take a shot though, I change the prices of the listings as Anthony had suggested. Maya texts me while I'm nearing the end of the task so I tell her what happened this morning. The next time I check my phone, it's a couple of hours and a million checks on Lenny later.

Maya:
No fucking way.
Are you serious??
My poor 4-legged nephew!!
I'm FaceTiming you as soon
as I get off work. I need to
see him. You're ok tho?

Nyasia:
Sooooo how'd it go last night?

Hayden:
How are you and your cat
doing? Need some company?

Need some company? Even after he saw me the way he did with Anthony this morning and I canceled our date, he hasn't been deterred?

Me:
Doing great! Much better than
this morning. I could definitely
use some company, though.

After sending my text to Hayden, I look through my other notifications and see that Anthony followed me on Instagram. Clicking on his profile again, I notice he posted a new picture. It's inside his house, right above his fireplace; a picture of my painting on his wall with my account tagged in the middle of it. There's no caption, only the photo of the painting, and it already has over two thousand likes since he posted it forty-five minutes ago.

Hayden texts back to let me know he's on his way and several minutes later he's knocking on my door.

"Come on in," I shout from the art room. I'm currently at a point in my painting where it's nearly impossible for me to set down my brush. "I'm in the back room." My house is a single floor with an open layout. When you walk in, there's the living room, which blends into the kitchen toward the back. A full bathroom and storage room are to the left, then my bedroom, which has another bathroom in it, and my art room are to the right.

Hayden finds his way in, holding a bag of food, and gazes around my room.

"This is your studio, huh? I like it."

"Thanks!" My hair is braided to keep my long hair from getting in the way and I have my painting overalls on over a tank top. I finish the detail I was working on, then set my brush aside to give him a friendly hug. Because that's the acceptable thing to do when you haven't even kissed yet, right? Or is he going to think I'm friend-zoning him now? "What have you got there?"

"Well, I figured you wouldn't feel like going anywhere without your cat today, so I brought dinner to you. And you mentioned on our date that you like scary movies, so I thought I'd bring one. I haven't seen this one yet, so I was wondering if you'd like to watch it together?"

I change out of my painting clothes into something a little less messy, and a few minutes later we're at the counter eating the pasta he'd brought for dinner. I've been eating in this spot for months now, but I can't stop smiling during my meal tonight. Hayden is grinning from ear to ear as he tells me a story about his vet tech sister — who helped Lenny this morning — and I feel myself becoming more and more enthralled with him. He's so *good* and makes me feel good in his presence.

When we finish eating, we're pulling the blinds closed to prepare for our scary movie when my phone dings.

I check the notification while Hayden puts the DVD in.

I made a sale. *No freaking way.* My fingers fly to unlock the screen and open my website. Sure enough, one of my paintings just sold for $5,000. *Oh my God.*

Chapter Eight

TATUM

Hayden and I are sitting side by side on the couch, and we're only ten minutes into the movie when I flinch at a jump scare on screen.

Hayden laughs and grabs some popcorn from the bowl we made. "I thought you said you liked scary movies?"

"I did, but that doesn't mean I'm immune to their creepiness." Hayden laughs again then takes my hand in his. If he can feel the way my heart is beating faster and comments on it, I'll blame it on adrenaline from the movie. *Seriously, Tatum? You're holding hands. That's it. Are you back in grade school, or what?*

What is it about Hayden Williams that makes me get all giddy over the tiniest things? I feel like I live in a period drama whenever he's around.

Oh, Mr. Darcy helped Elizabeth Bennett into the carriage!
How absolutely swoon-worthy!
Did you see how Anthony Bridgerton and Miss Kate Sharma stretched their pinkies toward each other? I'm dying over it!

If my life were a period drama, I wonder what moments would have people reacting like that.

The movie intensifies, and the main character finally feels like someone is watching her. Although I already know how this will play out since practically all scary movies are the same, I'm sucked into anticipating what will happen next, anyway. As the main character rounds a corner and the music climaxes, Hayden abruptly squeezes my hand, sending my soul so far out of my body with fear that I might never get it back. I shriek loudly.

Hayden can hardly catch his breath from how hard he's laughing over my reaction, so I punch him in the shoulder.

"Sorry about that. Muscle spasm," he jests with a wink that lets me know it was anything but an accident.

I narrow my eyes on him. "Uh-huh."

"Hey, you can come a little closer if you're scared. That way, the monsters would have to go through me before they got to you."

It's my turn to laugh now, "Oh my God, Hayden, that was the cheesiest thing I've ever heard in my life!"

He's smiling along with me. "I was aware of that possibility as I said it. Did it work, though?"

My head bobs from side to side with mock contemplation. "It worked," I tell him. "Cheesy is your thing, isn't it?"

He shrugs. "Why mess with the classics?" Hayden puts an arm around me, and I cuddle up against his side, pulling the folded blanket toward me from one of the cushions and spreading it open to cover both of us. As the movie continues, his hand rubs my arm in tender caresses, making it hard to focus on what's happening on the screen. He smells so good, like amber. It's earthy with a touch of spice, and his scent brings feelings of cozy warmth with it. "You're staring," I suddenly hear him say.

I blink, and I realize my eyes had shifted from the screen to his face at some point. He's clean-shaven today, and I was admiring the view of his strong jaw that this angle provides before I got caught.

I'm trying to think of how I want to respond; sarcasm, flirtation, or perhaps I should make up an excuse about how there's popcorn salt on his face. But he leans his head down and presses his lips to mine in a tender kiss before I decide. He holds his lips still against mine for a few seconds before pulling away. We stare at each other for a split second before we both snap back to each other with intensity. The kiss is no longer slow and careful, but it's not fast and desperate, either. Our mouths move with a deep sort of perfectly matched rhythm that has him groaning quietly in my mouth.

The movie is long forgotten as we familiarize each other with our mouths. I eventually roll over so I'm practically lying on top of him and his arms wrap securely around me. My fingers find their way into his shaggy brown hair while my other hand slides down his arm. Thanks to his job, I can feel the difference in his bulk compared to Anthony's.

There's a thud nearby and my head jerks toward my bedroom.

"Oh no." I hastily untangle myself from my blanket and rush toward the noise.

"What is it?" Hayden asks. Panicked and remembering what happened this morning, I flip on the light switch and search for Lenny, only to find him yawning and mid-stretch on the floor. "Tatum, what's wrong?"

I sigh with relief. "I was worried he was having another seizure."

Hayden squats down and brushes a hand along Lenny's back. The cat instantly perks up at the touch, not caring at all that he's never met this man before.

"This is Lenny, huh? He's cute! Now that he's not wrapped in a towel, I can see that he looks exactly like a cat I used to have."

I perk up at this.

"Oh? Was it a family cat or your own pet?"

"He was technically the family pet, but he and I were so bonded he was pretty much mine. We had him since he was a couple years old. The two of us were nearly the same age. Then I took him to college with me." Any man that likes cats, especially enough to own one, is an instant green flag.

"What happened to him?"

"He passed away while I was at Stanford. Old age, I think. I mean, the guy was ancient in cat years." He stands back up and stops in front of me, tucking a strand of hair behind my ear and leaning in again. We resume our kissing in the middle of my bedroom until my phone starts to ring with another interruption. Hayden chuckles and puts his forehead against mine.

"Ugh, I'm so sorry. I think my friend from back home is calling for an update about what happened this morning. She said she was going to call when she was free."

"That's alright. Go answer it before you miss it."

"Are you sure?"

"Yes." He urges me back to the living room. Reaching my phone, I see Maya attempting FaceTime like I had guessed and answer the call.

"Hey, give me a minute, 'kay?" I don't wait for her to answer before dropping the phone on the couch, the call still going. Hayden is waiting for me by the front door, and I go up to him with another hug. This time, it's anything but putting him in the friend zone since I kiss him the second our chests meet. "Thank you so much for dinner and the company. It was exactly what I needed."

He reconnects our lips. "It was my pleasure. I'm glad I could see your studio before you get all famous."

"Maybe tomorrow you can come back and we can try to watch that movie again? We kind of missed half of it since we were occupied doing something else."

Hayden laughs. "That *something else* was the best part of my week. How about I take you to a theater tomorrow? Today was fantastic, but I'd love to take you on a real movie date." We set the date up and after a few more moments of heated kissing, Hayden leaves.

Returning to my phone, I pick it up and am instantly met with my best friend making a comical face at me.

"That man didn't have an English accent. So, who's the new Romeo?" she asks.

"Maya, I have so much to catch you up on." The last time we talked was before I met Anthony in the coffee shop a few days ago. She works as a model and has a chaotic schedule, so we talk when possible, but it's not as often as we'd like.

A few minutes later, there's another thump which interrupts our conversation. This time, though, it comes from the back of the house near the back door.

"Hold on. I need to make sure Lenny isn't having a seizure." I get up from the couch and walk into the kitchen. "That's weird," I say more to myself, but Maya replies anyway.

"What is?"

"Lenny isn't in here." I turn back, going for the bedroom and find him sound asleep on the bed when there's another quiet thud outside. My brows knit together and I slowly return to the kitchen. Realizing that the sliding back door which leads to the back patio is unlocked, I quickly flip the lock into place.

"Maybe there's a raccoon outside or something?" Maya suggests.

"Maybe. Should I go check?"

"Should you go—? No! Tatum, what the hell? You're a horror movie junkie. Why would you even ask that? You know what happens to people who go check out weird noises. Say *fuck the noise; it's none of my business,* and carry on with your night in the safety of your house. Oh, preferably with a knife or something by you."

"Fine, you're right. Anyways, where was I?" We pick up where I left off and then I listen to her as she tells me about what's been going on in her life. Like Grace, Maya likes to have all the finer things in life and go on trips often, but she puts in the hard work for what she's got.

Since we can't have sleepovers anymore like we used to, we fall asleep on our FaceTime call instead. It isn't until the morning that I check my notifications for the first time since Hayden and I started the movie. When I do, I nearly choke on the air I'm breathing.

All of my paintings have sold — every single one of them. After refreshing the page multiple times, I log out and log back in. I even delete the app and re-download it to make sure there isn't a glitch. On the off chance my phone is somehow broken, I check the website on my laptop and see that everything has indeed sold.

"How did..." I check my phone for other notifications and discover that my Instagram account has also blown up. *Anthony*.

I call him, and he answers after a couple of rings. "Good morning, Miss Davis. What can I do for you?"

"My website sold out! How did you do it?" I demand. I'm not sure what I'm freaking out more for; the fact people loved my work so much I'm completely out of inventory, or the amount of money making its way into my account now.

"What do you mean?"

"All of my paintings. How did you sell them all overnight?"

"I didn't. You did, and that's amazing, Tatum. I'm happy to hear that."

I huff into the phone. "No, I didn't. For weeks I've hardly been able to sell a single painting. Suddenly you post a picture of one and I'm sold out. What else did you do?" I realize I may sound a little ungrateful, but I'm not. I'm stunned. The amount of money I just made...it's more than I'd have ever expected doing this. But putting the excitement of that aside, I feel like I didn't earn it like I wanted to because someone else brought me this success. This is too close to what I was trying to escape with my parents.

Anthony must somehow sense my line of thinking because he shoots those thoughts down. "I truly didn't do anything. You are responsible for your success. All I did was post a picture of something in my house and tag the artist. There was no caption telling people to look at your website or praising you in any way. People simply liked what they saw and acted of their own volition. You doubt yourself too much, but look at what you're capable of. *You* sold your paintings, Tatum. The only thing I did was let people know you exist."

Anthony's right. As hard as it may be for me to see, my success is my own, and I'm one step closer to becoming who I want to be. Having people who take me seriously like this makes the feeling even sweeter.

"Well then, I guess I have a busy day of boxing up these canvases before my date!"

"Your date? We haven't had the chance to set another one up yet, darling." I grimace, not having thought about what I was saying before I said it.

"It's a date with Hayden," I confess. Judging by his previous tone, he was already aware of that fact.

Anthony makes some sort of noise to display his annoyance, but it sounds muffled, almost like he put the phone to his chest so I wouldn't hear it, but I did.

"I have some business to take care of this morning, but how would you feel about me coming over to help you when I'm finished?"

"That works for me. See you then."

After we hang up, I drive to Ragsburrow to get all the boxes I'll need for shipping. As I'm in the store, feelings of unease creep up my spine like I'm being watched, but no one sticks out whenever I look around. That doesn't change the fact that I can still feel the weight of someone's intense gaze on me.

My phone buzzes with a text while I'm pushing my cart through the parking lot.

Unknown:
14

14? 14 what? I delete the text, chalking it up to be a wrong number or something, then load the boxes into my car and return home, making myself busy with getting orders ready to ship.

It's nearly noon now, and Anthony lets me know he'll be

heading my way shortly. I tell him to take his time so I can stop at The Brewed Bean for a coffee and to say *hi* to Nick.

"Tatum! It's been a few days. I was about ready to send out a search party for you," Nick exclaims joyfully when I walk in. "How've you been? And you want your usual, right?"

"Please, and a large tea as well." He places someone else's order on the counter and calls out their name. "It's been a busy week. There've been ups and downs, but I can't really complain. How about you?"

"Oh, I've been good. Looking at buying a new place which has been exciting. So, you're not going to tell me yourself? You're going to make me ask about you and Hayden?"

I chuckle as he places the tea in front of me and starts my coffee. "I thought you and Hayden were friends? Hasn't he told you anything?"

Nick smiles that handsome smile of his. The fact that this gorgeous man is in some small town making coffee all day instead of working alongside Maya in front of dozens of cameras blows my mind. But he seems plenty happy to be here and has never had a bad thing to say about Maple Crest.

"Oh, he's told me everything. You're all he talks about now, pretty much. I believe the man is twitter-pated, but I was wondering how it went on your end."

"Hayden is fantastic, honestly. He's incredibly sweet. I'm seeing him again tonight, actually."

"That's right, for a movie date, is that correct?" He slides my coffee in front of me.

"He really does tell you everything," I chuckle.

"Well, not quite everything, but most of it. And I thought you should know that Hayden has had nothing but good things to say about you since the moment he dropped you off after the gallery. Literally. He called me on the way home." A customer walks up to the counter, so we say our goodbyes and he gets back to work. On my way to the car, I think about what he told me.

Hayden found Anthony at my house making me breakfast the

morning after our date, but that didn't scare him off. He saw Anthony and I together the morning of our second date after clearly having had sex, and then I kind of rescheduled on him. Still, he has nothing bad to say about me?

I know I probably shouldn't be bouncing between the two men like this and, at some point, I'll have to make a decision. But as for right now, I can't bring myself to choose between them. They couldn't be more opposite from each other, but I love spending time with both of them. I wish I didn't have to choose. But especially given how they feel about each other, I don't see any other option.

When I get back to my house, Anthony is already there, leaning against his car and waiting for me in one of his signature all-black suits. I hand him his tea and he follows me inside. The first thing he does upon entering is go straight for Lenny on the couch so he can greet him with a scratch under the chin.

"How's he doing?" he asks me.

"He's okay. I got him started on that seizure medication, so he's a little drowsy as his body gets used to it. Otherwise, he's been acting normal. I also called that specialist in Ragsburrow to schedule the rest of the tests." After some persuasion, I finally convince Anthony to let me pay him back for the vet bill using some of the mafia money from the safe.

Then we get started on boxing up canvases. Since each package includes a handwritten thank you note and a couple of extra things to make the unboxing memorable, it takes more time than I'd expected. My art room is beginning to look more like a USPS than anything else.

I take a short break from packing orders to get ready for the date while Anthony stays busy with the boxes. Shortly after 6:00, as I'm putting some of the boxed paintings in my car, Hayden's truck parks along my curb and I can hear the country song he was listening to during the drive over before the vehicle shuts off. Hayden fits in easily with the rest of the people in town as a logger who drives an old truck, and wears faded jeans and flannel. But the more I pay attention, the more I can tell this isn't truly where he wants to be. He has a subtle yearning for the life he had to leave behind when he dropped out of college to help his family here.

"Hello, gorgeous," Hayden greets me as he hugs me tightly, rocking our bodies from side to side. He's much taller than me and only a little bit taller than Anthony, who walks out of the house then, carrying another couple more of the packaged boxes. "What's going on? You're not moving again already, are you?"

"You really want to go on another date with someone who doesn't stay tuned in to the milestones of your life?" Anthony inquires with a quirked brow.

I remove my arms from around Hayden's waist and adjust myself so I can see Anthony better. "You know as well as I do that it's been a busy day for all of us. Besides, I thought it would be nice to tell him in person."

Hayden and Anthony speak up at the same time.

"Why?"

"Tell me what?"

I turn back to Hayden and tell him about my website selling out. He shouts excitedly before wrapping me in another hug and spinning me around making me squeal.

"Tatum, that's amazing!" he exclaims as he sets me back down.

I laugh when I say, "That's why I wanted to wait to tell you." Based on the noise Anthony makes behind me, I'd be willing to bet he just rolled his eyes. I may have missed witnessing the action, but Hayden didn't.

"Maybe you should wear less black. It might make you a happier person," Hayden suggests to him.

"Maybe you should stop breathing," Anthony retorts. "That would definitely do that trick."

"Okay, stop," I demand them both. "Anthony, thank you so much for your help today. You were a lifesaver. The post office is closed now anyway, so I'll take care of everything else tomorrow." I hesitate, awkwardness filling the space between us. "I'll...call you later, okay?"

Walking back up the steps to my door, Hayden stays put in the driveway while Anthony follows me up the stairs. He grabs his phone from inside, then stays next to me as I lock the door. When we reach the bottom of the driveway again, he leans down to kiss me in front of Hayden, then gets in his car. As he drives off, Hayden pulls open the passenger door of his truck for me before walking around the other side and seating himself behind the wheel.

My conversation with Anthony about why he doesn't like Hayden comes to mind, but it doesn't make any more sense to me now than it did when he told me. So what if Hayden had something he wanted when they were kids? They're adults now, so why keep the feud going? I ask Hayden for his side of the story in an attempt to get a clearer picture.

"Things didn't start that way. At first, he was sort of quiet, but Anthony was fairly nice whenever he did talk. But then, out of nowhere, he changed. I'm not sure why. My guess is that his dad spewed poison into his head about the difference between our families and our financial situations. Anthony didn't care about that when they first moved here, but his dad clearly did. I saw it in the way he spoke to my parents. It wasn't long before Anthony started treating me the same way. I'm not completely innocent about why things are the way they are, though. Once he turned against me, I got pretty annoyed over it. We continued to make life at school hell for each other. But our date was the first time I've seen him since he moved back here the second time. I'm over it all, though, ready to let bygones be bygones since there was no reason to stay in touch when he moved to England. But it's clear he still holds some of the resentment from when we were in school." He pauses briefly before continuing. "Either that or his resentment is made anew by my dating you."

My gaze shifts to my hands in my lap. "Does it bother you that I'm seeing you both simultaneously?"

"Are you in a committed relationship with Anthony already?"

"No, I've been seeing him the same way and for the same amount of time that I've been seeing you."

He considers my question for a few seconds. Meanwhile, I start to worry that he's about to turn the truck around any second now.

"Do you want to be in a committed relationship with either of us?"

My cheeks start to heat up. I know he's not asking to be my boyfriend right now, but it still feels a little fast for that type of question. Except, I'm pretty sure I have an answer to it. Though, it may be a complicated one. The problem is that I think I want to be in a relationship with *both* of them while also being the only person for them. Knowing it's not fair, I'm worried that if I tell them this, they'll decide they won't want the same thing and we'll all go back to being strangers.

But I don't want that to happen. I enjoy being around Hayden and Anthony. They make me smile, and laugh, and feel things I was worried I wouldn't feel again when I was with Lucas. In a short amount of time, they've both shown support for me in ways that matter most. Hell, they've already done more than Lucas could simply by being present for me.

In the end, though, I know it's best to be honest early on. Even if it means that I'll lose them because I don't want to waste their time any longer if this isn't what they want.

It isn't something I thought I'd ever want until I met them. I don't know what it is exactly, but there's something about these two that has my mind and body constantly craving them. Not even in a physical way. I just like having them around or being able to text them.

"Yes," I finally answer, "but I don't know how I could choose between you two." Speaking the truth out loud to him makes me nauseous.

"No, it doesn't bother me that you're seeing us both at the same time." My head lifts to look at him as he drives. His shoulders are relaxed and his hands are loose on the steering wheel.

Hayden's body language tells me he really is unbothered by both my current dating habits and this conversation. "And you don't have to choose between us. If you want us both then that's okay with me. He's not my favorite person, but...well, you just might be. If a poly relationship is what will make you happiest, then I'm okay with it."

Did I hear him right? The small-town golden boy would be okay with being in a polyamorous relationship?

"Are you being serious? Wouldn't you resent me a little bit for it?"

"Not at all. I've been in a relationship like this before. I'm totally fine with it." When I don't say anything, he looks over at me and chuckles. "It was while I was in college and I didn't mind sharing at all. And it didn't blow up in my face. It only ended because I had to come back here, and our relationship wasn't that serious to keep it going long distance. Anyway, Anthony will be the hard one to convince. I'm just letting you know you've got more options than you thought."

That explains *so* much. I thought his easy going reactions to everything were because he's not easily provoked. I would never have imagined the real reason.

Chapter Nine

TATUM

Maple Crest has a single movie theater. There are only six auditoriums, half of which are playing older reruns. But this place is cute. It gives off a nostalgic vibe of a simpler time, and I adore it. Hayden and I load up on snacks from the concession stand, then go to find our seats. He has his arm around me by the second trailer and we take goofy selfies on his phone until the rest of the lights dim and the movie begins to play.

Being in the dark and in crowded places are things I've never minded before, but for some reason, the hairs on the back of my neck are scared straight. I can't shake the feeling from earlier this morning of being watched. It feels like someone is directly behind me, staring at me, but I'm too nervous to turn around and look. Not that it would help much in the dark, anyway.

It doesn't make sense that someone would be watching me right now. Hayden greeted a few people before we found our seats, but I don't know anyone here. Plus, it's so dark in here now you can hardly see anything. I try to enjoy the movie, or at least focus solely on Hayden. Something, *anything* other than the uneasy feeling in my gut, but I can't.

At one point, Hayden leans into my ear to ask if I'm alright. I smile and nod, assuring him that I am because I have no reason to say otherwise. But still, the unease persists.

It's just your anxiety. Things have been too easy for too long, and you know it. Take a metaphorical chill pill right now, and you can take a literal one when you get home if you're still feeling panicked.

Taking my mental advice, I shove the feelings aside to enjoy the rest of my date with Hayden. Luckily, it works. The rest of the evening goes by smoothly. By the time Hayden kisses me on the doorstep, I almost completely forget about the pesky feelings I was having while we were out.

"Text me when you get home," I tell him.

He smiles. "I will. Goodnight, gorgeous." Since I know he won't leave until I'm safely inside my house, I lock the door behind me before watching his headlights drive off through the window.

In the morning, it's time to take Lenny to his MRI appointment which will determine whether he has epilepsy. I battle with him to take his medication and wrestle him into the kennel before we rush out the door. In my hurry, since I still have to drop off the car full of paintings, I nearly missed the strip of paper that fluttered down to my patio when I opened my door. Setting Lenny's carrier down, I bend to pick it up. When I do, I see that it's not just any piece of paper but a ticket stub from last night's movie. 'Row 13' in the bottom corner has been boldly circled at least twice with a marker. I pocket the ticket and make a mental note to ask Hayden why he came back to leave his ticket on my door once I get to Lenny's appointment.

When we finally get to the Ragsburrow and they take Lenny to the back for the tests, I decide it's a good time to text Hayden.

Me:
Good morning Paul Bunyan!

I've got a question for you…

Hayden:
Haha, that's cute.
Good morning, gorgeous!
What's on your mind?

Me:
What's the deal with you
dropping your movie ticket off
at my door in the middle of the
night? I mean, it's cute, I'll keep
it, but also a tad weird lol. You
could've given it to me the next
time I see you!

Hayden:
My ticket?
I didn't drop it off at your
door last night.

Hayden tells me he's got his ticket in between his phone and its case and even sends me a picture of it in his hand.

Hayden:
It might be a stretch, but maybe
ask Anthony what he was up to
last night?

The vet comes back into the room with Lenny who is starting to wake up from anesthesia, so I pocket my phone. Since we won't get the scan results until later, I start the drive back to Maple Crest and decide how I'm going to ask Anthony if he followed Hayden and I to the movies last night.

A little over an hour later, I'm back in my house with Lenny settled on the bed, but I still have a pile of boxed-up canvases that need to be taken to the post office. Since I know it's Nyasia's day off, I ask her to watch Lenny while I drop the rest of the orders off, promising to make food when I return. When it comes to cat-sitters, she's the best. Although he's a mama's boy, he seriously loves his new aunt Nyasia, and she loves him just as much. Those two are BFF's and will remain side by side from the second she walks through the door to the moment she leaves.

After my stop at the post office, I go to Anthony's place since we need to have a couple of conversations, and one of them is better to have in person.

My knuckles rasp against the door and several moments later, it opens. Even when Anthony isn't expecting anybody, he's perfectly put together and the house behind him appears spotless. *Something we don't have in common.*

"Miss Davis, what a pleasant surprise. Is there something I can do for you? Or were you just missing me?" His flirtatious grin wakes up the butterflies in my gut.

"Hello, Kensington. Do you have a few minutes?"

"For you? Always." He steps aside and offers me a drink and to get me out of the light rain outside, so I follow him to the kitchen for some water. "What's on your mind, darling?"

I lean my hip against the counter as he fills a glass. "Were you at the theater last night?"

Anthony hands the glass to me and crosses his arms, relaxing against the fridge at his back. "No, I'm not one for movies. Why?"

The familiar clutch of anxiety wraps around my heart the same way it did last night. Even though I knew in my mind that the ticket wasn't Anthony's, part of me was hoping it was because the alternative is unsettling.

"But if it wasn't you, then who was it?"

His brows scrunch slightly and he cocks his head. "What do you mean? If what wasn't me?" I pull the movie stub from my pocket and hand it to him. He unfurls his arms to examine the scrap of paper. "Darling, I give you my word. I wasn't there last night. In fact, I've never even been there before. This isn't my ticket. Why is 'Row 13' circled?"

"I have no idea," I shrug.

Anthony looks at the ticket some more. "Mind if I keep this? I'll see if I can find out who was sitting in this seat."

Maybe I had a reason to be unnerved last night after all. Was someone indeed watching me before following me home? Shivers spread through my body and I'm glad the coat I'm wearing covers my goosebumps.

I haven't cared enough about Lucas to check any of his social media accounts or ask Maya for an update about him since he was released. But it might be time to make sure he's still in Dallas where he belongs, and hasn't come too close to my new home. Same goes for his group of friends. It scares me to think about what Lucas can get people to do for him. He has some pretty shady friends who are all desperate to impress him. They'll do anything he says.

"I— I need to go," I mumble while starting for the door. Suddenly the second part of this conversation isn't important now that I know someone, and I don't know who, was at my door last night while I was sleeping.

I'm quickly pulled to a halt when Anthony grabs my hand.

"Whoa, what's going on?" Turning me to face him again, he cups one of my cheeks. His gray eyes scan over me. "Tatum, darling, your face is white. Do you know who left the ticket?"

I shake my head. "No, but there's a chance I might know who orchestrated it. My ex got out of jail a few weeks ago, and surely he's pissed at me."

Anthony's hand lowers. "Why would he be pissed at you?"

I clear my throat. "Because I kind of sent him there. Actually, no. He put himself in a situation where jail was a possibility. I only made sure he got what he deserved, even if justice was short-lived. But it put a stain on his reputation and that of his family."

Anthony's face hardens, the words barely making it out of his grit teeth. "Did he hurt you?"

"We got in an argument, things got heated, and he hit me." I hate telling him this. Lucas' actions don't define me, and I don't want Anthony to look at me differently. He's the one repeatedly reminding me of how strong and capable I am, so I hate him knowing about my weakest moment. Anthony closes his eyes and clenches his jaw, and I revert the conversation back to the original topic. "But I don't know what the ticket means or if he has anything to do with it. Right now, it's nothing but a ticket."

"A ticket to the same movie you were at last night which doesn't belong to me, you, or the lumberjack you went with, that was tucked into your door. I wouldn't say that's nothing. Do you want to stay here tonight while I look into it?"

"No, my friend Nyasia is spending the night with me. I'll be fine. Let me know if you find anything out?"

"It's really not a problem for you to stay the night. If someone—"

"Everything will be fine, Anthony." He doesn't look convinced, so I grip his fingers and give him a reassuring squeeze. "Is it weird? Yes. But it's just a scrap of paper. I'm not in any danger, so you can relax. If something else happens, or if I need any help, I promise I'll let you know. Okay?"

Anthony looks like he wants to object further, but resigns. "Alright, fine. I'll check in with you later."

On the way home, I listen to rain splattering against my windows and the sound of my windshield wipers rather than putting on music. It helps me think. I doubt the ticket is tied to Lucas. How would he even know where I live? Surely he could find out my city, but not my whole address. I try to convince myself this is all an accident caused by the wind pushing the ticket to my door. In reality, though, the most logical explanation is that someone from town is likely messing with me. Why? I have no idea, but it's a harmless act.

When I walk through my door, Nyasia has Criminal Minds playing on the TV with Lenny on her lap.

"Fuck, marry, kill Aaron Hotchner, Derek Morgan, and Spencer Reid. Go," she demands the second I walk in.

"Ooh, um, that's tough. Okay. Fuck Morgan, marry Reid, kill...wait, no, can we change it to kiss? That will make it easier."

She considers this strongly as if it were a serious matter.

"I'll allow the change," she finally determines.

"Okay then, Fuck Morgan, marry Hotchner, *kiss* Reid. You go."

"Fuck Hotch, hardcore make out with Morgan, marry Reid," she shoots out one after the other with no thought.

"Wow. Okay then." I hang my bag up on one of the hooks by the door. "Marry Reid? Really?"

She mimics the girl's voice from a viral video a while back to say, "I like them skinny and scrawny."

"Skinny and scrawny?" I laugh back.

"Skinny and scrawny," she finishes.

I check on Lenny, then get started on dinner. Cooking isn't my favorite thing, so I keep it simple by making fajitas. When I sit on the sofa again, I cave and check Lucas' social media. There are a few posts with passive-aggressive captions but nothing to indicate him being out of Texas, so I text Maya to see if she knows anything. That's also when Anthony calls to check up on me like he said he would which makes my heart feel all warm and fuzzy.

Wow, if someone doing something as simple as keeping their word makes me this happy, I seriously need to raise my standards. Then again, Lucas was my last boyfriend so no wonder I get so giddy over someone doing the bare minimum.

Some time after Nyasia and I fall asleep, I'm woken up by the flash of lightning and the crash of thunder. My eyes barely close again when I hear a thump similar to the one I heard the other night. The paranoia Lenny is having a seizure has me bolting up straight, but I find him asleep on the bed with me.

Another thump.

"Nyasia?" I call out unsurely, but I don't get a reply. Instead, there's an answering scrape of something against glass outside, giving me the feeling that whatever is causing the noise tonight is not a raccoon.

When I enter the living room to check the locks on the doors, I see Nyasia snoring lightly on the couch. I step quietly past it, careful not to wake her on my way to the door. To no surprise, the lock is in place. Flipping the nearby switch to turn on the porch light, I look through the peephole but see nothing unusual. Even though the noises have stopped, I still go to the backdoor to repeat the process.

The back door is the kind that slides open and closed rather than swings and is made entirely of glass. Because of this, I have a large curtain I pull over it every night to ensure my privacy. Pushing it aside now to glance outside, a flash of lightning lights up the sky for a fraction of a second, illuminating everything in sight. Including the hooded figure standing right on the other side of my door.

My hand immediately drops the curtain as I scream and retreat several feet to put distance between us, grabbing the chef knife out of the knife block on the counter.

"What's happening?" Nyasia demands as she flips on a light and rushes up beside me.

Breathing heavily, I point at the door with a shaky finger. "There's someone out there."

Nyasia whips her head to the back patio. "Are you sure?"

"I— I think so. I mean, I only saw them for a second." She takes a step toward the door but I pull her back. "No! Stop. What if they're still there?"

"Then you'll call the cops, and I'll kick their ass for being a creep until they get here." Nyasia pulls the curtain back, but the space is empty. With no one standing on the other side, she suggests the lightning and crime show combination before bed probably caused my mind to play tricks on me. Considering how worked up my head has been over the ticket, maybe she's right. Maybe I am fooling myself.

TATUM

Once Nyasia goes to work in the morning, I review my emails and DM's, trying to respond to two hundred inquiries, then get started on another painting. I want to go hiking again since it's been days since my last walk along the boarded trail, but I'm still nervous about last night. Part of me believes Nyasia was right. However, the rest of me is convinced I know what I saw, and what I saw was a hooded person outside, separated by only a handful of inches and a thin pane of glass. I don't know who they were or what they wanted. For all I know, they're still walking around the forest somewhere or hiding in the trees, watching my house.

I throw my paintbrush down, leaving a smear of paint on my pallet. Now I'm psyching myself out with scenarios that I don't even know if they're true or not. Before last night, I could stay in my house for a couple of days at a time without going out and be perfectly content since I have everything I need to keep me happy, healthy, and busy here. But now that I'm staying inside for fear of someone else? Someone who might not even exist? Fuck. That.

Shredding my overalls and replacing them with leggings and a hoodie, I kiss Lenny on the head before grabbing my phone and keys so I can get a coffee. When I open the door, I smile at the sight of a vase of roses on my porch, but my smile stutters a moment later when I truly take in the picture.

The vase they're resting in looks like every inch of it is cracked and ready to shatter in my hands, but that isn't the strange part. The strange part is that all the roses are already dead.

A note sticks out from the middle of the decaying bouquet, and its message is simple:

A dozen dead roses.

Okay...I can see that it's a dozen dead roses. But why? I flip the card, looking for the sender's name, but there isn't one. There isn't even a company logo or anything. Not that a business would deliver dead flowers. At least, not any business I know of. Which likely means it was dropped off by someone themself rather than sent to me professionally.

Although I know this isn't his style, I text Hayden to ask if they're from him and send the same text to Anthony. It's hard to tell if they're from the latter; he might be hiding a deeper meaning, but it's unlikely since it's not exactly his style either.

Hayden responds to me about ten minutes later, confirming my thoughts, but hours go by without a word from Anthony. It isn't until the early afternoon of the next day that he calls me.

"Hello?"

"Hello, darling. Are you available?" His voice sounds strained, not at all like himself, and his accent is much more prominent in this state.

"Yes," I state hesitantly. "Are you okay?" He pauses, and his sudden silence makes me nervous. "Anthony? Are you okay?" I repeat.

"I could use some help," he finally discloses. It sounds like he inhales through his teeth in pain a moment later. A couple breathes pass, then, "I need some supplies, I'm all out."

"You need...supplies?" That is not the reply I was expecting. In fact, everything about this call after his period of silence is strange and has me growing increasingly worried.

He breathes heavily through the phone, as if breathing is a chore. "Yes, if I send you a short list, could you bring the necessary items?"

"Okay..."

"And Tatum?" I wait for him to continue, a multitude of emotions coursing through me. "Bring Hayden."

"I'm sorry, *what?* Did you say, 'Don't bring Hayden?'"

"*Bring* Hayden, love. Don't come alone. Please."

Trying to remain calm, I explain that I don't know when Hayden will be able to join me since he's at work, but Anthony says he'll wait. Even after I explain that he sometimes doesn't get off right at five, Anthony remains adamant about my not coming alone. He would rather wait however long it might take for me to have Hayden's company. Though, he adds that a slight rush on things — as much as possible — would be nice, so I hang up and call Hayden.

The call goes unanswered, but I expected that since I'm starting to understand how things go for him at work. I'm also not surprised when he calls me back a few minutes later. My conversation with Anthony already left me on edge. Then he sent me the list of items he needs, and I've been pacing the floor and chewing on my nails ever since, waiting for this call.

"Hey Tate, is everything okay? Or can I ca—"

"I think something is wrong."

The noise from heavy machinery was loud when he first answered, but it starts to fade like he's walking away.

"Are you okay?"

"It's not me, it's...it's Anthony. I think he's hurt. He asked me to come over, but he told me not to come unless you were with me."

"That's odd. What makes you think he's hurt?" I hear some sort of door open and close, then it's completely quiet where he is.

"He called me and he didn't sound right. Plus, he wants me to bring him a bunch of medical supplies, including a suture kit."

Hayden curses softly. "Okay. Shit, okay, I need a few minutes to try to wrap some things up here. I'll swing by to pick you up as soon as I can."

When I spot Hayden's truck outside my house a little while later, I'm a nervous wreck. I got some of the items on Anthony's list together but have no idea where to grab a suture kit. Hayden claims he can handle that item, so he stops by the vet clinic to have his sister bring one out on the way to Anthony's home.

The gate that leads into his driveway is already open for us and as we turn into it, I call Anthony. The phone rings for so long I almost think he isn't going to pick up but after too long for comfort, he finally answers.

"Are you here?" He sounds tired, whereas my legs haven't stopped bouncing the whole ride over. I'm so nervous about what we're walking into that I feel like I could've ran the distance here with energy to spare.

"I'm here," I assure him, even though we haven't parked yet.

"Come in...come inside." Anthony sounds like he's falling asleep on the phone so the second Hayden pulls up in front of the house, I already have the truck door open before it's even in park. Hayden hurries beside me to the front door, which we find cracked open. Seeing that, he tells me to stay behind him before he pushes through.

Anthony's house almost feels like being in a cave since the walls and ground are both made of dark gray stone. Blue LED lights line underneath appliances, adding to the cave-like feeling of the house with their soft glow. It didn't bother me when I was here before. In fact, matched with the clean scent of eucalyptus and cypress, I loved how it all fit together to match Anthony perfectly. But the house feels cold and dark right now. It almost seems like the walls are closing in on us. My unease only grows when we don't immediately spot Anthony and notice that there isn't a sound in the large house.

Hayden calls out into the silence.

"Anthony?" The house remains quiet before we eventually hear the shuffling of feet. Hayden moves an arm behind himself to ensure I stay at his back and his body tenses, preparing for a potential threat.

Anthony comes slowly into view, stopping once he sees us, then leans against the wall for support. He's holding a light gray washcloth to his face, but even from across the room, I can see that it's covered in blood. And that's far from the only blood I see.

I gasp quietly.

"What the hell?" Hayden whispers. His head moves as he takes in Anthony's battered appearance.

"I'm glad you're here," Anthony admits to me. His silver eyes, one of which is now burdened with a splash of red as a result of some type of hit, settle on Hayden. "Just...don't touch anything. I don't want you to make my house dirty."

Hayden rolls his eyes. "Relax, man. I'm not going to get anything dirty by touching it." Hayden walks up beside him and, although I can tell it's a little awkward for them both, Hayden supports Anthony's body so he can help him down the hall. Presumably, they're headed towards a bathroom or somewhere for Anthony to sit since he looks ready to fall over any second now.

Anthony looks pointedly at the path Hayden took to get to him. "You're already doing exactly that, and all you've touched so far is ten feet of flooring." I look at where he's focused and indeed see specs of dirt from the bottom of Hayden's work boots.

Hayden only shrugs and continues further into the house. "You're telling me you've got all this money but can't afford a vacuum cleaner?" He tsks. "Shit, you should've said something. I would've taken you to the city thrift store for one. Now shut up and let me help you in peace."

Walking behind them, I spot droplets of blood on the floor. It takes everything in me not to start shaking Anthony by the shoulders, demanding to know what happened to him. But after he weakly points Hayden to where he wants to go and is sitting on the edge of a massive stone tub, Hayden asks the question we've both been wondering.

"What the hell happened to you, man?"

"Can you allow me the decency of letting me clean myself up first and bloody stitch myself up before I tell you a story? Or would you rather I keep bleeding all night to satisfy your curiosity?" Hayden solemnly nods so I set the bag of supplies down on the counter, pulling each item out and setting them on the countertop. As I do, Hayden helps Anthony out of his shirt and removes the shattered watch from his wrist. When he groans and grimaces from the pain the movement is causing, I have to look away. The sight of blood doesn't usually bother me. Only when it's coming from someone I care about, and Anthony has become one of those people.

Finally, once all his other wounds have been addressed, it's time for the stitches.

"Are either of you able to help me with this? The angle is a bit odd for me to do it myself."

"I can," Hayden surprises me by saying.

"You can?" I inquire uselessly.

"My sister taught me. I thought it would be a useful skill to learn since things at work can get a little hairy at times, and now look at where we are."

"Yes, well, do your best to remember I'm not a dog or a cat and try not to do a botch job at it," Anthony grits out. He's still in pain and likely will be for a while. Most of his body appears to be bruised, and multiple parts of his face are swollen and cut. Hayden starts to set up for the sutures that will go on Anthony's ribs, and Anthony grips tightly onto my hand. It's hard to tell whether he's trying to comfort himself or me, but I squeeze him back just as hard.

Finally, when the stitches are tied, Anthony gives directions to his bedroom so Hayden can grab him a hoodie to cover up with, leaving the two of us alone. Anthony grips my chin in a gentle grip and kisses me the second Hayden leaves.

"Thank you for coming, love. And thank you for bringing me what I needed. You are a blessing beyond measure for a damned man." He kisses me again, and I taste the faint flavor of copper coming from a small cut on his lip.

Hayden returns with the hoodie and I help Anthony into it. Once it's on, Hayden supports him while we walk to Anthony's living room, putting him down on the couch. I sit beside him, Hayden takes up a spot in the chair across from us.

"Tell us what happened," I tell him gingerly.

He rubs a hand on my thigh. "Some people broke into my house and robbed me. I didn't know if they would come back, so that's why I didn't want you to come alone."

"Anthony," I whisper, quiet shock filling my tone as I grip his hand. Hayden is quiet, so I look over at him, finding him staring hard at Anthony who's now meeting his gaze.

"You were robbed," Hayden states flatly — neither a question nor a statement.

"That's what I said," Anthony replies dryly.

"In Maple Crest?"

"*Yes.*" It's evident Hayden doesn't believe him, but I don't know why he wouldn't. Just because crime is minimal here doesn't mean it doesn't exist. And unfortunately, Anthony is the ideal mark since his wealth isn't a secret from the town. The same town where some families are struggling to pay their bills.

"Look, this isn't going to work if you aren't honest with us," Hayden states while he runs a hand through his hair, and my body stills. *Oh no. No, no, no, no. Anthony isn't ready for this yet. I haven't talked to him about it!*

"What isn't going to work?" Anthony's brows bunch.

"Us. This."

Hayden says with a twirl of his finger to indicate the three of us right as I say, "Nothing."

"The fuck do you mean *us*, Williams?" There are confused looks all around and I again find myself wishing to be swallowed up by a random sinkhole or something.

Unfortunately, my body isn't swallowed up by the universe so I'm left to lie in the bed I made, groaning lightly. "Look, I meant to talk to you about something sooner, but then that conversation with the ticket kinda ruined the moment. I was going to bring it up later, but there hasn't been a good time."

"Mind if I go grab some water?" Hayden asks, already standing up and clearly leaving just to give us some privacy.

Anthony waves him off uselessly since Hayden is already almost out of the room. "Talk to me about what, Tatum?" he asks when I start to pick at my nails.

How am I even supposed to start this next conversation? It's not like asking someone if they'd be okay with being in a polyamorous relationship is everyday talk. Hayden is perfectly fine with it and even has experience with this sort of arrangement. But I don't, and I don't know how Anthony will react. Especially considering what he's just been through and the fact he hates Hayden.

"Nothing," I chicken out. I can't ask him this. I really, *really* like him, but we're still getting to know each other. Even though I know it would be best to be honest about what I want sooner rather than later, I can't spring this on him. Besides, he's made it clear he wants a relationship with me. Not me and another man.

Anthony shifts so that his body is facing me more. He grimaces at first, but once he's settled, he cups my cheek with a bruised hand. It appears whoever hurt him didn't get away without getting hurt at least a little bit themself.

"Hey, if something is bothering you, then let me know. I want to help." This man has already been beaten bloody. I might as well get the rest of the damage over with so he can heal from everything at once in case this blows up in my face.

I swallow, wondering if this is my last conversation with him, but knowing I can't keep this from him any longer.

"I like you, Anthony." He grins as much as his bruised and swollen face will allow. "And I want to keep seeing you, but I want to keep seeing Hayden, too. I...don't want to have to choose between the two of you. I would *never* have imagined I would want something like this, and I know it's something people might hate about us, but I don't think I can lie to myself just to stay in line with society's typical standards. And I can't deny myself the chance to keep you both in my life this way."

The upturned lift of his lips has faded to nothing, but he doesn't look disgusted or angry. I actually can't tell what he's thinking right now. All I know is he's completely invested in this conversation.

"The chance to keep us both in *what* way, exactly? Just so we're clear." Even his tone gives nothing about his emotions away, and my skin flushes with nervousness.

Even though I've never done anything like this before, will he think I'm disgusting for wanting it? If we try this arrangement, will he think of me as used or cheap for no other reason than because I don't want to do things the traditional way? Is it really such a bad thing for three people to be together rather than two? As long as those in the relationship are happy, it shouldn't bother the rest of the world what we do with our lives. It's never made any sense to me that it does.

Maybe Anthony won't hate the idea, but rather, who I've chosen the third person to be. Even though my mind races, it's too late to stop now.

"I want to be in a relationship. With both of you. The three of us all at once. Or at least, both of you with me? I don't know. All I know is that some people might think it's still early to jump into a relationship. Let alone one like this, but I know what I want, Anthony. I know what I *feel*. It's because it's early that this comes up. I respect you too much to drag you along or trick you into something you might not want. You're amazing and I want to keep you in my life because we work so well together. But if you want to tell me to fuck off or if you're pissed off at me because you're hurt about this, then I get it. I do. And I will have no ill feelings toward you whatsoever. It's your choice."

I'm holding my breath. What I didn't tell him is I not only want this, but I'm crazy about him. Sexy accent, his talent in both the bedroom and the kitchen, and his insanely good looks aside, I'm obsessed with how my very soul feels when we're together.

Being with Anthony is calm like stargazing and chaotic like kissing in the rain. It's fresh like spearmint and soothing like a midnight walk. It's free like the waves during a storm.

Being with Hayden is like being bathed in the warm light of the setting sun. It's soft like crochet and flannel. Smooth like honey, sweet like citrus, and safe as the feeling of holding someone's hand. How could I possibly feel so much so fast and how could I ever pass up on the opportunity of having both the sun and the moon and choose one or the other?

"You want a poly relationship? Hayden knows this already and he's agreed?" I bite my lip and nod nervously. He stares at me for a few seconds longer. God, I wish I could tell what he's thinking but he keeps himself so carefully blank. "That's surprising. But if this is what you want then you can have it. There isn't a thing in this world you could ask for from me that I would deny you."

What was left of my breath that I'd been holding escapes me in a quiet and shocked gasp. "Are you sure? You don't have to say yes to this if you don't want it. I swear, we'll figure something else out and that's okay. I don't want you to feel pressured in any way."

He grabs the back of my head and pulls me in for a kiss, deepening it with a swipe of his tongue against mine and I melt into him. He's letting me feel his assurance, not just hear it.

"I'm sure," he smiles at me and finally, *finally*, he lets his emotions show to me. There's a sparkle in his gorgeous silver eyes. "I've seen a lot of works of art in my days, but none as breathtaking as you. The only thing that comes close to your beauty are the paintings you create. I want as much of you as you'll allow. Your time, your text, your call, your art. *You.* In any and every way. If that means dealing with him, then so be it."

Chapter Eleven

TATUM

"You can stop dawdling and come back now," Anthony calls over his shoulder after another kiss. I'd nearly forgotten Hayden left to get water, but he enters the room seconds later, carrying a glass for each of us. He hands out the cups and then returns to the seat across the space with his own, raising it to his lips. Anthony stares at him pointedly. "For the record, I still hate you."

Hayden takes his time to finish quenching his thirst, unbothered by Anthony's discourtesy. "You're welcome." Hayden's eyebrows lift and his brown eyes shift briefly, indicating the drink in Anthony's hand while ignoring the jab.

"I'm serious. I'm doing this for her. You mean nothing to me."

"And they say romance is dead," Hayden remarks as he makes himself comfortable on the cushioned chair.

"Why didn't you call your family, or go to the hospital, the police, or anybody else?" I ask Anthony, bringing the conversation back to the reason why we're here and listing other resources he could've turned to.

He's playing with my fingers when he answers. "I'd like to ensure no one finds out about this. If they do, it could cause a lot of trouble that I'd rather not deal with. You're all I have." Hayden clears his throat strongly and I know it's in order to get under Anthony's skin. Anthony shoots him a poisonous glare.

My phone dings with a text, and I pull my phone from my pocket to check the notification. It's Nyasia confirming plans for our night out tonight.

"Shit," I mumble. I'd forgotten I was supposed to go out with her, but with Anthony in the state he's in, I can't leave for a girl's night. I nearly complete typing my message to reschedule when Anthony takes my phone away from me, holding it in his other hand, out of my reach. "Hey!"

"You're going."

"Like hell I am," I object, leaning over him to snatch my phone back. I fail because he bares his teeth in pain. I pull myself back from him quickly. "Are you okay? I'm so sorry, I wasn't thinking."

He takes several steadying breaths through his nose with his eyes closed, then opens them, still keeping my phone out of reach. "When did you last have a night out with a friend? You're not going to cancel *because of me*, and I know you were about to. Even if you try to deny it by coming up with some other excuse to not go."

"Okay, fine, you're right. But I want to make sure you're going to be okay. I'm not leaving you alone like this to hang out with Nyasia. I can go another time."

"I'll stay here with him," Hayden provides. Not an offer, but a statement of certainty.

"What?" My head whips to him.

"Yes, *what?*" Anthony scowls, turning his head across the room much slower than I did. The act is menacing, especially with how his eyes are now narrowed at Hayden. One would think he'd committed a terrible crime against Anthony rather than offer to stay and help him out. "I don't remember inviting you to stay."

"Tough cookies. What was it you said earlier? Oh, that's right, *I'm doing this for her.*"

"Did you— you did. You said tough cookies. That's not happening. You can sleep in the tin can you call a truck if you're going to say rubbish like that."

"Anthony," I start, "the only way I'll go is if I know you're safe and cared for. You just told me you have no one else, so your options are him or me. What's it going to be?"

He sighs and rolls his eyes. "Fine." His eyes are soft and kind when he looks at me again. "You should leave soon so you have time to get ready. Walk with me to my room?" Hayden stays behind while Anthony and I walk to his bedroom. He moves slowly, showing me that each step is painful.

"Are you okay?" I ask after he lowers himself flat onto the mattress.

His eyes are closed when he replies. His breaths a little uneven.

"I'm fine, love. Just felt a little nauseous, that's all." Knowing nausea is a symptom of concussions, I'm a little worried about him sleeping. Since he claims the injuries happened yesterday, though, he insists he'll be fine.

Anthony was right. I should be leaving soon. Instead, I climb up on the bed beside him and adjust the pillows until we're both comfortable. Tucking his head under my arm, my fingers run through his hair until his breathing evens out. Even when I know he's asleep, I stay a little longer, running my fingers through his blonde hair.

I got more of him and learned how close I was to almost losing him on the same day. The only people he had to call for help were a woman he'd gone on a couple of dates with and a man he hates. Tomorrow I will get more answers from him. But today, today, I am happy he's alive. That's more than enough for now.

Carefully sliding out from under him when I can't stay any longer, I leave him fast asleep in the room behind me and close the door. Returning to the living room, I find Hayden messing around on his phone. Sensing my presence, he stands up and wraps me in a caring hug.

"I didn't know he wasn't aware yet. I am so, so sorry I forced that conversation, Tate."

I wrap my arms around him and let my head rest on his muscled chest, inhaling his amber scent. Like everything else about them, even his scent is the opposite of Anthony's. His smell is warm, just like he is in the otherwise cold house. Together, they create the perfect balance.

"It's okay, it ended up working out and now I don't have to worry about it anymore. I can't believe Anthony agreed."

Hayden laughs, his chest rumbling beneath my cheek. "Me neither. But you're happy?"

"I'm happy. I know he hasn't been the nicest person to you, so it means a lot that you're doing this for me. Thank you." I think about everything he's done today alone and decide I need to be a little more specific. "For everything. I can't pinpoint a singular action because everything you do is amazing. You're so *good*."

He uses two fingers to tip my chin back so I'm looking at his face. He's smiling at me. From that look alone, I can feel the setting sun, the crochet and flannel. I can taste the honey and citrus all at once; all the things which make the perfect blend of warmth and comfort that is Hayden Williams.

"Stop thanking me for things." His head leans down to kiss me, so I raise up on my toes enough to meet him halfway. "Check in throughout the night to let me know you're alright?"

"Of course." I kiss him again, more profoundly this time. Something about kissing him makes me weak. I don't get easily addicted to things, but I can definitely see his lips being an exception.

NYASIA and I are in line three hours later to enter the club. We went for a 'matching but not' sort of vibe with our outfits tonight, so she's wearing cutoff shorts and a backless halter top. I'm wearing a pleather skirt with a mesh long-sleeve shirt and a bra underneath. The matching part comes into play by every article of clothing we're wearing being black aside from our silver jewelry. Since we've never been dressed up like this at the same time before, we took lots of mirror selfies before we left and I made sure to send a couple to my boyfriends.

Boyfriends.

Jesus. My parents aren't religious by any means; still, they are seriously going to freak the fuck out when they find out I'm in a polyamorous relationship.

Hayden texts back quickly to tell me how gorgeous he thinks we are and to have fun. He also updates me on Anthony, who apparently had woken up long enough to use the bathroom and give Hayden the middle finger before falling asleep again.

After finally making it through the long line, Nyasia and I go straight for the bar. There, we each throw down a shot before making our way to the dance floor, getting lost in the blaring music and flashing lights. It's been so long since the last time I went clubbing, which was with Grace right before my move. Typically, sizable groups aren't my thing. But when I'm here, it's almost like I'm a different person. Here, I'm someone who doesn't worry about what people think and lets herself be truly free. It's okay if I make a fool of myself since, more than likely, I'm far from the only one who will look stupid at some point during the night.

We spend hours going back and forth between the bar, the dance floor, and, of course, the bathroom. Our night is filled with laughter and ridiculous dancing, on my part at least, since I don't know how to dance to save my life.

Nyasia and I are maneuvering through the crowd to get to the bar again when I accidentally bump into someone's shoulder.

Turning around to apologize, my words abruptly stop mid-sentence.

"Benjamin." My buzzed mind instantly begins to sober up. I don't know what it is, exactly, but something about this man is unsettling.

His narrow face fills with a smile, but even with the deep dimples, the expression feels more like a threat than a greeting.

"Evie! What a pleasant surprise it is to see you here!" He's wearing a dark t-shirt that shows his structured arms, and he's decked out in more jewelry than Nyasia and I together. Rings are on each of his index fingers, a couple of woven bracelets sit around his wrist, and a necklace rests against his chest. "Where's Anthony?"

"He went to the bathroom," I lie. I don't know why I do, but making him think Anthony is somewhere close by makes me feel a little better about Benjamin being right in front of me. He hasn't said or done anything malicious, but apparently, the feeling in my gut isn't aware of that fact.

When one of the flashing lights glides across his face, I notice what looks like bruising around his eye and cheek. He tried to cover it with product but I can still see hints of color. I take another glance at his hands, focussing this time on his knuckles. They're bruised too, yet he didn't bother trying to cover up the splashes of red that indicate he got into a fight recently.

"Is that right?" he inquires and checks his watch. "Well, well, look at that. It's 11:11. Make a wish." I just stare at him, and he smiles at me. "Time for me to get going. Make sure you keep an eye on the clock too, Evie. Everyone hates running out of time. Give my best to my buddy Anthony, will you?" He smirks at me before walking off. I watch his back as he leaves, shuddering once he's truly gone.

What the fuck did he mean by that? Was he trying to be cryptic or creepy just now?

Nyasia finds me again after apparently not noticing I wasn't behind her, then drags me to the bar. It's a little strange that he wants to leave now. The night is still young by club standards, but even so, I stop drinking after the strange interruption so I can start sobering up.

Three hours later, we start the drive home. Since Hayden had driven me to Anthony's house, he's letting me borrow his truck. After I drop Nyasia off at her place, I return to Anthony's, where Hayden opens the door for me as I arrive.

"How's he doing?"

"A little sarcastic, but he's fine. He's been asleep for a while now." I take a quick shower, then change into some clothes I gathered when I stopped at my house to check on Lenny. Entering Anthony's bedroom again, I find him still asleep on the bed; a faint blue glow shining dimly from lights placed behind a mirror on the opposite side of the massive room. Even in sleep, his face looks pained.

Moving to the side of the room with the light, I find his closet and venture inside. I say *venture* because his closet alone is nearly the size of my bedroom. It looks like a high-end boutique for men. My closet is crammed with clothes with no organization, while his is neatly categorized by sleeve length and color. Although, aside from either white or gray, I'd say about 97% of the clothes in here are midnight, onyx, raven, coal, or obsidian. Or in other words, just plain black. Maybe he's allergic to any other color in the rainbow.

Finding where he keeps his pajamas, I grab a pair of sweatpants and a plain tee for Hayden to change into.

"Thought you might be more comfortable in these," I tell him when I walk back into the living room. While I was in the shower, he settled onto the couch for the night without a blanket or pillow.

"Anthony approved this?" Hayden inquires after he sits up to take the clothes.

"No," I admit. "But it's the least he can do for making you leave work early to come stitch him up and stay the night to make sure he doesn't die." Hayden chuckles and when he goes to the bathroom to change, I return to the bedroom. Bending down over the bed, I kiss Anthony's cheek. He stirs, slowly waking up.

"You're back," he acknowledges sleepily, his accent thick. "Did you have fun?"

"I did. I missed you, though." He tugs on my arms to get me to climb into bed next to him and pulls me close so we're cuddled together. I make sure to keep a careful distance from his stitches.

"I missed you too, but I'm glad you went. You need to have fun and spend time with your friends." My fingers run gently up and down his chest. He's falling back asleep, but I don't know where I should spend the night. On any other occasion, it would be obvious; to spend the night with your injured boyfriend. But do you still spend the night with your injured boyfriend when your other boyfriend, who just became your boyfriend hours ago, will be sleeping on the couch alone?

"Where should Hayden sleep?" I ask.

"At his house."

"Anthony. It's extremely late, and he's done nothing but help you today. I know you don't care for him, but I do. I can't in good conscience stay in your bed when I know he's without a blanket and pillow."

His eyes are still closed and for a moment, I think he's fallen asleep. "I don't have a guest bedroom. He can sleep in here. But you're sleeping next to me."

I gape at him. "Really?"

"Really." I press a firm kiss on his lips, feeling a small smile spread on his mouth. When I return to the living room to tell Hayden what Anthony had said, he scrunches his brows.

"Did he take some new medication? Maybe we should take him to the hospital. He's probably got a head injury." I chuckle and take his hand, leading him to the room. "Are you dying?" Hayden asks Anthony when he enters the room.

"No. But I believe I'm currently living in some strange combination of a dream come true and a nightmare." Climbing happily into the king-sized bed, I crawl under the down blanket as

Hayden slides in on the other side, sticking close to the edge. I get the feeling it's for Anthony's sake more than his own. Later, the three of us will have to discuss any boundaries we might have. As for right this second, though, Anthony has an arm around me, and I have a hand entangled with Hayden's.

Chapter Twelve

TATUM

"Wow, look at you!" I exclaim as I walk into the kitchen, finding them seated on opposite ends of the counter, eating oatmeal and berries. They're sitting with their bodies angled away from each other and the house was so quiet when I walked in you could hear a pin drop. It's a fair assumption that even with our new arrangement, they haven't put their differences aside overnight.

Hayden is wearing one of Anthony's suits. It's slightly tighter on him than it would be on Anthony since he has more muscle and the suit has been perfectly tailored to someone else's measurements, but it doesn't look bad. Anthony is also in one of his signature black suits. If it were anyone other than Anthony who had their ribs stitched last night and looks like a truck hit him today, then this choice of clothing would be surprising. Surely most people would be living in sweatpants and loose shirts for the next few days, but it *is* Anthony, so I'm not surprised at all.

"If he's going to be here, then he might as well wear something clean," Anthony grumbles.

"That was nice of you," I tell him, even though he looks less than pleased about it. Hayden rubs his mouth with one of his hands, trying to hide the amusement on his face. Meanwhile, I place the tea I got for Anthony from The Brewed Bean in front of him, then do the same with a coffee for Hayden.

"Nick says *hi,* by the way," I say when I get beside him. "Do you guys report your every move to each other or something?"

He smiles at the mention of his best friend. "Oh yeah. We keep a detailed log of everything we do all day, then right before we fall asleep, we call so we can tell each other about every little thing. It's great. It's by far my favorite part of the day." Anthony gives him one of the most judgmental looks I've ever seen as I match Hayden's massive grin. "I'm kidding. About the detailed log part, that is. The rest is true. I fucking love that guy."

Anthony elects to ignore everything Hayden said entirely and changes the subject. "Where did you go this morning?"

Almost four hours after we fell asleep, I woke up again to get an early start on the day. Specifically, there was something I wanted to get before Anthony woke up. Due to the pain pills he took last night, I knew he wouldn't be awake as early as he once told me he usually is. Still, I knew there still wasn't much time for me to waste. The medication would only buy me a little bit of time.

"Lenny needed breakfast and his pill." I sit on the unoccupied stool between the two men. "I also wanted to go pick something up from the store." Pulling out a small box from my purse, I set it in front of Anthony.

He lays his spoon down in his bowl before picking up the box. With curiosity, he flips open the lid and reveals the watch inside. It has a titanium silver band, a navy-blue bezel, and an azure blue watch face. For someone like Anthony who dresses like they're constantly in mourning, it's like putting a pink lily amongst a bouquet of dark roses; it will definitely stand out.

I'd never seen him without his last watch until we removed the shattered piece in the bathroom yesterday. I knew he was going to be wanting a new one and thanks to the sales of my paintings, I'm far from strapped for money now. And since he likes everything he owns to be classy and sleek, I dropped a pretty penny on it. Or several. Not as much as I'm sure he'd have spent on one himself, but more than should ever be spent on something that just tells the time. Now that I think about it that way, it's kind of surprising the robbers didn't take such an expensive piece, but broke it instead.

I've been waiting for the chance to do something like this for Anthony. After what he's done for me already, I wanted to find another way to say *thank you* more than by simply voicing the words. So even though the circumstances for which he needs a new one are terrible, it gives me a chance to show him I care for him.

I couldn't help myself from adding a bit of flare to it, though. It's no secret he prefers his belongings to be black, but he gave me a piece of himself when he told me he likes blue. Part of me doesn't expect him to wear the watch because of the color, but I hope he does. Even if only around me. But people always say 'It's the thought that counts' so, that's what I'm counting on. Maybe he can place it on his bedside table and look at it before he goes to sleep and think of me.

Anthony doesn't say anything. He just stares at the watch in its box for a long minute, his finger tenderly running along the blue edge. I'm about ready to start feeling self-conscious and regret going with the blue, thinking I should've stuck with the reliable choice of black instead.

But I can see emotion written all over his face. His mouth has parted a little and his shoulders are slumped, but he doesn't look sad. He looks overcome with something else. Something I can't quite place. Looking at Hayden, he smiles warmly at me, nodding his head a couple of times as if to tell me that from where he's sitting, this was a good move.

Finally, Anthony breaks away from whatever is going on in his head and removes the watch from the box, fastening it on his wrist.

"I love it, darling. It's truly fantastic, thank you." He leans in for a kiss and when I straighten up afterward, he grabs my hand, squeezing it under the counter and holding it in his.

"Look at that," Hayden drawls, resuming his eating. "Now you look a little less like the grim reaper."

"I never looked like the grim reaper," Anthony denies with a leveled look directed at Hayden. "I dress much nicer than the grim reaper ever could."

"Sure. But you can't deny that you look like someone who almost met the grim reaper."

"Oh, speaking of people who look dead," I cut in, then immediately give Anthony an apologizing look before continuing, "I saw Benjamin last night." Anthony tenses.

"Who's Benjamin?" Hayden asks, glancing between us. I wait for Anthony to respond since I don't *really* know the answer to that, but he doesn't.

"What did he say to you, Tatum? Verbatim," he asks instead.

I try to recall his exact words, but I can't. At that point in time, I was still pretty drunk, so I tell him as much.

"He said something about watching the clock because everyone hates running out of time, and then said to give you his best." A couple of details come back to me as the conversation continues. "He looked bruised too. Is that a coincidence, or was he the one who attacked you?"

Hayden straightens in his seat, obviously intrigued by the question.

"Merely a coincidence," Anthony replies, but it sounds strained. "But not too much of one, since he's always getting on someone's nerves or getting into fights. It's more unusual to see him without any bruises than it is to see him with any. If he speaks to you again, tell him...tell him we aren't together. Say that I left you or something."

"Why the hell would I do that? We just started dating."

"Benjamin is a prat. He'll give you a hard time if he knows I'm close to you."

At this, Hayden chimes into the conversation. "You don't seem to like a lot of people."

"It's not hard."

"And a lot of people don't seem to like you, which is weird since you're such a likable person. Do you ever wonder why?"

"No. There's no point in wondering when you do what I do."

This lures me back with an inquiry of my own. "What do you mean? You're a software engineer. How does that make you enemies?" Anthony opens his mouth with a reply on his tongue, but his phone ringing cuts him off. He digs it out of his pocket, then excuses himself to take the call in another room.

The conversation we had doesn't make any sense. Why would he want to know exactly what Benjamin said to me, then immediately downplay his concern? And then there's the whole *there's no wondering when you do what I do* thing. I've never heard of people in his line of work racking up a list of people that don't like them. It sounds weird. But at the same time, he was the one who said honesty is key in a relationship. If he has something to say, I trust him to say it.

"Should I be worried about this Benjamin guy?" Hayden asks.

"I don't think so," I admit right before I kiss him. "I met him only once. He won't be a threat in any way."

He tilts his head back enough so he can meet my gaze. "What about an addition to the group?"

"Definitely not. Besides, I'm happy with who I've got already." Hayden grins and pulls me against him by my waist.

"So, you like me in a suit, huh?" He smirks after we kiss again.

"Eh. you look alright," I tease. But I do. I really, really do. The fine material is paired with his logger boots, creating a unique, stark contrast. Somehow, Hayden manages to make the look appear not only good but intentional, nearly opulent.

"I've got to head out soon. My family is pretty worried since I took off from work yesterday, and I have some things to take care of before work tomorrow. Do you want a ride back home?"

We wait until Anthony finishes his phone call before we leave so I can make him promise to keep me updated throughout the day on how he's feeling. Hayden swears to return the suit after it's washed, but Anthony tells him not to bother. He says he won't want it back after the material has been stretched out and ruined by his wearing it.

When Hayden's truck stops along the street in front of my house not long after, I turn to stare at him, letting all the emotions that have been welling within me be felt.

"How did you get so amazing?" I ask him as I push a lock of his shaggy brown hair from his forehead.

"I didn't do anything extraordinary, Tate. I acted the same way most people would when someone they care about needs help. You might need to improve your circle if you think that's a bold move I only used in an attempt to impress you," he teases lightly. Though he's not entirely wrong, I suppose.

"The fact that you think spending the night with someone you hate is something most people would do is adorable," I tell him.

"I don't hate Anthony. Anthony hates me." Guilt. Add that to the list of emotions. *Maybe this was a mistake. Maybe they don't* really *want this, maybe they—* Hayden's palms cup either side of my face and his thumbs stroke me tenderly. "Hey. Get out of your head. I know what you're thinking and you're starting to *overthink*. I'm telling you right now that you have nothing to worry about. I want you. I want this. Hell, I want that grumpy English bastard if that's what makes you happy. Trust me, gorgeous, I can handle the emo boy and his attitude. I've done it for years."

Hayden gets out to open my door for me, then escorts me to my front door. After I unlock it, he tugs me closer to him, planting his lips on mine in a passionate kiss that doesn't end until we're both breathless. The way he tastes and has his hands on me makes me painfully aware of the fact that kissing is the furthest we've been with each other. But there hasn't been a good chance for us to fix that yet. Maya is going to lose it when I tell her, not only about my two boyfriends, but that I made one of them my boyfriend before he's even so much as grabbed my boobs.

"Hey, think you'll be able to come over a little later? I'd like to take you somewhere. Just the two of us."

He smiles, giving me another peek at his dimples. "Yeah, I think I can do that."

I'm smiling back at him now. "Good. You'll have to ditch the suit, though." After we spend another handful of minutes kissing each other like the world is ending, he leaves. I try to get back to work on a painting, but I can't focus until after I spend some quality time with a certain pink, battery-operated object I keep in a drawer by my bed.

Once I'm in the right mind frame to work again, Lenny, my shadow who acts like he hasn't seen me in years, takes up residence in the art room with me. I'm still getting inquiries about when I'll have new canvases listed. Since pictures of all the previous paintings are shown on my website, many people are requesting that I print the designs on other things such as stickers, tote bags, and planners. It's not a bad idea honestly, so I write a note to myself as a reminder to look into it.

While I catch up on my responses, Maya calls to tell me about how much of a disaster an event she went to last night was since the organizers dropped the ball. In return, I tell her about my weekend. As expected, she loses her shit when I tell her about my situation with the boys.

Entering my kitchen for a soda from the fridge while still on the phone, I spot the vase of dead roses. I'd completely forgotten about them after Anthony had called me. Setting the card they came with aside, I take the roses to the trash and text Anthony to ask him again if they're from him. It's only when he informs me they weren't that I stop in my tracks to put some serious thought into things.

The ticket, the man that may or may not have been there, the flowers...are they all connected somehow? Is someone stalking me?

"Tatum? Are you okay?" Maya's voice pulls me back and I realize I've been standing frozen in the middle of the room.

"Yeah. I was just— some weird stuff has been happening." I tell her about what I've seen, and she bites her lip; an obvious attempt to hold something back. "What are you keeping from me?"

"Steph saw Lucas the other day while he was with some of his friends. He didn't see her, but she heard him talking about you. He said he had to see you again to make things right or some shit. Do you think maybe he was the one who sent the flowers?"

Make things right? It doesn't matter if he apologized a hundred times. What he did will never be 'made right.' I may move past it and stop thinking about it, but I'll never forgive it. You don't hurt someone the way he did and make amends just to make yourself feel better. One day, I'll be so happy with my life that that night will never cross my mind again. And I hope he feels regret for it for the rest of his life.

"Were you going to tell me what he said if I didn't bring up the roses?"

"I don't know," she admits truthfully. "I didn't think it was something you'd want to hear since you're done with him."

"He hasn't left Dallas, though, right?" I ask.

"Not that I'm aware of." Even if he was responsible for the roses — which he couldn't be because I'm sure a business wouldn't deliver those — that still leaves two other strange occurrences. If he still hasn't left the city, then that means someone else followed me home a few nights ago and wanted me to know it.

"Maya," I start seriously, "what do I do if someone is stalking me?"

"You think someone from Maple Crest is stalking you?"

"I don't know. No. Maybe?" I groan and rub my brow with two fingers. "I don't know, Maya. But it's weird, right?"

"It's weird," she agrees. "Maybe you should get a gun. Or a dog." We discuss the pros and cons of each and conclude one of each would be a good idea. A gun for protection and a dog because, come on, it's a dog. Why wouldn't I want one?

A little while later, we end the call and I return to my painting after checking up on Anthony. It's another large one, but not as hyper-realistic as some of my previous paintings have been. For this one, I'm allowing myself to be freer when it comes to the bright colors I use, and I'm using enough gold foil to make a dragon happy. This piece is feminine, alluring, and might be my favorite piece yet. Looking at it makes me think of strength, beauty, and feeling completely free in one's own skin. It represents everything I love about being an artist. From the entire process that takes place the second you grab your paint, to the moment you finish laying it down on the canvas, the feelings being creative is able to build in you is truly magical.

When my phone chimes with a message, I check the notification and smile. Now that Hayden's on his way, I wash my brushes and change out of my overalls before packing one of my late uncles' hiking backpacks with all the supplies I'll need once he gets here.

Chapter Thirteen

TATUM

"Where are we going?" Hayden asks when he sees me all dressed up and ready for a hike. He'd changed out of the suit like I'd advised and is now wearing a dark gray t-shirt under a dark flannel, some hiking boots, and jeans. As much as I like him in the suit, I love him in his casual everyday wear. It's rustic and cozy.

Although he quietly longs for a different life, Hayden makes the most out of the one he's living here and fits into it so well. Most people would never imagine that the man who drives the beat-up old Chevy, works with heavy machines all day, and has the most delicious muscles from swinging an ax, just wants to go to college and learn about people who changed the world with paint, glass, ivory, and marble. On our first date, Hayden told me that even though he's close with them, he doesn't talk to his family about wanting to go back to school. He doesn't want them to feel guilty for being the reason he dropped out. But he trusted me with his secret.

During the day when he's busy living one life, he sends me sweat and sawdust covered selfies while at work. All of which I immediately save to my camera roll because he looks so damn cute and I'm absolutely obsessed with the way he makes a different face in each one. Then at night, we find historical pieces of art we love and send screenshots of them to each other, discussing what we like about them with either a text or a call. Sometimes I forget I haven't known him for years because he's so familiar to me now. Like with Anthony and the watch, I want to do something special for Hayden, so I thought of the perfect way to combine both of the people he wants to be in one date.

"Somewhere special," I tell him. "But it's a surprise, so let's get going, Big Joe."

His brow quirks. "Big Joe?"

"Yeah, you know, the French-Canadian logger." I lock my door and put my keys in one of the pockets of the backpack.

Hayden chuckles. "I don't know him, actually. Do you sit and google random names to call me because I'm a logger?"

I throw the backpack over my shoulders and shrug. "No." Except that is exactly what I do, and surely my voice is much too high-pitched for him to believe me. "Come on."

I guide him down the wooden trail behind my house until we're about two hours in and nearing the final location. My surprise destination is a little loud, so I lose the element of surprise before we get there. That part's a little disappointing, but Hayden is grinning anyway. His smile only widens when the waterfall we've been listening to for the past couple of minutes finally comes into view.

Water pours over two different rock platforms, creating two waterfalls that flow directly into a lake. It's a truly spectacular sight.

"You look as in awe of this place as I was the first time I saw it," I tell him. "How many times have you been here?" Surely, he's been here plenty since he grew up in Maple Crest, and because, I mean, it's a waterfall. Why wouldn't you come see it?

He laughs lightly. "This is my first time seeing it, actually."

I scrunch my nose. "No, it's not. How have you not been here before?"

Hayden walks up and places a hand on each of my arms to steady me as he places a kiss on my forehead. "That thing you just did with your nose was the cutest thing I've ever seen in my life. But I'm being serious; I've never been here before."

We take several minutes to hike closer to the water: not too close that we get soaked by the spray, but close enough to feel a light mist on our faces. Hayden walks back several feet and holds up his phone, telling me to pose. I do so by putting a confident hand on my hip and leaning forward, blowing him a kiss with my other hand. Meanwhile, he's grinning widely, as if he were the one getting his picture taken. I race back to his side and flip his camera around so we can snap a few shots together, then we make our way toward the lakeside.

"Okay, I brought a few things for us," I say after we settle in comfortably on top of a blanket I pulled from the backpack, alongside a thermos. "First, cocoa. And don't worry, I have all the right things in case you want them Irish," I wink at him.

He laughs, surprised. "I didn't peg you as the kind of person that would like Irish hot chocolate."

"Are you kidding?" I pour hot cocoa into two little steel cups I'd found amongst my late uncle's things. They each have different mountain scenes depicted on them and cheesy little sayings, but they're cute and perfect for outings like this. "It's hot chocolate and liquor combined. It's perfect." Once both of our cups are ready and he has his in hand, I raise mine in a toast. "Sláinte."

Hayden can hardly stop smiling enough to take a drink, making my chest swell with joy.

"What else did you bring?" he asks once he swallows.

I pull two sketchbooks and a small, rolled case of pencils from my backpack next. "You've seen what I can do. Time for you to do the same thing. Show me what you've got, mountain man." I flip my sketchbook open to a blank page and immediately start my sketch.

"You just want to do art with me in the mountains?" His voice isn't condescending at all. Rather, the question sounds airy, almost like he can't believe it.

"Yeah. I love it here and know that you love the outdoors. Plus, I thought it would be fun to put all that art talk of yours to use." My head whips up from the paper, suddenly feeling like he hates what I planned. "We don't have to do this, though. We can pack up and leave if you'd rather do something else."

"No, no," he rushes. "This...this is perfect, Tate. I don't want to be anywhere other than here." His eyes shine in a way that seems impossible given that the sun is covered with clouds, yet I swear his brown eyes are glistening. And his smile...God, his smile. It's one I haven't seen from him before. It's like he's looking at something that fascinates him.

The softness of his face suggests he was being genuine when he told me this is where he wants to be right now, and I feel the same way.

"Well. Then good. I don't either." I start sketching again to hide my face since I can feel a blush on my cheeks.

"What should I draw?"

"Whatever you want. I'm sketching the waterfalls." Glancing at the waterfalls for reference, I take a moment to soak in the details, then return my attention to the paper to lay down in graphite what I saw. "But you can do whatever. It doesn't even have to be something you see. You can get creative and draw whatever you're thinking."

"Whatever I'm thinking?"

"Mhmm." I tend to get sucked into my work, and I can feel myself starting to tune everything out but myself, my subject, the sketchbook in my lap, and the pencil in my hand. My brow creases, and I lick my lips while studying the falls. That's followed by me biting my lip in concentration when I try to replicate things.

Neither Hayden nor I speak as we sketch, but it's not uncomfortable between us, it's peaceful. It's him and I, the sound of the water, and the singing of birds. Days like this are what long-lasting memories are made of.

"Ta-da!" I exclaim a little while later as I flip my book around for him to see.

"That's incredible," he exclaims. "Wow, it's a good thing you're already selling your stuff."

I chuckle. "Thank you! Let me see what you've got." I bend forward to look at his sketchbook, but he flattens it against his chest and leans away, hiding it from me.

"Nuh-uh. Not yet. I need a couple more minutes to finish shading first."

"Fine. At least tell me what you're working on."

He smiles a mischievous smile. "Nope. You're going to have to wait." As he continues shading the paper, I admire the look of concentration on his face. He's wearing a baseball cap over his hair and when he flips it around to concentrate better, or see better, or something, I nearly swoon. Perhaps that was the reason for the adjustment. I don't care. I'm just thankful the universe has blessed me with this sight. I swear he gets more and more attractive every time I set my eyes on him. "Okay, I'm ready. But you've got to come sit by me to see it."

I'm broken from my dazed stare and when I finally focus on his face and expressions, I can tell he knows exactly what's been going through my mind. Hayden is not a self-conceited person in the least, but he's giving me a smug smile now. And damn if that doesn't reaffirm my last thoughts.

"Why do I have to sit by you to see it?" My body is already moving closer to his as I speak, so it's not like I wasn't going to do it. But I'm still curious to know.

"Reasons," he states simply. When I'm settled beside him, he looks down at where I'm seated and inhales a deep breath, suddenly seeming a little nervous even though he's trying to hide it. "Alright, go easy on me. I took an art *history* class, not life draw-ing." He finally shows me what he was working on and my mouth parts before slowly spreading into a grin.

"This is what you were thinking, huh?" I ask.

"Still am. I think about it all the time. Morning, noon, and night." Right in the middle of the paper, drawn in a square a fraction of the size of the page, is a detailed sketch of two faces. The people in this drawing appear to be mid-kiss. Both of their mouths parted. The man's more so than the woman's, and it's as if I can hear the very breath they separated for, before they return to passion. Except, this isn't random people being depicted. Based on the sharp jawline, firm chin, and perfect lips, I can tell the man in the drawing is Hayden. I've admired these details about him often. And judging by the plump lips, button nose, and light hair that cascades slightly over what can be seen of the faces due to her position above him — or rather, *my* position above him — I can tell the woman he drew is me. And damn. The sketch is good. *Really* good. So good, in fact, it has stirred up emotions that didn't need any help driving me crazy because I've had similar thoughts in my mind just as often. "You've got to say something, you're killing me here." I pick up a hint of nervousness in his soft chuckle.

"Sorry, I was...lost in thought." I'm still smiling whilst staring at his page. Honestly, I want to be the version of myself that's on that paper so badly right now it almost hurts. I want *him*. "This is *really* good, Hayden."

He adjusts himself and when he speaks, I feel his breath cascade against my ear, sending shivers down my spine. "What were you thinking about?"

"This. And...that maybe you need some more inspiration. Just in case you wanted to make this the first of a series of sketches."

His brows raise. "You know what? Now that I think about it, I could seriously use some help with the modeling. You know, to give me a clear idea."

I set my supplies aside and straighten my back before squaring my shoulders. "Alright, Jack Dawson. How do you want me?"

His eyes rave over my body at a sluggish pace. "Careful what you ask for, Tate. Are you sure you want to know the answer to that? Because I can tell you right now I can think of several ways to answer that question, all of which I think you'd be a fan of."

Oh shit.

My body reacts to his words in multiple ways. One of which is the rate of my breathing increasing due to desire. Hayden and I haven't had sex yet, but I want to. I want to, *so bad.* Putting a hand on his brawny chest, I lay my palm flat against him and push until he's on his back. Swinging one of my legs over him so I'm hovering over his hips, I lean down slowly and stop when my mouth is an inch from his.

"Is this how you pictured us when you were drawing?" My voice is low and sultry.

His lips part and he's breathing quicker now, too. Chocolate eyes focus on my lips, and he swallows before meeting my eyes again.

"Yes," he admits. Hayden puts his warm hands on my hips, pulling me down so the lower half of my body is no longer hovering above him. Instead, our bodies are connected now, and I can feel his erection through his pants and in between my legs. "Except you were like this instead."

"Mmm," I hum, nodding my head slowly several times. Each time my head dips, it closes more of the distance between our faces, leaving only a whisper between us. His chin ticks up once, suggesting that he's fighting the urge to end my teasing on his own, but manages to let me stay in control. For now, anyway. "What else?" I whisper against his lips.

His eyes flutter closed with a soft sigh but when they open again, he starts rocking my hips against him. Even through the material of his pants, I can feel that his size is impressive, so I bite my bottom lip. He's not the only one trying to restrain themself.

"You were doing this." Hayden's voice sounds so lust-filled it's hard to focus on anything else. We're both fully dressed, and we haven't even kissed yet, but still he's got me close to feeling euphoria. My lips graze against his in a gentle touch as my hips continue to rock. When he moves to deepen the touch, I pull away, still enjoying the effect my teasing has on him. "God, please, end my misery and kiss me already, Tate," he begs.

I indulge him, our mouths crashing together. His powerful hand runs up the back of my neck, burying itself in my hair, holding me to him. I lower myself a little more, so my chest is pressed against his, needing more contact as we nearly devour one another. Minutes or hours go by. I'm not sure which since I can't think of anything other than the feeling of him when he suddenly flips our bodies so that he's the one above me. The move was so sudden and skillful that our lips didn't separate, even for a breath.

Hayden slips a hand under my shirt, bracing it firmly against my ribs. I detach myself from him so I can shed my jacket and he follows my lead, leaving him in a light gray t-shirt which shows off his pecs deliciously. As he starts to come back down over me, I meet him halfway and press my mouth to his neck, licking and kissing the tender skin. He rewards my action with a deep groan and a hand slips beneath the waistband of my pants, but he stops once his fingers meet my underwear.

He pulls his head away from mine so he can look at me. "Is this okay?"

"Yes," I whisper, pulling him back to me and undoing my pants to make it easier for his hand to slide in. When his fingers touch my slit, he curses softly at the moisture his fingers find. Then, finally, *finally*, Hayden starts to work his fingers both in and on me, all the while whispering words of praise.

That's it, Tatum.

Keep riding my hand. You're doing such a good job.

Look at you. So fucking gorgeous.

It isn't long at all until I'm writhing underneath him and whimpering.

I need more. I need *him*.

Pushing him up so he's on his knees, I sit up and undo his pants, pushing them down enough to expose his impressive length. I grip him firmly before licking from base to tip, then putting as much of him in my mouth as I can, give it a good suck. Then another, and another. Then, I work his shaft with my hand as I lick and suck his tip.

When I tilt my eyes up to look at him, I find him panting with his eyes clenched tight. He cusses again, every muscle in his body clenching tight before he pulls himself out of my mouth suddenly.

"If you keep that up, this is going to be over long before it's even started," he says while rubbing my cheek with his thumb. Hayden lays me back down, gripping the top of my pants on either side and yanking them down to expose me entirely before covering my body with his.

I feel his skin against mine in the most intimate places of our bodies and I barely have a clear enough mind to remind myself I don't have a condom, so we can't have sex. I won't do this without one and tell him as much.

"I've got one in my wallet."

"You do?" I ask as he reaches for his wallet. He pulls out the proof. It surprises me he has it since he's never made a move before in the way he has today. In fact, I had nearly convinced myself he was a virgin. But that theory went so far out the window the second his fingers were inside me. There's no way a virgin could do the things he was doing. Not with how good he was doing them, at least.

He laughs. "I might take things a little slow at first, but I'm still a guy. One who likes to be prepared since you never know when you'll need one." Hayden gestures around us for emphasis. Which is another thing. I'm far from new to sex, but I wouldn't say I'm adventurous. As in, I've never had sex outside during the day where we could be caught at any moment. But Hayden doesn't seem bothered by the idea, giving me the impression this isn't a super popular trail, so I choose not to be either.

"Fair point," I grin.

"So," Hayden cocks his head, his eyes heated and a knowing smirk spreading on his lips, "was that your way of telling me you don't want to have sex or should we open this?" He holds up the condom packet already fully aware of how badly I want him right now, but getting my consent one last time before we cross this next line.

"Hayden, if you don't put that condom on right now and fuck me already, I'm going to—"

His mouth crashes against mine, but his hands are noticeably absent from my half-covered body. A second later, I vaguely hear the tearing of the condom wrapper. A few more seconds after that, Hayden's large hand wraps around my throat. Not squeezing, just holding.

"Ready?" he whispers, a breath away from my mouth.

"Mhmm." It's the only response I can muster. He brought me so close to the edge with his fingers, but I switched things up before he could bring me my release. It was worth it, though, to have him in my mouth. He's warm, thick, and I loved the way his velvety skin felt against my tongue as it ran over the veins of his shaft. But I'm on the verge of losing it if at least *one* of us doesn't come soon.

His tip is at my entrance, then Hayden slowly starts to push himself inside of me. Before he even comes to a stop, a satisfied breath leaves me as my body stretches to accept him.

Once fully inside me, Hayden slowly starts to pump his hips, letting my body take its time to adjust. When I start to roll my hips to meet his rhythm, he picks up his pace and his hand tightens slightly around my throat when he kisses me again. Hayden's other hand moves to my hip and he grabs me firmly in order to hold my body against the ground.

Now that he's coated in my slickness, he picks up the pace of his thrusts again, pumping into me even harder. My body rocks with every plunge, so I grip onto his shirt-covered shoulders to help steady me.

The combination of the strength he's fucking me with, his hold on my neck, and his passionate kissing, has me losing my breath. I rip my mouth from his so I can breathe, but I end up moaning loudly instead.

"That's it, gorgeous. Don't hold back." Hayden buries his face in my neck, his rhythm not letting up, and nips at my pulse point before kissing away the sting.

Holy shit.

Running my hands down his sides, I gather the material of his shirt and pull it over his head so I have more skin to touch.

Jesus. That body.

It's all tan, tight skin. I'm mystified by the sight of watching his toned body bend with every thrust into me. Needing to see more, I lift my back several inches off the ground to see where we're connected.

Having had to remove his hand from my throat when I took off his shirt, Hayden snakes his fingers into my hair in order to hold me at this angle. "You like watching, baby?"

"Yes," my response breathy. When he tightens his hold on my hair, I feel myself reaching the edge. "Hayden." A plea, a warning, I'm not sure.

"You can take it, Tatum." His hand leaves my hip and moves to my clit, massaging me. Hyden's other hand moves from the back of my head to the back of my neck, allowing my head to fall back as another loud moan leaves me. The second my neck is arched and exposed to him, he latches his mouth onto it bringing out a surprised gasp from me.

"Hayden! I'm— Fuck, I'm going to—" I can't my panting and moaning long enough to form a solid sentence. Jesus. Before this, the part of me that wasn't convinced Hayden was a virgin was convinced that sex with Hayden Williams, though it would still be good, wouldn't really stand out from my previous experiences. I was wrong. Oh, I was *so* wrong.

"If you can say it, I'll let you do it," Hayden says into my ear.

"I'm going to—" Again, the rest of the sentence is cut off by a moan.

Hayden, through his own panting, chuckles. "Come on, baby

girl. You can say it. It's not that hard." Except, it is. All I can think about is the pleasure he's bringing to my body. Even if my own sounds of enjoyment gave me enough of an opening to speak, I don't think my mind is coherent enough to form real words anymore. "What's wrong, Tate? Is something distracting you?"

What. A. Dick. I lift my head to attempt to glare at him, but a particularly hard thrust into me has my eyes rolling back in pleasure instead. Then, he stops. His whole body stills, and when I look at him again, I find him smirking at me.

"Hayden!" This time, I know it's a plea. I *have* to come. Soon. "*Please.*" Bracing myself up with my forearms, I roll my hips once but grabs hold of either side and stills my body and gives me a playfully scolding look.

"Please what? I want to hear you say it. Say you want to come and I'll let you."

My back falls back against the blanket in defeat. "Please, Hayden. I want to come."

"That's a good girl," he praises, then slams back into me.

Chapter Fourteen

TATUM

I'm going to be sore tomorrow. I can't be sure whether it's in between my legs because of the way he pounded into me in the best way possible, or from all the other glorious things he did to my body when he made me come, not once, but three times. Or, maybe the soreness is all over because of the fall I took during our hike on the way back. Two out of the three, I wouldn't mind too much because it's the best kind of soreness that comes from the best kind of circumstances. The other option out of the three though...yeah, let's just say it was mortifying for me and absolutely hilarious for Hayden, and move on.

After we get back to the house and he leaves, I spend some time cleaning since I've been in and out a lot lately. My laundry pile was already quite large since it's one of my least favorite chores to do, but now it's especially impressive. Turning my music on shuffle, I get started on the household duties I've been neglecting. Productivity lasts for a solid seven minutes before '*18*' by One Direction starts playing. The next thing I know, I'm using a spatula as a microphone and sliding around the kitchen in my socks as I throw my head around, singing along to the words. The laundry is long forgotten as I put on the performance of a lifetime in my very own kitchen.

Lenny watches me perform three more songs in concert, and I manage to finish loading my dishwasher before I decide it's time for a well-earned break.

"Hey," I chirp when Anthony answers my FaceTime call. The poor guy looks a little rough, but he smiles back at me anyway.

"Well, well. If it isn't my beautiful new girlfriend. To what do I owe the pleasure?" I sit on the couch and prop my phone up on a pillow.

"I'm just checking in again. How are you feeling?"

"I'm doing fine. I'd be better if I was spending the day with you, but I was a little tied up the past couple of days, unable to work. Now I'm too close to reaching the end of a deadline I'm, admittedly, unprepared for."

I frown. "You're working today? You should be taking it easy."

Anthony chuckles, then grimaces at the pain it caused him. "I'll be fine, darling. I'm only going to be in my office in front of a computer, not doing anything strenuous."

"Okay, fine. Let me know if you need anything. I'll let you go so you can get back to your project and try to meet that deadline. Call tomorrow?"

"If I can wait that long." We hang up with his promise to call me later tonight.

I'VE GOTTEN a little used to hearing bumps in the night, so I no longer immediately assume the worst about Lenny, which is nice, but the alternative is far less comforting. This time, the bump was so loud against the window beside my bed I almost thought the glass would break when I first heard it.

After calming my racing heart, I gently pull the curtain aside to reveal.... nothing. No one and nothing is on the other side. Once the emptiness is exposed, I hear another thump against the glass. Except, it's not the window by my bed anymore. It's one of the windows in the living room. Slowly, I move to stand in the bedroom doorway. When I get there, the thump sounds again near the bathroom across the room. Whoever it is, they're moving around the house. If I want to catch them, I have to get ahead of them. So, as they move for the kitchen windows, I hasten my steps to get to the art room while dialing 911.

"911, what's your emergency?" the operator asks.

"Hi, I think someone is outside of my house," I whisper into the speaker.

"Do you know who it is? Are they trying to get inside, or do they have a weapon?"

"I don't know. They're moving around my house, hitting the windows." As I say that, I hear them hit the kitchen windows and I flinch, chills running up my arms. I give the operator my address. Maybe I shouldn't be sitting by this window to wait for them, but I can't help it. I need to see if I know who this is.

"Is the person still there?" the operator asks.

"Yes," I tell her. My body shakes with anticipation because I know they'll be here any second.

"Okay, ma'am, a unit will be on its way. An officer will be there in about—" The slap of sudden hands on my window inches in front of me makes a scream burst from my body. My phone drops to the floor and crashes against the wood, but I don't move to pick it up. I can't. I'm face to face with the person who's been skulking around my house at night.

Or, I would be, but they're wearing a mask over their face and underneath their hood. I remain frozen in a combination of shock and fear. Both of their hands are planted flat against the window on either side of their head. With the white mask and how their hands are placed on the glass; they resemble the painting hanging up in my house. The height of their hands compared to their body and the distance they are from their face is almost *exactly* the same as it is in my painting. It looks like my painting escaped the abstract world of the canvas and jumped into the real world. The world that's right on the other side of my windowpane.

"Ma'am? Ma'am?" I can faintly hear the 911 operator calling to me from where my phone is lying on the floor.

The masked figure and I stare at each other. Neither of us is moving or attempting to speak, but with each passing second, my body begins to shake more and more. *Are they going to try to get in? What happens if they come inside?*

It's that last thought which snaps me into action. Bending down to get my phone, I snatch it from the ground. The person on the other side of the window is gone when I straighten back up. Putting the phone back to my ear while keeping my gaze outside, I elect to ignore the fact that I let the call stay abandoned while I stared the person in the face for who knows how many long moments.

"How much longer until they're here?" I ask.

"About fifteen minutes."

"Okay. Please hurry." I hang up the call before they have the chance to say anything else and before I have time to think, my phone is back to my ear.

The ringing ends a few seconds later, and an English accent fills my ear. "Tatum? Are you alright?"

"There's someone outside my house," I blurt out. "I don't know who it is or what they want, but they're pounding on my windows, and I'm scared."

I hear shuffling on the other side of the phone. His voice is filled with urgency. "I'm on my way. Did you call the police already?"

"Yeah, they said they're like fifteen minutes out, though."

"I'll beat them there. Where does Hayden live? Is he in town, or does he live somewhere outside of it?" I hesitate. Now I feel like a bad girlfriend because I never even asked him that. Anthony must read my silence because he speaks again. "Call him. Maybe he can get there faster than I can."

Faster than less than fifteen minutes? I call him anyway and explain the situation to Hayden, who sounds like he's already out the door before I finish talking. Watching out the window, I see he and Anthony show up within seconds of each other and I open the door for them. They come in and hastily shut the door behind them, making sure to switch the lock into place. Anthony storms outside again and is searching the backyard when the police show up a couple of minutes later. They ask me questions and search the area but end up telling me no one is there and that they can't do anything about it.

"There weren't any shoe prints or anything to suggest someone other than Mr. Kensington was ever out here. If you're menstruating right now, then your emotions are heightened. Being this close to the forest, perhaps you saw an animal and mistook it for a person." My eyes widen and my mouth gapes.

If I'm menstruating right now? Is he being serious?

"Are you kidding me?" Anthony bursts, his apparent anger boiling up inside of him.

"Easy, man," Hayden warns him. His arms are wrapped around my shoulder, and he hugs me to his side. From the tense set of his jaw, I can see he's as irritated over the man's comment as Anthony and I are.

"No, that's complete rubbish. You're seriously going to try to make her feel crazy? Make her think she doesn't know what she's talking about? You won't believe a woman's word that someone is pestering her until she winds up dead or missing, is that it?"

He's right, and I know this because I have heard too many stories and read too many articles about women suffering with their lives after they've been ignored when they tried reaching out for help. But it's unsettling to hear those words when I'm the one who had to call.

Sometimes I feel like I got lucky with the way things went down with Lucas and the fact I got immediate results when I was in danger and needed help. But what are the odds of it happening twice? This is a man's world. That is a fact that is proven time and time again. Of course, they're not going to take me seriously over this.

"Anthony," I press quietly. When he looks at me, I shake my head. There will be no changing the police's minds that someone was out there even though there's no mistaking what I saw tonight. But Hayden and Anthony believe me, so that will have to be enough for now.

When the police leave, both of the boys refuse to leave my house for the rest of the night. We lay shoulder-to-shoulder in my bed, myself in the middle, and I get the feeling I won't be the only one not sleeping even though it has barely reached midnight.

"Whoever it was, they mimicked my painting *exactly*. They've been inside my house."

Both heads turn to me in the dark.

Chapter Fifteen

TATUM

"I really think you should consider staying at my place for a while," Anthony tries to convince me through the phone. Both he and Hayden left this morning for work. I've triple-checked the locks since then and have only looked out the window about a hundred times since I started painting.

"Everything about our relationship has been moving so fast," I tell him plainly as I drag my paintbrush through a blotch of paint on my palette. "I can't move in with you this quickly. I have to take some things slower, at least."

"Then don't call it that. You can define it as coming to reside in a safe house until we find out who's been sneaking around your place at night and why. We don't even have to sleep in the same room if you don't want to. I could set one up where you could stay for as long as you wish. Whatever would make you the most comfortable."

"I can't, Anthony. Whether you call them pancakes, flapjacks, or hotcakes, they're still the same thing. It's too soon for that, Kens." He's not the biggest fan of the nickname I started using a couple of days ago, but I keep taunting him with it regardless. Someone has to keep that ego of his in check. "Besides, your house just got broken into and robbed. You still look like shit from what they did to you. No offense. So, I don't think I'd be much better off there, anyway."

"I promise you; you'd be safe here. No one is getting into the house again." My silence is his answer, but I have to appreciate the fact that someone who cares so little for company in his home is offering me his own. "Fine," he resigns. "I don't want to push you on the matter but remember that the offer always remains open should you want it. However, I am prepared to push you for a security system and some cameras for your place."

"I was looking into that this morning after you guys left," I assure him, stepping back from my canvas to see how the details I added look. He seems surprised by this. "Of course, I did. I'm a woman who's living alone, who doesn't have neighbors close by, who weird stuff has been happening to. Why wouldn't I look into getting security for this place?"

"Did you pick out which system you want?"

"Not yet." I pick a clean brush from my collection and dip it in a blob of color on my palate. "But I'll get around to it."

When our call ends a short amount of time later, the rest of the day is quick to become a little hectic. The vet from Ragsburrow calls with test results, telling me Lenny has epilepsy and will need to continue medication for the rest of his life. Which is thankfully expected to be a long and otherwise normal life so I can stop imagining a tear-filled goodbye in some vets' office due to the worst-case scenario.

But where there's good news, bad news often isn't far behind. I told Grace about what happened last night earlier this morning and asked her not to tell our parents so they wouldn't worry about me. But one thing about Grace is that she loves tea. And I'm not talking about the drink. Turns out a couple of hours is the longest she can go before she spills my story to them because I spend an hour and a half on the phone with my parents while they continuously tell me to move back to Dallas. Since I *defi-*

nitely don't want to do that, I downplay the whole situation to them until they finally accept it.

On my way home from picking up an afternoon coffee and catching up with Nick, I stop beside my mailbox to gather today's mail. Among the regular junk mail and electric bill is a thick, kraft paper envelope with my full name written on it.

My name, and *nothing else* written on it.

There's no name saying who it's from or an address for a return to sender. There's not even my address on it: only my name.

I can feel an electric pulse of anxiety shoot down my arms as my heart rate picks up. Tucking my finger under the paper on one side, I rip it open, first noticing a folded-up piece of paper with several holes in it. When I unfold the paper, I lose my breath. It's a shooting target with the outline of a person that's been shot repeatedly. Dropping the target on the passenger seat, I look inside the bag and then tip the rest of the contents out in my hand.

Nine empty shell casings clatter into my palm.

Hastily dumping them back in the mailer, I don't bother folding the target before I put my car in reverse and drive to the police station. My windshield wipers are working overtime to fight off the heavy onslaught of rain. After I'm parked, I grab the shot-up target from the passenger seat and rush through the doors up to the woman sitting behind the glass partition.

"I called last night about someone walking around my house and banging on my windows, but the officers pretty much told me I was hormonal and making things up since there was no evidence. Then today, I came home to find this in my mailbox." I hold the target up against the glass.

A handful of minutes later, I'm giving a report to some officers who have taken the casings and the target as evidence. That's twice now I have made a report in twenty-four hours, so on my way home, I make a stop at Maple Crest's gun store. Unfortunately, it doesn't do me a lot of good since there's a three-day waiting period before I can take the thing home.

Before I start for the house again, I create a group message between myself, Hayden, and Anthony. It'll be more effective to text them like this than it would be to keep telling them things separately.

After letting them know what I found, I ask Hayden if he owns any guns.

Hayden:
Yes. Do you want me to teach
you how to shoot?

I've been around guns before and have a mild understanding of them, but I want to ensure I'll feel completely confident while using my own once these mandatory three days are over.

Anthony:
I have a range under my house.
If you're able to come over
tomorrow, I'll teach you.

Hayden:
Dude. You have a shooting range
in your basement?

Anthony:
*Tatum, if you're able to come over
tomorrow, I'll teach you.
Also, I'm sending someone to your
house. Let me know when you get
home, please.

I follow through with his request and about forty-five minutes later there's a knock at my door. Opening it up, I find

Anthony's sister, Zara, standing on the other side with a couple of people behind her.

"Anthony is busy with some work stuff, so he asked me to oversee the installation of your new security system." She gestures behind her at the two people wearing apparel representing the company they're with.

"Oh. I didn't pick one yet, so I didn't schedule anything."

"You didn't? It must have been Anthony then. He can be a little overprotective sometimes, but don't worry, this company is the best. Pricey but good. At least they charged it to his card. Can we come in?" Her voice is accented like Anthony's and flows so smoothly I could picture her being a book narrator plenty of authors would want to commission.

I hesitate. I didn't want Anthony to buy me a security system since I can do that myself. Then again, I take a long time making big decisions because I repeatedly go over every pro and con. It probably would've been several more days before I decided on one. And who knows? By that time, it could be too late.

Stepping aside, I invite them in. The two security workers immediately start setting things up. Anthony spared no expense in getting me cameras for both the inside and outside of my house. They will be an immense relief since I suspect someone has come inside at some point.

While they work, Zara and I take a seat on the couch.

"So, you're the artist," she starts. Zara looks nothing like her brother or their dad. I assume she gets her dark hair and green eyes, like mine, from their mom. Just like her brother, though, she's gorgeous. She's wearing black skinny jeans and an emerald green sweater to offset the cold weather. Her lips are painted with crimson lipstick, and her eyes are winged with sharp liner. Even though she's in high-heeled boots with cheeks that sparkle from an abundance of highlighter, she looks like she could kick anyone's ass and look good while doing it.

"I am," I say, following a drink of water. "Anthony's mentioned me?"

"Only to me. He and dear old Dad don't talk much these days unless it's about business. He's told me a lot about you."

"All good things, I hope." I chuckle a little nervously, hoping she can't sense my unease. *What is the proper response to comments like that? You can't say that kind of crap without me getting awkward and overthinking it for 5-10 business days.*

Another issue is that I don't know how much he's told her. Does she know about the relationship he's in now and how it's not solely with me? Or does he want to keep it a secret? My palms start to sweat when I think about Hayden randomly stopping by and what she'd think about it if he did.

Deciding to take charge of the conversation in order to steer it in a safe direction, I ask her about what she does for work. From there, the conversation flows relatively effortlessly. Before I know it, we both relax into our seats, breaking out the wine coolers once the security team leaves.

"You know, I thought you were Anthony's girlfriend when I saw you two at the gallery opening," I chuckle.

Her mouth gapes before she cringes. "No, did you really? Ugh, that's dreadful. Didn't you see me with my girlfriend at all?"

Girlfriend? "Um, no, I must have missed the part where you had a significant other. Otherwise, I wouldn't have thought you and Anthony were together." *Unless, of course, you were in a poly relationship like I currently am, with your brother, in fact. But that wasn't even on my mind at the time.*

"Oh. Well, she was there, looking gorgeous on the side of the stage. It's strange you didn't see her." That's the thing about Anthony, though. When he's in the room, he sucks all my attention solely to him. I suddenly get tunnel vision, and he's all I see. The rest of the world falls away, becoming a blank white canvas with him, the standing masterpiece, front and center.

The only one that could, and ever does, compare to him is Hayden. One is the sun, and the other the moon, and together they create the perfect balance to keep me filled with life.

Zara tells me about her girlfriend. How long they've been

together, how they met, and by the time she finishes telling me about her, I feel like I've known the woman I've never even met forever. Zara goes from an intimidating badass to a badass with a *major* soft spot for the girl who's a massive Marvel fan. Her smile is soft and wide as she recalls taking her to the latest Spider-Man premiere. Her girlfriend met Tom Holland, and her look at the memory almost makes me forget that she gives me the feeling she's carrying multiple knives. I can't tell for sure if she is — *I don't know if that's a comfort or not.*

After a couple of glasses of water and another hour later, we exchange numbers as she gets up to leave, and she tells me to call her if I need help with the cameras. Once she's out the door, I reply to Anthony's two texts. One is him asking if everything is going okay with the camera set up, and the other is him telling me that if his sister is too much, to say the word and he'll save me.

I found it odd she hadn't mentioned what happened to Anthony while she was here. Then again, he'd said he didn't want anyone to find out — her included — about what happened to him, so maybe she still doesn't know.

Since Hayden should be off work now, I call him, putting the phone on speaker. While I set up everything I need for the security cameras to give me access to them on my phone and laptop, he tells me about his day.

Chapter Sixteen

TATUM

Since Lenny's first vet appointment, every day now starts with me chasing him down to shove Zonisamide and Gabapentin down his throat. He's a quick learner of what the sound of pill bottle caps being removed means, apparently, since he makes each day increasingly more difficult than the last. Luckily, my big tomcat, who has brutal weapons on the top of each toe, and teeth that could shred just as easily, is too much of a softie to ever know what to do with them. Instead, he runs around from room to room until I catch him, making it a game of chase neither of us enjoys.

Once the game is over, I'm on my way to The Brewed Bean for a much-needed iced coffee when my attention snags on a stop sign at the end of my street.

ARE YOU COUNTING?

The words are written in white, dripping paint covering nearly the whole sign. I don't want to call it dumb graffiti because I'm an artist and know all things have value and meaning in some way. But the message of this piece is lost to me. Whoever did this should have made their point more clear. What are people supposed to be counting?

"There she is!" Nick proclaims when I walk into Maple Crest's best stop for caffeine. If anyone's personality could chase away this dreary weather, it would be Nick's.

He is Helios — the personification of the sun. As Helios is said to have brought the sun across the sky with his chariot, Nick brings light into the lives of those in the city with his smile and bubbly personality. Along with cups filled with coffee.

During my first couple weeks of adjusting here, his joy and willingness to get to know me helped me immensely. He gave me a sense of belonging; I don't think he even realizes that. It's not something I will tell him, though. Not now, at least. Maybe sometime down the line because I'd hate to make things weird between us.

We fall into conversation as he makes my drink, and luck is on our side, giving him a break from the usually steady flow of customers so we can have some time to catch up. Hearing the bell above the door chime a few minutes later, I'm smiling as I bid him goodbye. I'm mid-laugh as I turn around, crashing into someone's chest and nearly spilling my drink.

"Oh my gosh, I am so—" My words fade into nothing when I look up into steel-gray eyes and see who I've encountered. Clay Kensington. He's looking down at me as if — well, as if he were truly looking down at me. As if he were disgusted by my existence. I know being shoulder checked isn't something anyone wants to have happen during their day, but this seems to be far beyond that. Suddenly, Nyasia's and Nick's warnings about this man and his family start to sound in my head. His intense stare alone makes everything they said about him thinking he's better than everyone else, seem true. He shares the same-colored eyes as his son, but the color is all they have in common. "Sorry," I finish.

Clay brushes a hand at his shoulder, wiping off droplets of my coffee which aren't even there. Other than that, neither of us moves, and I know what he's waiting for. He wants me to step aside so he can continue forward on an unblocked path, whilst I'm waiting for him to do the same thing. Sure, I was the one that bumped into him. But that only happened because I was turning around, and he wasn't giving me my proper space. It wasn't like I was walking distracted and looking at my phone or something. For that reason, I'm not about to cower and give some asshole of a man the right of way simply because he's a man. That may have been how things used to be, but it's a stupid and outdated practice.

Sorry, Anthony, but meeting the boyfriend's parent didn't quite go as I'd hoped.

We remain standing in a stare-off for much longer than necessary before finally, Clay steps around me and up to the counter. The strange thing is, I swear I glimpsed an amused smirk as he passed by me. Not one that suggests he's amused with himself, but one that suggests I was amusing him in some way.

Looking over my shoulder before leaving, I see Clay talking to Nick, but it's apparent he isn't ordering a drink. Nick's posture is far too defensive for that, with his chin tilted up slightly, his gaze hard, and his arms crossed. Nick doesn't just work at The Brewed Bean. It's his own business. It makes me wonder if Clay, as Nyasia mentioned, wants to buy the company and kick Nick out of it. That would explain why Nick seems upset about his presence, but I don't want to linger, so I continue towards my car.

When I turn on my street, I see the black and green accented motorcycle I saw in front of The Brewed Bean a little while ago. Except now it's parked along the curb in front of my house. The rider is decked out in dark protective gear that doesn't show a sliver of skin, making it impossible to tell who the rider is.

Who the hell? I slow my car to a crawl as the rider swings their leg off the bike. When the helmet gets removed, Megan Fox's half-English doppelgänger, Zara, is revealed. Only then do I pull fully into my driveway.

"What are you doing here?" I ask as I step out of my car. Zara is walking up the driveway and undoing her braided dark hair, pulling it up into a high ponytail.

"Are you going in to paint, or do you have a couple of free hours?" Zara is taller than me by about three inches, but the biker boots she's wearing make it seem like half a foot.

"Why?"

"Have you ever been kickboxing before? Since you've got a creep coming around, I thought it might be a good idea to take you in case they get too bold and try something stupid."

Not even ten minutes later, we're both in my car headed towards Ragsburrow and the gym Zara is a member of. She uses her family name to get me past the front desk, and we walk further into the building. When she'd said *gym,* I was expecting a couple of spacious rooms filled with workout equipment. This place has that, but it also has a pool room, a fencing room, a CrossFit room, an indoor soccer field, and a room for boxing and wrestling.

In the locker room, we pass by a sauna until she comes to a stop in front of a row of lockers. She sheds off her thick biking jacket and steps out of the matching pants until she's left in a sports bra and leggings like me. To my surprise, both her arms and stomach are covered in tattoos.

"Are those all new? I didn't see that you had any back at the gallery." She'd been wearing a spaghetti-strap dress that night, and her arms were bare. Yet not a single tattoo appeared to be etched into her skin.

She chuckles. "No, no, these are not new. I've had them for quite a while. I started getting them at sixteen, actually. My dad despises them, says it isn't proper for me to have marked my skin like this, blah, blah, blah. I didn't let that stop me from ever getting more, though. But since he's the boss, I have to follow some of his rules. Hence, the bottle of foundation used to cover my ink during important public events."

"He's the boss? So you're not like Anthony, doing something

independently? You work directly for your dad doing...I don't know what he does, actually."

Zara's arms pause in mid-air for a second as she's pulling a pair of Nike shoes from her locker, then resumes the motion again. "Oh. I meant to say he's the boss, as in he's our dad. So, he's kind of the boss of us in that way, you know what I mean?" After slipping her feet into them, she finishes tying the knots on her shoes. "Ready?"

ZARA WANTED to start by teaching me what she believes are some of the most imperative self-defense moves that aren't kickboxing related before we get started on our actual workout. She teaches me how to get out of various holds an assailant may attempt, such as someone grabbing my wrist, hair, or neck. After repeating them several times, we start on our intended workout.

I'm in fairly decent shape. I keep my body healthy, but I also enjoy having several rest days and eating snack food. As for Zara, it quickly became apparent she dedicates a lot of time to bettering her body. She's more flexible with her kicks than I am, and her punches pack more of a hit. By the time we're done, I'm exhausted, and we're both soaked in sweat.

Returning to the locker room, I shower before changing into the clothes I brought while Zara does the same. When we're both ready, we start the drive back to Maple Crest.

"Anthony is going to be teaching me how to shoot when we get back," I tell her once we make it onto the freeway. "He's letting Hayden and I use his shooting range. You should come!"

"Hayden?" she questions. "I don't know who that is."

"Oh, Hayden Williams. He's a...very close friend of mine and Anthony's," I inform her. I suppose it makes sense she wouldn't know who he is since he didn't get along with her brother, and she didn't go to school with him.

Zara scoffs quietly in the seat beside me. "Anthony doesn't really have friends. He's only ever had two, and I know them both. Whoever Hayden is, Anthony must only be keeping him around for your sake." *Well, she's not wrong.* Not wanting to give away too much information that Anthony might not want her to know, I laugh lightly before changing the subject.

The boys and I had previously determined a time to meet, but thanks to my surprise kickboxing excursion, I'm running late. Zara and I stop by my house long enough for her to get on her motorcycle, then she follows me to Anthony's place. With Maya calling me on the drive over, I don't get the chance to call one of the guys.

Pulling into the large, circular driveway, I see Hayden's truck is already here. As I park behind him, I send up a quick prayer, hoping they're both still alive and that one hasn't killed the other in my absence. Zara parks beside my car, an unreadable expression on her face as she walks up beside me. Her cheerfulness from earlier seems to have dissipated and I'm not sure why.

Several moments after I knock on the door, it opens, revealing a still-healing Anthony. He's wearing all black, as usual, but his clothes are more relaxed. Rather than a suit, he's wearing jeans with a belt and a sweater that covers up much of the damage he received a few days ago. The only bit of color aside from the bruises on his face is the blue watch I'd given him resting on his wrist.

He looks immediately at Zara, appearing more than slightly surprised. "Why are you here?"

"What the fuck happened to you?" she returns. The question sounds almost defensive and when I look at her, she has her arms crossed. "Other than asking me to look after your girlfriend yesterday, I haven't heard from you. You've practically been MIA. Now I see why. Tell me what happened."

Anthony inhales an annoyed breath and looks over our shoulders at nothing before returning her gaze. "It was nothing. I slept too hard, that's all."

"An obvious lie. Not even a good one. What happened?"

"Filchers." He glances at me, then looks back to his sister. "Money makes people cheesed off."

Behind Anthony's back, I spot Hayden approaching us from the living room.

An awkward silence ensues after he comes to a stop beside Anthony, so he sticks his hand out to Zara. "Hi. I'm Hayden Williams."

She takes his hand. "Zara Kensington."

His brows lift slightly. "Kensington." His head twists to Anthony. "Your sister?"

"Only when he needs me to be, apparently," she snarks before he can answer, but based on the look on Anthony's face, I don't think he was going to say anything. Several emotions war on his face. Annoyance. Denial. Defeat. Heartache. The combination hurts me to see alongside the bruises that are bursting with the colors of healing. "You can keep your secrets all you wish, *brother*. But had you bothered to answer my calls, you'd have realized I needed you too."

I don't know if I should turn around and return to my car or go inside. I just know I shouldn't be standing in the middle of this. After a moment of consideration, I make a decision.

"I'm going to go," I mutter, fearing if I speak too loudly, I'll set something off. But as I turn to leave, Anthony gently grips my elbow, turning me back to face him.

He wants me to stay, that much I can tell, but when he speaks, it's to Zara. "What do you mean, you needed me?"

Zara pulls her phone out of her pocket and taps a few buttons before flipping it around. I only catch a quick glance before it's turned from my sight. From what I saw, she's showing Anthony some sort of symbol. It has the top half of a raven over a kind of shield or plaque, surrounded by ivy.

"If you want to know more, then you have my number. Use it for more than a wellness check." She turns to me now. "I'm glad we went out today. You have my number too, text me. Especially if you want a *real* shooting lesson. Anthony is a fine shot, but I'm better. Much better. See ya!" Zara walks confidently down the steps and back to her bike.

"Zara," Anthony calls after her, but she doesn't stop. "Zara!"

"Use your phone, Anthony," she shoots back without looking. "If you give a shit about me, you'll do what needs to be done." After pulling on her helmet and settling onto the seat, she revs the engine before peeling around the circular driveway and riding away with her front tire in the air.

I don't know what the hell just happened, but I feel used. It's hard not to after she came here with the sole purpose of tearing into him and leaving immediately after. Not to mention her calling me a wellness check. I didn't need her to come over and babysit me while the security system team was over. *Had ending up here to confront Anthony been her plan all along?* And I wonder what she meant by '*you'll do what needs to be done.*'

Then again, maybe she does actually care about my well-being. After all, she did stay longer than necessary yesterday, and took hours out of her day today to teach me self-defense when she didn't have to. We had some real bonding moments that surely couldn't have been faked.

Anthony sighs softly before tipping his head toward the open door. "Come inside."

Stepping in, I greet Hayden with a hug and he keeps a hand on the small of my back after I turn around. The door clicks shut and when Anthony turns around, he's running a hand through his perfect hair. I had no idea he had a rocky relationship with his sister. I figured he didn't want her to know everything about his life, but I saw them together at the gallery opening and everything seemed fine between them. Then again, Hayden has a great relationship with his family. I suppose it would only make sense that Anthony wouldn't since they seem to be opposites in every other category.

"Well, that was awkward," Hayden remarks when no one else

speaks. I suck in my bottom lip slightly, unsure how to respond because he's right.

"Shut up," Anthony hisses, dropping his hand.

"I'm just saying," he comments with a small shrug, "wanna… talk about it?"

Anthony shoots him a glare. "With you? Absolutely not." He gives Hayden directions to the shooting room so he and I can talk to me alone for a minute.

We wait for Hayden to walk down the hall and once his back disappears I put a gentle hand on his cheek. "What's going on?"

He leans into my touch, his hands settling on either side of my waist. "I'm sorry about Zara, darling. She's miffed with me for not calling her since the robbery, but I promise you she's not upset about being there for the camera setup."

"What did she mean when she told you that you need to do what needs to be done?"

He pauses, his gray eyes lowering momentarily. "I'm going to have to go out of town for a couple of days for work. My business sometimes overlaps with that of my dads. She knows I hate it when it does. But if I don't do this, more work will be put on her. That's all she meant by that."

"Oh. She made it seem like a big deal," I laugh lightly. "When do you leave?"

"I'll leave tonight and be back in two or three days. I'll let you know for sure when I do."

I lean up on my toes to give him a quick kiss. "I'll miss you."

He smiles. "I'll miss you too, darling. But I'll see you soon." The look in his eyes changes then as he scans my face. My body heats from his stare alone, but he doesn't keep me wanting. His lips latch onto mine and he backs me into the nearby wall. Anthony's hands roam over my body before stopping over one of my breasts and squeezing.

I sigh into his mouth. *God, I missed his sensual touch.* I haven't gone more than a day without seeing him lately, but we've only had sex once. Finding time for that passion kind of is a little hard since we share so much of our time with Hayden.

I need to make this moment last a little longer. My hands find their way into his hair on either side of his head. His lips move to my neck, and I gasp softly at the sensations shooting through my body as he licks and kisses at the skin there before returning to my mouth. He parts my legs with his knee and lifts his leg enough so that I'm seated on his thigh.

"Wait, won't this hurt you?" The pressure against my center makes my clit ache for more, but I'm worried about his injuries.

"Darling, I would crawl through shards of glass just to be near you. If you think I'm going to let some bruises stop me from feeling your pussy throb as you find your pleasure, think again."

This man's tongue will be the death of me. As passion grows between us, I find myself rocking my hips against him. I'm careful with his body at first, still not wanting to hurt him despite his last words, but Anthony is quick to put an end to my caution. He grabs my waist, pressing me onto his leg harder so I get the firm contact I need. Soon, I'm nearly desperate for release and he knows it.

Anthony pulls the top of my shirt down to expose one of my breasts before sucking on it. I should stop this. Hayden could come back for us at any moment to see what's taking so long. Yes, he knows I'm dating Anthony just as much as I'm dating him, but that doesn't mean he'd want to see us being intimate. But I can't stop. It feels too good.

"Look at you riding my thigh," Anthony says, his voice gravelly. He rocks me harder and faster against his leg. "What I wouldn't do to see you ride my cock like that right now. Are you going to come for me, Tate?" *There it is.* I gasp loudly as an orgasm explodes through me. Anthony quickly covers my mouth with his hand, smothering my satisfied moan. Once my orgasm settles, he kisses me tenderly and steadies back on my feet. "As you know, the bathroom is down the hall to the left. The shooting range is down the stairs at the end of the hall. Take your time cleaning up. I'll meet you down there."

He walks away with a cocky, pleased grin, and I stay rooting in place with my mouth slightly agape. Without even taking off my clothes, he managed to make a mess of me in a matter of minutes. I want to get on my knees and return the favor for him, but he's already at the top of the stairs, shooting me a wink before starting his ascent down them.

A couple of hours later, I'm not the most skilled shooter around, but I'm perfectly capable. Zara said Anthony was a *fine* shot and that she's better. If what she said is true, she must be the next Annie Oakley because Anthony is a great shot. Hayden is too. At one point, it almost seemed like they were starting to have fun together. The hint of a smile ghosted on Anthony's lips as Hayden joked with us before shooting the paper target. After going through a couple more magazines, we wrap things up for the night and split up for the night. I'm both confident and ready, excited to be able to pick up my new gun soon.

Chapter Seventeen

TATUM

Hours later, in my bedroom, an alarm starts going off. *That's strange.* I don't remember setting one. Pulling my phone out from underneath my pillow, grogginess makes it take a couple of seconds to realize the alarm isn't coming from my phone. Eyeing my bedside table, I see an older digital clock facing me. That's the one ringing so loudly it could wake the dead.

Shutting it off, I examine the device. I've never seen it before in my life. I especially didn't set its alarm to go off at 7:00 in the morning. Hastily setting the clock back down, I roll back so I'm once again lying flat on the mattress and let my hands rub over my face with a sigh. When I let my arms fall wide on either side of me, there's a slight crumpling noise, and I feel an odd texture against one of my arms. Rolling my head to see the other side of my bed, I notice glossy squares of pictures scattered across the blanket. Picking one up to see it better, I see it's a picture of me walking out the door of The Brewed Bean.

What the hell?

Sitting up, I grab another one. It's Hayden and I on our hike.

Another one is of me painting in my art room taken from outside.

There's one of me walking out the door with Lenny, the vase of dead roses I'd found that day visible in the picture.

There's a picture of Nyasia and I laughing in my car.

There are three more pictures, seven in total, of me going about my day-to-day life. Someone has been documenting my movements and wanted me to know it by leaving these pictures next to me while I was sleeping.

Grabbing my phone, I immediately check my cameras and the recorded footage. There's absolutely nothing out of the ordinary recorded all night long. None of the cameras caught any unusual movement. Not even the one set up in my room. The entire night, it shows me being the only one in the house, but clearly, that's a mistake. I wasn't alone. Someone stood right next to me in order to put these items here.

The exceedingly strange part is that at one moment, my bed is empty. No pictures. The next, they're lying beside me. Meanwhile, the timestamp is continuous. It looks like the photographs impossibly appeared out of thin air.

I start to dial 911 again but stop myself. There's no point. For them, these photographs won't be enough evidence. Especially since there's no explainable video proof to go along with it. The odds are I'll be called hormonal again or be told some other misogynistic bullshit. So, I call who I know will believe me.

The only problem with having two boyfriends is choosing who to call first for things. Usually, it ends up being Anthony since, alphabetically, his name is first. He answers after a couple of rings.

"Anthony," my voice breaks and my body begins to shake with the fear I've been trying to control. Tears fill my eyes. My personal space has been violated. With the footage somehow missing, I'm unable to know what else the person who came into my house did whilst they were in my room. How long were they in here? They could have touched my skin and I'd have no clue.

"Tate, what's wrong?"

"They came back," I cry into the phone. "Someone was in my house last night. They were *in my room* with me, but my camera didn't catch any of it."

I can tell he's trying to reign in his panic as he asks, "How did you know they were in your room? Did they touch you?" That question makes my tears fall. I already considered the possibility, but having to say *I don't know* out loud makes it much more real. "Damn it," he curses. I hear something clatter from his side of the phone as if he's just thrown something. Since he's already gone on his business trip, he can't be here physically to help me right now. Instead, I settle by giving him all the information he'll need to access my cameras himself. That way, he can try to recover the missing footage since his knowledge of computers is greater than mine.

While he's still on the phone, I slip on a pair of cabin socks and leave my room. The first thing I notice is the door to the wall safe wide open. Hurrying over, I find the space behind it empty. All the money I kept inside is gone. Thousands of dollars, all of it, gone.

"Tatum, breathe for me, love. I texted Hayden, he'll be there shortly. Breathe. Breathe. That's it." My mind races, and I can't speak because I don't know what to say. Thankfully, Anthony stays on the phone with me for over a half hour anyway, giving me occasional words of comfort. Between him and Lenny, who has curled up on my lap, I'm able to settle slightly, despite my gut still twisting with unease. When my phone chimes with its declaration of movement in the front yard, I jump. Anthony assures me it's only Hayden since he's already logged into my system, trying to find the lost footage. Once Hayden is in the house, we end the call.

Not even a minute later, he's kneeling in my room beside my bed, examining the pictures without touching them.

"What the hell?" With how quiet his question is, I assume it's meant more for himself than anything else. He reaches for one but stops himself before his fingers touch the polaroid. "We should take these to the police to see if they can get any prints off them."

"I don't want them to call me crazy again," I argue. My arms are wrapped tightly around myself in an attempt to smother the goosebumps which are hiding underneath my sweater.

He lifts his gaze to look at me. "They won't. They said that shit once, but they won't get away with repeating it. I promise."

Hayden accompanies me to the police station and I report the misdeed, leaving out the parts about the camera footage for now. Thankfully, he was right about them not calling me hormonal, and they took me more seriously today. Probably because I was here two days ago reporting what I received in the mail. I think I would've lost it on them if they had spewed that misogynistic nonsense at me today.

Strange things are happening more often. My sense of security is flying out the window and I hope that it won't be out of reach before whatever is happening gets settled. When I ask them about the bullet casings they took as evidence, they inform me the only prints on them were mine. Whoever is taunting me is being smart about it and leaving no trace behind.

"Can you stay with me today?" I ask Hayden as we exit the police station. He opens his truck door for me and puts one hand on top of the vehicle to brace himself once I'm seated, the door still open.

"I'm sorry, Tatum, but I have to go back to work." He looks regretful, and I want to tell him it's okay and that I understand, because I do. But I can't. I don't want to be home alone. "I can come back when I get off, though. Maybe spend the night if that's okay?" I nod eagerly and he closes the truck door, walking around to the driver's side. *One more day before I can get my gun...*

I have him drop me off at the diner, where I spend the next several hours waiting for Nyasia's shift to end. Luckily, the majority of my money is still in my bank account. Regardless, I should be working on a painting. After all, I run a business. But I can't be home alone today. Part of me feels guilty for leaving Lenny there since someone is able to bypass the cameras and get inside my house, but what would I do with him all day? He can't sit in the car for hours on end, and I highly doubt the café would allow a cat inside.

When her shift is finally over, Nyasia and I pick up some food and she takes me home, deciding to stay until Hayden arrives. I can't express how thankful I am to have her company, even though we're doing nothing more than sitting in front of the TV on our phones. It feels a little odd that this is how we're spending our time considering the way my day started, but I'm not sure what other type of response we're supposed to have. We already talked about the photographs and my displeasure with the police department, but aside from that, what are we supposed to be doing? I've done all I can do, and Nyasia is just as helpless. Everything about today makes me feel helpless, and I hate it. I want to be doing more, but don't know what else can be done at this point. The only thing bringing me comfort right now is her company. I tell her how much it has meant to me today, and she immediately drops her phone.

"This is what friends are for, Tay. You've been there for me a dozen times already. It's about time I was able to return the favor." She smiles at me. "I know I might come off as a little intense sometimes, maybe even a little mean, but I love you."

"I love you too." And I do. She said it's about time she returned the favor of being there for me when I needed help or support, but she has been since day one. She's like a second sister to me.

MY PHONE CHIMES with the announcement of someone in my front yard. Hayden had informed me he was on his way after stopping by his place after work to shower and grab some essentials for an overnight stay. Good thing he did, because his heads up prevented me from immediately getting nervous by the notification.

Nyasia decides to stay a little longer, and it's strange to watch them interact immediately, not as strangers, but as old acquaintances. In my mind, though I'd been told they went to school together, they were strangers since I'd never seen them in the same room before. I'm quickly reminded how untrue that is when they begin recalling stories from their school years, bonding over things even though he'd been a couple of grades ahead of her. I suppose one of the perks of going to school in a small town — depending on how you look at it — is that everybody still knows everybody, even in adulthood.

The three of us make dinner together, and this becomes one of the best nights I've had in Maple Crest. The only way it could be better than it is now is if my English man was here.

After dinner, we turn on some background music and spend more time talking before Nyasia goes home. When it's just the two of us, Hayden turns up the volume of the song that's currently playing — '*Feel So Close*' by Calvin Harris.

He saunters over to me from the speaker and takes my hand with a handsome smile on his face. He looks happy. Better than that, I *feel* happy. "Come here, gorgeous."

I angle myself more toward him and he takes my other hand, pulling me closer to him and our bodies begin to sway to the up-tempo rhythm of the music. His brown eyes, their charm being heightened by his smile, are focused solely on me as he sings along. When I throw my head back with a laugh, he smiles even wider before he lifts our conjoined hands in the air, twirling me around a couple of times. When I'm done spinning and our chests meet again, I think my smile might be permanent. Which is really saying something considering all the unpleasant things I'd been feeling for most of the day prior to this.

Hayden closes his eyes and brings our foreheads together, our bodies still moving, but it's more intimate now. More emotional as he brings me back my sense of safety that I felt starting to slip from my grasp.

The music changes and starts to build as it begins to repeat the same seven words.

The phrase repeats once. Our noses brush.

Twice. I inhale a breath and feel him do the same. This close, it's almost as if he were taking the same breath as me.

The music continues to build, and then the lyrics change and the beat drops. Our lips meet and suddenly, we aren't dancing anymore. I feel my heart beating as hard as the beat of the music as we let our kiss deepen.

Suddenly, he pulls away and lifts me by the waist, spinning me around as I laugh loudly and our dance party continues.

Chapter Eighteen

TATUM

After Hayden leaves in the morning, I set myself to work. Painting has been a comfort therapy for me for years now. Sometimes it's hard to start a project when I'm in a mood, but it's hard to stop after I get started. My troubles get swept away with every sweep of my brush and my mind clears of everything but my canvas and paint palette.

I hear my phone go off but pay no attention to the notification so I can make a perfect brush stroke and watch as thin, runny paint drips down exactly how I wanted.

My doorbell rings next. After a glance at my screen and seeing it's a delivery person, I opt to leave it for later. But my doorbell rings again.

I groan. "Coming!" I call out reluctantly. Setting my brush down, I wipe my hands on my overalls, going for the door. Swinging it open, I'm met with a friendly smile from an older man. He appears to be from a bakery, judging from the giant pastry on the delivery vehicle's side and the design stitched onto his shirt.

"Tatum," he pauses to check the card, "Davis?"

"Yep, that's me." The man hands me a light blue package before tipping his head at me.

"Have a good day, miss," he says, then starts the short walk back to his van.

"You too." I close the door and set the rectangular box on the counter on my way back to my art room. I'm still too focused on my painting to think about anything else. Half an hour later, though, I finally reach a point where I feel content enough to take a break. Returning to the kitchen, I finally examine the bakery box and read the note on top.

I'll see you soon.

My heart flutters. Anthony. That's what he'd said to me when he first told me about his work trip, and it's as if he could sense me missing him last night.

Flipping open the lid, I see half a dozen red velvet cupcakes with the tops covered in cream cheese frosting and either a raspberry or strawberry drizzle. Plucking one from the box, I remove the cupcake liner from one side before taking a bite. With that one mouthful, I know the cupcakes won't last the night. They're *amazing*.

I take another, larger bite. This time, there's something foul, musky, and a bit metallic in the mix. Pulling the cupcake from my mouth, I look down at it and immediately spit the food out, gagging. A mini, bloody heart sits in the middle of the pastry. I chuck the remaining cupcake back into the box and practically throw myself at the sink, spitting and rinsing out my mouth.

Rechecking the card, I search for a company name. There's no way these were from Anthony, which is a problem I will address when I finish my current task. But first, I want to look up the company's menu to see if raw animal hearts are a usual filling. It turns out — to no surprise — they're not.

Calling the company, I try to keep my panic and temper in check as I explain what I bit into. They're as surprised as I am. The small business owner apologizes profusely, swearing up and down they have no idea how the cupcakes got delivered like this. When I ask who placed the order, they say it was a Mr. Anthony Williams who used cash.

What the fuck?

Not Anthony Kensington or Hayden Williams, but a combination of their names. Whoever did this knows about our relationship, which leaves me even more confused. There's only a handful of people who know about us. Aside from my immediate family, there are only two people who know that I'm not related to: Maya and Nyasia. However, I know for a fact they haven't told anyone. They'd have no reason to.

I get off the phone and send a picture to the group chat with all the information I received from the business owner. Needless to say, the guys are pissed. So am I. In fact, my anger might be winning as the superior emotion right now, more so than fear, because who the actual hell does this? As if breaking into my house and stealing thousands of dollars the day before isn't enough.

The only thing I don't like about working from home is that I don't want to be here right now. In fact, this is the second day in a row I've felt like this. I'm starting to want to be here less and less. Home should be where you feel safe, not where you're trying to get away from. I want to be around people who can witness the crazy I'm experiencing, but I'm not. There aren't neighbors close enough to help look over my property. I can't even call Hayden or Nyasia to come over because both of them are working, so I'm stuck.

Taking the box of heart cupcakes, I walk them outside and toss them into the garbage can with a little extra ferocity. When I think of what's in their center, I feel bile rise in my throat and it's an effort to throw up my breakfast. Getting back inside, I pack my laptop, a notepad, and a pen into a small backpack.

"I've got to get out of here for a little while, buddy, but I'll be back." I kiss Lenny's head and tell him I love him before walking out the door, locking it behind me. The feeling I have that I'll come back to something unsettling on my porch nearly makes me want to pack up and leave town. Nearly. But I'm not about to give up everything I have here because of some coward who's too afraid to show me their face or stick around for any sort of confrontation.

Besides, it's day three. So, my first stop when I get to town is the gun store to pick up my pistol. When I walk out of the building with my new piece concealed in my bag, I feel a hair more secure than I did before I went in. Hopefully I'll never be in a situation where I have to use it, but I'm glad I have it.

With my new form of protection finally in my possession, I go to The Brewed Bean. Nick is lively as ever until I ask about his interaction with Clay.

"Ah, that. Yeah, Clay wants to buy my business, but I've seen how he works. Even if I wanted to sell, which I don't, he'd end up putting me in a miserable situation no matter how well I read the fine print. Clay isn't a person you can say *no* to, though. And since I don't want to sell, I'm getting myself ready for misery, anyway." His shoulder bounces up and down as if knocking his problems away with a quick shrug and his smile returns. "But hey, business is still great. I still get to be here and help the town I love wake up in the mornings. Life is good." *Not for someone who got a butcher shop delivery from a psychopath today, but maybe for everyone else.* Obviously, I don't say that, opting to keep things light in my little utopia even though I don't have my usual energy. The evil and the creepy can't reach me here — just the sun.

Still avoiding home, I sit at one of the tables where I spend some time online looking into turning my designs into new merchandise. When my phone chimes with a text from Hayden telling me he'll be getting off early, I finally pack my things up and go home, calling Anthony on the way.

"I miss seeing you," he tells me after we've been conversing for a while. We switched from a regular phone call to FaceTime when I got home and determined nothing had been tampered with while I was gone. A stroke of luck hits me when I discover I caught Anthony after a shower, so I have the blessed opportunity of watching beads of moisture slowly roll down his defined chest. He sits shirtless on his hotel bed, wearing only a towel around his waist and the watch I gave him on his wrist. "Thankfully, I'll see you soon."

Those words make me stop daydreaming about all the things we could be doing on that bed together and stiffen. "Please don't say that. It's too soon. I can still taste the blood in my mouth."

He grimaces. "Shit, I'm sorry." A slight pause. "I wish I was there, Tate. This is my last night, though. I'll be there, hopefully, by this time tomorrow. I'm leaving as soon as I can so I can get back to you."

"Good."

"I'm glad Hayden is there so you haven't been alone. I still hate the bloke, but at least he's good for something."

I roll my eyes with a small grin. "You can't keep talking like that."

"Why not?"

Something mixed between a scoff and a chuckle leaves me in response, and then I stare at him through the screen. Really, truly get a good look at the man who seems to like no one in the world. *No one other than me.* The light shines brightly through the windows where he is. He isn't ghostly pale, but his skin is light and almost seems to glow in the sun. He's beautiful. Strikingly so. From his fine features and sculpted muscles, to his confidence, he makes me think of Adonis, the Greek god of beauty and desire.

"I miss seeing you too," I tell him after soaking up his appearance a little more. I can't help myself from adding a little more to my statement. "I miss seeing *all* of you." I've been thinking about the time we had sex nonstop and have been craving more. He's been the image in my head when I touch myself and the reason why I come when I'm alone.

His brows lift. "Oh yeah?" His voice is breathy, demanding, curious, and knowing, all at once.

I nod. My body immediately responds to the way he said that, and to the images that my head has had on repeat. I want him so badly. I want to feel the velvety skin of his length in my mouth. I want to taste him.

"Show me?" Even I notice the lust in my voice, and he obliges my request with the perfect angle. He's already hard and gives himself a slow stroke. My mouth waters and I swallow thickly.

"Your turn. Show me." It nearly sounds like a demand, and I feel its effects ripple through me down to my center. It sparks a fire within me.

With my phone resting on the pillows, I sit up and grip the edges of my shirt to pull it off when I hear Hayden's Chevy pull up. My hands stop at my belly button as I glance out the window.

"Hayden just got here, I've got to go."

Anthony groans and throws his head back against the pillow. "Just when I thought I couldn't dislike him any less. That man could not have worse timing."

"Relax, I won't leave you without throwing you a bone first." His blonde head whips back up like it's on a spring and I flash him my tits. "Better?"

"My god. I am the luckiest fucking man on this earth."

Dropping my shirt, I feel my cheeks instantly begin to flush. "I should probably go get the door for him before he gets soaked from the rain."

Anthony has that satisfied grin of his that lets me know he's getting a kick out of my reaction. I love it and hate it at the same time. Love it, because he looks so damn cute when he's pleased with himself. Which, actually, isn't as often as I first thought it'd be. As for why I hate it? Well...I don't actually have a reason to hate it at all. I suppose getting flushed isn't all that bad as long as he keeps making it happen like this.

"Alright, fine. I'll call you later, darling."

"Okay, sounds good." I move to get off the bed, then stop. "But maybe put on some clothes before you do," I joke.

He glances down at himself before meeting my gaze again. "Why not remain naked? I'm going to fuck you when I get back, whether he's around or not. And if we're going to keep spending all of our time together, then he might as well get used to seeing my cock in you."

My mouth falls open. "I— I don't even know what to say to that." Hayden knocks on my door then.

"I've been trying to be a gentleman, but I've been craving you since the night I first tasted you. As long as you want it, I don't see a reason to hold ourselves back."

My mouth clamps shut in an attempt to hide my shock from his dirty mouth. But he's right. Why have I been putting sex off? We both want it, and they each knew sex was part of the deal when they agreed to this. Not between the three of us, of course, but surely they knew there would be one-on-one time.

"Fine. Don't wear clothes. But I'm going to hold you to what you said when you get back to Maple Crest."

"Darling, you won't need to. That's a promise." We say our quick goodbyes and then I open the door for Hayden.

I know he's going to ask me if I'm okay, but I want to exist in the head space where I'm not worried about someone trying to terrorize me for a little while longer. So I kiss him deeply and drag it out. My hands dip into his open jacket and I slide it down his arms.

"Take me to the bed," I whisper against his mouth. Part of me feels an inkling of guilt over Anthony being the one to turn me on and Hayden getting to finish the job, but there's nothing I can really do about that.

Hayden pulls back. "Don't you want to talk about what happened?"

"No." Another deep kiss.

But Hayden stops again, putting his hands on my arms to hold me in place as he creates a small space between us. "Tate. Are you okay? Don't get me wrong, this greeting is amazing, and I *really* want to take you to bed. But...you're okay?"

"I'm okay," I confirm. "Please. Take me to bed, Hayden."

He has a second of contemplation before he pulls me back to him, lifting me so my thighs wrap around his waist. When we get to the room, he lays me down and our mouths move so in sync it's like a dance. His hands drift across my body and brush down the side of my face.

I pull away this time. "I'm okay, I promise. You don't have to treat me like I'm going to break in your hands. I know what you're capable of, and I want *that.*"

"Are you sure? That's what you *really* want right now? This isn't just a distraction?" It kind of is a distraction, but I've also been craving his cock. His concern for me is cute, but right now, I want to be fucked. Not loved.

"I'm sure, Hayden." He doesn't need any more convincing after that. My handsome man snaps back into action, his once light touches now turned possessive. Hayden likes it a little on the rough side. He's the other reason I come hard when I'm alone.

Hayden undoes the button of my pants and I move my pants to my thighs before he pulls them the rest of the way off of me. As he strips himself, I remove my shirt and bra, rejoining our mouths when we're both naked. I'm wet in seconds, a fact he shows his appreciation for with a hungry groan as he feels the slickness when he slips his fingers inside me.

"Fuck," he practically pants. Removing his fingers, he brings them up between our faces and inserts them into his mouth. "The taste of you could bring the gods themselves to their knees." Moving his face down to my clit, he licks, kisses, and sucks me; nibbling the sensitive area and dragging it out with his teeth.

I gasp, my hands flying into his shaggy brown hair. His teeth release my clit and he kisses the sting away before repeating the action.

"Hayden," I pant. I'm not sure why. I want nothing more than for him to keep doing what he's doing. He bites me again, a little harder, and I yelp. My hands tighten in his hair and he groans, sending vibrations through my body which have me throwing my head back.

His mouth is on my pussy when I finally look back at him and the first thing I see is his earthy eyes latching onto mine. Seeing him between my legs like his has me coming hard on his tongue. Hayden doesn't lift his head until he's finished tasting my arousal. Then he sits up with a smirk on his face, grabbing a condom from my nightstand and sheathing himself with it.

Twining our fingers together, he climbs back over my body. Encapsulating my wrists in one of his large hands, he pins them on the bed above me, covering my body with his. His other hand runs so slowly down my body it's as if he's trying to memorize every curve as his mouth tastes my neck. A sudden nibble makes me gasp and my body lifts, but his body over mine doesn't allow for much movement. Hayden likes to use his teeth and my body never fails to show him how much I like it when he does.

When his hands reach below my stomach, he uses his middle finger to massage my clit. Even though it's already tender from what he did with his mouth, I roll my hips to meet his movements anyway, intensifying the feeling even more. I want to touch him. My fingers crave the feeling of him, but he continues to keep my hands restrained with his.

"Hayden, please," I beg breathlessly.

Removing his talented finger from my clit, he guides himself inside me. When he's fully in, he starts to pull out at a torturously slow rate all the way to the tip before rolling lazily back in. He repeats this several times before I lift my hips, trying to make his movements quicker and harder, like what I know he's capable of.

He stops, grabbing my hip and pushing it down against the bed. "Mm-mm," he hums with a scolding shake of his head. "You want more? Then use your words. Let me hear you say it, Tate." This is another thing he seems to like; me being vocal.

"I want more," I say without hesitation.

"Tell me how you want it."

"You know how."

His playful and heated eyes quickly scan me, lingering a moment longer on my breasts before returning to my face. "Tell me, Tate. How do you want it?"

I stare at him, my body igniting from the heated look in his eyes as he gazes down at me. "Wild."

Chapter Nineteen

TATUM

Lenny's meowing sounds like screaming. It's not a panicked or painful meow like the terrible yowl that woke me up the morning of his seizure. It just seems abnormally loud. My head feels groggy. Much more than the usual kind of morning fog, and there's already a headache building behind my skull even though I woke up two seconds ago. It almost feels like I'm insanely hungover, even though I didn't have a drop of alcohol last night.

Hayden has his arm draped over me and when Lenny jumps on the bed, I feel him shift. Lenny meows again, the sound seeming to echo through my ears. I groan, and Hayden rolls onto his back. When I look at him, his eyes are squeezed shut and his fingers are pinching the bridge of his nose like Lenny's breakfast call is too loud for him too. His shaggy brown hair is messy, tossed this way and that. He's so cute, and I want to continue letting him sleep, but despite not checking the time yet, I'm also fairly certain he's late for work.

"Morning," I say, touching his bare chest and leaning over to kiss him.

"Good morning," he returns, his voice gravelly from waking up. His eyes open as I pull back, smiling. He blinks several times before squinting at me. "What the hell?" He jerks up into a sitting position and grabs my chin lightly, turning my face to the side.

"What?"

"Tatum, what is this?"

"What's what?"

"This...is this paint? Where did this come from?"

I tenderly touch my cheek and feel a cracked, rough substance where nothing but my skin should be. Rushing to the bathroom, spooking Lenny with my speed, I stop in front of my mirror. A hand made from red paint is imprinted on my face.

My chest heaves with panicked breaths as Hayden comes up beside me, confusion and fear on his face. Judging by his uplifted hands which hover several inches from my body, I can tell he's unsure whether or not to touch me for how I'd react to it right now. I'm thankful he didn't, to be honest. I didn't put this print on my face, and I know he didn't either, which leaves me more unsettled than I've ever been before.

Turning on the sink, I don't wait for the water to warm up before I start scrubbing at my skin. Lathering soap on my cheek, I scrub harshly in an attempt to get this paint the hell off of me. Finally, it's all gone. My face is red from friction and rage, but at least it's no longer red from the paint. Hayden hands me a towel that I use to pat my skin dry. Spinning back toward the bedroom, Hayden flattens himself against the wall to get out of the way. Once on my phone, I pull up the security footage for the night. I don't expect to find anything since there was nothing to show the morning I saw the photos, but I try anyway. Try, and end up finding footage that sends chills down my body.

Everything is normal until 5:55 in the morning. One second, it's just me and Hayden asleep in the bed with Lenny curled up against me. The next, there's someone in a hoodie standing beside the bed. They just stand there staring at us for a minute. When Lenny notices him, he stretches and walks up to the stranger who picks him up and walks out of the bedroom with my cat. The stranger returns, their face hidden from the camera. Then they hold up some sort of canister, and Hayden and I watch the screen in horror as smoke starts filling the room. When the smoke stops, the stranger walks up to me, somehow unaffected by the gas. They push my hair out of my face before pressing their hand against my cheek. The stranger then turns around and looks directly at the camera like they knew exactly where it was all along. They're wearing a gas mask, which explains how they remained unaffected. Then they wave at the camera before walking out of the room.

After the intruder has left and everything is still like it had been before their arrival, Hayden and I remain frozen for what feels like an eternity. We are still trying to determine what to make of what we just saw. We were gassed. That must be why my head feels like this.

Hayden reaches for my phone and rechecks the footage, changing angles to different cameras throughout the house and skipping time stamps.

"It doesn't show them coming in or out of the house," he says with his brows scrunched, focused eyes still on the screen. "Just like with the photos, the timestamp is unbroken. It's as if they just appeared and disappeared."

"Like a ghost?" My voice is a whisper.

"Maybe that's what they want us to think, but it's not a ghost. Ghosts don't need to wear gas masks." The tone he uses suggests he's pissed, and rightfully so.

"I'm so sorry, Hayden," my voice breaks and I avoid looking at his face. He was trying to make me feel better by staying the night. He did, but look what happened to him because of it. In my peripheral vision, I see Hayden look at me.

"What are you sorry for?" He sounds genuinely confused.

"For putting you in this situation."

His head cocks slightly to the side, and his eyebrows pull

together. "You didn't put me in any position. You have nothing to be sorry for, Tate. This isn't your doing."

His phone rings on the other side of the bed; yet he lets it ring.

Tears well in my eyes, and I feel the heat of them as they fall down my face. "I'm so sorry," I repeat with a cry. I am truly sorry. Truly. Regardless of what he said, I still feel bad because he wouldn't have been gassed if he had been at his place. I'm also overwhelmed, nauseous, scared, and confused. So many thoughts and emotions run through me, resulting in my current breakdown.

Hayden sets my phone down and pulls me into him. "Hey, hey. It's going to be okay. I know this is scary, but we're alright." His phone starts to ring again, and he continues to ignore it, keeping me tucked against him. "We're okay; they didn't hurt us. We'll figure this out. Okay?"

I nod. I want to believe him, but I need a little more time before I do.

"You should probably see who's calling you," I say. Tipping my chin up with his finger, he makes me look into his softened eyes.

"I promise you, Tate, you're going to be okay." Then he kisses me. It's a firm kiss that seems to reaffirm his promise. Something about this kiss makes me believe him entirely.

Leaning back and twisting around to grab his phone, he checks the screen. I hear him curse lightly. As he calls whoever has been trying to reach him, I feed Lenny and give him his medication. No wonder he seemed so needy, it's a little after noon. The gas had kept us out for hours. I'm filling up his water fountain when I hear faint music. It's so quiet I'm trying to determine whether it's my imagination when Hayden comes up beside me. His sudden presence makes me jump since my nerves are shot this morning.

"Sorry," he apologizes, his hands in the air as he steps back to give me space.

"It's okay. I'm fine." *I'm not. I'm scared and don't know what to do next but I'm alive.* "I'm guessing that was work calling since it's so late?"

"Yep," he confirms, running a frustrated hand through his hair. "We're going to the hospital. We have no idea what was in that canister. The doctors will get ahold of the police while we're there, and you might want to let Anthony know what's going on. He tried calling me, so I imagine he tried to get a hold of you first."

Anthony. After grabbing what we'll need for the hospital and we're seated in his truck, I check the notifications on my phone. Anthony had tried calling half a dozen times, texting me twice that amount. However, when I try to call him back, it goes straight to voicemail.

My finger hovers over the button to call my mom, but I don't let it connect with the screen. I'm scared and want to hear her tell me everything will be alright, but I also don't want to scare her. One of the worst things I can imagine is dragging her into this mess and my family getting hurt because of me. It's that thought that makes me lock my screen.

The warm weight of a hand stills my bouncing knee before moving up to hold my hand.

"It's okay, Tate. We're okay." Hayden holds my hand the rest of the way to the hospital. His calmness in this situation is truly a godsend. Without it, I'd surely be a wreck.

Not long later, we're sitting in a hospital room getting blood drawn for tests and talking to police officers. Our doctor returned to inform us the gas that knocked us out was a halogenated anesthetic. Likely sevoflurane, and we'll feel the side effects of it for the rest of the day, but will be fine. Though, it's recommended Hayden doesn't drive again and that we drink plenty of fluids.

Anthony finally calls me back as we're filling out discharge paperwork, telling me their plane just landed at their private airport and he'll be here in a few minutes. I hadn't realized how worried I was about something happening to him until we ended the call. Then it was like a weight was lifted off my shoulders. He's already in the loop with all the crazy that's been happening, and he's not intimidated by it. Worried for me, yes; but not for himself. Perhaps that will change once he discovers Hayden was endangered simply by existing in my presence.

We meet him right outside the hospital doors, where he hugs me, and kisses the top of my head. Anthony keeps a protective arm around me as he tells us he'd been working on regaining lost footage from the morning I found the photos when, suddenly, he was locked out of the system. Someone was actively putting up blockers to keep him out as he fought to get back in. He managed to do so for only a split second before his screens went black. But in that split second, he saw a hooded person in my house. Since he couldn't tell for sure if it was Hayden, that's when he first tried calling me. The more he couldn't reach us, the more he began to worry. It wasn't long before he dropped everything and practically forced Zara onto the family plane to come back early.

"You're staying at my place," Anthony says with finality. His assertive tone leaves no room for argument, but I have none to give. After what happened this morning, there's no reason for me to stay at the house while the intruder is on the loose. Not when they can easily get inside, and we have no idea how.

"Lenny is coming. I know you like your house spotless, and he can be a little messy at times, but I'm not leaving him behind or boarding him," I state with as much finality as he had.

"I wouldn't expect you to, darling. You and the cat are a package deal. I know this and accept it." His arm is still around me, holding me like he never wants to let go. He looks at Hayden. "You're welcome to stay as well." My head jerks to stare up at him. He's still looking at Hayden, who just nods.

"Come with me to the house?" I ask him.

"You don't even have to ask. Of course I am. I'm not leaving your side until we figure this out." He turns to Hayden, "Zara is here. She can drive the decomposing thing you call a vehicle wherever you need to go."

"That's really sweet, man, thanks." Hayden puts his hands

over his heart mockingly, his voice filled with sarcasm, although I can see the hint of genuineness in his brown eyes.

I ride with Anthony in his Audi while Hayden and Zara take off in his truck. Anthony doesn't let go of my hand from the hospital to my house. Then he barely gives me enough space to breathe as we move from the car to my door. Whilst I pack a duffel bag and get Lenny ready, Anthony walks around the house looking for anything out of place.

"Was this broken this morning?" I hear him call out to me. Finding him in the bathroom, I see what he's referring to. My perfume bottle of Chanel No. 5 is shattered against the ground.

"No. No, it wasn't." I stare at the broken pieces of glass. If things continue going as they have been, I worry that this broken bottle and I will have a lot in common. "Let's get out of here."

We leave the perfume on the tile and walk out of the house. I'm eager to get to his place to have a sense of security again. That's what my new gun was supposed to provide, but how can I protect myself when I never see the attack coming? When I'm put to sleep? I've done everything right. I've contacted the police on multiple occasions. I reached out to people close to me for help. I got multiple security items, and still, it wasn't enough. I don't know who I offended or what I did to grab someone's attention enough to cause this. Did I do something wrong? Or was I just in the wrong place at the wrong time for someone who's sick? I hope this temporary stay at Anthony's, on top of everything else, will be enough to keep me safe. And if my guys are in danger now too...hopefully it's enough to keep them safe as well. Because if it isn't, and they get hurt, I will become my stalker's worst nightmare.

Anthony and I are the only ones at his place. Hayden is taking time to explain to his family what's going on before he comes to join us, and Zara is kind enough to wait for him as long as he needs. I'm happy to have this time alone with Anthony. We haven't had much of it lately. I get Lenny situated and when I'm done, I find Anthony in the primary bathroom. The sleeves of his black dress shirt are rolled up to his elbows, his wrist which isn't wearing his blue watch dips into the water pouring into the bathtub before turning the faucet off.

"Hey," I say.

"Hey," he responds after he turns and spots me. "I was about to go find you. I drew you a bath. Hopefully, this will help ease the ache from the anesthesia and help you relax." The aroma in the room is incredible. It smells like fresh flowers. As I near the large tub, I realize why. Dark flower petals sit atop the abundance of bubbles in the water.

I wrap my arms around his neck and tenderly kiss him. His hands brace themselves lightly on my waist, but he doesn't attempt to take the kiss any further. Anthony seems off. He hasn't been right since I saw him outside the hospital. I think I scared him today. It's not hard to guess why he'd be upset, but I wish he would tell me exactly what was going on in his mind.

"Stay with me?" I whisper against his lips.

"Of course," he whispers back. Anthony's touch is feather-light as he helps me get out of my clothes, then holds my hand for support as I step into the massive tub. When I'm settled, he perches himself on the side. It should feel weird to be completely naked in the water, utterly vulnerable, while he remains dry in his suit, but it doesn't. Even more so when he tips my head back so it's resting against his thigh. Yet I'm completely at ease in his presence. Especially when he starts to massage my scalp.

"Tell me about your business trip," I say quietly. I want to talk about anything *but* the reason why I'm here. He doesn't reply for a moment, like the topic I'm trying to avoid is exactly what he wants to talk about but finally, he indulges me.

"It was terrible," he mumbles. And the answer catches me off guard. I scrunch my brow and open my eyes to look up at him, but he tells me to close them again and smooths the crease with his fingers. His hand rubs at my scalp again, easing the ache in my skull as he talks. "My dad is an ambitious man, and sometimes his ambition backfires, leaving Zara or me to clean up his messes. I don't want to work for him anymore, but I can't leave. I'm in too deep."

"I thought you didn't work for your dad?"

"I'm allowed to do my own projects, but ultimately, I still have to do as he commands or I pay the price." I hear him swallow. I want to open my eyes, but I get the feeling he wants them to stay closed to help me relax. And also so he can hide whatever is on his face right now. Were I to open them, I'm sure I know what I'd see. Sadness. And guilt, for some inexplicable reason. I can hear traces of it in his words, but I don't understand why it's there. "I'm a Kensington. There is no *other life* for me, though. I was made for what we do, and I need to accept that this is how things are. For a moment there, I was ready to. Then I went for a hike and met you."

The combination of the anesthesia still in my system, the relaxing bath, and his fingers in my hair has me on the verge of falling asleep and I hate that. This is an important conversation. *But I'm so tired....*

"What do I have to do with any of that? If you're not happy working for your dad, then don't work for your dad." My statement comes out slightly slurred from my drowsiness, but I find myself too tired to care or attempt to clarify it.

Anthony seems to have understood me though. He sighs lightly. "I fear you might have everything to do with it, love." I don't know how much time passes from that moment, and the moment when I feel my head against his chest as he walks. Then, again, from that moment to the one where I feel myself laying in a bed and hear his whispered voice saying, "Stay. She'll want you here as well."

Chapter Twenty

TATUM

I feel the heat of a body beneath my cheek. One of my hands is draped over someone's chest, and I can feel their arm wrapped around my shoulders. Opening my eyes is hardly helpful since the room is mostly dark. Apart from the soft blue glow across the room that originates from the lights lined behind a mirror. After letting my eyes adjust to opening, I recognize I'm in Anthony's room. It's his arm I'm tucked under.

Hearing someone else's quiet, steady breaths behind me, I glance over my shoulder. Hayden is asleep on the other side of me. That must've been who Anthony was talking to last night when he said *stay*. A smile spreads on my face knowing he said that when it would've been incredibly easy to cast Hayden aside last night.

Turning back to Anthony, I press my lips against his cheek. He stirs, opening his

eyes.

"Is everything alright?" he whispers.

"I'm fine. Thank you, Anthony." He glances over at Hayden

like I had moments before, understanding the meaning behind the words, then looks back at me.

"Of course, darling."

Leaning over him, I pick up my phone to check the time. It's barely after 5, meaning I've been asleep for about ten hours. I guess being gassed and spending the day at the hospital really takes it out of you.

I can't believe that happened to us. I should probably talk with someone about the trauma I experienced. I'm more of a 'conceal don't feel' sort of person, though. The police are searching my house and investigating the situation. I bought protection for myself, I'm staying at a different place, and I have my two so-called guard dogs. Hayden is definitely a golden retriever while Anthony is probably a fawn-colored doberman or something. The point is, I've done everything I can do to protect myself. They can't touch me anymore and I'd *really* rather not think about it or the fact I had a nightmare of someone in a mask running their hand down my face. So, problems, meet broom. Broom, introduce my feelings to rug as you sweep my problems away. Is that healthy? Probably not. I'm doing it anyway, though.

"I'm hungry," I whisper. "Can I raid your fridge?"

He chuckles softly. "Yes, you can raid my fridge. You don't need to ask next time." Anthony stands up and takes my hand to help me stand. Together, we walk toward the kitchen. One would think the floor would be cold since it's made of stone in a place where you almost always have to wear a jacket. To my surprise, however, they're heated — an incredible perk of having money to spare. When we get to the kitchen, he turns me around and lifts me by the waist to seat me on the counter as he opens the stainless steel fridge, staring inside.

"Anything in particular you're in the mood for?" he asks softly, his voice a little louder now that we're not next to a sleeping Hayden.

"Pancakes?"

He looks over his shoulder at me with a smile, then hums a laugh. "Pancakes it is, love."

It feels so domestic to make early morning pancakes with him in the low light of his kitchen; honestly, I could get used to this. I love it.

"You know what I was thinking about the other day?" I ask. He hums his response as he mixes ingredients in a large bowl. "The day we met you were hiking, and wearing jeans and a beanie. Now that I know you, that seems so out of character."

He shrugs his shoulders lightly. "I hike." I give him a look that I hope calls him out for being a liar. When he sees it, he laughs. "Okay, fine. I don't hike, but I was having a bad day and wanted to see what all the fuss was about."

"Why were you having a bad day?" His hand stops stirring. "I'm sorry if that made you uncomfortable. You don't have to tell me."

"No, it's okay." Anthony resumes mixing the batter. "It was just family business. Something really frustrated me that day. Good thing too, otherwise I'd have never met you." He grins cheekily at me and I playfully roll my eyes.

When the pancakes are ready, we top them with powdered sugar, syrup, and various berries.

"Do you have a TV?" I ask him as I finish topping my stack of food with a couple of raspberries.

"Yes, I have a TV," he chuckles. Anthony guides me to a mini in-home theater. And when I say mini, I'm referring to the number of chairs in the room. There are only two lounge chairs in front of a massive screen.

"I thought you said you weren't one for movies? Why do you have a home theater, then?"

He shrugs, the action cute coming from a man like him. "I'm not, but Zara used to come over for occasional movie nights. She used to complain about the screen being too small. Then the windows were causing too much glare, so I put this room together for her."

"Used to?"

He clears his throat. "We don't spend as much time together as we once did." When he doesn't elaborate, I don't press for details. We've been having a great morning, and I don't want anything to ruin it. I start my favorite rom-com movie and cuddle up with him after breakfast. I laugh as the cute Irishman and the pretty American give each other a hard time as they try to get her to her fiancé in time for a Leap Year proposal.

But only a fraction into the movie, my eyes close again. Anthony must have fallen asleep again because he seems just as surprised as me when the theater room lights turn on, and Hayden walks in.

"This looks cozy," he says. His hair is disheveled in that perfectly messy sort of way. And though he's smiling, it doesn't reach his eyes. I can't help but start to wonder if he's unhappy with our arrangement until Anthony questions him.

"What's the problem?"

"I went out to my truck to grab a couple of things, and, well, I think we have a problem." My anxiety wastes no time declaring its presence as my arms tingle before almost going numb entirely. I swallow thickly.

I can feel Anthony glance down at me and see Hayden do the same.

"What happened?" I ask him this time.

"All four of your tires have been slashed." It feels like the beat of my heart has changed. It's not beating faster, but harder. Louder. Almost painfully. I'm not all that worried about my tires. They're easily replaceable, and I've got the money for them. The problem is they need to be replaced at all. There's only one person who would have done this. At this point, they're as familiar to me as they are a stranger. I came here to separate myself from them, but somehow, whoever it is still knows exactly where I am.

"You have gates at the end of your driveway. How did they get through?"

"Not only gates, but security cameras all around the property as well. I don't know how they went unnoticed," Anthony says as he removes his arms around me and checks his phone. Several taps and a minute later, Hayden and I watch over Anthony's shoulder as the footage begins to play. A silver car stops in front of the closed gate that separates Anthony's house from the road. A moment later, the gate opens, and the person drives right in, parking beside my vehicle. A hooded figure steps out and proceeds to slash my tires, taking their time getting to each one as if the thought of being caught doesn't bother them. And when they're done, they stroll back to their vehicle with their hands in their pockets before driving away, the gate closing behind them.

"How did they get in the gate?" Hayden asks.

"And why weren't you notified?" I follow.

Anthony's breathing seems stiff, and his face looks a little pale. His pink lips part on an uneasy breath.

"I need to make a call," he says before standing abruptly and leaving the room, his phone already to his ear. I hear him say Zara's name as a greeting before a door closes down the hall, cutting off the rest of his conversation.

Hayden is staring intently out the open door like he wants to follow Anthony, or like he has something to say. Perhaps even both. I just pull my knees up to my chest on the cushioned seat.

"You trust Anthony?" he asks suddenly.

My eyebrows pull together. "Why wouldn't I?"

"He's hiding something. I just can't tell what." Hayden is usually always positive and happy. To see him like this now is unsettling because I know it's serious.

I think things over for several seconds. "He's a little cryptic sometimes, and sometimes I'm not completely sure what he's talking about, but I trust him. If you're worried about him being like his dad, then I don't think you have to worry. I don't know Clay, but I know Anthony, and he's a great guy."

I grab his hand and pull him over until he's sitting in the seat beside me.

"Even you can't deny he's a little weird, but maybe you're

right. Perhaps, given our history, I'm looking for something wrong." He sighs and runs a hand through his already messy hair.

I rub my thumb along the top of his hand which is still enclosed with mine. "How are you feeling? I didn't mean to fall asleep so early last night, and I especially didn't mean to sleep that long."

He laughs. "Hey, it's okay. As soon as I got back from grabbing my things and stopping at my parents to let them know what was happening, I fell asleep, too. I think Zara even snapped a picture of me nearly drooling in the car, but I don't even remember if I fell asleep or not. I swear I could hardly walk through the door by the time we got here. Whoever that person is gave us one hell of a drug."

Though clouds cover it, the sun is up when an hour later there's a knock at the door. Anthony had been in his office the whole time, only leaving it to answer the door. Since Hayden and I migrated to the living room to sit in front of the large windows, we hear Zara enter the house but don't see her.

"Where do you want to do this?" she asks her brother. He must have gestured for the living room because two sets of footsteps begin coming our way. Zara walks into view seconds later, her motorcycle helmet under her arm.

"Hi!" She greets us chirpily. Zara has always been nice to me before, but this greeting is a little too over the top. She's *too* cheery from what I've experienced with her so far.

I smile back anyway. "Hey."

"What's going on?" Beside me, Hayden's defensive tone has made a comeback. Though, this time, I completely understand why. The two siblings are giving off an uncomfortable energy that makes me want to plug my ears and close my eyes to prevent me from knowing what they will say or do next. Whatever it is, I get the feeling I don't want to know.

"Let's all take a seat for a moment, please." *Oh shit. Anthony said* please *to Hayden. Now I know this isn't going to be good.* Hayden and I sit beside each other, his arm draping over my shoulders. Zara shoots a glance at Anthony, but he doesn't acknowledge it. Instead, he takes a seat on the other side of me. Zara unzips her biker jacket and sets it aside. She's so much like her brother. They both favor the color black, but let little bits of their personalities show through a single color. Blue is Anthony's. He used to only show his favorite color through his car with its subtle accents on the outside and the color of the seats on the inside. For Zara, it's emerald green. She shows off her color more often than her brother and in more ways. Today, she's wearing a simple but expensive necklace with a green gem over her black turtleneck shirt.

"Anthony," she urges.

"We think we know who's been toying with you," he starts. "We believe it's Benjamin."

"The guy she ran into at the club?" Hayden asks. "Who the hell is this guy?"

Anthony looks at Zara and she nods. The joyful expression from when she came in is gone. "Do you remember when I told you he used to do business with my dad and that there was a falling out?" I nod. "Well, he wasn't simply fired from the company."

The air is thick with tension now. "Tell me what happened," I demand, even though I don't think I want to know it. His arms are braced on his knees, and he looks between his hands at the floor. He takes one, then two steadying breaths before speaking.

"Benjamin wasn't just fired. He was ruined. We found out he was stealing money from our dad. Had that been everything, he may have gotten off a little easier than he did. But that *wasn't* everything. Benjamin had a girlfriend, and when we learned he was stealing from us, we also learned his girlfriend was running a trafficking ring. Our family was enraged by what we found, so we worked with the authorities to shut the ring down. However, my dad kept the ringleader, Benjamin's girlfriend, for his own sort of justice. He killed the ringleader in front of Benjamin, then beat him nearly to death before leaving him in the gutter with nothing but his girlfriend's corpse. Now, it appears he wants revenge and is targeting you."

The silence is deafening. I feel everything and nothing all at once.

"I thought...I thought you were a software engineer," I state dumbly.

"I am. Yes, I do software engineering. But...as I've told you before, there are many things Zara and I have been trained for and are tasked with."

I add an even more bizarre question to my last statement. "Are you...in the mafia or something?"

"I wouldn't say 'mafia,' but not everything we do is legal," Zara says from across the space.

"Like murder." Hayden's face is straight, his tone hard.

"Yes. Like the murder of someone who caused the pain, suffering, and deaths of far too many people. Trust me. She deserved what she got, the world is a much better place without her in it."

"Why me?" I whisper.

"Because you're his girlfriend," Hayden grits out. "Isn't that right? Her life is on the line because you *lied* to her."

We were standing in this very room when he said *honesty is key in a relationship*. Remembering what he'd said infuriates me, sending anger in place of the shock and I feel it spread through my veins.

"You told me honesty was important, yet you've been lying to me!"

"I didn't lie, love. I omitted some truths, yes, but I never lied!"

I gape at him. "Are you fucking serious right now?"

"I know, I know, I should have told you everything, and I am so sorry. I thought I was keeping you safe!"

Hayden lets out a bitter laugh. "Yeah, how's that working out for you?"

"Piss off," Anthony's face turns from pleading to furious when he looks over my shoulder at Hayden.

Hayden returns the fury. "Jesus Christ, man. She's being terrorized, all because you're a murderer? Then you turn around and say keeping the truth from her was for her own good. What the *fuck*? Do you even realize how easily we could have died yesterday? You don't even care, do you? You're just like your dad. You don't give a damn about anyone but yourself."

Anthony shoots to his feet, Hayden doing the same. In a blink, Anthony has Hayden's shirt gripped tightly in his hands. "I am nothing like him. Don't you even question it. *Of course,* I care."

"We were at the mercy of that guy. He could have easily slit *our* throats because he was mad at *you,* and we could've done nothing to stop it. You killed his girl, so now he wants to kill yours. Just say it as it is. Stop trying to make the truth sound prettier than the reality."

"I didn't kill her!" Anthony bellows.

"I did," Zara states as if she were sitting at a restaurant, saying she was the one who ordered the salad. "I killed the girl. I'd do it again too. Anthony was present, but he didn't do so much as lift a finger. But I'm untouchable for someone like Benjamin. He doesn't have the skill it would take to kill me, so he's going after the next best thing; the person who means the most to Anthony."

Hayden wrenches Anthony's hands from his shirt and shoves him off, but neither of the men goes back to fighting, both remain standing. I massage my temple with my fingers.

"The business trip you were just on. Was it *your* business, or was it stuff for your dad?" I have the feeling I'm going to regret asking that.

Anthony pauses before answering, "It was for my dad."

"Was it legal?"

Another pause. His mouth opens with a breath to reply, but Zara is the one who answers.

"No, but no one died. Our dad is barely more lenient with his children than the rest of his employees. There are less than pleasant consequences if we don't do as we're instructed.

Anthony went on that trip to keep me from doing something he knows is hard on me. He went because he knew I wouldn't have done it and would have been punished. Anthony was protecting me." I think of the day they argued on the porch. She'd told Anthony she needed him and that if he cared about her, he'd do what needed to be done. I didn't realize it then, but she was scared and pleading for her big brother's help.

Hayden pinches the bridge of his nose, surely in an attempt to ward off a headache. "So you Kensington's aren't just rich pricks, you're killers too?"

"Don't forget to add hot if you're listing our qualities," Zara says, her voice light and upbeat. Hayden drops his hands and gives her a stern glare.

"What am I supposed to do?" I mean that question in more ways than one. Aside from feeling helpless, I can't name the other emotions flowing through my body. How should one feel after learning the truth their boyfriend has been hiding? Does it make him any better that he stood by and watched a murder happen in front of him but didn't partake in it? Does it make enough of a difference that the person killed was horrible? From the second Hayden walked into the theater to now, there have been too many questions I don't want to deal with. I don't want this to be my life. I'm always waiting for the next thing to happen, and I hate it. I want to go back to hiking, drinking coffee, and painting. My life was so good then and it wasn't long ago at all that that was how I spent my days. I'd rather have that than fearing for my life on top of finding out my boyfriend is a murderer. Or...not a murderer, but a liar? Not a mafia man, but something close? Maybe I can still go back to the way things were before.

But...if I do, then I'll lose the moon. I'll never get to experience stargazing and the chaos of kissing in the rain again. Spearmint will no longer be fresh, but a bitter reminder; midnight walks will become tragic; and the waves during a storm will feel like a trap. I'll still live if all those things change. It may take some time, but I will still be happy without them. I just don't want to live without those things being the way they currently are.

Anthony kneels in front of me and tries to take my hand as I pull away.

"Tatum, I am so sorry I didn't tell you. And you have no idea the guilt I feel for dragging you into this. But I'm telling you now and I am begging, *begging* you to please forgive me. You have to understand, it's not like I could just come out and explain the dirty parts of myself to you the moment we met. Despite the signs I shouldn't be with you, I ignored them because I want this to work between you and me, Tatum. Please."

"What signs?" I ask.

His face softens even more. "Our first date. Or, what was supposed to be our first date. You got stood up. I never gave you a reason, and you were gracious enough not to ask. You were pissed, as you should've been, but you hadn't asked. I wasn't there because I had something to attend to for my dad the night before. By the time it was over, there were several hours before we were supposed to meet, but I couldn't. I felt...dirty. I felt like I would have tainted you just by being in your presence so soon after I did something so horrible. I couldn't tell you because I didn't know what to say, and I needed time to cool off after what I had to do. Then when I came to your house after I saw you with Williams at the gallery, I knew for sure that I should leave you alone because nothing good in my life stays. I always mess it up. Even if by some miracle I didn't mess it up, then my dad would do it for me. He can't stand to see me happy, and I knew you would undoubtedly make me happy."

"You tried telling me last night, didn't you? Before you knew it was Benjamin and what all of this was a result of." He nods. Another odd occasion comes to mind. "When you were beat up and robbed, that's not the real story. Is it?"

Anthony shakes his head. "No." Hayden scoffs lightly from where he's standing with his arms crossed by the window. I'd nearly forgotten that we aren't alone. A glance at Zara shows she's giving Anthony a considering look, but she's otherwise relaxed in her seat. When my gaze meets Anthony's, I silently urge him to continue. "I was robbed. As I said, I've never lied to you. I just omitted some truths. But the full truth is that Benjamin came here, and he wasn't alone. For the entirety of the night, they kept me tied to a chair and, well, you saw what they did."

"What did they steal?" Hayden asks, still sounding hostile.

"Hardware containing all of my important coding software. They took a lot of my gear. It must be what he's using to hack into your cameras so easily." My mouth gapes. "Yes, he's been hacking your cameras. I could tell that much and have been slowly getting flashes of footage back, but it's been difficult. I didn't want to come to you until I had something to offer."

How can he be talking about what he's been doing for me after what he just told us? Tears well in my eyes, and I cup his cheek. He freezes beneath me like he expected me never to touch him again.

"You were tortured?" My voice breaks a little. He looks from one of my eyes to the other.

Again, words seem to fail him, so he only nods. Slowly this time. I launch myself at him, wrapping my arms around his neck and burying my face in his hair. His arms wrap around me, holding me to him tightly. With our bodies pressed together, I can feel the shuddering breath he lets out and the coldness of his skin. It's easy to tell how difficult this conversation has been for him.

"It's okay, love. I've been through worse. It wouldn't be the first time."

"That doesn't make it okay." My mouth is still against his scalp. While he was being beaten, I was sitting at home, living my life like normal. He could have died, and I wouldn't have known. I'd just be sitting on the couch wondering why he didn't return my text.

"Why didn't they kill you then?" I hear Hayden ask.

But it's Zara who answers. "It wouldn't have been enough. He was in love with the monster he called his girlfriend, so he wants someone to suffer the way he has suffered. What he did to Anthony was just for fun." Anthony's hand holds the back of my head now.

"Are you still in this?" he asks quietly.

"I'm still in this," I confirm. I don't know if that's the smartest decision or if I'll regret it later, but right now, it feels right. When I pull back from his hug and sit back in my seat again, I look at Hayden. Conflict consumes his taut features. Anthony sees it too, so he stands and moves to be in front of Hayden.

"Are you still in this?" Hayden's jaw tightens, I see the muscle tick, but he doesn't say anything. "Remember, we're doing this for her." Anthony barely has the last word out before Hayden punches him in the jaw. I gasp and Zara sits up, but we remain in place. Anthony uses his thumb to wipe a spot of blood from his mouth, but doesn't strike back. They glare angrily at each other, tension filling the space between them, and then Hayden strikes again. This time, Anthony fights back. Their fists continue to fly, connecting with the other's flesh regardless of the fact Zara and I are trying to pull them apart now.

Finally, I manage to squeeze between them and push my palms flat against each of their chests. They could easily push me aside and keep fighting one another, but they both stop, not risking the chance of hurting me like I'd expected.

"Stop it!" I shout at them. Their chests heave beneath my fingers as I twist my head to look from one of their faces to the other, inspecting the damage they managed to inflict. "That doesn't do us any good, so just stop."

Two minutes later, we're in the bathroom, where I'm wetting washcloths so they can clean their faces. Hayden's scowl has left him. What's left is an impassive look as I hand him one of the gray towels. On the other side of the bathroom, Anthony has a resigned expression.

"Hayden," Anthony begins, "I'm...sorry. Okay?"

"Oh, well, that fixes everything, doesn't it?" Hayden snaps.

Anthony unfurls his folded arms, then closes some of the

distance between them. "You know how I feel about you, so you must know how hard it is for me to say this." He dips his head and lifts his eyes to intensify his stare at Hayden, sticking out his hand and letting it hang in the air. "I'm sorry. For everything. I truly am."

The room is quiet for a long time. So long, in fact, I begin to think Hayden is done with Anthony, me, and all of this when he takes Anthony's hand and voices his forgiveness.

"We can't choose the paths our fathers paved for us."

Another pause, then Anthony asks again, "Are you still in this?"

"I'm still in this," he responds as their hands shake.

Chapter Twenty-One

TATUM

"I think it would be best if you left town for a bit," Anthony says a little while later as we all sit around a table on his back patio for lunch. As usual, clouds cover the sun, but it feels good to be sitting outside. Anthony's home is tucked away, surrounded by trees like mine. There's a pool behind his house he claims to use for laps, other than that and a raised fire pit in the lawn the mountain is his backyard.

"Just like you thought I should stay here?" He clamps his mouth shut. "Are you both coming with me?" It's just the guys and me now. Zara left once the hard part of the conversation was over, and we knew no one would try to kill each other. When I look at Hayden, he nods his head.

"Given the circumstances, they gave me time off work. But even if they hadn't, I'd follow you out of here anyway. There's no chance in hell I'm leaving you to deal with this all alone."

I look back at Anthony. "And you?"

"No," he says. "Trust me, I'd rather go anywhere you go, but all that would do is stall things. He'll pick up where he left off the second we return, so I'm going to stay here, try to find him, and stop him."

"Then I'm staying too. I think the lesson from today is that it doesn't matter if I move locations or not. Benjamin will still find me, so if that's the case, I'm staying put too."

Anthony turns his head to Hayden. "Williams, you know she's safer if she leaves. Help me out here."

"I'm not going to run and hide while you remain in harm's way as bait. No, that's just not going to happen," I interject before Hayden can answer.

Hayden shrugs and leans back in his chair, bracing an arm along the back of mine. "You heard her. She doesn't want to go." He addresses me now, "If you don't want to leave, would you at least be fine with us acting as your bodyguards whenever you leave the house for a while?"

"Yep," I agree easily.

Hayden looks at Anthony again. "Good. It's settled, then. We're all staying here until further notice and we're enforcing buddy rules for everyone, not just Tate."

"You're absolutely useless," Anthony mutters under his breath. Hayden hears him and responds by laughing, showing me his teeth in a perfect smile. One I haven't seen for days.

THEY WEREN'T JOKING about having a bodyguard *whenever I left the house*. I haven't been able to so much as open a window without someone staying next to me, and it's only been a single day. Anthony's house is enormous, especially for usually only being occupied by one person. It has everything you could ever need or desire. Everything except for art supplies so I talk Anthony into taking a break from his work and going to my house with me to pick up some of my painting materials. If I'm going to stay at his place for however long it may be, I need my materials to keep myself sane.

When we park in front of my house, Anthony barely gets out of his Audi when my phone rings. The number is unknown and only rings three times before it stops. Anthony opens my car door, and I pocket the phone, but it starts to ring again when we're walking up the steps to my porch. It stops by the time I pull it from my pocket.

"Who was that?" Anthony asks.

"I don't know. That's the second time they called, though." When we reach the door, Anthony holds a hand up to stop me. "What's—"

"Shh," he hushes me while holding a finger to his lips. He points to the door, and I see it's cracked open. I know for a fact it was left locked. Anthony pulls a gun from a holster I didn't realize he was wearing under his black dress jacket and instructs me to stay behind him as he slips inside. Since I didn't get a gun for nothing, I pull mine out too so I can cover his back. We check each of the rooms but find no one hiding inside. "I'm going to search the backyard. Stay inside. Lock the door behind me."

When he walks out, I lock the door and turn around to gaze at my home. Something in my art room catches my attention, so I start toward it when my phone rings for a third time. Lifting the screen, I see it's an unknown number again. This one ends on the third ring, as did the other two calls. I continue for the art room again but only make it a single step when something else makes me stop. Quiet music. I recheck my phone to ensure it's not coming from my device, but the screen is blank. The rhythm of the song that's playing sounds vaguely familiar, although it's hard to tell for sure what the song is since the volume is so low. I stand in place, trying to pinpoint what the song is and where it's coming from. I've heard music that wasn't mine before. It doesn't make sense with no neighbors and low traffic on the road in front of me.

Knocking on the glass door behind me makes me jump until I see Anthony on the other side.

"There's nothing back there," he says once I let him inside. I'd gotten so distracted I forgot he was looking for my stalker back there.

"Do you hear that?"

He pauses to listen, but everything is silent now. "Hear what, exactly?" He's not asking dubiously by any means. Rather, he's genuinely trying to find out what to listen for. I tell him about the music and he closes his eyes to try to listen better, cocking his head to focus on different areas of the house, but it's unsuccessful. I don't even hear the music anymore.

"Nevermind," I sigh with slight frustration. "I thought I heard something." Walking to the art room, this time I make it inside without getting interrupted. To anyone else, this room might look like a bit of a mess, but there's an organization amongst the chaos for me. Even when I haven't managed to put things back in their designated spots, I still know exactly where everything is and how to find it. That's how I know someone has been in here, messing with my things.

Stepping further into the room, I see a reference photo I had taped to the wall crumpled on the floor. The jar holding my brushes is tipped on its side. One of my sketchbooks is opened on a page I didn't leave it on. I don't bother checking for footage. There's no point. It'll probably be blank. Besides, we can guess who it is now, so I just pack what I'll need and return to the car.

"Is there anywhere else you want to go while we're out?"

"I'd love to see my friend." Anthony takes me to TreeCutter Cafe and waits patiently with me as I visit with Nyasia. It isn't busy when we get there, so she sits in the booth with us, getting up every few minutes to do things for her job before returning. As usual, she complains loudly about the place. Enough so that I look around a couple of times, half expecting her boss to pop up out of nowhere to fire her. But even though she hates this place, she's a damn hard worker in order to keep it running smoothly, so when it starts to get busy, we decide to leave. Anthony leaves her an exquisite tip, and she declares her love to him on the way out. Though he should be used to the public eye by now, he blushes. It's extremely subtle, but I'm always looking for hints of the feelings he keeps to himself.

"Why are you still staring at me?" he asks with a charming little smile once it's just the two of us and he's hidden behind the tint of his car's windows. What I've come to learn is that with Hayden, what you see is what you get. He gives no false pretenses or tries to be anyone other than his true self. Meanwhile, Anthony wears masks which change depending on the crowd he's in. For example, there's the mask I saw him in when he was a gallerist. His attitude and entire demeanor were far different from the mask he wears around Maple Crest. At the gallery, he was charming, funny, and full of smiles. Around town, however, he's stoic and cold. Then there are different variations of his mask depending on who he's around. With me, I get a version of the gallerist Anthony. Only, he's more flirtatious and vulnerable, which I love. With Zara, he's half gallerist and half Maple Crest versions. And with Hayden...poor Hayden. He experiences a more grumpy version of the Maple Crest Anthony. Everyone in his life gets an altered version of Anthony Kensington. He doesn't let himself be the same, or even his true self, with more than one person.

Or, rather, he's not allowed to be.

Clay is responsible for Anthony's mask. From what I've learned about his dad, I know I don't have to ask him about it to confirm my suspicions. Too many expectations have been put on him. When to smile, when not to smile. Intimidate people, but not these people. Anthony can't simply live the way he wants to.

"I like seeing you like this, is all. I wish everyone could see the you that I see. I wish you would *let them.*"

"You see me. Isn't that enough?" I do see him. Meaning I saw him half smiling in the diner at something Nyasia had said. I know what the town and Nyasia think about the Kensington family as a whole. A kind, genuine half-smile is a big deal.

"It's enough for me if it's enough for you. But I know if you gave more people the chance to know you, the real you, they would like you just as much as I do." Anthony's face softens before he leans over in the seat and runs his thumb along my cheek before cupping the back of my head, pulling me in for a kiss. It's slow and sensual at first, but a tender swipe of his tongue instantly heats my stomach making me pick up the pace a little bit.

We kiss like that until we're both breathless. When we pull back to fill our lungs, I can tell by the heated look in his eyes we both have the same thing in mind. I want him just as badly as he wants me.

"Take me to your room, Kens." He lifts his brows. "Seriously. The things I want to do with you can't be done in a car, so take me to your room. Now." He wastes no more time before putting his Audi in drive and speeding toward his house. Hayden isn't in the kitchen or the living room when we get there. Instead of finding out what he's up to, Anthony and I head straight for his bedroom.

Closing the door behind us, our hands immediately start to remove the other's clothes. When we're both down to our underwear, he breaks apart our sealed lips and pulls away. "Get on the bed." It's a quiet command, but a command nonetheless, and I feel an immediate response to his words in my gut.

"Yes sir," I say in a sultry tone. His head turns to the side and his eyes only heat in intensity.

"Oh, love, if you start talking to me like that, you're going to have an entirely new experience than the last couple of times." Chuckling, I turn around and ease my knees onto the bed. Placing my hands on the soft material underneath me, I slowly slide my arms forward until my chest connects with the mattress and my back is arched.

"Like this?" I ask. Anthony comes up behind me and I feel his featherlight touch start at one of my ankles and run leisurely up my leg until he reaches the curve of my ass. I hear a breath of satisfaction come from him, then he uses his fingers to hook into the material of my panties and slide them down my legs. Cool air touches me for only a second before Anthony's warm tongue replaces the coldness. I jump slightly at the sudden sensation and he grabs my thighs in order to hold me to his mouth.

Anthony licks me from slit to clit, then back again before inserting his tongue inside me. Throwing my head back, I gasp for the breath he just stole from me. When he groans, I moan at the vibrations that are sent through me. My whole body flushes with heat. Hooking one of his arms further around my legs, he uses his thumb to massage my clit as his face pulls away in order to catch his breath. My legs immediately start shaking as my hands fist the blanket. I have my face buried in my arm in order to keep myself from screaming out.

"Look at you," he hums reverently. "You're doing so good, love." My body writhes beneath his touch, and just when I think I'm about to explode, he stops and flips me over. I have no idea where he grabbed the condom from, but he's rolling it down his shaft. The second it's on, he pulls me forward and lifts me up, holding me securely by my thighs. Anthony kisses me deeply as my legs wrap around his waist and he walks us toward the floor-to-ceiling windows. The glass is cold against my back while the rest of my body is on fire from his touch, his kiss. *Him.*

Removing one of his hands from my thigh, he uses it to guide himself inside me. Anthony's perfect lips part with a moan as he slides in easily inch by inch. The stretch of my body accepting him makes me moan and my back arches the deeper he goes.

"Anthony," I whimper. I need more. Planting his hands on my hips, he holds me in place as he starts to fuck me fervently. His mouth latches onto my neck and my appreciation for his tongue on my pulse spot is loud. "Fuck, Anthony, I'm—" I don't get to finish my sentence because I'm too consumed with the feeling of finishing on his dick. He groans as my body clenches tighter around him.

"That's it. Good girl, Tatum," he pants as he fucks me

through the orgasm. He picks up the pace and loses his rhythm shortly after, his own orgasm about to crest over him. He's so close. Anthony throws his head back. His eyes are clenched tight and his mouth is open. He looks like he's in pain, but I know that that's the last thing he's feeling. I can't help myself. I bend forward and lick from the base of his throat to his ear and then I nip it.

"Oh God," he grunts, and then he comes hard.

Chapter Twenty-Two

TATUM

Making our way toward the kitchen for a much-needed drink of water before we shower, Anthony and I spot Hayden on the living room couch with his phone in his hand. When he notices us, a grin spreads along his face before he checks the time on his phone.

"You're done already? You just got home about ten minutes ago. Jesus, Tony. Quick off the mark, huh?"

I stifle a laugh, trying to cover up my smile with the sleeve of my sweatshirt.

Anthony gives him the finger and keeps walking. "Bugger off, Williams. And if you ever call me 'Tony' again, I will bury you."

Hayden scrunches his nose. "Yeah. I thought I'd give it a try, but I didn't like it either." Hayden follows me into the kitchen and Anthony groans with annoyance when he sees him enter the room.

Half an hour later, after Anthony and I have showered the sweat off our bodies, we're all settled in the living room. I have my easel set up beside the floor-to-ceiling windows whilst I work on a painting I started several days ago, but haven't been able to spend much time on lately. Anthony is sitting in the chair closest to me with a book, whilst Hayden is doing whatever it is he's doing on his phone with music playing through the speakers. I'm adding streaks of sunlight to my painting a couple of hours later when Hayden speaks up, starting a conversation for the first time in over an hour since they both let me focus on my work, free from distraction. He's lying on the couch, his feet still on the floor and his phone in front of his face.

"Is that pool heated?" I glance at Hayden in time to see him jerk his chin at the pool in the backyard.

"Obviously. I wouldn't have an outdoor pool here without having it heated. I have no interest in catching hypothermia."

Hayden puts his phone down and sits up, a grin quickly growing on his face as he flips his ball cap around. One of his legs bounces up and down like he's excited, and he bites his bottom lip. His brown eyes meet my green ones.

"Want to go for a swim?" I quickly put my brush down and wipe my hands on a rag, catching Anthony's attention.

"Can we?" I ask him, so much excitement packed into those two words.

"You need not ask for anything, darling. If you want something, take it. If you want to do something, then do it. What I have and who I am is yours." Anthony could take a moldy slice of bread and somehow turn it into something that makes my heart swell. How he does it, I have no idea.

To the rest of the world, he has this tough outer shell that blocks everyone from getting past his defenses and seeing who he really is. People in town know I'm associated with him now. I hear the whispers of what they think about him, but it's all false. It's just the mask he wants them to see; the mask his dad instructs him to wear around that particular crowd. Despite that, there's hope he'll someday wear only his true face. No more masks, or pretending. Why do I think this? Because, like now, the mask slips from time to time in front of Hayden.

"We should invite friends over to join us. It would be good for your public image. Plus, I think it would do us all a little good. You know, bring some light into our lives after the past few days," Hayden suggests.

Anthony's mask snaps back into place, and his tone quickly changes to convey his annoyance. "My public image doesn't need any help. Especially from you."

"Oh, that would be amazing! It would be nice to do something normal like," I interact. "Would that be okay?" Anthony settles his attention on me, giving me a prompting look. It takes me a moment to realize why.

If I want to do something, then I do it.

What he has is mine.

And who he is, is mine.

I smile brilliantly and pick up my phone to text Nyasia. "Who are you inviting?" I ask Hayden.

"Nick," he replies, pressing buttons on his phone to text his friend. Seeing Nick outside of The Brewed Bean will be weird, but I'm also kind of excited for it.

"And you?" I turn to Anthony. Immediately, I regret letting the question leave me. He won't call anyone to tell them to come over. The only person he has aside from me is Zara, and their relationship is strained. From what he said in the theater room, there was a time when they were close, like all siblings should be. Something happened somewhere along the line, though, leaving them both with stares of longing for it to be remade that the other never notices. I quickly ask another question and hope it will cover up my slip. "Will you be joining us in the pool?"

"Pool parties aren't my style, darling. Now, I'm not stopping you from having your gathering, but I don't suppose either of you packed swim clothes? I would love nothing more than to see Tatum in the pool without one. You, on the other hand," he addresses Hayden pointedly, "I would not. What's your plan?"

"It'd be too much of a temptation for you, would it?" Hayden shrugs when Anthony doesn't bother responding. "Swim trunks, boxer briefs, there's not much of a difference." Anthony continues to stare blankly at him, annoyance growing in his eyes. "I'm kidding. I'm having Nick bring something over for me."

NYASIA and I are changing into bathing suits with our backs turned to each other in Anthony's bedroom. Since I didn't feel like returning to my house and refused to send my friend there in my stead, she's letting me borrow one of her bikinis. I'd much rather squeeze my chest into this patterned triangle top of hers than worry about what horrors might be waiting at my cabin. Luckily, there's just a sexy, tasteful bit of side boob instead of me spilling out of the material like I thought I would.

"Is boy toy number one allergic to colors or something?" Nyasia asks as she starts to snoop around Anthony's room. I hope she wasn't expecting much because there's hardly anything in here. Windows take up an entire wall, a massive bed with nightstands on either side, and a dresser across the room with a large mirror lined with lights hanging above it. That's all there is. There's nothing personal about the space, making it look like a luxury hotel room or something.

"Yes," I tell her. "It's quite tragic."

She opens the door to his closet and walks in to examine its contents. "He sure has a thing for fashion, doesn't he?"

"Another yes," I chuckle. "Are you ready?"

She walks out of the closet and picks up her phone. "Almost. Come on." We pose in the mirror and spend the next ten minutes taking pictures. It isn't until one of the guys knocks on the door that we finally walk away from the mirror.

Kissing Hayden's cheek after opening the bedroom door, I grab his hand and practically drag him along in my hurry to get to the pool. Anthony follows us all out, walking with his hands in the pocket of his black pants. Nick and Hayden are in their swim trunks, leaving Anthony the only one still dressed in normal clothes.

With the push of some buttons, beautiful blue lights turn on beneath the surface. The sun is setting, and the air is cold, but when I dip my toes in the water, I find it warm. The rest of my body starts to shiver since I'm only wearing a long sleeve shirt made of thin material over the bikini, so I pull the shirt over my head and dive in. When I resurface, I find both of my guys staring at me with completely different expressions as Nyasia gives an excited shout. Anthony is staring at me with a sort of desperate hunger despite the fact he thoroughly had my body mere hours ago. Whereas Hayden is smiling at me with undeniable joy and that impossible sparkle in his eyes.

"Well? Is anyone else joining, or will I be the only one?" I ask the group.

Hayden pulls his shirt over his head, and as he does, the setting sun shines through a break in the cloud cover as if spotlighting his perfectly sculpted body. It's like the world is moving in slow motion now as I watch his muscles shift with his movements. When he drops into the water, droplets splashing onto his chest, I'm suddenly thankful for the chilly air. It helps cool my heated cheeks. Unfortunately, it does nothing to cool the heated thoughts in my head. Now is *not* the time to think about getting physical in the pool. Not with our friends coming into the water with us.

Nyasia must have given her phone to Anthony before getting in because one of her favorite playlists starts playing on the speakers surrounding us about a minute later. Nick brought drinks with him, so we each crack open the poison we chose, and I let my worries drift away as the sky grows darker.

Stalker? Never had one. Creepy gifts? Nope. Threats to my life? Nuh-uh.

Tonight, I'm just regular old Tatum Davis. Just a girl jamming out to party songs that came out around 2010, treating her wine cooler like a microphone. When Nyasia and I finish a rap chorus which nearly got me tongue-tied, Hayden picks me up by the waist, spinning me around before setting me back down and kissing me. He tastes like the beer he's been drinking. It's odd, because normally I can't stand the taste of beer. Apparently, when he's involved, my preferences change because I can't get enough of it when it's on his tongue. I kiss him like I could get drunk on him. The way he's making me lightheaded with lust makes me think that maybe I could.

Hayden's hand drifts to my lower back, continuing to move further down when we're splashed with a wave of water. I shriek. Hayden just laughs and shakes his wet hair like a dog.

"Did you forget we were here, Romeo?" Nick asks him playfully.

"Nope. Just had to kiss my girl." *My girl.* I already know what I am to him. He's never shy to let me know. But it feels good to hear him say it to other people. Hayden wades through the water over to Nick and a playful brawl breaks out between them. Hayden manages to hook an arm around Nick's neck. "Uh-oh, we're going down!" He pretends to act surprised as he leans backward, causing them both to crash below the surface.

I laugh before telling Nyasia I'm going inside to use the bathroom. When I step out of the pool and wrap myself in a towel, I notice Anthony isn't out here anymore.

"Kens?" I call when I get inside the house. The heated floors feel amazing. I almost want to lie down entirely.

"I'm here." Anthony rounds a corner wearing only black swim trunks. His torso is muscled, yet lean. Like the surrounding house, his skin is cool-toned and light, indicating he rarely gets much sun. Not that anyone really does in Maple Crest, I suppose.

A grin spreads quickly over my face. "I thought pool parties weren't your style?"

"Seeing you nearly naked and wet? I couldn't resist." He approaches me and pulls me into him, kissing me deeply.

"Nearly naked and wet, huh? Want to find out where else I'm wet?" My words sound like a dare: a dare he eagerly accepts. I bite his lip and drag it out. He groans, then dips a finger beneath the material of my bikini bottoms, inserting it inside me. Although I was expecting it, his touch makes the breath leave my body. Sparks of heat and energy surge through me from just his single finger.

"Wet indeed," he whispers. Pulling his finger out of me, he brings it to his mouth and tastes it. Tastes me. *Fuck.*

"There you are. Are you joining us?" Hayden asks Anthony as he steps into the house, clearly having noticed his swim trunks. I bite my tongue to keep from asking him the same thing, but for another situation entirely different from a pool party. "We're out of drinks out there. Do you have anything in that fancy fridge of yours?"

"Impeccable timing," Anthony mutters. He looks like he's about to shoot Hayden down, but I bat my eyelashes and say *'Please,'* so he leaves to lead Hayden down the hall instead.

"You are gorgeous," Hayden whispers against my ear as he walks next to me, as if it were a secret even though we're the only ones in the room. I know Hayden wouldn't hesitate to shout those exact words to the world, but there's something special about the intimacy of this moment.

"Williams." We hear Anthony call from down the hall. Hayden winks at me before walking off.

Chapter Twenty-Three

TATUM

"Your car is ready," Hayden announces as he hangs up his phone and strides into the living room the following afternoon. After Benjamin shredded my last set of tires with his knife, we had it towed to get new ones. I would have gotten the point if he'd slashed just one. Doing all four was overkill to prove his point that he knew where I was, and he clearly wasn't too happy about it.

"Oh, great!" I reply as I finish cleaning away some of the gold foil I just added to my painting. As if it didn't have enough already. *Maybe I should add more.* It can go around the border or something. *No. It doesn't need any more gold foil. Any more, and Smaug will take over Anthony's living room.*

I stand up, wipe my hands on my overalls, then take them off so I'm left in leggings and my henley. Or, rather, Hayden's henley. I will admit, it's not as weird living with them as I thought it would be, given how fast it happened. That could be because it hasn't even been a week yet, or the fact we're living together out of necessity for our safety. I don't like to think about the latter, though. Instead, I'm going to say things aren't weird because we

222

all work so well together. For the most part, that is. Things are always interesting between Hayden and Anthony, although I stopped feeling bad for Hayden. He seems to enjoy their bantering and sometimes even eggs it on.

It took only a day for Lenny to warm up to our new, temporary living situation. Giving him his morning medications has been more difficult because the house is so big, but we manage. Anthony is a great help with it, and I have to contain my laughter as I watch the otherwise well-composed man chase my cat.

As for the sleeping arrangement...let's just say I'm glad Anthony has a king-size mattress. Otherwise, things would be a little tight with me, the guys, and Lenny who claims a good chunk of the space for himself, all sharing the same bed.

Pulling my hair out of the bun I'd placed it in to paint, I'm combing it with my fingers when Anthony walks into the room. My arms freeze midway through a ponytail when I notice the expression on his face. The way he's staring down at his phone with his brows drawn together makes me feel unsettled.

"What's wrong?" I query.

"I just got a hit on Benjamin's location."

"And?" Hayden questions as he puts on a flannel over his t-shirt. "I thought that's what you've been trying for, so why do you look like it's bad news?"

Anthony flips his phone around, showing a grainy picture that appears to be from some sort of cheap security camera. "Because he's not in the same state as us. A gas station caught this image in Colorado yesterday. That's not the same car I caught on my cameras when your tires were slashed, and it wouldn't make sense for him to be so far from Maple Crest if he was targeting you. We're looking for someone else. Benjamin is the wrong guy."

Hayden's face, a mix of irritation and confusion, matches Anthony's now. "Do you have any connections to Colorado?" he asks me.

"None," I reply. I should be relieved my stalker isn't Benjamin because if it were, we know his endgame consists of my death.

Knowing it's not him, though, isn't comforting at all because now we have no idea who's following me or why.

WITH THE MECHANIC about to close, both of the guys come with me to pick up my car. That way we can continue discussing the new development, but the conversation leaves us in the same position as before; which is nowhere. Whoever is doing all of this is being smart and covering their tracks extremely well.

Since Anthony drove us here, he returns to his car after we've sorted the paperwork, while Hayden walks with me to where mine is parked in the lot.

I hear Hayden's hands hitting his jeans before he speaks up. "Shit, I left my phone in Kens' car. One sec, gorgeous." I chuckle at the fact he's picked up the nickname now, too, as he jogs off.

After sitting behind the wheel and turning on the ignition, I spot a postcard on my dash. The picture on the front is an artistic, patterned hand holding up a peace sign. It's likely some generic thank you note from the mechanic telling me how much he appreciates my business. Flipping it over, however, the card is blank.

The passenger door opens a moment later, with Hayden plopping down in the seat beside me.

"Let's go on an adventure," he suggests as he buckles his seatbelt.

I snort a short laugh. "Yeah, right. Anthony would probably piss his pants over the lack of security if we did that."

"He already agreed." My eyes widen in surprise as I stare at him. "Staying locked up for days on end isn't good for any of us. We can't live in constant fear. Besides, with each of us carrying our guns, I think we'll be pretty secure." He leans over to kiss my cheek, and I smile. "I won't let anything happen to you."

We go home to drop the Audi off, then pile into my

Mercedes. Anthony is driving, though, since he picked the spot and I don't know where it is. Once we leave town, trees with burnt umber bark and green leaves fill the spaces on either side of the winding road. Thirty minutes later, glimpses of the ocean peak out occasionally through the branches.

Anthony pulls over and parks in a random space on the side of the road. "Everybody out, or we're going to miss it." He pulls the keys from the car and is already getting out before I have the chance to unbuckle.

"Miss what?" I ask.

"You'll see...if you're fast enough. Come on, love." Our eyes lock, and he gives me an upside-down smile. His mask is slipping in front of Hayden again. As if recognizing the same thing, he glances at Hayden, who's stepping out from the back seat. "You too, Williams. Hurry up."

Hayden just lifts his eyes to the sky like he's searching for strength from the clouds, but looking closely, I notice the corner of his mouth is lifted into a smirk as he does it.

Walking around to the front of the car, Anthony leads us down an unmarked trail. The sun is close to setting, and I can hear the ocean below us. Sea-scented air blows around us with the breeze, hitting us even stronger when we reach a cliff's drop-off that overlooks a beach. After pausing for a second to take in the sight, Anthony ushers us further down the path that meanders down a steep slope, over a small bridge, and then finally, onto the beach.

A large piece of beached driftwood is where the three of us sit to watch the now-setting sun. We made it just in time for the most breathtaking sunset I've ever seen. Massive rocks form small islands further out in the water which are covered in trees, among other various plant life. Silhouettes of birds fly in front of us.

Since the ocean isn't too far from Maple Crest, I've visited a nearby beach a couple of times with Nyasia, but this spot isn't like the others. There are no fire pits with stacks of driftwood nearby or empty bottles as evidence of polluting assholes. It's just us surrounded by the seemingly untouched earth. The combination of wearing shorts and a hoodie, seeing the sun set over the ocean for the first time, whilst being here with them; it's all perfect. While I watch the colors of the clouds change, Hayden takes my hand. His fingers intertwined with mine.

"How did you know about this spot?" I ask Anthony. You'd never think a perfect path to this ideal beach spot would be here since there are no signs or a parking lot around. Except, Anthony knew precisely where to go, like he's been here plenty of times. Even when it looks like other locals don't know about it.

"My mum showed me this place. We used to come here and sit for a couple of hours at a time. There's nowhere else like it."

"Oh my God," Hayden gapes in quiet shock as he peels his gaze off the masterpiece before us. "You almost sound human. Tate, check his temperature. He might be sick."

Anthony looks past me at Hayden with a flat, unamused stare. "I won't hesitate to sic my sister on you."

Hayden's face straightens. "You wouldn't." Anthony threateningly cocks his chin. Chuckling, I playfully push both of their faces to watch the ocean. Anthony captures my hand with his and kisses the top before letting it go again. It's moments like this that make me stop and think about how glorious life could be here if only I felt completely at ease. But I don't. No matter how much I like to pretend otherwise, someone is tracking me. For all I know, they could be standing in the trees watching me right this second. With the way it feels like spiders are crawling along my back, I'd be willing to bet I'm right. Suddenly, sitting out in the open as things start to darken around us doesn't seem all that great of an idea.

"Come on, guys. It's time to go," I mutter quietly as I stand up, brushing the sand off my butt. I catch the glance Hayden and Anthony share before they follow me back to the car.

Chapter Twenty-Four

TATUM

"What's so hard about it for you to understand? It's a two-letter word. *No.* Are you truly that thick?" I can hear Hayden and Anthony talking — more like fighting — in another room as I walk down the hall after waking up from the 'nap' I excused myself for earlier. I've been in a mood since the beach yesterday, which meant a lack of hunger for two meals, and only taking a few bites from another. On top of that, I haven't really felt like talking much or even seen the point in getting out of bed.

Curiosity slows my steps until I come to a stop against the wall, out of sight so I can listen to their conversation. From my spot around the corner from them, I can hear Hayden as he releases a heavy breath through his nose.

"No, I know what the word means. See? I just used it myself. What I don't understand is why you said it."

"Because I don't want to talk to you."

"Holy shit," Hayden sounds exasperated. "*Still*? You're still going to keep this feud between us going? What's the point, man?" Anthony stays quiet and I inch forward to get closer to the corner so I can hear better when either of them talks again. Just in time, too, because Hayden lowers his voice, and it sounds like he's speaking through his teeth. "You're not in charge here. No one should be. We're all in this together, so it's time you act like it."

"What the hell do you think you're doing here standing in my kitchen if I'm not being a so-called team player? Let's get something clear; I don't give a shit about you. Everything I do, I am doing for her. She's the one that wants you here, I don't. You eat my food, sleep in my bed for God's sake, you fill this space in my home. Fine. But I don't have to keep you informed about anything."

It's so quiet in the house I can hear Hayden's angered breathing. Part of me wants to announce my presence and interrupt their fight so I can help Hayden. But another part of me wants to listen and see *exactly* what they're talking about. Something sparked this conversation. I need to know what it was.

"I just think we should come up with some sort of game plan, is all. We've been sitting here playing house pretending nothing is wrong on the other side of these walls, but we can't keep doing this. Something *is* wrong, and I know you're trying to figure it all out. I want to be included in that, by the way. But Tate and I can't move in with you permanently and keep hiding away. I need to go back to work and see my family. Plus, I think the reality of all of this has caught up with Tatum. She needs more than a life in a cage, however gilded it may be." My gaze drops to the floor with guilt. For the life of me, I can't understand why Hayden is still here. I know that being in a relationship with me at the moment isn't easy. Plus, he just said it himself, though in different words, that I'm keeping him from living the life he wants to get back to.

Hayden is right about the reality of the situation catching up to me, though. I'm paranoid about everything. I'm terrified to sleep because when I do, I have dreams of the night we were gassed. When I close my eyes, my mind tricks me into seeing a dark figure filling my doorway, so I lay with my eyes open for hours. Sometimes I feel the phantom touch of fingers on my cheek exactly where I once woke to find paint. I've been hiding it all from them really well, but I'm losing the energy to keep up the illusion that I'm fine. It seems Hayden has already noticed.

Anthony inhales, getting ready to reply, but music suddenly starts to play from my phone and the lyrics are being sung at full volume.

Only two words repeat over and over; 'one day.'

Scrambling to pull my phone from my pocket, I curse, knowing my cover has just been blown and they'll know I was eavesdropping.

The same two words repeat several more times before my index finger slams against the screen, hitting pause on Matisyahu's song '*One Day*' just as Hayden turns the corner in front of me.

I smile guiltily at him. "Hi."

He gives me a pitying little grin in return. "Hey. Don't you hate it when your phone presses random buttons while in your pocket? It's so annoying." He shakes his head and rolls his eyes, playing off the whole situation, saving me from well-deserved embarrassment. When he lifts his arm for me, I tuck myself underneath it and look at my screen again as we walk into the kitchen.

"I don't even have this song in my library. Plus, it skipped the first fifty-three seconds. I mean, it's a good song so I'm adding it to my music library now, but still. That's weird, right?" I lift my head before asking so I can see Anthony. He has his hands braced on the spotless island counter. His dark sleeves are rolled up and his blue watch is on his wrist.

Concern creases his forehead. "Indeed, it is." He glances at Hayden, then the countertop, then me again. "The stalker probably hacked into your phone. They've had no problem doing so with cameras, so I wouldn't be surprised. But if you have no attachment to the song, then I'm not sure why they chose that one in particular to play."

"To show us they could," Hayden chimes in with a shrug of

his shoulders like it's the most obvious answer in the world. "I bet it's a scare tactic to mess with her." Here it is. The fear I'm becoming all-too familiar with. It's like there's a fist clenched around my heart right now. If the stalker hacked my phone, then that means they have access to everything. All my texts, my photos, my bank account. *Everything.* Seeing how they already stole money from my safe, with access to my account, what's stopping them from stealing every penny I've got?

"Let me see your phone. I'm going to try to counteract them and install some protection." Anthony extends his hand for the device. Although it's not him I'm mad at, I drop my phone carelessly on the counter and start storming out of the room. I didn't do anything to deserve someone obsessing over my life like this. Taking pictures of me, messing with my property, terrorizing my home...I can't keep dealing with this.

"Tatum," Anthony calls after me, but I keep walking.

"Let her go, man. Let her have some space for a little bit." Hayden steps in to stop him.

I go back to the bedroom and stop in front of the massive windows. Like in the living room, the entire wall is made of glass. Staring out, I let my eyes wander over the forest that's a stone's throw from the house. *I wonder if my stalker is out there right now. Watching. Waiting.* Just in case they are, I use both hands to flip them off before I decide to lay under the covers for the rest of the day. I knew there wasn't a point in getting out of bed. I did it anyway, and look what happened; my phone was hacked in the first five minutes. So now there *really* is no point in getting up. Not even to tap the buttons on the fancy wall device to black out the windows for privacy. I'm sure it would get overridden anyway, so I might as well just leave things as they are.

I was having the time of my life in Maple Crest before all this. Sure, I missed my family sometimes, but damn was life amazing. My independence was at an all-time high and things were just how I wanted them to be. Now, I can't do anything on my own.

She needs more than life in a cage.

Hayden understands me so well.

Although I know they're only trying to help and it was my decision to be here as much as it was theirs, I do feel caged. It's not the guy's fault. It's my piece of shit stalkers. Whoever it is, *they* made me the caged bird I am.

Chapter Twenty-Five

TATUM

Today is the second day in a row where I've barely moved at all. I don't even want to use my phone. Anthony told me it's secure now, but I don't trust it. The thought of my stalker staring at me through the camera freaks me out. So, I've pretty much been an emotionless statue. Anthony suggested we all watch a movie earlier in the afternoon, which was great, but didn't break me from my stupor.

Now, I'm sitting on the couch in the living room with Lenny, watching the rain run down the windows as Hayden and Anthony walk into the room. Surely, they've been talking about me, but I don't ask. Anthony stays standing in the spot where the hallway meets the open room, but Hayden comes and kneels in front of me.

"Hey," Hayden addresses me softly with his voice just loud enough for me to hear. "Let's go for a night drive. We'll grab cocoa from the gas station, roll down the windows, turn up the radio, and blast the heater. Want to?"

When I look at him, I find him smiling sweetly. During one of our phone calls before bed, I mentioned that was something I loved to do before leaving Dallas. The effects of a drive like that are therapeutic. Even when I went on them by myself, I would always return home with my cheeks sore from smiling so much. For some reason, though, I never got around to doing it in Maple Crest. God, I mentioned that to him weeks ago in a conversation which wasn't even face-to-face. How did he remember? Then again, I shouldn't really be surprised. It is Hayden, after all.

"Yeah." I manage to smile back at him. "Let's do it." He grabs both of my hands and helps me stand. It's not like I didn't have the choice to go for a drive before. The problem is that I've been so stuck in my head I couldn't think of anything other than the fear.

Anthony has my hoodie draped over his arm and he looks pleased as he passes it to me. "Have fun darling, I'll have dinner waiting when you get back." My heart melts a little as I stare at him. He's maskless right now. At this moment, in front of Hayden, he's just him; no false pretenses. It's not lost on me how he hasn't said to 'be careful' or mentioned any risks and I'm glad he hasn't. I'd be willing to bet the absence of those words is intentional and solely for my sake. Had he said them, I'd be focusing more on his warning than anything else, and Anthony is aware enough to keep that in mind. Lifting myself up onto my toes, I kiss his cheek.

Rather than running through the rain, Hayden takes my hand and instead, we walk to his truck. Tipping my head back, I embrace the feeling of the water as it splashes against my face. Hayden just stands alongside me with a curve to his lips until I've had my fill.

"Whoo!" he exclaims once he shuts his door and is behind the wheel. His hands rub together excitedly. "Let's go, baby!"

When we get to the gas station, we split up once we're inside. He asks me to fill a cocoa cup up for him while he goes to grab us a snack. He isn't back by the time I fill up both of our medium-sized mugs, so I set out to find him. Luckily, with him being so tall, and aside from the fact the gas station is empty of people besides the cashier and us, my handsome tree-cutter is easy to spot. His back is to me when I join him in the snack aisle.

"You ready?" I ask. When he turns around, I can't stop the loud, surprised laugh that escapes me. "I thought you said you were going to grab *a* snack. What is all that?" Hayden's arms are almost overflowing with a variety of chips, chewy things, and chocolates. Though tall and strong-shouldered like a pro football player, his gentle eyes hold an innocence to them like that of a teddy bear.

Those muscled shoulders of his bounce up and down in a shrug. "Oh, well...I only meant to grab a couple of things, but I didn't know what you were in the mood for. Then the more I looked, the more it all sounded good. Come on, let's go check-out." Hayden starts to walk by me, but I just laugh again. It makes sense he has a sweet tooth. He's such a sweet guy!

"I'm not *that* hungry. You can put some of it back." Not to mention gas station snacks are always more expensive than they need to be. I already know he will refuse to let me pay even though I have more than enough money, and he's still splitting his paycheck to help his family.

He stops and shrugs again. "I like to be prepared. You never know when you might change your mind. Besides, I can think of a fun way to burn off the extra sugar if that's what you're worried about." He winks those caramel-colored eyes at me.

"I'll hold you to that." I point at him seriously.

"You won't need to, gorgeous. Now that I know you're down for a workout, all I'll be able to think about is—"

"Okay, I get it!" I interrupt loudly. I don't need the cashier staring at us to overhear our plans for later, and I know Hayden well enough at this point to know he was about to give a very detailed description. Still, I'm smiling. *Leave it to Hayden to manage that.* He's so good at getting those out of me and distracting me from all the scary moments. Grabbing his shoulder, I turn him back around so he can start walking toward the counter again. "Just pay already."

Hayden chuckles as he starts to turn around but then stops *again* mid-twist. Jerking his head at something, he asks, "Can you grab one of those, too?"

Turning to see what he's referring to, I spot a display of powdered donuts at the end of an aisle. Rolling my eyes with mock annoyance, I grab a package. He smiles triumphantly as he *finally* makes it up to the counter. I'm pretty sure we just bought enough junk food to supply a movie theater for a night. There's no way we're going to eat all of this on our drive.

OKAY, we haven't eaten all of it, but we made a pretty impressive dent in our supply, if I may say so myself. Grabbing a SweeT-ARTS rope, I take a bite out of it before offering some to Hayden. He keeps his hands on the wheel and leans toward my seat. Hayden stops singing along to the song that's playing and leaves his mouth open. With the candy now resting on his teeth, he closes his mouth and rips a piece away.

This drive is exactly what I needed. I feel good. Like *me* again. The pre-girl-with-a-stalker version of me. I liked her. *I missed her.*

Hayden and I are belting the words to Macklemore's song '*White Walls*' at the top of our lungs. Using my closed fist in place of a microphone, I pass it between us and throw my head back, laughing when Hayden puts his heart and soul into his performance. When I lean forward to turn up the radio, Hayden looks out the window at the car next to us and something he sees makes him do a double-take.

"What the fuck?" I barely hear him say. "SHIT!" His foot punches the gas, and he swerves to the side. The excess rainwater on the road causes us to hydroplane. I grip the handle above me. Our velocity from the speed we were traveling at on the highway continues to carry us, right toward the beginning of a concrete divider we're surely about to hit head-on. "Come on, COME ON!" The tires regain traction mere seconds before we crash. Hayden turns the wheel and presses the gas pedal again to try and prevent the collision, but it doesn't work. His side of the truck slams into the concrete making our bodies jerk violently right before the entire vehicle is thrown into the air.

After crashing against the pavement and landing upside down, the truck slides to a stop. My chest strains against the seatbelt that's keeping me from being on the ground, which is actually the truck's glass-covered roof. My head pounds and my body hurts.

"Hayden? Are you okay?" Looking to my left, I see him hanging limp with a large amount of blood running down his face. "No, no, Hayden! Please be alive!" My fingers feel nearly numb as they work to undo the seatbelt. Using one hand to grab onto something above me helps me catch my fall when it comes undone, but when I'm loose, my door swings open. Someone thrusts their hands into my hair and yanks me out roughly. Shrieking, I try to grab onto the door, but it's a useless attempt. I'm pulled flush against someone's body, but I can't see who it is due to the way they're still holding my head.

"Evie, Evie, Evie," they say in a sing-song voice I can barely hear above the rain. *Evie?* Only one person I can think of would use that name around me, but I thought we determined it couldn't have been him. A wave of goosebumps flushes over my covered skin. Lifting my foot, I slam it back down on his, then throw my elbow into his gut. Benjamin doubles over, and I run back for the truck. I barely have the glove compartment open to get my gun when Benjamin wraps a hand around both of my ankles. Before I have the chance to grab the weapon, he yanks hard, dragging me across the wet pavement and broken glass.

"No! Hayden!" He remains unmoving in the truck and there are no headlights around us to suggest help is coming from a passerby. I'm on my own in getting myself out of this situation.

"Pretty little Evie," Benjamin taunts as he wrestles me towards him. I kick, punch, and squirm, but he still manages to pin my arms on either side of my head and straddle me so I can't thrash around. "Did you get my gifts? Tell me, how long did it take you to realize there was a countdown to this moment? It was all very clever, I think."

Countdown? What? Oh. My. God. A countdown. The weird occurrences, the unexplainable gifts, all of it, has been a *countdown*. Now that I know this, I know exactly when it started. Fourteen days ago, with a text.

Fourteen. The only thing in a text I received from an unknown number.

Thirteen. The number circled on the movie ticket.

Twelve dead roses.

11 o'clock. The first time I was told to watch the clock.

My head starts to ache as I try to figure this all out.

Ten; the number of fingers held against the glass when I saw my stalker.

Nine bullet holes in a target and the number of casings in my mailbox.

Eight...eight...the stop sign. What I thought was graffiti was actually a message specific to me written on an object with eight sides.

Seven pictures of me found at seven in the morning.

Six chicken heart cupcakes.

Five...what was five? *Shit.* The night Hayden and I were gassed. The stalker, *Benjamin,* wasn't waving at the camera. He was showing me how many days were left.

Four of my tires were slashed.

Three missed calls, which only rang three times.

Two; the peace sign postcard.

One. The song. It literally repeated the words '*one day*' over and over.

How could I be so stupid? There's been nearly two weeks' worth of a countdown which I've been completely oblivious to!

My lip quivers so I bite down to stop its persistent shaking. "Not really," I lie. "I knew you were coming. That's why I got the cameras and the gun."

He laughs, his grip tightening on my wrists. I feel the circulation of blood to my fingers being cut off. Then he leans forward so he's mere inches from my face. "STOP LYING TO ME! I could hear your conversations with your friends. Your *boyfriends,* too. You had no idea it was me or what was happening. I could hear you every night as you talked to that model friend of yours about what I had done for you that day. Don't pretend the cameras did you any good; it's way too easy to hack into someone's system, and I'm too good at clearing footage for you to have seen anything I didn't want you to see. Anthony tried hard to work around me, but I was always five steps ahead of him. The most obvious thing of all is that I know your name isn't Evie. Isn't that right? Tatum Connelly Davis. I did my research, and I learned a lot."

"H— how did you hear me talking at night?"

"Your conversations aren't the only thing I heard, you know." He ignores my question. Moving my arms further above my head, he takes hold of both my wrists in one of his large hands, making me feel completely powerless. Benjamin squeezes my cheeks so hard my teeth cut through my skin, then leans in even closer so his mouth is barely above my pursed lips. "I could hear you every time you pleasured yourself. I would access those cameras you got to make yourself feel safe and watch—"

I jerk my head forward, colliding my skull with his nose. He shouts and backs up, grabbing his face, giving me the opening I need to scramble away from him and grab the gun from the open glove box. When it's in my hand, my body simultaneously raises and twists, ready to shoot the pervert. Instead, I get a fist to the face.

I let out a shout made of equal parts pain and surprise but manage to keep a hold of the gun. Raising it to aim again, Benjamin kicks me square in the chest, sending my body careening into the side of the truck. The crash of my body against it matches the clap of thunder that rumbles loudly. My breath leaves me in a gasp. Again, I start to aim my pistol, only for him to knock my arm aside, holding it against the long side of the truck bed. Gripping my throat, he holds me in place, my other arm trapped painfully between my back and the metal.

"Were you going to shoot me?" He leans his bleeding face into my ear. "That's kind of hot." Benjamin barely dodges my attempt to knee him in the groin and laughs at my failed attempt. Moving forward, he pushes his full body against me to restrain me further.

I can hardly move an inch, and barely even breathe with the combination of the angle and his tight grip on my neck. The way he's toying with me reminds me no one is on their way to help. If he takes me, God only knows what plans he has in store. And that's *if* he even attempts to take me anywhere. Whatever evilness he has planned, he has waited fourteen days for. More than that, even, since that's just how long the countdown was. Those two weeks don't include the organizational time involved, so he's had who knows how long to plan what to do with me. I don't intend to find out what he came up with.

His fingers trail down my neck and then leave me. He must have reached into one of his pockets because the blade of a knife replaces the spot on my neck where his fingers had just been.

"You really are beautiful," he tells me as he scrapes the knife tip lightly across my skin. My body shivers beneath him, and I fight to control the shaking. "But even beautiful women have to be taught lessons." A sharp pain slices through my neck, and I cry out. The fresh cut at the base of my throat isn't deep enough to cause any life-threatening damage. It's just deep enough to hurt like hell and make me bleed. I can feel the warm drizzle of blood mixing with the cold rain as it descends my neck.

My chest fills with a couple of quick breaths while I try to think of what to do next. "You think I'm beautiful?" I once heard it could save your life to play along with delusions in situations like this. Although, I never thought I'd be in a position where I'd have to decide whether or not to do that.

My question appears to catch him off guard because he just stares at me for a moment before answering. Then he uses the tip of his knife to push some hair out of my face. "Yes. It's a shame things have to go this way. Waste of a perfectly fine woman, if you ask me."

Doing the only thing I can think of to lower his guard, I kiss him. At first, he seems shocked, and when he presses the knife to my throat again, I think my plan has failed. But then he swipes his tongue into my mouth, deepening the kiss with a quiet groan, and I know I have him. He's far from being the man I want to kiss in the rain. Despite that, I have to keep this moment between us going. I run my tongue along his and I roll my hips as much as I'm able. The taste of his blood from when I head-butted him enters my mouth, nearly making me gag. At the same time, the urge to bite through his tongue or rip his lip fills me. A few seconds later, his hand on my arm slides up to my elbow, as he starts to lose himself in the kiss, just like I need him to.

Angling my wrist, careful not to move it too much so he remains unaware, I stop when I think I have the gun pointed at his gut. Though, I can't be sure where the barrel is aimed. All I know is it's pointed at him, and that's good enough for me.

I pull the trigger. Benjamin screams, nearly as loud as the shot itself, dropping me immediately to hold his wound. As he bellows in pain, so do I, and the gun falls from my hand. The recoil and angle I had my wrist at when I took the shot must have caused me to tweak it.

"You fucking shot me!" he yells as he grips his thigh. It's not his gut, but it did the job. Thanks to his injured nose and gunshot wound, Benjamin is soaked in crimson blood nearly as much as he is with rain.

"I thought you said it was hot when I tried. I must be a goddamn vision now." The adrenaline that has been fueling my body since the crash is fading. My whole body hurts and it feels like my bones are made of heavy metal.

Overwhelming rage consumes every inch of Benjamin's face, and he finds the strength from his anger to snap toward me, crashing my head against the truck so everything turns black.

Chapter Twenty-Six

HAYDEN

An obnoxious ringing in my ears fluctuates in volume. My head pounds. Everything is blurry and hard to make sense of when I open my eyes, and...and I'm upside down. How...?

The crash.

My chest heaves as it painfully fills itself against the tight restraint of the seatbelt holding me in place. I look to the passenger side of my wrecked truck, expecting — sincerely hoping — to see Tatum *inside* the truck.

I don't.

No, no, no!

Eyes flying to the windshield, I assume I'm about to see a body-sized hole in the glass, even though I know she was wearing her seatbelt.

There's no hole. Just a badly cracked window, a breeze away from crumbling.

"You fucking shot me!" A man's voice shouts in the dark somewhere on the other side of the crumpled metal. Given the circumstances, I can't see much, and the panic at not knowing what's happening is formidable.

Despite it being jammed, I still struggle with the seatbelt, needing to find Tatum.

"I thought you said it was hot when I tried. I must be a goddamn vision now." *Tatum.* Thank fuck. Not only is she okay, but it sounds like she's defending herself from whatever the hell is happening out there. Later, when we're out of this mess, I'm going to kiss her so hard and tell her how proud I am.

Then I hear the man's vicious growl and the loud crash of someone's body against metal. The impact makes the truck rock and suddenly Tatum's hand comes into view as it falls against the pavement.

"NO!" I bellow. Jerking at the seatbelt with ferocity does nothing to help me get unstuck from my position. I see Tatum's hand get jerked out of view like someone is pulling her. I growl and curse as I dig into my pants pocket with difficulty. Retrieving my knife, I finally cut myself loose from the strap. My body instantly falls on top of the glass littering the inside of the truck, and I groan at the pain that accompanies my sudden descent. Pressing a hand to my aching ribs and crawling out the open door on Tatum's side, the first thing I see is a man with his hands around Tatum's ankles. It's obvious the man is struggling just to be upright right now, let alone drag an unconscious Tatum to his car. I have no idea who the fuck this guy is, but I know I'm going to kill him. "Let her go!"

His head snaps up at the sound of my voice. We hold eye contact for only a second before I go for the discarded gun on the pavement. By the time I reach it, the man is already driving away, leaving Tatum behind. I empty the magazine, firing shots toward the fading tail lights.

What is happening right now? This has to be an unconscious dream caused by the crash, right?

But that still doesn't explain what I saw that caused the crash in the first place. I remember looking over while driving and seeing someone holding something. When I looked closer, I saw it was a gun, and it was pointed right at me.

With the gun now empty and the tail lights out of sight, I drop the weapon and go for Tatum.

Cupping her cheek, I scan her body to take an inventory of her injuries. Seeing blood coming from her neck, I panic. *The bastard cut her throat!* Fingers flying to the wound, I wipe at the blood that's mixing with rain and find it's not as deep as I'd initially thought.

"Tatum? Honey, can you hear me?" Leaning forward, I put my ear to her mouth to listen for breathing and watch her chest to see if it's still rising but can't tell through the rain. Hand trembling, I grab her wrist and feel for a pulse. Tears fill my eyes when I feel it and a relieved sob bursts through me.

I feel in my pocket for my phone with my free hand, then cuss when I realize I don't have it. Carefully setting her hand down, I stand to go back to the truck, but a sharp pain shoots from my ribs. I clasp a hand over the area as I fall to my knee. After taking a couple of breaths, I start to move again, crawling into the wrecked vehicle. Finding my phone, I dial 911 as I return to Tatum.

When I get off the phone, I move Tatum's upper half onto my lap and hold her close to me. Using my jacket, I drape it over one of my shoulders, holding the other side over her head to protect her face from the rain.

"Tatum, please wake up. Please," I plead hopelessly. I'd punched the gas out of instinct when I saw the gun being pointed at us. If I hadn't done that, we wouldn't have crashed. If we hadn't crashed, she wouldn't be left alone to fight someone injured while I was blacked out. If I hadn't fucked up, she'd be awake. "Somebody help me!" I yell as loud as I can into the night, hoping beyond hope I'll get an answer, but knowing we're all alone.

Leaning down, I press my shaking lips to her head and hold my face beside hers, my eyes squeezed shut, as I wait for the ambulance.

Chapter Twenty-Seven

ANTHONY

My knee won't stop bouncing. *That's strange.* I'm usually in such control over the movements of my body. Thanks to my dad, I've trained myself not to let a muscle so much as twitch unless I determine it's an acceptable situation to do so.

Yet right now, my knee won't stop bouncing.

I've always hated hospitals. Ever since I visited my mum for the last time, and she had more tubes than she did skin, I've hardly been able to stand going through one's doors. Especially this one. I nearly entered Ragsburrow's hospital for the first time in over a decade after Hayden and Tatum had been gassed, but by some sort of mercy, I had met them on their way out. But this time there was no other option than to come in and it's killing me because I can't even be by Tatum's side.

Before now, the night my mum died was the last time I was inside the building. I still remember exactly how to get to the room where her heart stopped beating. Everything changed in that moment. Only when she was gone did my dad lose his mind, becoming a whole new person. He became someone she would have hated. I know this because he became someone *I* hate. When she left, she took all the best parts of him with her. With him unable to let go of her, I lost both of my parents the day she died.

I was the reason my mum became sick in the first place. That's a fact my dad never let me forget and that I never forgave myself for either. If it weren't for me, she'd still be alive today. My dad wouldn't have become the man who would hold a loaded gun to my head with his finger on the trigger, blaming me for her death. Zara wouldn't have been sent away to boarding school for no other reason than for looking like our mum.

I remember holding Zara's hand on the day of the funeral. It was raining that day, as it does most days in this place. But it was different this time, like the world was crying too. Like together, we were mourning the same loss. Her funeral was the last place I wanted to be, but it wasn't solely because of the typical reasons people don't want to go. The last time I saw her, she was connected to so many machines that I was scared of her. My own mother. Guilt from feeling that fear consumed me, but I was a little kid then. Too little to know what was happening to her when I saw her like that. All I knew was that I didn't want to see her again, and I didn't want to say that last, forever goodbye.

A piece of that fear resides in me still, which is why I ensure everything remains clean and do all I can to keep myself healthy. I avoid being in close proximity to people when possible, and I avoid hospitals at all costs: being here brings up too many memories I try to keep buried.

Right now, the hospital has me sitting in a chair in some hallway, waiting for clearance to see Hayden and Tatum. If you aren't family, visitation is challenging to get immediately after an emergency. Using my family name gave me some leverage, but they still have to check with Hayden to make sure I'm not someone he doesn't want to see.

Hayden. Not Tatum, because I can't get so much as a simple update about whether or not she's even alive. I'm beginning to think Hayden told them I could bugger off, and that he doesn't want to see me. I wouldn't blame him at all if he did, but he's being daft if he thinks I'll leave.

When a door opens nearby, I pay no attention to it. There have been lots of doors opening. People are walking in and out, in and out, repeatedly. I rest my forehead on my cold knuckles, my arm propped up on my knee, my eyes squeezed shut.

"Anthony." I know that voice. Even now, when it's a little more gravelly than normal, like he needs a drink, and when it sounds utterly depressed, I recognize it. There is something different about hearing it now, though. Before, his voice would immediately ignite feelings of anger, jealousy, and annoyance. But now, I hear it and none of those emotions come to me. Instead, my entire body fills with relief. And...something else. Something I'm sure can't be right because there's no way that's what I'm feeling toward him.

I stand up quickly to greet Hayden. He's going to have a shiner tomorrow, and he's a little banged up in other places, but he's standing on his own. *Most importantly, he's not made up of tubes.*

A massive sigh leaves me, my shoulders sinking as it does. Tears well in my eyes and the next thing I know, Hayden rushes up to hug me. One of his arms wraps around my shoulders whilst the other grabs onto the back of my head. No one has hugged like this before. At least, not since before my mum died. He's hugging me like...like he loves me. *Truly* loves me. Tatum and I have had our share of embraces, but nothing like this. When she and I held each other, it was always comfortable, and we were happy. We did so because we wanted to. But this, this is desperate. It's a need.

I cling back to him, my fingers digging into the back of his jacket, but my panic doesn't cease. It builds. My lungs demand more air than I suddenly find myself capable of giving them. They're asking too much of me. I can't— I can't breathe. It's a silly thing, not being able to breathe after never having trouble with it before, but I can't stop this. My head feels like needles are pricking my brain and the edges of my vision are beginning to blacken. Hayden is attempting to talk to me, but it sounds like I'm underwater. I can't hear what he's trying to say to me. I notice he's moved us inside one of the rooms and closes the door, giving us some privacy. That's the only thought that registers before my mind whips back to more important matters.

Hayden's okay. He's fine.

Hayden is okay, but what about her?

What if she's gone?

She could be okay too, but what if she's not?

But Hayden is okay.

My body feels like a vice is crushing it, it's still so hard to breathe. Bringing a hand to my chest, I apply more pressure than what already feels like is there because, for some reason, that helps.

"I'm so sorry. I'm so sorry, I'm so sorry," I repeat breathlessly, over and over. "I'm so sorry for bringing all this shit into your lives." My knees crash against the ground and I know it should've hurt, but it didn't because I can't focus on anything else.

I'm having a panic attack.

Hayden follows me down, wrapping his arms around me again. I should tell him to let me go and not get too close to me, but I can't. It's too late for that. The damage my presence around people can do has already been done. I let myself lower my guard and have what I want, and I shouldn't have. I knew better, but didn't listen to my head when it screamed to leave them alone.

I can't escape all the truths that are crashing down on me. All of this, everything they've been through, is my fault. This is my mess, but now they are the ones lying in the very grave I dug for myself.

I grasp at Hayden's arms and the comfort he's trying to offer me, but these overwhelming feelings stubbornly persist.

"Help me, Hayden. Please help me." I'm still struggling to breathe normally and am beginning to think this panic might be permanent.

"Tell me how," he pleads, his voice sounding as broken and defeated as mine.

Then it hits me. And I mean the realization seriously hits me so hard my whole body just freezes.

I can't lose him.

He's holding me against his body like he's afraid to lose me, and I realize part of the reason for all of my panic was because I was *terrified* I would lose him, too. Not just Tatum.

All this time, I pushed and pushed to try and keep him out of my life. Then, when I couldn't, I pushed to keep him from meaning something to me when Tatum said she wanted him just as much as she wanted me. Even though I was being stubborn, still set on being a bully to him, he didn't budge. Hayden matured, putting up with my bullshit while I stayed stuck in the past.

It's easy to see why Tatum was drawn to him. Hell, I was too, for years. I just tried to block it out. I'm done doing that now. This is it, I'm giving in. To hell with what my father will have to say about it and all the potential repercussions. This right here is rock bottom. The demons from my past can't possibly do them any more harm.

My body has stopped shaking and the breaths have come easier to me since the epiphany. Hayden managed to pull me from my head. Removing myself from his embrace, I stand up, finally registering the ache in my knees. He rises too.

"You're okay," is all I say.

He pauses. I think he's waiting for more, but there isn't any. "Yeah. Yeah, I'm okay." He searches my face for something and, whatever it was he was looking for, I think he found it because his mouth moves. Except, no words come out. I stare at him with a look I've never given him before. Never gave anyone other than Tatum. I almost tell him about my newfound thoughts toward him, but now is not the time. I need to know Tatum's okay.

I make myself busy by readjusting my suit jacket, but it's not because I actually give a shit about how I look right now. It's a force of habit. Something to keep my hands busy and my eyes averted.

I clear my throat. "Is she alive?" There are a hundred other questions I want to ask, but this one takes precedence over all of them. It feels like my life depends on his answer and whether it contains two letters or three.

"Yes. Tatum's alive."

JUST MINUTES after he and I leave the room, Hayden's parents and two of his sisters show up at the hospital. To say they're surprised to see me here would be an understatement. But, they're Williams', which means they're kind and accepting of me being here for their son and brother regardless of our families' histories.

Although he's walking, Hayden is in no condition to be doing anything other than sitting still. He tries convincing everyone he feels better than he does, but no one believes him in the least since he looks like absolute shit. It irked his parents when they discovered the doctors wanted Hayden to stay the night for observation, but against medical advisement, he checked out. Since we're still in the waiting room of the hospital should he take a turn for the worst, I have kept my mouth shut about it.

The Williams family and I have been in the waiting room for about twenty of the longest minutes of my life before a nurse in dark green scrubs finally comes to take me and Hayden to see Tatum. Visiting hours are technically over, but they're allowing us ten minutes before we'll have to come back in the morning. As the nurse leads us down the hall, he explains she was put in a medically induced coma so her brain can rest as it heals from the swelling and bleeding endured by the trauma. Due to Hayden's injuries, we're moving at a fraction of the pace I'd like to be going. The nurse must agree Hayden shouldn't be walking in the condition he's in because he offers to grab a wheelchair for him, which Hayden denies.

When we turn down another hallway, a lump rises in my

throat, and my steps stutter. This is the hallway holding the room my mom died in; nine doors down on the left.

Fuck. Each step forward is painful, like a large pin pushes itself further into my chest with every movement forward. Keeping my eyes away from the end of the hall, I follow the nurse and silently plead that he doesn't take us into *that* room. Three doors down the hall, the nurse stops to give us one last reminder that even though she's in a coma, they have her on a fentanyl drip so she can't feel any pain. Anxious to see my girl, I step around him and into the room before he's finished speaking. Then I stop dead in my tracks.

Tubes. Tatum is connected to tubes.

Chapter Twenty-Eight

HAYDEN

Anthony is standing unmoving in front of the door, but I don't waste any time getting to the hospital bed. *Jesus.* Tatum is intubated, connected to monitors, and has an IV. Shallow cuts, most likely from shattered glass, scatter around her face. There are some bruises on her arms, reminding me of the way our bodies thrashed around during the crash. As I get closer, though, the bruises on her wrists look more and more like hands. No doubt these were caused by the man who tried to take her. Same with what's underneath the bandages on both her head and neck.

Taking her hand and one of the seats beside the bed, I press a hand to my mouth. The memories of seeing someone trying to abduct her, of checking for a pulse when I thought she was dead... of holding her unconscious body on my lap...it's all too fresh. Even now in the still room, I can hear the echoes of crunching metal and pouring rain. I have never known fear like what we experienced out on that road. Five years from now, or even fifty, I know those scenes will still be as vivid in my mind.

Maple Crest is special. A little boring, perhaps, but that's part of what makes it exceptional. Bad things aren't a typical part of living there; there's no crime or evil. It's a place where parents don't immediately assume the worst when their kids are late for curfew. Assumably, that's why Tatum wasn't taken seriously by the city's police. *Maple Crest* was *special.* The perfect bubble the town was in has popped now. I don't know when it happened, but at some point, the perfect place I grew up in became just as dangerous as everywhere else.

I hear Anthony break from his stupor as his footsteps near the bed, making their way to Tatum's other side.

"Should we call her family?" I question a minute later.

"No. It's already handled. Her family will be here in the morning." Anthony holds up his phone, showing me a picture of a man I recognize as the piece of shit from tonight. "Is this who you saw?"

My jaw clenches, biting back my anger before I answer. "Yeah. That's him." My mind replays the moment our gazes locked after I crawled out of the truck and saw him dragging Tatum on the pavement. He was illuminated only by the headlights of his car, but his face has been etched clear as day into my memory. "Who is he?"

"That's Benjamin. What happened?" Anthony finally asks me. He wasn't here when I gave my report to the police. Then, between what happened when we first met up and my parents not giving me a second to breathe, now is the first chance he's had to hear my account of what put us all here.

I tell him everything, starting from when I looked over and found myself staring down the barrel of a gun, not attempting to make any excuse for my actions that resulted in things being the way they are.

I won't let anything happen to you.

I told her that yesterday. Fucking yesterday. I failed her in barely over twenty-four hours.

Inhaling a shaky breath, I squeeze my eyes shut again. I'm trying to block everything out. The guilt, the pain, the sight of seeing her like this, the sound of her body hitting the truck, and the image of her lying on the pavement when I thought she was dead. Tonight will leave me haunted.

I was putting on a brave face, pretending I was okay in front of my parents, but I'm not. As if Tatum's situation isn't bad enough, seeing the effect it had on Anthony was its own form of torture. For as long as I've known him, nothing got to him. No matter what I threw at him during school, no matter the stares and whispers from the town when we got older, he has remained composed through it all. Sure, he'd get mad when I messed with him, but he never broke.

Today, he broke.

I don't know why I rushed to hug him when I saw him. That's not something we've ever done before. I was just so damn relieved he was there, and then the way he was looking at me...but then he had a panic attack. The strong and stoic Anthony Kensington was brought to his knees with a panic attack because of a hug.

I'm such an asshole. I should have reacted differently and thought clearly in the face of danger to save everyone from this pain. If I hadn't pushed in that peddle and—

"It's not your fault." I hear him say.

"Yeah, right," I reply with a dry, humorless laugh. There's nothing funny about any of this. In fact, tonight is the worst night I've ever had in my entire life.

"Look at me," he instructs firmly. After a second's hesitation, I meet his gray eyes. There's that look again. The one I can't read because it's new and so different from what I'm used to coming from him. "It's not your fault," Anthony reiterates each word slowly and with discernment.

It wasn't that long ago when Anthony exposed his truths to us, and I did the opposite of what he's doing now. Rather than giving him understanding, I blamed him. For the first time in years, I lost my composure and punched him because he was telling us his truths and exposing his wrongs. Now Anthony, the last person I'd expect to hear those words from, is offering me release from self-imposed culpability.

"When my time with her kept getting interrupted with you, I knew things were about to get interesting." I recall seeing them together outside the gallery, then the morning after at her house, and yet again at the vet. "We hardly see each other at all the past few years, then suddenly, here you and I are bringing the same girl flowers in the morning."

"Just because we're in a hospital room doesn't mean we have to have a heart-to-heart, Williams. We can sit here in silence."

Ignoring his comment, I continue. "Then when she brought up the relationship, I almost laughed. Not at her, or because I thought the idea was funny. I almost laughed because I knew you were going to hate it and the fact that it was me she wanted too."

There's a long pause that makes me think he is, in fact, just going to sit in silence.

Then, "I did. Fuck, Williams, I did hate it. But even you couldn't stop me from being with her. When she brought it up to me, the only reason I hesitated to answer was because I was considering the best way to get rid of you permanently."

I wait for him to make any sort of sign that he's joking, but it never comes. "Wait, are you being serious? When you say permanently, do you mean, like...you were thinking of ways to kill me?"

"Tatum's happiness is all I want, though, and as much as I didn't like it, that includes you. So, of course, I agreed."

His choice of words catches my attention. "*Didn't*? Past tense?"

We spend the rest of our allotted ten minutes in silence before rejoining my family in the waiting room.

Chapter Twenty-Nine

ANTHONY

Hayden wants to go home. To his home. But his parents and I all give a very adamant 'no' to that stupid idea. When he suggests going to stay with his parents, I'm all alone when I say 'no' to that as well. I seem to be the only one thinking logically. Though Tatum is Benjamin's focus, Hayden has now been attacked twice. He'd be safer if he stayed at my place since I have a security system and cameras which cover the entire property that I recently upgraded, and they don't. Benjamin got bold tonight. Bolder than I'd ever seen him. Until I get all the details, I can't feel safe in the knowledge that Hayden and Tatum are unguarded. Should things not be over tonight, and Benjamin lashes out over the failed attempt to kidnap her, Hayden could be putting his family at risk by being around them.

I'm one second away from pulling him aside and informing him of this when he finally seems to realize it on his own. While he talks to his parents, either forming a lie to comfort them or convincing them it's better he stays away from them, I step away and pull out my phone.

My finger hovers over Zara's number for longer than it

should. Calling my sister shouldn't be this difficult. Every time we interact, I hate our dad a little more because it was his business that drove this wedge between us.

The line rings and then stops when she picks up. "Yes?"

"There's been an accident."

"What kind of accident?"

"Tatum." I glance behind me at the Williams family, still in mid-discussion. "And Hayden. Benjamin almost took them out tonight. We're at the hospital."

There's silence on the other side of the line. "Were you hurt?"

"No. I'm letting you know, because—" *because the last time something happened, you nearly bit my head off for not informing you. And because I need your help* — "I'm just letting you know."

"Okay," she replies quietly.

"Okay."

"Thanks."

"Yep." She hangs up and I'm slow to lower my phone. When I turn around, Hayden catches my gaze and jerks his chin, signaling for me to come back. His hand is clutching his ribs. It has been for a while now. He should be sitting.

"They're going to give me a ride over there. Are you coming?" he asks.

"No. I'm going to stay here and shoot Benjamin myself if he comes through those doors for so much as a band-aid." Hayden's family all share various looks of unease, but he just nods. "I'll text you the new codes." Without waiting for him to respond, I turn and walk away, sitting in a chair where I can see the whole room, including Hayden and his family leaving. I wish I was leaving too. Not to be with them, but so perhaps the embarrassment of what happened with Hayden earlier and the nausea from being here will leave me.

Using my phone, I search the cameras throughout the city trying to find where Benjamin disappeared to. The problem is that the highway where Tatum and Hayden crashed doesn't have any cameras. It's impossible to know which direction he went, if he switched vehicles, or if he pulled off somewhere. Benjamin has disappeared. Hopefully, he's bleeding to death somewhere since Hayden said Tatum shot him.

Going to my Audi in the parking lot, I grab my spare laptop and bring it back inside. That way, I can watch the hospital's cameras as I work on my phone. Though, since cameras are sort of Benjamin's specialty, I make sure to keep a constant eye on the door as well. Because of this, I'm aware of Zara entering the building long before she sits beside me.

"Hey," she greets as she crosses her legs and sets her black helmet on the empty chair beside her.

I go back to searching the hospital records of every hospital within 200 miles for patients matching Benjamin's description.

"Hey." A pause. "What are you doing here?"

"Thought I should check on you. Pulling security?" I nod, feeling her stare at the side of my head, but don't acknowledge it. "Where's Hayden?"

"At the house."

She closes the laptop on my hands. "Go home, Anthony. I'll take things from here."

Sitting back with a sigh, I finally look at my sister. "I can't go home, Zar. I need to stay here in case she needs me. What if Benjamin comes for her again and I'm not here?"

"I'll be here. Besides, there's someone else who needs you. I don't know exactly what the three of you have going on, but I know it's something. I'm not stupid. You've been here for hours. Go check on Hayden." Her concern for him stings with the reminder that when I was hurt, I couldn't call her. Although she rebels against our dad, her rebellions are only minor infractions. She's still immensely loyal to him and if I had called her for help, she would've told him about it. I wanted to postpone his punishment for as long as I could. "Go, Ant. I'll still be here when you get back."

There's another minute of reluctance before I get moving. I thought that once I was out of the hospital and in my Audi, I'd be able to relax at least a little. Yet I don't. My body is tense the whole drive from Ragsburrow to Maple Crest. Approaching my house while I roll up the driveway, I don't see any lights inside. It's nearly three a.m. now, so I'm not surprised to be met with darkness. Hayden's family's car isn't out front either, but I wasn't watching the house cameras to see if anyone stayed with him. That part will be a surprise for me.

I don't like being around people. My house is my sanctuary. I don't care to leave it much and I don't like people being inside. That's why I never bothered to set up a guest room. Until Tatum came into my life, if someone was here long enough to sleep, then they'd have been here too long. End of story. Having— *what is he?* Tatum is my girlfriend. Does that make Hayden my...*goddamnit. I think it does.* My nemesis has become my fucking boyfriend. Whatever he is, having him at the house without Tatum will already be bad enough as it is.

As my feet carry me through the house, I soon find the only light left on is coming from my room, which faces the back of the house. Pushing the door open, I see Hayden pacing back and forth. The bedroom lights illuminate the light sheen of sweat coating his brow and I notice the slight limp in his walk.

"What the hell are you doing?" I figured I would find him in here since this is where he was told to sleep, but that's exactly how I was expecting to find him; *asleep.* Like Lenny, who's stretched out on the bed.

"I think better when I'm moving," he replies without looking at me. He's moving anxiously around the middle of my room wearing the same rain-soaked and bloody clothes he left the hospital in. The pacing finally stops when he turns to look at me and I wonder for a minute if the minor cuts and bruises on his face have somehow gotten worse since I'd seen him just a couple of hours ago. "Did you find out anything?"

"No." Hayden purses his lips and grinds his jaw as he nods his head. I can't tell for sure, but it almost looks like tears are brimming in his eyes before he blinks them away. I reset my tone, softening my voice. "Not yet. Nothing tells us where the bastard is and there's nothing new about Tatum's condition, either. The doctors are unsure how long she'll be in the coma. Zara is staying at the hospital and will make some calls for added security. You and I can return in a few hours when visiting hours start again at 7:00."

"Fuck, this is all so messed up." Hayden's face looks green. I can't be sure whether the color is from his injuries or the situation. Out of nowhere, Hayden chuckles.

"What's so funny?" I'm starting to learn that's something he does when he's overwhelmed, but I ask anyway. Though I don't mean it anymore, I'm still breaking the habit of speaking to him in a bitter tone. Unfortunately, I have nearly twenty years of practice doing so, so it might take a little while to readjust.

"You realize there is absolutely nothing normal about our relationship, right?" His voice raises to a near shout. Our relationship being atypical is something I am, in fact, highly aware of without him pointing it out. But he's asking rhetorically, so I keep my mouth closed. "One of us always seems to be hurt. Then there's the stalking and near abduction…this is all normal to you, though, isn't it? Maybe not with someone you care about, but isn't this all a little familiar?" A pause, then a sigh. "This is a lot for me, Anthony. I'm just a logger. Not the kind of guy who has ties with this stuff on the regular. Tatum almost died. The closest I've come to death is when my grandparents died of old age. I can't…this is a lot to try to comprehend."

"Is that what you think of me, then? That I go around killing people all the time? That I regularly put the people I *love* in situations like this? That I'm heartless?" The urge to slam my fist into his jaw is overwhelming, his injuries be damned, but I opt to clench my fingers instead. "This isn't *familiar* to me. Nothing about this is familiar."

His face softens. "Anthony, I didn't mean—"

"You have no idea how much I have hated the life I've been forced to live for years. I didn't want to get close to her, to you, to anyone *because* I was worried about things like this happening. But I did it anyway. Every second since we realized the reason for her torment, I have hated myself for staying in her life." I can't stand the weight of his stare, so I look away and swallow down the lump in my throat. As I do, I think about the hospital and the two of us in that room. "I understand it's a lot for you. It's a lot for me too. If you were anything other than a logger, you'd still be feeling the same way you are now."

"I'm sorry. I'm just...I don't know what to do." When I look at him, his shoulders are drooped, and he's favoring one side of his body to keep the weight off the other. Although his face still seems discolored and there are bags under his eyes, he's holding his head up high. For multiple reasons, I have no idea how. Throughout everything, Hayden has been like a lighthouse in a storm; showing strength after getting hit by wave after wave and still providing light.

"You can start by sitting down before you fall down."

"I'm fine." The son of a bitch goes back to pacing, and for a brief second, I think about pushing him over for not listening to me. I know it wouldn't take much. Just a single one-handed shove. Hell, a small breeze would do the trick just as effectively. I swallow my sigh before I enter my closet and find him something to wear for the night other than the disgusting clothes he currently has on. Perhaps he already has clothes somewhere in the house, but I leave the closet with something, anyway. Stopping outside the door, I toss the shirt and sweatpants I collected at him. Surprisingly, he catches them. As expected, however, he nearly loses his balance and falls over.

"Sit. Down," I tell him firmly. He stares at me for a moment before he starts to remove the zip-up jacket he's wearing. The action takes three times as long as it should, and his face is contorted with pain throughout it. Hayden moves stiffly to remove his shirt next. Quiet groans accompany this action. He moves so slowly that the sun will have already risen by the time he's done.

Walking up to him, I knock his hands away and neither of us says anything as I take the hem of his shirt and pull it over his head. With the material gone, the explosion of dark colors that form the shape of a seatbelt stares loudly back at me. The bruise starts at his shoulder, going diagonally all across his torso, disappearing below his pants line. The surrounding skin looks heated and swollen.

He lets me examine the damage for several seconds, then speaks quietly when he says, "Not too pretty, is it?"

"How are you...feeling?" Hayden breathes a small laugh through his nose. Unlike the last two times, this laugh is different, making me glare at him. "What?"

"Nothing, it's just that I was the one who got into a car crash, yet four words make you sound like you're the one in pain."

"Shut up." I grip him by his uninjured shoulder and shove him down on the bed so he's finally off his feet. Instinctively, one of his hands flies to my hip and digs in to stop him from being pushed flat against the mattress. Even though layers of clothes are between his skin and mine, there seems to be an electric buzz emanating from him. I feel that touch everywhere. He must feel it too, because when I take my gaze away from where his hand is on me and meet his eyes, I find him staring quizzically at me.

Loosening my grip on his shoulder, I don't know why, but I let it brush softly down the curve of his deltoid. "How are you feeling?" The words come easier to me now.

"I'm fine." Now he's the one who sounds like he's in pain. Not from his injuries, though.

I cock an eyebrow at him. "Are you?"

Hayden clears his throat and is quick to remove his hand. I instantly note the coldness that replaces the heat of where his palm had been resting on my hip.

"Yeah. Yep. I'm fine." His tongue pushes through his pressed lips to lick the bottom one as he nods at me.

Jesus. Has Hayden always been this easy to read? I feel confident with my guess that if I were to make a move on him right now, he wouldn't reject me. Is this a recent development? Or had it always been an option when we were constantly messing with each other in school? Imagine the sort of mischief we could have gotten into for all those years if we knew then what we know now. Perhaps he's as aware as I am that something has changed between us. I have sudden desires for things I want to experience for the first time when this is all over. Things I know he's the only one I want to experience them with. But not now. First, we wait for Tatum to wake up. Everything else comes after.

"Good." I take a step away, creating some space between us. "Do you need help getting the other shirt on?"

"I figured I'd sleep without one, actually."

Turning away to give him privacy as he changes into the sweatpants, I say, "I'll get the light." I stand beside the switch and wait until he's settled on his side of the bed before flipping it off. Knowing my way around the room, I easily find my way to my side of the bed and lay down. I hate that Tatum isn't here. Oddly, though, I'm glad that Hayden is.

Chapter Thirty

HAYDEN

We barely got three hours of sleep before we were awake and heading back to the hospital. Thanks to Anthony's punctuality, we got here right at seven to be by Tatum's coma-sated side as long as possible.

"I've got to be honest. I thought one of you would have killed the other by now without a mediator around," is the first thing Zara says as we walk through the hospital doors. Anthony and I share a glance. His face is unreadable. I want to know what he's thinking about...well, *everything*. It's clear he's felt uncomfortable with the vulnerability he's shown since the accident, but what else is he feeling?

Last night, emotions were running high for both of us. Something happened between us in the bedroom. Hell, something happened in that first room here at the hospital. Mixed in with the mess of all this other crazy bullshit, I need to know what those looks have meant. *I wish I knew what the look he's currently giving me means.*

"As you can see, we haven't," Anthony replies as he turns his head away from me. Had we been in any other situation right now, I would've made some sort of joke to get under his skin because, so help me, I think I'm addicted to his side-eyed glances and plotting stares. There's just something about his face when he's looking at me and I know he's thinking of ways to get back at me that I can't get enough of. But we're not in another situation, so I say *hello* to Zara and keep walking to Tatum's room. Even though I'm anxious to get there, I'm exhausted and my body hurts, so getting around takes me longer than I'd like. Anthony takes a couple of minutes to talk to his sister and then catches up with me right before I enter Tatum's room.

A couple of hours later, I'm feeling the effects of minimal sleep after a mentally and physically draining night. Moving to get up from the chair I pulled next to Tatum's bedside, I smother a groan of pain that rises inside of me.

Hearing it, Anthony spins around from where he was looking out the window. "Where are you going?"

"To get a coffee. My energy is completely spent."

"Then sleep. You shouldn't have a lot of caffeine after an accident. It will slow your healing." He walks up to me and grips my uninjured shoulder, shoving me back down in my seat like he did last night. "I'll see if we can get you a smoothie instead. You look disgusting. I'd hate for your healing to be delayed and have to look at you like that any longer than necessary."

"What are you, my doctor, now?" He glares at me, just like the good old days, before leaning against the nearby wall and pulling out his phone. Since he took a jab at my appearance, I take a few seconds to soak in his. Today, he's switched his regular suit for a black long-sleeved shirt and pants. Although seeing him out of a suit is rare, seeing him with his hair a mess the way it is now never happens. It's unsettling. But since there's one hell of a reason for him not to care about the way he looks, I don't say anything, taking a more gentle but sarcastic approach instead. "Thank you for your concern about my appearance. You're a real softie. But I think I can handle it."

"No. I'm not getting it for you."

"That's fine. I didn't ask you to. I can get it myself."

"No."

"Well, I wasn't asking your permission, actually, so—" I try to stand up again, and again, he pushes me back down. My teeth clench together. *This man is impossible sometimes.* I curse my body and the fact that it hurts every single muscle to just breathe since it's keeping me from shoving him aside. "Anthony—" I start to warn him, anyway.

"If you leave this room, you'll more than likely fall in the hallway. Your muscles are so stiff you can't even stand up straight."

"I'll be fine," I grit out.

"No."

"Yes."

"No!"

"Ye—" The door opens, and a nurse walks in with two people behind her, interrupting our bickering the second I get to my feet.

"Oh, hello," she starts. Anthony gives her what I think is supposed to be a small smile, but it looks more like a grimace than anything else. I try to give her a polite wave but hiss at the pain it causes to do so. Anthony shoves me back down in my seat and it takes everything in me not to glare at him. I'm usually pretty tolerant of his shit. Unfortunately, my tolerance is all gone at the moment. "Miss Davis' parents are here and there are only two visitors allowed in the ICU at a time so you're going to have to leave now, gentleman."

"Yes, of course," Anthony agrees, every inch his composed self again. "Do you mind granting us a couple of minutes to talk to them and then we'll leave? On behalf of the Kensington Foundation, it would be my honor to make a donation to the hospital on the way out as a thank you for taking such great care of Miss Tatum." The way he's smiling at her makes him seem like a whole new person than the man that was fighting with me over coffee versus smoothie mere moments ago. It doesn't even matter that his hair isn't styled. He looks every bit the well-established multi-billionaire. I can tell he isn't giving her a flirtatious smile.

Still, the woman in scrubs blushes regardless as she smiles back at him.

"Of course, Mr. Kensington. Take your time."

The nurse closes the door behind her, leaving us alone with Tatum's parents. She takes after her dad in terms of hair color and eyes. But the shape of Tatum's nose, cheeks, and everything else really, is entirely from her mom. Unlike Anthony, they took the time to make sure they left the plane, or hotel, wherever it is they came from, looking perfectly presentable. My mouth twitches down in disgust at my deduction that they cared more about their appearance to the public than about getting to their daughter.

"Mr. and Mrs. Davis, it's a pleasure to meet you. I just wish it was under different circumstances. My name is Anthony Kensington. This is Hayden Williams." I give a flat, close-lipped smile to them. To their credit, her parents look like they couldn't care less about us now that they're here and I don't blame them. I wouldn't either if my kid was in a coma. Tatum's mom walks around us to get to her bedside, but her dad remains standing by the door.

"Yes, we've heard your names before," her father replies, his southern accent much stronger than Tatum's. "Who are you two to our daughter? She's been very hush-hush about her life here."

"We're, uh—" Anthony stumbles over a response, so I painfully stand and move up next to him, extending my hand to her dad.

"We're dating her. I was with your daughter during the accident, so I can answer any questions you might have about what happened."

Tatum's mom speaks up behind us. "You're both dating her? And you know about each other?"

"Yes ma'am," I reply. "Though, it's more than dating, really. We're in a relationship."

"Two boyfriends?" I confirm her question and she sneers at us. "We thought her sister was pranking us when she told us about this little arrangement. It's not right."

I try to make sense of this conversation but it's difficult. I just told her I was with her daughter right before she ended up in a medically induced coma and I'd talk them through what happened, but she's more concerned about her opinions on our relationship status. What the fuck?

"Okay...well, the doctors are optimistic the coma won't last too long, but it's hard to tell for sure. She—"

"We have the information we need already. You two can go home," Tatum's dad interrupts. "We'll have her call you when she wakes up."

'When she wakes up?' Is he trying to say he doesn't want us to visit with her the rest of the time she's under?

"Actually, we'd like to switch off having visitation with her," Anthony interjects. "She means too much to us to sit at home and wait for some kind of update. We understand she's your daughter and that you want to be with her, so we'll gladly wait in the waiting room until you need to take a break to get food, or breathe fresh air. We'll take what we can get so long as we still get to spend some time at her side."

Tatum's dad pushes past us, joining her mother at the bedside. "I don't think so. Two boyfriends? That means both of you were only giving her half of your effort so she felt she needed more to make up for what you weren't giving her. Go home. You won't be seeing our daughter."

"Sir, I promise you that's not the case. Please reconsider. We want nothing more than to be here for Tatum. Please, just let us be here for her," I join in, damn near pleading for the chance to be with our girl when she's at her most vulnerable.

Her father pins his green eyes, a replica of Tatum's, on me. "As if running off to that ghost town to paint all day like a child and getting two boyfriends wasn't enough, she picked you as one of them." My brows pull together in silent question. "College dropout. All you have to show for a resume is odd jobs of physical labor before joining the company you're currently with. There's nothing impressive to show on it. You come from a family that can barely keep their house. And if you were with her during the incident, why didn't you stop it? You are not the kind of man our daughter needs. If she means as much to you as you claim she does, then you'll let her go. She belongs with someone who can financially support her when her so-called art business inevitably fails. That will never be you. You barely make enough to feed yourself. I did my research on you two and I am very disappointed with her decision to be with you."

My mouth clamps shut. From the second we met; I knew I was lucky for every second of the time Tatum gave me. But when we're together, our social classes never mattered to either of us. I may not have extravagant things, or a bunch of extra stuff that only serves the purpose of impressing others. I have everything I need and that's fine with me. Plus, Tatum's art business will never fail. She's far too determined and talented for that to ever happen, so those words didn't hurt me. It's just really damn infuriating that her parents are so unsupportive of her goals.

What really fucking hurts, though, is knowing Tatum's parents also blame me for what happened. Like a knife to the chest, I feel the pain deep inside me, reawakening part of the guilt Anthony had managed to put to rest. I would have done *anything* to have kept her from being in that bed. Had there been the chance to take her place, I would've done it without a second thought. But there's no excuse for my mistakes so I won't even try.

Anthony straightens, his voice hard when he speaks. "I'll have you know that Tatum has more talent than I've seen in a while, which is a truly impressive feat considering I recently opened one of the largest art galleries in the Pacific Northwest. Regarding your opinion of her, it's no wonder she found somewhere else to be appreciated, even if it is a ghost town in your eyes. As for Hayden? To overlook him simply based on what's in his bank account would be one of the stupidest things you've ever done. Loyalty, friendship, and dedication like his can't be bought. Yes, he was with Tatum when the crash happened. But he also cut himself free when he was stuck upside down in the vehicle and crawled over shattered glass to get to her. Look at him and tell me you think what he did was easy. Yes, Tatum is here because of him. She's here *because* he did everything he could to get to her and shot at the son of a bitch, who's actually responsible for the accident, before he could drive off with her. If you looked into us, then you know I have met more than enough wealthy families. Not one of them can hold a candle to Hayden's character. If it's a good man you want for your daughter, then you won't find any better than him." Anthony puts a hand on my back and urges me out the door.

"Where are we going?" I ask as we start down the hall, his hand still guiding me.

"To the waiting room. And to get you a cup of coffee."

Chapter Thirty-One

ANTHONY

I'm in the waiting room with Hayden, wondering how such an amazing woman came from such unpleasant people when my cell phone rings. Since it's an unknown number, I ignore the call and pocket the device when it rings again with the same unknown number.

"What?" I demand when I answer.

"Ew, watch that tone with me. I was just starting to like you. Where's Tay?" I lean forward in my chair, placing my elbows on my knees.

"Who is this?" The voice on the other line is a woman's voice which sounds familiar, but my head is running with too many other thoughts at the moment to place who it belongs to.

"Nyasia. Where's Tatum? Why isn't she answering her phone?"

"How did you get my number?" Hayden straightens in his seat a little, worry starting to show on his face as he stares at me. I shake my head in silent assurance that the conversation isn't something to worry about.

"I got it from Tatum's phone in case she went missing and I

271

had to question you as a potential suspect. And it seems like I was smart to do so. So, where's my girl?" I fill her in on what happened, but she demands to talk to Hayden for confirmation I'm not lying to her.

Several hours later, Hayden is asking a nurse if we can join Tatum's parents in the room only to be reminded that only two visitors are allowed at a time on the ICU floor and we'll have to 'sit tight.' I'm not the praying type, but in the past twenty-four hours, I've prayed enough to make up for all the years where I didn't. Every second where I just *sit tight*, I'm praying that even though she's connected to tubes and wires, and only six doors away from where my life changed, she won't end up with the same fate as my mom.

When visiting hours end, Hayden and I are still in the spots we've been occupying for most of the day. Across from me, Hayden's asleep with his head propped up on his hand. Since we hardly got any rest last night and he only fell asleep about forty minutes ago, I'm not ready to wake him up yet. I'll rouse him when it's been a complete hour.

Tatum's parents come into view on their way out from being with Tatum, and I note the way her mother glances at Hayden before looking ahead again. It was the same kind of scornful sneer you usually see come from compassionless people as they pass a stray dog.

"Stay home next time, boys," her father quips as he strides by.

"See you tomorrow, Mr. Davis," I respond. Twenty minutes later, Hayden and I are getting up to leave. All day, it was clear he was uncomfortable sitting in the hard chair, and I know he should be lying down somewhere soft. But I didn't want to not be here by driving him back to Maple Crest, just in case Tatum's parents changed their minds and gave up some time so we could sit with her. Plus, I know he wouldn't have wanted to leave for the same reason, had I even suggested it. The only thing he and I have ever had in common is our admiration for the woman in the hospital bed.

Once back at the house, I feed Lenny while Hayden showers. I'm finishing a call with Zara when he comes into the living room in plaid pajama pants and holding a hand to his aching ribs. Hayden's lack of a shirt shows that awful seatbelt bruise of his and his lingering stiffness from the crash is evident as he sits on the sofa.

Zara concludes our call by telling me there's still no sign of Benjamin and why she thinks he slithered off and died somewhere, then hangs up. Frustrated, I drop my phone on the table. The damn thing collides with the glass platform so loud I'm surprised it didn't crack either object. Dropping down into the chair, I slump into its cushion. This is my first time doing so since I bought it years ago after I first had this house built. It's hard and uncomfortable. Its rigidity could be due to minimal use, or the tension in my body. But it's also very likely that, though it had too many numbers on its price tag for a fucking chair, the stupid thing just isn't comfortable to sit in.

"Did you mean what you said about me back at the hospital?" Hayden asks suddenly. I run a hand over my face, then stare at him. It was stupid to hope and want him not to mention it. *My control is slipping.* This situation is causing me to keep being vulnerable around him. "If all of that is true, then why did you hate me? One day as kids we were fine and the next, we weren't. I've always wanted to know."

Of course, he has. Precious Hayden Williams. For years, Maple Crest has crowned two young men as its ultimate golden boys: Hayden Williams, who has been here his whole life, and Nick Madden who moved here in high school. They, of course, were drawn to each other and quickly became best friends. Everyone likes them.

Almost everyone.

My family had been normal when we first moved from London in the summer. We were happy and healthy, but then by fall, the sickness that has plagued the Kensington family ever since came. School had only been in session for a month before my mum died. I was allowed two weeks away from classes before I had to go back; everything felt different when I did. When I left, I was a kid with a happy family. When I came back, I had only one parent, and he terrified me.

My dad became someone I could no longer recognize; he became a monster. One day, after he stopped hiding his hateful nature from Maple Crest's public, Hayden's father and mine discussed something while Hayden and I were both present. I can't remember what it had been about. Whatever it was, though, hadn't gone how my dad had hoped. He used awful words, some of which I didn't understand the true meaning of until later, to describe the Williams family. Yet Hayden's father didn't appear to be phased by any of it. Despite my dad's insults, Hayden's dad remained proudly standing. When we were leaving, I saw him turn to Hayden and smile at him in spite of the verbal beating he'd just received. Then I watched as he shrugged off everything my father had said, as if it were nothing. Even as we were walking away, I couldn't stop staring at what I'd witnessed. I was in shock at the lesson of kindness Hayden had received rather than being the brunt of someone else's frustration. That was the first of many occasions where I saw Hayden interact with his perfect family.

So why did I hate Hayden?

I never did. I was jealous. I was jealous of his joy. Jealous of his family life. Jealous of his safety. Just...jealous of everything he had.

"Whatever, man," Hayden sighs, rolling both his eyes and shaking his head when I still don't reply. "I figured after all this time, and with everything that's different now, we could clear the air between us entirely. Guess not."

An ache has taken up residence in my chest. Too much is happening too fast. There are too many changes. Too much fear for Tatum. Too much annoyance at her parents. Too much out of my control. Just too. Fucking. Much.

He stands up and starts to walk out of the room, but I don't want that. I breathe easier when he's around. His presence is no longer something I loath, but something that helps.

The truth is long overdue. I've been a coward for too long by holding it back. Weak. Pathetic. He's right. After everything we've been through and, God willing, everything we will experience together when Tatum wakes up, he deserves to know it.

Closing my eyes, I try to pretend I'm admitting it aloud to only myself. If I don't see him, he's not here. That's what I used to tell myself with my father, at least.

"I didn't hate...*you*. Not really," I start. He waits silently for me to continue. "I hated that I wasn't you."

Opening my eyes, I dare myself to look up into his brown irises. People often associate blue with daytime and light. Yet that's all I see when I look deeper into the color brown right now. It reminds me of a warm setting sun in various landscapes. On the water, making it gold as it washes against the sand, as it shines through treetops creating slices of light along an autumn path. They're not a deep, dark brown shade. Rather, they're a shade that almost resembles precious gold on rare occasions when the sun hits them. I let the warmth of his stare wash over me after feeling cold from my admission, but I don't react to it in any way.

Hayden rapidly blinks a couple of times as he tries to make sense of the words that just filled the space between us.

There's a long pause, and then, "What?"

I huff a breath. "Yeah. So...after all this time, now you know."

Hayden lets out an uneasy chuckle and I guess his question before he even asks. "Why would you want to be me? You heard everything Tatum's dad said. I mean, I've had a pretty great life, but you've always had more than I did. More opportunities, more money. You had the chance to go to college doing something you liked and were actually able to finish all your classes."

"You had your mum. And happiness. At the end of the day, isn't that what really makes you a wealthy man?" His lips part, ready to free the words he's holding back in his mind, but then they close again.

Silence rests over us like a too-heavy blanket until, "I don't know how you put on a suit every day after you were beaten to hell. I can barely tolerate anything other than a loose sweatshirt. I'm going to bed. You coming?" My mouth pulls into a small grin and I nod, telling him I'll be there, as he continues forward to the bedroom.

I can count on one hand the people who have ever truly known me. My mom, Zara, Tatum...and Hayden. It's strange that someone I once couldn't stand to be around isn't just on that short list, but he proves his spot repeatedly. Like now, when he changed the subject after my uncomfortable confession. Without a doubt, I know that was solely for my sake. Not his.

Several minutes later when I walk into the bedroom, Lenny is curled up underneath Hayden's arm. Hayden is already asleep. Walking quietly to the bed, I slide onto the other side of the mattress. When my hand touches Lenny's soft fur, he lets out a small, tired chirp. I fall asleep with my hand on his back.

Chapter Thirty-Two

HAYDEN

Every day is the same. Wake up, take care of Lenny, ride to Ragsburrow, sit in the waiting room until visiting hours come to an end without us ever seeing Tatum. My parents have been extremely supportive and have brought us meals the past few days. They even bring enough for Tatum's parents, which nurses have been kind enough to take to them. Anthony doesn't think they deserve it. I was on the fence about it myself at first, but they're Tatum's parents, and she loves them. And I love Tatum.

Anthony has his laptop open, and he's tapping away on his keyboard when someone walking toward us catches my eye. I nudge his arm with the back of my hand to get his attention and straighten in my seat. Anthony looks at me, then follows my gaze to Tatum's parents as they come to a stop several feet in front of us.

"We don't agree with your relationship choices, but it's obvious you care for our daughter," her mom admits. Anthony closes his laptop. "There's still an hour left for the night. We'll see you tomorrow." As they start to walk away, Anthony and I meet each other's gaze before springing into action. We've been gifted an hour with our girl and I don't want to waste a single second.

Although Anthony's tried to convince me I shouldn't bear any, a wave of guilt washes over me anew when I see her. Like mine, Tatum's bruises are fading since it's been five days since the accident. Someone, either a nurse or one of her parents, has brushed her hair and put it in a neat braid.

"Hey Tate," I start. She looks like she's sleeping, which, I guess she is. It almost feels like if I talk too loud, I'll wake her up. Although if that were the case, why the hell am I nearly whispering?

Anthony doesn't say anything. He just sits in the chair beside her bed, props his elbows on his knees so he can rest his chin on his hands, and stares at her contemplatively.

This fucking sucks. All I want is to see her smile. The image of it has been engraved into my mind and even though there's no way I could ever forget it, I *have* to see it again. If begging and pleading could get her to wake up, then I'd spend as long as it took on my knees.

When our hour ends, I rake a hand through my hair, giving her hand a squeeze. "Wake up, Tate. Please." I look at her anxiously like that would actually have done the trick, but to no surprise, it doesn't. After kissing her fingers, I stand, feeling defeated and not yet ready to leave this room.

On the other side of the bed, Anthony still holds her hand even as he stands. The way he's looking at her is exactly like what you see in the movies where the guy looks at the girl when she isn't paying attention; his eyes filled with love. It's how everybody wants to be looked at.

"You need to wake up tomorrow, love. Lenny is waiting for you. So are we." It's the first time he's spoken in hours.

THE NEXT MORNING, we're walking back to the same seats we've been occupying for nearly a week now in the waiting room. Except, things are different this time. As they pass us on their way in, Tatum's parents stop to give us coffee and tell us we can see Tatum when they leave at noon for lunch.

It happens again the following morning. I'll admit, having days like this on repeat is much more tolerable than how the previous days had been. At least now we get to see her.

For the number of hours Anthony and I have spent sitting next to each other, one would think we'd now know everything there was to know about the other. But that's only if you didn't know Anthony at all. The truth is, we've hardly talked. Even after things changed between us, nothing *really* changed. Anthony doesn't act like being close to me will kill him, and when we do talk, it's a little nicer than what I'm used to coming from him. But still, it's Anthony. He's always quiet. As the days drag, he's got his attention buried in the pages of a book or the work on his laptop.

It's officially been a week since the coma started. Anthony and I have been in the waiting room for three hours today when a nurse walks in.

"Anthony and Hayden?"

"Yes?" I stand to meet her and can hear Anthony setting his book aside to do the same.

"Follow me, please." She starts walking away even as she's still giving us instructions. My large strides have me catching up to her pretty quickly.

"Is Tatum okay?" I ask. With the exception of that first day, we haven't been led by hospital staff like this so the change makes me nervous.

"Yes. Her parents asked me to grab you two. They said there's something you need to see." I glance back at Anthony and see him staring at the back of the nurse's head. He doesn't look happy. I can't say I'm too pleased with her either. She's being short and a little cold-shouldered. "This way," she corrects me when I start on the path toward Tatum's room.

We're led in another direction and I feel a lump in my throat. *If Tatum's fine, then why are we going to a different level of the hospital?* I try to school my features so the worry I'm currently feeling doesn't show on my face.

"Where are we going?" Anthony asks when we take another turn into a new part of the hospital.

"Right through here." The nurse gestures to a room at the beginning of the hall which has hope swelling in my chest.

The first thing I see after entering the new room is Tatum's parents. The second thing is Tatum staring back at me. Despite the fact she just spent the past week unconscious, she looks exhausted. But oh, she looks so beautiful. The color green never looked as good as it does now as she looks first at me, then at Anthony, then at me again. Nothing could wipe the massive smile off my face.

Confusion contorts her face. "Who are you?" *Nothing could wipe the massive smile off my face except that.* Like anchors have been tied to either side of my mouth, my smile falls. It fucking drops the deep dark depths of the earth. My mouth parts. *What did she just say?*

Beside me, I see Anthony's body tense in my peripheral vision. Tatum's voice is low and raspy after having a tube down it for seven long, miserable days. Maybe I didn't hear her right? Perhaps if I give her water, I'll be able to hear her clearly when she talks again.

A quiet, gravelly chuckle leaves her before she winces and touches her throat tenderly with her fingers. "I'm kidding. I remember you guys. How could I forget?"

"What the hell, Tatum?" I'm stunned. Mildly confused. A little angry, maybe? "That was really the first thing you wanted to say to us?" I scold.

"Come on, that was probably the only chance I'm ever going to get to mess with you like that. Besides, it's a classic. You love classics. You can't tell me you wouldn't have done the same thing," she croaks.

Just like that, the anger falls away and I'm smiling again. Shaking my head as I fill up a cup of water from the table in the room, I walk it over to her.

"You're right. I would've." She smiles up at me as she takes the cup and I brush her hair back before kissing the top of her head. "I'm so fucking glad you're awake."

Tatum swallows some water down then hands the cup back to me. "Mom? Dad? I'm really craving some Ben and Jerry's. Is it too much to ask that you get some for me? Please?"

"Sure, honey. We'll be back." Tatum's mom releases her hand, then grabs her purse. It was an obvious dismissal, but I'm glad for it. Anthony moves aside enough for her parents to get past, but no more than that.

"Kens?" Tatum questions. "It was just a joke. I remember you." She and I both take in the way his eyebrows are curved and how there are creases on his forehead. I can't tell if the look in his eyes is worry, relief, or something else entirely.

"You have an IV. That's it," he breathes.

She nods, unsurely. "Yeah. I have an IV and that's it. Are you okay?"

"You're okay." He breathes out in relief, but he still doesn't step forward. *What's going on?*

"Are you? I know I am." It's only when she confirms she's alright that he breaks from whatever it was that was holding him in place. Anthony grabs both sides of her face tenderly and kisses her.

"I am now, love." He kisses her again.

Chapter Thirty-Three

ANTHONY

Tatum is in surprisingly good spirits after her ordeal. She fell back asleep shortly after her parents returned without even eating a bite of the ice cream she'd asked for and has been in and out of sleep since. With her being moved out of the ICU to this new level of the hospital, more visitors are allowed, so we spend the day here with Tatum and her parents.

The next time she wakes up, she calls Nyasia but is asleep again by the time her friend arrives. Since Hayden and I hadn't been expecting Tatum's sudden return to consciousness, we weren't prepared to spend the night in Ragsburrow. But now that she's been relocated to the new floor, she doesn't have to be alone at night anymore and there's no chance in hell I'm leaving her. I just got her back.

Someone still has to feed Lenny and give him his medication in the morning though, so I give Nyasia my house key before she leaves to return to Maple Crest, along with the security codes to both the gate and the house.

Late the following morning, Tatum is sitting in a wheelchair being pushed by Hayden on her way out of the hospital. It's a moment I've been wishing for for days, and yet, was beginning to think wouldn't happen.

"Meet you two at my house?" she asks us once she's seated in her parents' car.

"Absolutely, gorgeous." Hayden kisses her cheek.

"Is there any chance you can bring—"

"Lenny?" I interrupt with a small grin. She smiles back, surely thinking about reuniting with the furball. "Of course. We'll see you there, love."

WELCOME HOME is written in obnoxious, colorful, bold letters across a banner that's been strung up in Tatum's living room. Nyasia went all out in terms of decorations to welcome her friend back. She and Tatum's parents are all in the living room with her when Hayden and I come in with Lenny's carrier in hand.

"Lenny!" Tatum shouts excitedly. He starts meowing and pawing at the door of his kennel to get to her as soon as she calls out to him. He doesn't stop purring or move from her side for hours.

Though mine and Tatum's homes are vastly different, they are the same in the way that neither have been set up to house guests so her parents elect to stay at the motel in town. They leave fairly early in order to check-in. Meanwhile, Nyasia declares she's staying the night, essentially kicking Hayden and I out so she can have a sleepover with Tatum who's just as happy to see her.

We kiss her goodnight, then he and I return to my house so he can pick up his duffel bag and the truck his parents are letting him borrow before he returns to his own place for the night. It'll be the first time in about two weeks he'll be going home. It will also be the first night in the same amount of time we won't be sleeping in the same room, and the first time in a week we won't be sleeping side-by-side. To be honest with myself, I'm not as thrilled about that as I thought I would be. Part of me stupidly wants to ask him to stay with me one more time.

Following me inside, Hayden doesn't go straight for his

belongings. He stops in the kitchen when I go to fill up a glass of water. His hands are placed flat on the island as he watches me.

"Want one?" I ask, holding up an empty glass. He nods, so I fill it up, placing it in front of him once it's full. It's so quiet here. There's no music, no indistinct chatter, no hum of machines. It's dark around us, too. The only light is coming from the room we're in. After spending a week worrying and wondering, it feels odd now to be standing here like there is with nothing to worry about. Benjamin is gone. Tatum is awake and back home where she belongs. I've even been given space from dealing with my dad in light of the circumstances. For the first time in a while, things are utterly normal.

So why does my chest feel so tight?

"Are you okay?" Hayden questions. He still hasn't touched his glass. I take another drink of mine. It's been a mentally draining past couple of days filled with surprises and people. Lots of people.

I'm beyond happy Tatum has been surrounded by love and support since she opened her eyes. I love that she has Nyasia with her tonight and her friend went above and beyond with the decorations to let her know she's been missed. I would have gladly stayed had she wanted me to. Without question, I would stay wherever she wanted me to.

But I'm not used to any of this. Hayden's parents driving an hour for the sole purpose of bringing us home-cooked meals. Tatum's parents bringing us coffee the last couple of mornings. Spending endless hours on the hospital floor where my mum died. Spending so much time around people when I usually seclude myself...I'd never tell anyone, but it was a lot to handle. Isn't that all so stupid?

"I'm fine," I state definitively. His bruises from the crash are fading, now showing in shades of yellow and green. I also note the bags clinging underneath Hayden's usually bright eyes. Perhaps he's as drained as I am. Finishing my water, I start to wash my cup in the sink. "I'm happy she's awake," I say, surprising myself a little for letting my feelings escape me into the space between us and creating an opening for conversation.

He heaves a sigh of relief. "Me too, man. Me fucking too."

His closed fist bounces against the granite countertop a couple of times, and I feel him looking at me. The moment our eyes meet, Hayden starts rounding the island quickly. Strong, calloused hands plant themselves on my cheeks. The next thing I know, I feel firm lips landing on mine as he starts to kiss me.

My eyes widen and I see how his are clenched tight. I stand frozen in place, trying to make sense of what's happening before my free hand lands on his hip. Giving in, my eyes close as I let the kiss continue. Deepening our connection, my mouth opens up for him. When it does, Hayden groans softly and I clench my fist into his shirt.

Holy shit. I can't believe this is happening, but now that it is, I realize I've wanted to feel his mouth on mine for so long. Hayden's kisses are fast and strong. He drags out my bottom lip as he pulls away. Almost as soon as he started, he's done.

"Figured it was about time we got that out of the way," he drawls, a breath away. Hayden's head dips for one more kiss, then walks to the bedroom to get his things. I'm still standing in front of the sink when he walks past the kitchen half a minute later, calling out that he'll see me tomorrow. Then the front door closes behind him.

Just like that, he's gone. Hayden kissed me and then left as if those ten seconds didn't just change everything. Or perhaps they didn't. Maybe, to me, the world stopped turning when our lips met, but it was nothing more than another kiss to him. Before I can give any more thought to what I'm about to do, my feet are carrying me swiftly to the door. It opens right as Hayden reaches his parents' truck.

"Hayden." He stops, still holding his duffel bag, but I keep walking forward. I only stop when I'm right in front of him, kissing him again.

"I'm Hayden to you now, huh? No more of my last name?" the prick jests when we're both breathless.

"Shut up," I instruct before pushing him against the vehicle and reconnecting our mouths. I hear the thump of his bag as it falls to the ground and then feel his hands start to explore my body. His mouth is demanding and strong, fighting mine for dominance. But his hands explore reverently. The combination of fast and rough in one place, with soft and slow in another makes me shiver. It's hard to focus. My attention bounces from his mouth to his hands repeatedly, unable to pick a sensation to focus on entirely.

Hayden's phone starts to ring, but neither of us stops what we're doing. I don't even think he hears it because his movements don't stutter. If anything, they increase in urgency as his body presses against me more. His hands are dragging lower down my hip toward where our groins are pushed together; where I can feel both of our hard-ons meet through the layers of fabric we're wearing. But when it starts to ring with a second call, he pulls his mouth away and puts his forehead on mine.

"I should probably get that," he mumbles, like it's the absolute last thing he wants to do. I know it's the last thing *I* want him to do right now. Hayden's eyes are closed and he's panting, taking a moment to collect himself, but he's still holding me to him when he digs into his pocket for his phone to answer the call. "Hello? No, I'm fine. Sorry, I didn't mean to worry you. Who's there right now? Okay, I'm on my way. See you in a few. Love you too, bye."

"Your parents?" *Great, bring up his parents as if your dicks weren't just rubbing up against each other.* I put some distance between us now that the moment has been interrupted.

"One of my sisters. With everything that's happened, they're a little paranoid when I don't get back to them quickly." I think of my own sister. She contacted me multiple times to see how Tatum was doing during the past week, but aside from that first night, she's shown no concern for me. Not that I want or expect her to.

It just feels odd when I get reminders of what typical sibling relationships should be like.

"I see." There's an awkward pause between us. "How many times were there just ten inches between us? You had every chance to make a move before now, but you never did. Why?" This is something I've been wondering about since the shift in our relationship a week ago.

"I would have moved the other nine if you had just moved the first one. All I needed was a sign that you wanted the same thing I did. After all this time, I got the confirmation I needed last week. Neither of us would want to start something during the uncertainty of Tatum's condition, though. But don't think I forgot the way you looked at me that first night. Now that everything's looking up, I didn't see a reason to hold back any longer. I don't know about you, but I've been holding that back for years."

I'm stunned. I shouldn't be. His tongue was in my mouth for fuck's sake and I can feel pre-cum leaking out of my dick because of him. Still, to hear him say he's been holding back for years surprises me.

"Oh," is all I find myself capable of saying. My sudden loss of vocabulary is frustrating since I'm not normally one to be speechless. I usually *choose* to be quiet. Not this time.

"I need to get going. My family is all waiting for me. I'll see you tomorrow at Tate's." Hayden throws his duffel bag into the bed of the truck.

"See you tomorrow."

The door of the old vehicle shuts loudly once he's seated and I watch him drive off, toward his family who's anxious to spend time with him after he distanced himself for everyone's safety for so long. When I get back inside, I text Tatum to see how she's doing. The fact I can ask her now makes it easier to breathe than it had been for an entire week. Tatum waking up and having no negative long-term effects is the biggest blessing I've ever received in my life.

A couple of minutes later, she sends a selfie of her and Nyasia cuddling together on the couch in front of the TV. She also tells me Maya bought a plane ticket and will be here in two days to spend some time with her as well. I smile, knowing how much her friends mean to her, and place my phone back down once I send my reply.

My home has always been my sanctuary. Aside from Zara and Tatum, I never liked people being here with me. But tonight, it's too quiet. Suddenly, the space is too big and empty. Everything else is changing. It might be time to make some adjustments around here as well.

Chapter Thirty-Four

ONE MONTH AND TWO WEEKS LATER

TATUM

"Stop it," Anthony directs from the doorway of my bathroom. I can see him in the reflection of the mirror. He's dressed immaculately. His suit is fancier for tonight's event than his usual everyday suits, and he's wearing a white shirt beneath his jacket rather than his usual choice of black. "You're thinking about the scar again. Don't. You look beautiful."

He's referring to the spot where Benjamin's knife had cut my throat. It's about four inches long and it's not the most gnarly scar, but it does draw attention. I'm lucky he didn't cut any deeper or a quarter of an inch to the side. That's what the doctors had told me, at least.

"She already knows that," Hayden chimes in as he comes up beside him. He's dressed in a suit as well, but this time it's one of his own, and he has a navy-blue tie around his neck. The color of which matches Anthony's watch, and my satin, floor-length sheath gown. "So, what's bothering you?" he asks me.

I vaguely remember the night Benjamin caused us to crash. I remember drifting in and out of consciousness after he'd attacked me. I remember my body being jerked and dragged along the pavement as he tried to move me, right before everything went still. The way it ended was the first thing that came back to me about that night, but there are still a lot of holes in the details. From what the doctors say, memory loss is completely normal, and things may come back to me over time. Honestly, though, I don't know if I ever want all the memories back.

One thing I didn't forget was how scared I was that night. Sometimes I have nightmares where everything is dark but yet the fear remains. Then suddenly, Benjamin springs out at me from the darkness. I've woken up several times screaming. So yeah, if I'm that terrified while I can't even remember the whole story, then I don't want to know what else happened. I'm probably better off without it.

In addition to the police still looking for Benjamin, Anthony has been doing what he can to search for him too. He told me how he asked Zara to join the search right away. Though, with how concerned she was for me, and how pissed off my story made her when I saw her after the attack, it was easy to tell she was going to join the search regardless of whether Anthony invited her or not. However, though he's not going to stop looking, Anthony is convinced we're searching for a corpse. The police showed me the crime scene photos. There was enough of Benjamin's blood on the road to suggest he more than likely died somewhere since he never showed up at any of the hospitals. Still, I can't sleep alone.

Hayden and Anthony don't bicker like they used to. And by 'they,' I mean Anthony, since he was the one to start things the majority of the time. Two words that would describe how I felt when I learned how the tragedy had brought them closer would be *shocked* and *thrilled*. It was Hayden who did most of the explaining, but I knew he was keeping some details to himself. Most likely for Anthony's sake. I could tell they thought I might be mad that things evolved while my brain was busy healing from trauma, but that isn't the case at all. The fact that we all share the same adoration for each other is incredible to me. With so much love between us, I can't understand why anyone could ever hate people in relationships like ours or think it's wrong.

At first, neither of my guys left my side for weeks, despite everything else going back to normal so quickly. Hayden returned to work shortly after I woke up. Even my parents and Maya left about a week later. I don't expect the world to stop turning because I went through some crap. It just feels weird. My life nearly ended.

"It's not the scar I'm worried about," I start to explain. "I'm worried about him coming back." There have been no more mysterious gifts or unexplainable events, but I still can't help but think 'what if' sometimes.

Both of my guys don somber expressions.

"I know, love. We're still looking for him. We'll find him, but for now, remember you're safe," Anthony assures me.

I turn around. There's a small swish from my dress dancing lightly across the floor with the simple movement. "Promise?" I ask.

Anthony steps forward, taking my hand. His silver eyes stare into mine as he raises our joined hands to his mouth and kisses my knuckles.

"I promise."

TWO HOURS LATER, we're entering a ballroom in Ragsburrow where Anthony's dad is hosting a gala. I have an arm linked through my men's, one on each side. This is our first time making an official statement about our relationship status. For me and Hayden, it doesn't really matter. All of Maple Crest pretty much already knows, and no one cares what we do. But for someone like Anthony who holds high status out of our small-town bubble, it does. Our relationship is no one's business but our own. Still, it makes me happy that tonight, they're both making a show that they're with me, and I'm with them.

Though, I suppose the point would be clearer if it were only the three of us. Nyasia is on Hayden's other side. She may be a little on the short side, but she is fierce and loyal. Maybe even a little intimidating at times. I'm not sure who was more concerned for my safety after what happened with Benjamin; my guys, or my friend.

Since she's never been to an event like this before but told me she's always wanted the chance to dress up like a princess, I thought this might be a fun way to try to pay her back. The black satin gown she's wearing looks like it was made specifically for her with the way it fits tightly to her figure. It has one sleeve that extends up to her neck, wrapping around it delicately, and sparkling crystals adorn the dress. They're thicker in some areas and more spaced out in others, creating beautiful designs which sparkle in the light. Undoubtedly, she'll be pulling a lot of atten-tion tonight. She deserves to.

"Come with me to grab some drinks?" Hayden asks her. Nyasia links her arm through his and he tells us they'll be back before disappearing into the crowd.

Anthony and I continue further into the room, away from the door to make room for more guests. We don't make it far before I notice Zara standing beside her dad. Zara's emerald-green gown leaves her arms uncovered and I can see they're bare of tattoos as well, not just material. She covered them up for tonight's event. Unfortunately, avoiding Clay the entire night isn't an option, so Anthony decides to go up to him now and get it over with.

"Ah. My other disappointing child," Clay declares just loud enough for Anthony to hear him and with no apparent regard for his son's feelings. His English accent is thick, and he doesn't attempt to sound any other way but patronizing.

It's a fight to restrain from making a face at his callous words. A disappointment? Anthony is anything but. He has several accomplishments and skills. But more impressive than that, he was raised by a bitter, greedy, dreadful man and still grew up to be good-hearted. Sure, he's a little sharp around the edges, but he isn't razor-blade sharp.

"It's good to see you too, Dad," Anthony replies, though there's no emotion in his statement. He turns his attention to his sister and gives her a small smile. "You look beautiful." Standing next to Zara is, I assume, her girlfriend. The young woman is as pretty as Zara explained. Her skin is dark brown, as is her hair, though it's mixed with red in stunning locs which have been pulled back.

"Thanks." Zara returns the smile. "You look good too." *Goodness. I don't know what kind of crap happened between them, but it's so fucking obvious they both want to fix it and get things back to normal.* In public, they act like the perfect siblings. But away from curious eyes and cameras, they're so cold with each other. They each have defensive gates up, not knowing that all they have to do is open the door because it's unlocked.

"You're late. You were supposed to be here twenty minutes ago," Clay scolds before taking a sip from his champagne glass.

Anthony dips his chin. "I'm sorry, I lost track of time."

Clay's gray eyes slip to me, looking me up and down, before returning to his son. "You mean your girlfriend was slow to get ready."

"I meant what I said." Tension in this group is thick and while father and son stare each other down, Zara's girlfriend and I share an uncomfortable glance. I want to introduce myself but feel like it might be awkward to stick my arm between the two men for a proper handshake. They might lunge at each other and my arm will become nothing more than a casualty of war.

"Oh, for God's sake," Zara mutters as she pushes Anthony

back a little so she can step between them. *As if you and Anthony are any better.* "Tatum, that dress is fantastic. It suits you well. Meet my girlfriend, Kiara."

With the tension broken, I extend my hand to greet Kiara. Not twenty seconds later, Clay interrupts me as I'm talking to her.

"Cameras are coming this way. Anthony, Zara, it's time for a picture. Tara should stand out of the shot." *Ouch. Okay.*

Before Anthony has time to say anything, a reporter for the event begins to ask Clay questions about the gala and the fundraiser it's for. When the camera is raised, Clay gives Anthony a quick, pointed look before posing with his daughter, smiling at the lens. I start to step away, but Anthony grabs me by the waist and pulls me into him. Instead of looking at the camera, he looks at me, a small smirk on his face right before he plants his mouth on mine. After the flash goes off signaling the picture has been taken, Clay and the reporters share a few more words before they move on to other people.

"Care to explain what that was?" Clay questions Anthony once we're alone again.

"Did they take the picture already?" Anthony asks, pulling away from me, but not moving far. "I didn't notice, my attention was entirely on *Tatum*." Clay steps closer to him and I can see the barely restrained rage in his father's eyes. My smile falters. That action and how Anthony holds his breath now makes me realize Clay is a man worse than I had initially thought. It's easy to tell now that Anthony has kept dark pieces of his past locked away.

"Tonight is about more than making money for the fundraiser. I'm making money for the family as well. Meaningful connections. To do that, I need you to look available tonight." He looks at me and grabs Anthony's arm, pulling him away from the rest of us. I look at Zara, but she shakes her head. I barely hear the rest of Clay's words above the noise in the room. As he starts to speak again, I'm joined by Hayden and Nyasia, who seem to have read the tension because they stay silent. "I told you to come unaccompanied, and yet you brought a brothel. There's a bid on you tonight and I expect you to follow through as usual. Understood?" Clay doesn't wait for a response. He walks away, leaving Anthony behind.

At first, Anthony doesn't move. But a moment later, he returns to me, taking a champagne flute from Hayden. After swallowing nearly half of his glass' contents, he and Zara make eye contact and she raises her eyebrows in question. He nods, and she excuses herself and Kiara a second after their silent communication ends.

"What did he mean by 'a bid?'" I ask Anthony quietly as he slips an arm around my waist again.

"Think of it like an auction for a date," he answers casually.

"Oh." Every woman in this room is rich and pretty, and haven't stopped staring at Anthony since we walked through the doors. Not that I could blame them. I wonder how many of them have bid already. Or plan to. "And...are you going to go on this date?"

"No, of course not," he replies as if it were already obvious. Perhaps it should have been, but I'm beginning to understand how much Clay controls his children's lives. I wasn't sure *no* would even be an option for Anthony.

His reaction when Clay got close to him and his and Zara's previous mention about punishment for disobedience comes to mind. "What will happen if you don't? Should we leave?" I gesture to myself, Hayden, and Nyasia.

"Nothing I can't handle, darling. I promise. And no, don't leave. He said to look available, but I'm not, and I don't care to say otherwise."

"Are you sure?"

"Kiss my lapel."

"What?" His statement throws me off. He doesn't want me to kiss his cheek, neck, or lips like any normal boyfriend would. Nope. He said lapel. As in his shirt.

Hayden chuckles at my reaction. Even Anthony smiles.

"Kiss my lapel," he repeats. "Right here." He taps the collar of his white shirt. This is only the third time since we met months ago that I've ever seen him in any other color besides black, excluding the silver and blue of his watch.

Leaning forward and grabbing his arm to steady my balance, I press my lips firmly against the bright fabric. When I pull back, there's the perfect impression of my red-painted lips staining the material.

"There. Now there will be no reason for people to question if I am involved, if for some reason you find the desire to leave me at any point tonight." I grin up at him. His smile is so bright I swear his gray eyes shine as if they were stars and suddenly the chorus of Taylor Swift's '*Lover*' plays in my head.

"And how do you want me to leave my mark on the other side?" Hayden voices beside us, a teasing lift to his dark eyebrows. "Unfortunately, my lips are naturally this perfect shade, no lipstick required, so I can't pull the same move."

Anthony uses his middle finger to scratch an itch on his nose I'd be willing to bet was never really there. When his hand drops, he fixes Hayden with a severely sarcastic grin. "Piss off."

Hayden laughs and I wish I could bottle the sound. "Don't worry, I'll make my mark later," he quips with eyes filled with promise. I see the corners of Anthony's mouth twitch into a smirk, a real one, and something in my core heats up with excitement.

Beside Hayden, Nyasia is struggling to stop giggling long enough to take a drink. "Atta boy," she grins behind the rim of her glass.

Chapter Thirty-Five

TATUM

Since we all knew it was going to be a late night at the gala and none of us would be up for the task of driving back to Maple Crest, let alone be sober enough, we reserved two hotel rooms in the city ahead of time. There's one for Nyasia across the hall, and one for me and my guys. Both rooms are Anthony's treat. Hayden and I insisted we split the cost three ways, especially me because he's taking care of my friend too, but he wasn't having it. He set us up in some fancy building that has too many rooms in our reserved space for us to only be staying a few hours since we'll be driving back in the morning. I mean, seriously, our hotel room has a living room with an amazing couch. Nyasia wouldn't have minded sleeping there at all.

Walking to the large windows, I gaze out at the abundance of city lights filling the view far below us. After spending so much time in my small, cabin-like home in Maple Crest on the outskirts of town, I nearly forgot what a view like this looked like.

Anthony comes up behind me, placing his hands on my waist before kissing my neck.

"You look so beautiful in this dress," he murmurs into my skin and I angle my head to give him better access.

"Your dad looked pissed before we left. Was it about you not partaking in the date auction like he wanted?" I can't help but ask. The cold look his father gave Anthony when he didn't respond to his instructions promised retribution. I don't even know the man. Still, his angered stare sent chills down my spine.

Anthony turns me away from the window so I'm facing him and hovers his lips above mine. "Let's not talk about my dad right now," he whispers before kissing me. The kiss is slow and relaxed, like we have all the time in the world and tonight will never end. I hope it doesn't.

I'm so engrossed in this kiss and the slight taste of champagne on Anthony's tongue that I don't hear Hayden come up behind me. I only realize he's there when my loosely curled hair is being gathered and draped over one of my shoulders. Anthony continues to caress his tongue over mine as Hayden presses his lips to my pulse point on the other side of my neck.

The zipper for my dress is located right on the curve of my ass since it has such a low back, and I make a satisfied sound when Hayden starts to pull it down. With the zipper undone, he runs his hands leisurely up the bare skin of my back until he reaches my shoulders. Then, he pushes the thin straps of the dress over the curve of my arms and pushes the gown down my body until it pools at my feet, all while kissing my neck and shoulder. Standing between them, I'm left in only my heels since I didn't bother wearing a strapless bra or want to run the risk of panty lines. I can feel the warmth of Hayden's surprised breath when he realizes what I'm wearing. Or rather, not wearing.

Pulling away from Anthony, I turn so I can kiss Hayden and Anthony's hands take over running across my bare skin. The room is cold, but Hayden's amber scent fills my nose and warms me. As does his tongue and hands, which are now cupping my cheeks. Several moments later, I move my lips away from his.

"Thanks for the help undressing." He smiles and moves to

kiss me again, but I put a finger to his lips to stop him and he freezes. "I'm going to go take a shower now." I leave him gaping as I walk toward where I assume the bathroom will be. The sway of my hips is definitely being exaggerated, but when I look over my shoulder and see them both practically salivating at the sight of me, I know it was worth it. Having both men stare at me like I'm the most incredible thing they've ever seen does wonders for my confidence. "Well? Are either of you joining me, or am I going to be showering alone?" After a quick glance at one another, both men snap into action, taking large steps toward me as I continue for the bathroom.

A couple of minutes later, the three of us are naked and stepping under the warm spray of the shower. Luckily, and to no surprise, the elegance of the room didn't end at the bathroom. The shower is huge, with glass walls on three sides and gray tiles on the back. There are two shower heads, each on opposite walls. Both are massive with excellent water pressure.

There's hardly any space between me and the guys as my body once again becomes sandwiched between theirs. Each man has soap on their hands that they start rubbing into my skin. Anthony is massaging the soap across my arm and breasts while Hayden moves up my legs at a lazy pace up to my hips. Both men are over six feet tall. I should feel small being trapped between them when Hayden stands back up to his full height, but I don't.

"I can't believe you weren't wearing anything under that dress all night and I had no idea," Anthony groans.

I give my head a sassy little jerk. "I figured it would make a fun surprise."

"Oh, it was," Hayden chimes in. Based on the fact I can feel his hard dick against my back right now and Anthony's against my stomach, I have no doubt that it was. But they're lucky because they had no idea. For hours, I was turned on and wanting them but couldn't do anything about it at the gala. I've been so desperate for relief for so long that my pussy is practically throbbing.

"Remember the hallway during our little pool party?" I ask Anthony. His ashen eyes widen before flashing with unmistakable heat.

"How could I forget?" he purrs. Anthony lifts one of my legs and holds it against his hip. With his other hand, his fingers move to my center and rub a couple of circles around my clit before inserting them in-between my legs. I've been wet for hours, so his two long fingers slide in easily. He's barely to his knuckle when a satisfied moan leaves me. Once his fingers are as far as possible, he starts to pump them in and out. It's not long before I'm breathing heavily and rocking against his hand.

Hayden runs a hand into my hair and grips it enough to not hurt, but so he can tilt my head back and kiss my jaw. His free hand reaches around and massages one of my breasts.

"I knew I'd interrupted something that day." One would think he'd be bitter, but he's not. There's a slight smirk on his perfect lips before our mouths connect. Pleasure floods through me, coming from both the man at my front and the one at my back. Having to ground myself, I grab hold of Anthony's wrist. He immediately stills.

"No, don't stop. Keep going," I pant. His fingers start to work inside me again and when he crooks his finger to rub against the perfect spot, I cry out in pleasure and bring my other arm over my head to crook around Hayden's neck. "Oh my God," I moan loudly into Hayden's mouth. I let go of Anthony's wrist and grip his dick instead. When I run my thumb over the tip, he shudders.

Lifting my head to watch Anthony's fingers work, I let my eyes enjoy the journey down his body. Water is beaded on his arms and chest where little streams run down and over the muscles of his torso. They're not as dark or defined as Hayden's but impressive nonetheless, and I get the urge to run my tongue up his body, drinking in the taste of the water and him.

Hayden must have felt a similar urge because the next thing I know, he's leaning forward, pressing me even tighter between them, and latching his mouth onto Anthony's collarbone.

Anthony gasps softly but his fingers don't stop pumping, bringing me closer and closer to euphoria, and I start pumping him, too.

"What are you doing?" Anthony asks him, his voice strained with pleasure. Since the accident, I've seen them get intimate from time to time but not often, and nothing major. It's all been very middle school between them. With me, these men are experts at the craft. Each touch of their hands on my skin is confident and skillful. But when it comes to each other, they're overly cautious. It's easy to tell they want to experience what it's like to pleasure the other person, but they usually act nervous of how the other might react. Yet there's nothing hesitant about the way Hayden is kissing and sucking at Anthony's collarbone now, making him throw his head back against the glass wall of the shower.

"I'm marking you. I said I would." Hayden pulls away from Anthony long enough to say before going back to licking him.

"Oh fuck," Anthony groans. Removing his fingers from me, Anthony grabs my hips and plants them firmly down against his thigh, rocking me back and forth. I know he'd rather pick me up and sit me down on his dick, but he knows I don't like the idea of having sex without a condom. It's not that I'm worried about whether or not we're all clean, because I know we are. It's because I'm not going to risk getting pregnant and I'm not taking birth control. But neither of us is about to stop what we're doing here long enough to run to the other room for a condom.

Between my pumping him with a tight fist and Hayden's attention, Anthony's whole body becomes a shaking mess as he nears release. He curses again breathlessly as he spills into my hand. Seeing him get his pleasure from us brings me close to my own release. Sensing this, Hayden quickly drops to his knees and spins me around so my back is now pressed to Anthony's front. I can feel the rise and fall of it underneath me as he tries to catch his breath.

"Give me your leg," Hayden instructs with a pat on his shoulder, showing me where he wants me to put it. Anthony supports my body so I don't slip on the wet shower floor while I drape one leg over Hayden's shoulder. His tongue is on my clit in a second and in less than a minute I'm a grinding, whimpering, pleading mess. My fingers are clenched into his wet hair so tightly I have the brief thought I might be hurting him, but I can't stop myself and the thought gets swept away with the next swipe of his tongue.

"I'm...so...close," I pant, though it sounds more like a whine.

Anthony has been nipping at my jaw and tenderly kissing my neck this whole time. "You didn't tell us you were bare beneath your dress tonight. You still think we should let you come?" His hands are massaging my breasts as he talks.

"Mhmm," I whimper. If I don't come soon, I'll probably combust. I've been waiting all night for this.

"Say please," he instructs. I'm too lost in the pleasure Hayden's tongue in my vagina brings to reply. That is until he pulls out and bites my inner thigh, just enough to cause a slight sting to make me focus.

"Say it, gorgeous," Hayden directs.

"Please," I beg now, my hips rolling forward, looking desperately for more contact. Hayden buries his face between my thighs again as a reward for my answer. He licks me with more fervor this time and I can feel my legs getting weak from the amount of shaking they've been doing.

"The next time you decide to leave the house without anything underneath your clothes, you will tell us and give your panties to either me or Hayden beforehand. Got it?" *Holy. Shit.* I love this side of Anthony. It's hot as hell. Between the two of them, Hayden is usually the more dominant one when it comes to sex. Both men know exactly what they're doing, they just have different styles. Since I can't possibly form any words right now, I nod. Thankfully, he accepts it as enough of an answer. "Make our girl come, Hayden." Fuck. Yeah, those five words are going to be what takes me over the edge during my alone sessions from now on.

Hayden inserts a finger and crooks it at the right angle, right as he sucks hard on my swollen clit. I don't bother muffling myself. I scream my release. Hayden remains on his knees with his tongue on me as I ride it out on his face. When I start to come down from my high of the orgasm, I feel him gather my come on his tongue. Then he stands and holds the back of Anthony's neck. Both men lean forward and when their mouths meet, Hayden shares with Anthony the taste of me during their intimate kiss. There's nothing cautious or hesitant between them now and if I hadn't just barely come, the sight of them would get me right where I needed to be.

"It's your turn," Anthony mutters to him through half-closed, lust-filled eyes as he pushes Hayden back a couple of steps. As Hayden had done for me, Anthony goes to his knees in front of him. The mark Hayden left on his collarbone is clearly visible to me now. I'm not the biggest fan of hickeys since they seem juvenile to me in most cases. *Most* cases. Not this one. In this instance, I am hickey's biggest fan.

I watch as Anthony tilts his head back to meet Hayden's shocked gaze. The way Hayden's eyes are wide and his mouth is forming a little *o* is so at odds with the way he was moments ago. The difference almost makes me laugh, but I manage to hold it in.

"You don't have to do that," Hayden reminds him, a hand pressed against Anthony's wrist to stop him from touching his dick.

"I know. I want to." A playful grin spreads on Anthony's face. "It's not quite ten inches, but I'm making a move, anyway."

Hayden laughs at the reference I don't fully understand, his white teeth showing thanks to the size of his smile. He takes his hand off Anthony's wrist, allowing him access to his body. Anthony resumes his progress towards Hayden's rock-hard dick and when his large hand fists around Hayden's shaft. I hear the quiet gasp that leaves Hayden's mouth at the touch. Knowing this is a big moment and wanting to watch it unfold, I take a couple of steps back so I can get a better view. From my new angle, I can clearly see Anthony lick up the shaft. Hayden's chest is practically quivering already. The moment Anthony takes him in his mouth, Hayden groans.

"Holy. Fucking. Christ," he grunts as Anthony sucks him down.

Hayden doesn't seem to know where to put his hands. I see him reach for Anthony, but he seems unsure about the movement, so I step forward and bring his hands to my breasts. Our tongues connect a second later, and he kisses me with a new form of desperation and hunger.

"You usually have such a dirty mouth when your clothes are off," I tease him. "Stop biting your tongue."

Hayden's whole body jerks from something Anthony does. "Fuck that's good. That's so good. Shit," he moans loudly and grips my hair with a firm hand, bringing me back in for more kisses. Anthony runs a hand up my leg and squeezes my ass as he continues to suck Hayden off. We stay in our positions for another couple of minutes before Hayden finally comes. He was the last of us to reach that point, but he came the hardest. But this is just the beginning.

I'm really fucking glad Nyasia has her own room because we end up using the couch once we're out of the shower and the condoms are within reach. Then the counter. Next, the floor. And, of course, the bed. The three of us remain occupied with each other for hours and don't get a minute of sleep by the time we have to leave in the morning. I'm exhausted, but I wouldn't change a single thing.

Chapter Thirty-Six

TATUM

"Y"ou're going away so you can murder someone?" I demand.

"Wha—? No, I'm not going to murder anyone, love," Anthony assures me on my porch two days later.

"I might," Zara chimes in from where she's standing, leaning against Anthony's Audi. "But we haven't received the assignment yet, so I'm not certain." Anthony clenches his jaw and looks at the sky before turning around and wordlessly pointing at the car. She rolls her eyes and flips him off but gets in. When he turns around again, I look at him with my eyebrows raised and eyes screaming, *See? I knew someone was getting murdered!* I remember what happened the last time his dad sent him away. I don't like this.

He chuckles. *Chuckles* at my worry over this and tugs me gently toward him until I'm comfortably being held within his arms.

"Darling, look at me. Zara is only messing with you. I'm not going to be doing any 'shady mafia shit' as you like to call it, and no one is going to die. I'm just going away for some low-level grunt work no one wants to do."

"Then why do you have to go?" I assumed that by being the head man's son, he was far past doing grunt work. What even was grunt work for the mafia, anyway?

Wait, not the mafia. *But close enough.*

I don't know. I don't ask for all the information. Anthony told me he would tell me anything I wanted to know whenever I wanted to hear it, but I kind of like being in the dark. So, I told him not to give me the dirty details about anything. At least, for now. Further down the line, maybe in a few more months, I'll be ready to hear all the truths. But not now. I'm still recovering from my own madness. It's probably best not to add on to it.

Anthony's jaw ticks. "The gala. You were right about your assumption in the hotel the other night. He's pissed I disobeyed his orders."

It occurs to me that as far as I know, Zara did everything he asked. "Why is your sister being punished?"

"She's not," he corrects me, taking a second to kiss the top of my head before continuing. "She's repaying the favor of when I went for her. Plus," he takes a quick glance at the Audi, "we're working things out. It's been...nice."

Unease fills me, but it's hard to tell if it's because I'm worried about what type of potentially illegal activities he'll be up to, or if it's because the brewing storm is starting to get worse. Rumbling thunder is starting to get closer, and the clouds getting darker as the storm moves into Maple Crest. I used to love this weather. It was one of the main reasons why I moved here in the first place. But ever since everything happened with Benjamin, it scares me. Thunder reminds me of Benjamin moving around my house. Rain makes me think of the crash. Lightning has two effects on me now; I'm either scared the flash is someone's camera taking a picture of me, or I'm scared the momentary light is going to show me something I don't want to see. I hate that he ruined something I loved so much on top of everything else.

"I'm really happy to hear that, Kens." Leaning up on my toes,

I kiss him. "You better get out of here before the wind picks up, and the storm gets worse. Be safe. Text me."

He kisses my lips again, then my cheek, my nose, and my forehead. "No need to worry about my safety, love. There's not a single thing in this world that could stop me from coming back to you. Ever. I'll *call* you every chance I get." Anthony kisses me one more time and then leaves. As I watch him drive off, there's a single word that echoes quietly in my mind. It's the same one I've thought about with both of my guys so many times lately, but it can't be right. Surely, it's too soon to be feeling something this strong. Then again, maybe it isn't, given the circumstances we've been through together. We've gone through a lot. More than most couples will ever experience in a short amount of time. Every single one of us has been individually tested by the universe. As has our relationship, but we've remained intact and resilient.

Maybe it isn't too soon. Maybe it's — *we're* — meant to be. Maybe I should tell them that I am completely, utterly in love with them.

Nyasia is house and cat-sitting, so I can spend the weekend with Hayden at his house. The cabin he calls home is beyond adorable. It's small, with only one large room and a bathroom on the side. Unlike Anthony's home, there are framed pictures of family and personal belongings everywhere. The place looks very much lived in. Not in a messy way, but a comfortable one. Well-worn work boots line up on a shoe rack by the door beneath hung-up jackets and flannels. Colorful quilted blankets he says his mother made are stacked in a pile in the corner. There's a pile of wood beside the cast iron fireplace that can double as a small stovetop. The place is warm and smells earthy, most likely from the woodpile and cracked open windows. Everything here was chosen with the intention of comfort, and Hayden's home definitely fills that role.

Unlike Anthony and I, Hayden doesn't have bookshelves filled with books. But he does have a small pile of them stacked on top of his dresser. A couple of which are left over from his time in college. The rest are about art he got on his own accord with the one on top being open to a picture of an 1850 painting by artist William-Adolphe Bouguereau. The piece is titled *Dante and Virgil in Hell* and, although it's slightly terrifying to look at, the detail is astonishing.

The first time I was here, Hayden was shedding himself from his jacket and shaking rain from his hair when he said, *"It's not a mansion, but it does the job."* No, it's not a mansion, but it's perfect. It's a mix of all the things that make Hayden who he is and it's the ideal place to be creative. Anthony has a luxury house full of impressive and convenient things. But Hayden has a home.

Once we put my stuff in the house and eat a quick lunch, one of his sisters meets up with us so we can go for a hike. I've met a lot of Hayden's family in the past few weeks. The entire William's family is so accepting and fun, it feels like we've been friends for years.

His parents? They're the most amazing people I think I've ever met. My own parents are great, but they're a little distant sometimes. Supportive, but really only if you're doing what they had planned for you. I get the feeling Hayden's parents would accept their kids no matter what they did, so long as they weren't hurting themselves or others. In return, they have unwavering love and respect from their five kids.

Upon returning from our hike and saying goodbye to his sister, Hayden suggests I paint while the memories of the excursion are still vivid. After the accident, I didn't have the desire to pick up a paintbrush for weeks. My mind was occupied with trying to understand what happened and how things went from a text to an attempted abduction so quickly. The day I picked up a paint brush again was a couple of weeks ago. I was by myself and didn't move for hours. Reuniting myself with my passion was healing and continues to be exactly what I need. Which is why Anthony surprised me with a transport box for my paints and brushes, and Hayden packed it for the weekend so I can paint while I'm here.

I spend the next half an hour or so sketching my design onto the canvas he had me bring before I sit back and gaze at it to make sure I've got my idea down perfectly.

"Got it down?" Hayden asks. His muscled arm comes into view, along with the ceramic mug filled with some sort of steaming liquid.

"Yeah, I—" My eyes widen when I look at him and I start to laugh but quickly cover my mouth. "What are you doing?" I ask between chuckles. Hayden is bare-chested, his jeans hanging low on his hips, and he has my paint brushes tucked into the waist-band. The handles are hidden behind his jeans while the bristles are lined up along his abs.

He looks down at himself and then back up at me, planting his hands firmly on either side of his pelvis. "I've got to be honest, honey, that was not the reaction I was expecting. In fact, it was a bit of a blow to the ego. Nyasia said I should try this sometime, but I think now she was messing with me."

I pin him with a stare. "Trust me, your ego will be just fine." Setting my pencil down, I swivel in my seat so I'm facing him. "You surprised me, that's all. Don't worry, *honey*, I think this is hot."

The corner of his lip lifts up and his brow raises. "Yeah?"

"Yeah," I confirm, my voice taking on a sultry tone. Standing up, I take the necessary step to close the majority of space between us. He's so much taller than me that by being this close, I nearly have to tilt my head all the way back to meet his eyes. Picking a brush at random without taking my eyes off of his, I start to pull it from his pants. *Slowly.* I also make sure to angle it so the tip of the handle drags lightly against his skin. When I feel his muscles clench and see goosebumps arise on his skin, I know it has the desired effect. "Thank you," I whisper against his ear, having leaned up on my tiptoes.

I hear him swallow, but his voice is steady when he answers. "My only request is that the brushes aren't removed so lightly."

The reason why dawns on me quickly, and I chuckle again. "Are you...no. You are, aren't you? You're ticklish!" His mouth opens. Closes. Then opens again with denial, but it's too late. His secret has already been discovered. "You're really going to say I'm wrong?"

"Yes," he lies to me loudly.

"Let's put it to the test then," I dare him.

He pauses and then agrees. "Let's." Hayden adjusts his stance while I look at the brushes in his waistband. Finally selecting one, I repeat the same move I'd done with the first brush, but get a reaction so small I'm not sure there even was one. But I know I read him correctly before and that he is in fact ticklish, so I try something else. I run the feather-soft bristles across his sharp jawline. His eyes flutter closed before opening again. "That doesn't tickle, but it sure as hell turns me on. If you want, we can switch roles and I can be the one running the brush up and down your body. You can even put a blindfold on if you're feeling daring. We can see how your nipples and pu—" he stops talking when I carefully pat his cheek with the handle.

"Shh. We'll do that later. Right now, I'm on a mission." He laughs and lets me continue my exploration. Hayden's body is addicting. It's fitting that he loves famous pieces of art, particularly marble statues. Had a sculpture been carved with his body as a reference, it would no doubt draw crowds.

The soft bristles run lightly over every curve and muscle I admire. To his credit, Hayden stands perfectly still. *Maybe I was wrong about him being ticklish after all.* After taking my sweet time exploring his body, I make eye contact with him again. Then he snaps.

Lunging forward, Hayden pulls me into him. Our kisses are

wild and energetic. Exactly what I need after being so up close and personal with his skin but not touching it myself.

"You have no idea how hard it was to stand still," he admits as he pulls my shirt over my head, leaving me in my bra.

"I knew it!" I shout victoriously a second before he crashes his mouth against my chest. Apparently being ticklish is Hayden's weak spot and the perfect way to get him in the mood. His hands run all over my skin as we start to move toward the bed, but the next thing I know, we're falling through the air and crashing against the ground. Shocked, I look for the problem and discover Hayden slipped on the rag I use to dry my brushes after I wash them.

He and I see it at the same time and he pinches the bridge of his nose, laughing. "Are you okay?"

"I'm okay," I assure him. A phone starts ringing then and Hayden looks first at the clock on the stove then moves quickly to get up.

"That might be Nick," he announces hopefully, more to himself than to me. Nick picked up and moved out of town a few days ago. There was no warning or anything. He just left. Hayden has tried to call him a dozen times, but all he gets in return are text messages. From what I heard, Nick is now with his girlfriend and wants some time alone after so long apart before he resumes his nightly phone calls with Hayden. It makes sense, I suppose, but I still feel bad for my boyfriend. I can't imagine what it would be like to have my best friend since childhood pick up and leave without so much as a goodbye. When I see the hopeful look fade from his face, I know it isn't Nick on the other line. "It's Kens." I give him a sad look as he hands me the phone, but he just shrugs it off.

Chapter Thirty-Seven

TATUM

I wish I could say it was a cloudless night as Hayden and I cuddle on his hammock. But it's not. We only catch occasional glimpses of the stars but when we do, they're bright and beautiful. The bugs surrounding the area create a symphony for us as I lay in his arms. The music from the insects reminds me of nights back in Dallas at my parents' estate. It's nearly as loud as a summer night in the South.

Hayden has his arms around me in a firm hold. He's not clutching onto me, but it's not a relaxed hold either, so I know something is on his mind as we lightly sway.

My mind has been a little occupied tonight too. The dark scares me now and my guys know this, but I was the one who insisted we sit out here. I only agreed to it because Hayden loves the way things gleam out here. Stunning lights are wrapped around the trees holding up either side of the hammock and there are more strung around his back porch. It puts me more at ease, but I still wonder occasionally if there's someone lurking where the orange glow can't reach.

"Do you ever think it's weird?" Hayden snaps out of wherever his thoughts were and hums in question. "That everything went back to normal so quickly," I voice the thought I've been having on and off for a while now.

He thinks about his answer for a few seconds. "Yes, I do," he answers honestly. "My first day back at work after the crash and after you woke up was...weird. One day, I'm practically in protective custody, then end up in a crash that could have killed us. I *shot* at someone. Emptied the damn magazine. After that, I sat in a waiting room while you were fighting for your life. Then, suddenly, I'm cutting wood again? I mean, you know what it's like. You don't want people fussing over you twenty-four-seven. It's just a little hard to comprehend."

My shoulders slump into his body, the weight of guilt pressing on me again. His life was so normal before he became a part of mine.

"Yeah," I mutter, reaching for his hand, intertwining our fingers. "I know how you feel."

He tilts his head to look down at me. "I'll tell you what though, I'm also glad things are back to normal. Because normal means that we get to do this and I'm pretty damn happy to be here with you right now." Hayden tries to fight it, but the smile that curved his mouth falters. "For a little while there, I was starting to think we'd never get the opportunity to do something like this again."

I tilt my neck up so I can kiss him. No tongue, or any sort of heat. Just the press of my lips against his.

"But we are here, and I'm not going anywhere, so we'll have so many opportunities to do things like this. So much so that I'm going to make you sick of me, Hayden Williams." He laughs and shakes his head, the rumble in his chest making my heart flutter.

Hayden looks down at our joined hands where his thumb is rubbing circles on my skin. "Tate, I know you told me I didn't need to say this before, but I do. I have to. These words have been eating at me for weeks and I can't stand the feeling of you not hearing them any longer." I know what words he's referring to without even having to ask. He tried to say them the day I woke up, but I wasn't having it. Those were the last words I wanted to hear from him. Although, now, seeing how much it's affecting him to keep them to himself...I nod my head and brace myself for the emotional impact this conversation will bring. "I am so, *so* sorry for what happened."

Even though I was telling him I'd hear him out when I nodded my head, I can't stop myself from interrupting his apology. "You really don't have to say that to me, Hayden. You didn't do anything wrong."

His brown eyes are so full of hurt as he no doubt recalls the night of the crash. "Yes, I do. Please, just hear me out. I was driving the truck. It was raining. I mean, what the hell was I thinking? I should've slowed down, not sped up."

"You were thinking that there was danger and you wanted to get us the hell away from it. Do you have any idea how many people would have pressed the same pedal you did?"

Hayden shakes his head and I see him gnaw his bottom lip. Cupping my palm to his cheek, I sit up straighter while trying to keep my balance on the hammock.

"You saved my life. You have nothing to be sorry for." I look from one of his chocolate eyes to the other. "I love you," I tell him earnestly.

I heard him say those words to me when I was in the hospital. It was the first night after the coma was reversed and they had moved me to another floor of the hospital since I was stable. While fentanyl was running through my veins, I woke up to find Hayden holding one of my hands in both of his. His shaggy-haired head was resting on top of our joined hands, and I heard him whisper the words before kissing my fingers. I didn't just hear the words then. I felt his love, too. But I didn't know for certain what I felt back. Plus, I was too tired to say anything in return and my throat was too sore to speak from being intubated while I was under. I let the drowsiness of the medication take over me again and I never let him know that I heard him.

I needed to heal from things first, both physically and mentally. As thrilled as I was, and still am, of course, that he told me he loved me when he did, I'm glad I didn't say the words back to him straight away. During this time, I have done *a lot* of thinking about Benjamin and Lucas. That's something I didn't want to do since they're both despicable human beings, but it was necessary. In the end, I concluded that I am not weak. Maybe that's something which wouldn't have even been a question to some people about themselves. It was an important revelation to me, though. Everyone I care about in my life has aided me in some way over the past few weeks. I am deeply, deeply grateful for every act of love that has been shown to me. But it was important for me to realize that although people, especially my guys, helped me, I did not *need* them.

The whole point of coming to Maple Crest was for independence. Some people back in Dallas believe I left because of what happened with Lucas, despite the fact I got myself out of that situation already. At the time, I was questioning if being around people you cared about made you soft. I saw it time and time again. That wasn't something I wanted for myself and *that's* why I left.

Then came Anthony and Hayden. Those two...God, these two are like getting caught in a summer storm you didn't see coming. Intimidating at first, but then beautiful. Strong. *Important*. With two truly incredible men suddenly entering my life and becoming cardinal at a pace I could barely fathom, I worried I was going to grow soft.

That's why my period of reflection was vital.

I realized I would have eventually been okay if I had to heal on my own. I'm just really damn glad I didn't have to. Because, like I said to Hayden, I love my guys. I just needed to ensure my self-value was completely in check before I tried loving other people first. Love will make you soft if you let it. But the right love will help you see the strength you didn't know you had. Or that you forgot existed.

"I heard you when you said it at the hospital, you know," I finally tell him. "I needed some time to figure some things out first, but I do. I love you, Hayden."

Hayden is grinning so widely right now I'm sure his cheeks must be hurting at least a little bit. After I was nearly taken, Hayden was the first one to make me smile again. He was right; I am glad things are returning to normal because everything about tonight feels so freaking good. Hayden takes my hand he'd been running circles on and kisses the top of it deeply.

"I love you too, Tatum."

Chapter Thirty-Eight

TATUM

I've been looking forward to Sunday. The whole long weekend with Hayden has been incredible, but I'm especially excited about today. Hayden's family is having a birthday party for one of his sisters. I've been to a couple of family dinners now where everyone is all together and it's such a positive environment to be in. By the time we leave, my body is practically buzzing with good energy.

The last Williams family gathering had me a little worried since Anthony begrudgingly came with us, but it went better than I could have imagined. This leads me to the next reason I've been looking forward to today. After being gone for four days, Anthony and Zara are returning to Maple Crest.

"You ready?" Hayden asks as he shrugs on a thick flannel over his gray tee. It's a shame the weather is acting up the way it is today because it feels like a crime to cover up how the sleeves hug his biceps. I make a suggestion that he strictly buys shirts that are a size too small from now on so I can admire his body even while he's clothed and he laughs. He follows up by suggesting I only wear v-necks because he likes to admire my body too. His eyes run up and down my body as he starts stalking toward me. "In fact, I'd love to thoroughly admire my girlfriend's beauty right now."

Hayden has one hand sliding into my hair from the nape of my neck and his face buried in the juncture between my neck and shoulder.

"Hayden, we need to go," I whine quietly, even as my hands do the opposite of what I say and rub along his body. I want to stay and do all the things that are running through our currently sex-filled minds. But, the idea of showing up anywhere late is enough to make me crazy so with some mental effort, I step away from his hold. "Tell you what, we'll take care of each other in the car now, and when we come back with Anthony later, we can pick up where we left off. Deal?" It's a win-win-win situation, so Hayden doesn't even look mildly upset when he grabs his keys off the hook.

He's got a cocky grin on his face when he asks, "So, who's going first? You or me?"

THE PARTY IS in full swing by the time Anthony pulls up in front of Hayden's parents' house. He greets me with a kiss and Hayden with a jerk of the chin before handing Hayden's sister a small, wrapped box. Since he's late and presents have already been opened, she quickly rips the paper off and finds an expensive pair of Bluetooth headphones. Her excitement is contagious, and I find myself smiling as Anthony asks me to accompany him to the kitchen to get a drink.

"My dad would be pissed to know I'm here," he chuckles while he fills up a plastic party cup with water.

"How did things go in New York, by the way?" Anthony turns around and braces a hand behind him on the sink as he drinks from the cup in his hand.

"Tate, do you recall when you said you didn't want any of the dirty details?" His face is straight. Expressionless.

"Yeah, it wasn't that long ago." It occurs to me after I reply that he's asking because after I woke up from the coma, my memory wasn't all that great. Thankfully, it improved with every week.

"For days, I've been trying to determine whether what I'm about to tell you is indeed a 'dirty detail' or not. In the end, I decided that it is, but it's something you should know, regardless." I set my drink down and cross my arms, preparing myself for whatever he's about to say. When I'm done moving, he continues. "The auction. It wasn't for a date. It's basically glorified prostitution. I have no foul opinions about people who use their bodies to make money. Just as long as it's consensual. The night of the gala, and every year since I was eighteen, it was not. For me, at least. With you and Hayden at my side, I finally had a good enough reason to put an end to it."

I swallow the ash on my tongue and try to make sense of the words I just heard. "Why didn't you tell me?"

He smiles and I can't imagine why on earth he'd be smiling after telling me something like *that*. I'm horrified by the revelation.

"You already wanted to punch my dad as it was. If I had told you then, you absolutely would have done it. The only reason I'd have a problem with that is because then you would've been kicked out. And darling, you looked too good for that. I didn't want the night to end before it had to." My heart plummets to the floor. Anthony inhales a little nervously. "I already know you're going to ask why I didn't tell you later, once we left. The answer to that is because...I was embarrassed I let it go on for so long."

I finally find my words. "You didn't *allow* it. Your dad has power over you. Whatever he would've done when you defied him was worse than a night with someone who—" I have to look away from him in order to blink away the tears. God, he didn't tell me this because *he* was protecting *me.* It should have been the other way around. Instead, I told him I didn't want to know the bad stuff when it came to his father's group. But had I known the truth would ever contain something as awful as this, I would never have asked him to hide it from me. Especially to protect my own feelings. Unfurling my arms, my hands reach for his. Tenderly gripping his fingers, I stare deeply into his eyes. On the outside, he looks as resilient as ever, yet I see the storm brewing within. Like the sea during bad weather, I can spot the waves of anger and hurt. "You never have to be embarrassed to tell me anything, Anthony. I am so sorry. For all of it. No more half-truths. Ever. No more hiding the dark parts. One hundred percent honesty from this moment on."

I'd forgotten we were in our boyfriend's parents' kitchen during his admission and there's a flow-blown birthday party happening on the other side of the wall. Still, we spend a few more minutes in solitude before Anthony insists we rejoin the group. He acts like what he's been through isn't a big deal. I can usually read him really well, but it's hard to tell now if that's how he truly feels or not. If it is, then surely that means he's experienced worse.

That thought makes me nauseous to think about. Anthony was right when he said I wanted to punch Clay. Now I'm ready to go full-on homicidal if I see him again. All the talk people have about respecting your significant other's parents? Yeah, not going to happen in this case. I don't have it in me to play nice around someone like him and I don't give a fuck what he thinks about me. Which clearly isn't much since he basically called Hayden and I prostitutes at the gala. That's pretty ironic now that I think about it, since he was trying to get Anthony to put his body up for sale the same night. Now, all I can think about is what his and Zara's lives must have really been like after their mom died.

About an hour later, we're on our way out the door to go home. I make it to my car first since Hayden got pulled back for one more hug from his mom and Anthony is almost to his Audi. When I sit behind my wheel, I spot a note folded up by my speedometer, my name inscribed on the front. Forehead creasing, I open the note and see familiar handwriting that makes my heart stop. Familiar, because I've seen it before on a note that was accompanied by the chicken heart cupcakes and dead roses.

SURPRISE!

Did you really think I was done with you? You thought I was gone, didn't you?

It has been most amusing to watch you loosen up and think you were safe. But here's a little newsflash for you: you're not as good of a shot as you think you are.

Now, let's get back to business. While you were eating birthday cake, I took something you love very dearly. If you want your cat back, then we must first have a chat. Just you and me. No boyfriends, best friends, or law enforcement allowed. I'm not much of a people person, you see. If anyone asks, say...the cat has got your tongue. You won't be too happy about the consequences if you don't obey.

It is my sincere hope you had as much fun as I did with the games we played but sadly, all good things must come to an end. When the sun sets tomorrow, meet me at home. Make sure to keep it our little secret.

—Benjamin

(P.S. If your little buddy isn't leverage enough, next week you'll be attending the funeral of someone you love if you don't show up. Can't tell you who, though. I love surprises. See you soon!)

My blood has been replaced with ice. My body is shaking violently.

He's not dead.

I had a feeling he was still around, but I thought that was just my paranoia. It wasn't. He really was there, watching me while I was convincing myself I'd killed him.

Do you want your cat back? What the hell? I reread the middle paragraph. *Lenny.*

I throw my car in reverse and press on the gas right as Hayden reaches out his hand to open the passenger door. I don't stop for him. Instead, I speed back home. I don't know what I'll find since he said to come back here tomorrow night, but I can't *not* check. As I turn onto my street, I hear the engine of Anthony's Audi behind me. I don't bother waiting for them. Throwing the vehicle into park without pulling into the driveway all the way, I don't even take my keys out of the engine before I start running for the open front door. I barely make it through the threshold before I hear the Audi coming to an abrupt stop along the street.

"Lenny!" I call, trying to sound approachable and calm so I don't scare him off, yet failing miserably because I am anything but calm. "Come here, buddy!"

Anthony grabs my arm and whips me around, stopping my frantic rush through the main room. "Tatum, what the hell was that?" Hayden is beside him, looking just as worried.

"Lenny is gone! He took Lenny!" I shout, twisting out of his grasp. I step to continue my fruitless search for my shadow when Anthony regains his grip on me and spins me around again. This time, he plants both hands on either of my arms to hold me firmly in place.

"*Who* took Lenny?"

"How did you know he's gone?" the guys ask one after the other.

'Make sure to keep it our little secret.'

I know I should tell them about the note, especially since I just told Anthony no more half-truths, but I can't. I don't know what will happen to Lenny if I do. Plus, the thought of staring at someone's coffin, knowing I could have saved them, makes me physically sick. I'm not willing to risk their lives or anyone else's.

Swallowing thickly, I finally answer. "I guessed."

"You *guessed*?" Hayden is giving me the same disbelieving look he gave Anthony when he told us he was robbed. He knows I'm lying to him and the knowledge of that makes me feel like shit, but I don't know how much Benjamin would allow me to share with them. The note instructs me to come alone. Does that mean they can know but not come with me? But then, it said to keep it a secret. Did Benjamin mean the fact that he wants me to meet up with him or that he's back? Did he tap my phone again? How would he know what I say?

"I just knew. I can't tell you how, but I knew. Please let that be enough for now," I beg them with tears in my eyes. Hayden nods slowly. I look at Anthony when he doesn't respond and I find his lips forming a flat line.

"Tate, I don't like thi—"

"Please, Anthony. Please, just trust me. Can you do that? Can you let this go for now?" He doesn't look happy with my request at all. Regardless, he finally nods too.

As I'd guessed, nothing on the cameras shows anybody other than ourselves was ever in the house. Evidence proves otherwise, other than the obvious facts of Lenny missing, and the front door being open when I returned. Smears from a hand being dragged are present on various surfaces. There's an empty glass on the counter and a shattered bottle of red wine on the floor, and music. Music is playing softly throughout the house. It's a haunted sort of tune that makes the hair on the back of my neck stand on end.

Memories of when I was being stalked resurface. Along with the memory of shooting Benjamin. I knew I shot him because Hayden said I did, but I couldn't remember doing it. The note seems to have brought that part back for me, filling another piece of the puzzle. It feels like I'm being haunted now. He wants revenge for me killing him and he finally got enough paranormal juice to pierce through the veil and exact his revenge against me.

But since it isn't a ghost, Anthony asks where I would feel safer; here or at his place. Just like old times, I'm packing a bag a few minutes later to stay at his house. Sure, his cameras got hacked once too, but no one ever made it inside the house after the attack on him. Somehow, even though Anthony got me the same upgraded security he has, his systems haven't been breached since my tires were slashed. Whether it's for lack of trying or not, I can't be sure. But it still feels safer there than it does in this godforsaken cabin.

The fact that Hayden, Anthony, and I once again find ourselves under the same roof while I'm being terrorized makes it a late night for all of us. Even though Hayden knows I'm hiding something from him, he's cradling me against him. He's half lying down on Anthony's couch, my chest against his. Our legs are tangled together and he's rubbing my back. I managed to stop crying, but only if I force myself not to think about what will happen to Lenny. Or think about the conditions he could be in right now, or what will happen if he has a seizure. Or who would be Benjamin's target if I tell my boyfriends everything I know.

Hours later, Anthony brings me a cup of tea and I sip it in hopes that it will bring me a sense of calmness. By some miracle, or maybe with the help of something Anthony added to my mug, my eyes drift closed.

Chapter Thirty-Nine

TATUM

The entire morning, I remain in the same spot I was in before I fell asleep. Not physically, exactly, but in the same chaotic mental space. My mind won't stop running. It tries to remind me of the risks and all the things which could happen if I don't tell the guys about my plan to leave tonight. I'm quick to shut it down when it does that, though. I switch my mentality so the part of my head screaming about reason gets reminded of Lenny, and a person-sized box that would be buried six feet deep.

Glancing at Hayden, who's off work for the weekend, makes my persistent questions resurface. How mad at me will the guys be after I walk away unharmed tonight? *What will they do if I don't walk away from this?* On the bright side, all of it comes to an end tonight. Although, I thought it had once before. This time, I'll make sure my bullet ends up in between Benjamin's eyes. My heart has been pounding for hours thinking about it and I wonder if it's possible for the organ to stop working at some point due to overload.

The doorbell rings, and our heads turn toward it, but neither of us moves. It appears we're both unnerved, not only me. Anthony casually enters the main room, but he's carrying a pistol in his dominant hand, showing that he's not at all relaxed, either.

"It's a delivery worker. I saw them on the cameras and let them through the gate," he informs us. Still, he looks out the window before opening the door, the gun in his hand and his finger ready to pull the trigger. By that time, the worker has already started to drive back toward the main road.

"Thanks for the heads up," Hayden mutters, bitterness in his quiet tone as he sinks back into his seat.

Anthony doesn't apologize, but he brings the box inside and sets it on the glass table in front of where I sit on the couch. "It's for you."

We all stare at the damn thing for nearly a minute as if we're all too afraid to open it and see what's inside. Except, I know something the guys don't. Benjamin has plans for me tonight, so I doubt he would send anything that could hurt me. Plus, he wants me to come of my own accord, so it's unlikely we'll be knocked out with gas again. With that knowledge, I start cutting the tape with Hayden's pocket knife. The second I flip open the lid, I barely manage to gasp before Hayden yanks me toward him and covers my head with his arm, telling me not to look.

Sobs wrack my body and I vaguely hear Hayden demand that Anthony get the box 'the fuck away from us.'

I don't understand. I didn't tell them about the note. I was going to show up tonight. I'm supposed to have more time. So why did the bastard kill my cat, put him in a box, and have him delivered to Anthony's door?

"It's not Lenny," Anthony states.

"It is. I saw him," I cry into Hayden's chest.

"No, love, it's not him. I promise. It's a tabby cat that looks like him, but it's not Lenny. See for yourself." His tone is gentle and urging, as if he were telling a kid to try something completely harmless for the first time.

"Take the box away!" Hayden yells, his shout vibrating through his torso.

"Wait." Anthony stops turning away with the box when he hears me. I look up at Hayden. "I have to know." He takes a couple of breaths and I can see on his face that he wants to spare me from the sight, but he loosens his protective hold on me. Anthony brings the box back over, and I peer into it. Fresh tears flow down my cheeks. Not for the loss of *my* cat, because Anthony was right. It isn't Lenny. But for the loss of the cat's life in the box and the fear that Lenny is still with the man who did this.

Benjamin knew I would come here after he took him. This box was a warning that he's still watching me and will know if I tell anyone of what's to come.

Hayden and Anthony are inconceivably mad. Mostly at the fact that Benjamin is back and didn't die, but also a little bit at me. Since Benjamin made his return obvious by having the box brought to Anthony's doorstep, I told them that I knew he was the reason behind Lenny's disappearance all along. I don't fault them for being upset with me now. I would be too if I were them. But I still can't tell them the part where I'm going to meet with Benjamin tonight and shoot him. Again. Making it a kill shot this time.

A storm brewed early this afternoon and rain has been pouring heavily for a while now. The dark clouds make it seem like the sun has been gone for hours when, in reality, it's only just set. Meaning I need to start finding a way to leave the guys behind.

As I'm considering different options I'm sure wouldn't even work, the motion sensor spotlights in Anthony's backyard illuminate the night. Immediately, the three of us go on alert and we all make our way to Anthony's wall of living room windows that overlook the backyard from a higher level. Being this close to the forest's edge, the light could have easily been triggered by an animal. But we all know what else, or rather, who else, it could be.

It's hard to see much through the heavy onslaught of rain but I scan the yard anyway trying to find what caused the light to turn on. I'm just about to chalk it up to being caused by the storm when Hayden stiffens and then points out the window.

"Right there. Do you see him?" I know the moment Anthony sees what Hayden's pointing to because he stiffens on the other side of me. Looking urgently now, I lift my gaze from the middle of the yard to the edge of the property. Right on the edge of Anthony's grass, where the light barely hits them, stands a dark silhouette. "Motherfucker," Hayden mutters angrily.

Both men immediately snap into action, pulling guns out of the holsters they're constantly wearing.

"Stay inside," Anthony instructs me sternly. His voice is stony, but his gray eyes are filled with his concern for me. I want to tell him I will and mean it because the truth is, I don't want to leave. I have to, though. So, I nod, unable to lie to him verbally. Anthony kisses the side of my head swiftly, then he and Hayden run out into the rain to go after the silhouette that has now disappeared.

My phone beeps with a new message.

Unknown:
This is what people call a diversion.
Time to go.
You're welcome for making things
easy BTW.

Staring at the message, I feel a lump growing in my throat making it hard to swallow. *It's time.* I take one last look at the men who mean the world to me as they rush through the rain, their feet pounding the earth, toward the spot where someone was on the property. They're out there for me, and now I'm leaving for them.

Grabbing my keys and throwing on my hoodie, I know the diversion Benjamin created won't last long, so I run out the door. With him having been standing on the edge of the forest a minute ago, I hope that means I'll have the upper hand by arriving back at my house first. That hope is quickly crushed the moment I walk through the front of my home.

I can't see or hear him, yet I can feel his presence somewhere in here with me. Somehow, he beat me back and is already in the house. Flipping the light switch by the door proves to be useless. The power is out. Whether the bastard cut it himself or if it was a casualty of the raging storm outside, I can't be sure.

Keeping my movements quiet, I grip my gun tighter as lightning flashes on the other side of the window. The boom of thunder follows shortly after. There's already a round in the chamber of my pistol, so I don't have to worry about racking it back and drawing attention. Instead, I quietly flip the safety off, bringing the weapon in front of me as I tiptoe further into the main room, making my way to the wall. That's when I hear the whispering.

It's impossible to make out what's being said. I can't tell whether Benjamin is alone or which direction the unrelenting whispering is even coming from. It sounds like he's all around me. I spin around, aiming the gun at random shadows, trying to locate the source. It isn't until I close my eyes and focus hard that I'm able to pinpoint that the whispers originate from my art room.

One quiet step after another, I inch toward what was once my mental safe space. My heart is pounding, and my breathing is getting faster. Adrenaline is already preparing my body for a fight. When the whispering suddenly stops, so do my feet.

There's a long moment of silence.

Then, "Let's see if you still bleed as pretty." I hear the whistle from some sort of rod whipping toward me through the air a fraction of a second before it smacks me across the chest, right below my neck.

The impact brings me to the floor as I try to regain the breath that was stolen from me with desperate, airless gasps. The stinging burn from where I was hit spreads through me like lightning and intense nausea floods my throat. I'm blinking, stunned, gasping like a fish when I hear a thud followed by a step, repeatedly. Barely managing to fill my lungs again, I stand up only to be whipped with the rod again and it sends me sprawling back down to the floor, the gun falling from my grip. After crashing against the floorboards, my shaking fingers hover over my face where I was struck this time. They want to touch the spot, but knowing the pain that will accompany the tender touch, I decide against it. Spitting out the blood that has welled in my mouth, I roll over, coughing as I move onto my knees. When I try to stand completely, I'm hit on the shoulder. This time, pressure continues to be applied even after the impact.

"Stay. Down." My eyes focus on the shape that comes in front of me and when lightning flashes, I see Benjamin's face staring down at me. The object he'd been using to hit me with lifts from my shoulder and he uses it to caress my stinging cheek. "Look at that. You *do* look good bloody. On your knees, no less."

"What do you want with me?" I seethe. My lip is swollen and blood enters my mouth when I talk.

"Canes," he cocks his head to better examine me and ignores my question. "Who would've thought they'd make such effective weapons?" Then I hear the whistle of his cane as it flies through the air, one last time, too quick for me to dodge.

Chapter Forty

HAYDEN

> *His job is done. All I needed was your girlfriend.*
> *You may think I'm mean, but I'm not a monster. Did*
> *you know I'm actually a cat person?*
> *—Benjamin*

That's what the note said when Anthony and I got to Tatum's house, only to find her missing and Lenny perfectly fine. While searching for any reason why she would have run off the way she did when we were distracted, we found a separate note in her car. I knew she was lying to us when she'd first found Lenny was missing. It was obvious. I made several attempts throughout the night to try to get the truth out of her, but she kept it clamped down behind a wall of iron will.

It hurt thinking that after everything, it was because she didn't trust me. But after reading the note, we discovered it was because there was a promise of death hovering over someone she loves. She was trying to protect us, and in doing so, put herself in danger.

Now, I'm staring at her house with yellow tape surrounding it that says 'CRIME SCENE — DO NOT ENTER' as lights from police cars flash obnoxiously in the dark. They don't even need the tape. It's overkill. I'm sure it's only up because some gung-ho officer got overly excited for the chance to use it since no big crimes happen in Maple Crest. Be that as it may, I welcome every precaution made to ensure things are done right. Even if, rather than holding back dozens of people, the tape is only stopping a handful of nosy onlookers from contaminating potential evidence.

It took only one look at them muttering their guesses on what happened before I had to turn away, fists clenched and mouth clamped shut. *What the hell is wrong with them?* My girlfriend was attacked and went missing here. Her goddamn blood is on the floor and half of these people are whispering like they're in school, afraid to get caught by a teacher.

The sound of a motorcycle gets closer and then shuts off not far from where Anthony and I are standing in the street. I turn to watch Zara approach right as two more people join the other spectators.

"Don't you have any place better to be?" I shout at them. Anthony grabs my shoulder and spins me back around.

"What the hell happened?" Zara asks when she finishes jogging up to us. I wait for Anthony to say something, but he doesn't. I can't say I'm surprised by his silence, though. Since we discovered the note, he hasn't said a word to anybody. He was, however, texting someone earlier. I now assume he was telling his sister there had been an incident.

"Benjamin is alive. He took Tate," I answer when Anthony doesn't. Pulling up the picture I took of the note on my phone, I show it to her.

"What? He took her? Is she still alive?" Zara's tone becomes more aggressive with each question. She looks to her brother with wide eyes and that's when Anthony finally faces her.

"Get the whole company on this. We need to find her *now*," he instructs.

Zara looks unsure as she holds her bottom lip between her teeth. "But dad won't—"

"I don't care what he thinks. I'll deal with the consequences. Just get everyone looking for her."

"Anthony..." Zara starts when her brother cuts her off for the second time.

"Go!" he shouts. Her eyes flick to me before she walks away. When we hear her motorcycle start, Anthony rubs a hand harshly over his face.

"Are you okay?" I ask.

"What the hell do you think?" he spits. It's a stupid question, I know that. I knew that before the words left my lips. Of course he's not. *I'm* not. But I don't know what else to say.

We were frantic before we called the authorities. I was completely livid. I was thinking of how I'm going to make Benjamin suffer for this. Anthony may have more experience in the torture department than I do, but in a matter of minutes, I've thought of a thousand ways to make Benjamin hurt for a hundred years. Then a hundred more after that.

Now I think I'm in some sort of numb state of shock. I'm still enraged. There's no changing that. Shock is just another feeling that has been added onto the pile. Tatum's time in the hospital was one of the scariest times of my entire life. It's only being beaten by what's happening now. At least when she was in the hospital, we knew she was alive and being taken care of. We don't know anything now except for who has her and it's the last person on earth we want her to be with.

He heaves a sigh and drops his hand. "I'm going back to my place so I can get to my computer. I don't trust these officers to do us a bit of good. They failed Tatum before, I'm sure they'll do it again. Where do you want to go?"

I run a hand through my hair. I don't know what to do with myself right now. All I want is to find Tatum alive. The problem is; I don't know how to start. Anthony can actually be helpful. He's going to lock himself away in his office with his fingers flying across the keyboard. He's a genius with computers. What do I know how to do? Nothing. I have no skill that can help get Tatum home and it's killing me.

"Tell me something I can do to help. Anything. I can't sit around and do nothing but wait. Give me something to do."

SINCE LENNY IS ALREADY familiar with Anthony's house and we needed to come here anywhere, we decided it would be best to bring the cat here. Plus, though neither of us has said it, I don't think either of us were in the mood to take Lenny to my place and leave him behind. Anthony hasn't said it, but I know he's relieved to see the furry bastard alive. I am too. And I know how much Tatum loves him. Having him near brings me a bit of comfort I desperately need right now.

As soon as we got here, Anthony locked himself in his office like I suspected he would. The first task he gave me? Calling her parents to let them know what happened. After dealing with that miserable call, I let Nyasia know as well. My head hurts. My fucking heart hurts. I feel like any sort of joy has been sucked from every corner of the earth now that Tatum's in danger again. No one, whether they knew her or not, will know peace until she's found. That's how vital her life feels for me.

I drop onto Anthony's couch, which is about as comfortable as a rock, and grip the roots of my hair in a tight fist. After a shaky breath, I hold up my phone again to make one last call for the night. At this point, I've gotten used to hearing the line ring and could match the voicemail he made perfectly.

"Hey, buddy. I uh...I don't know where you're at, or what I did wrong. I have no idea why you're avoiding my calls, but, um, I need...I need you to call me back, Nick. I need you to call me back. Please. Okay. Love you, man. Bye." Lenny hops up next to me when I hang up the phone and when he rubs against my arm, I fucking lose it. One hand holding up my head and the other on Lenny, tears pour like a damn river down my cheeks. I end up having to press my fist against my mouth to keep Anthony from hearing me cry.

Chapter Forty-One

ANTHONY

Tracking Tate's phone was an immediate dead end. It's in her house which does us no good since it doesn't give us a direction to start looking in. The device must have fallen and slid underneath some furniture during the struggle.

During the struggle.

The thought of what she went through, what she *will* go through, makes me back away from the keyboard like it's on fire and squeeze my eyes shut. *Fuck!* It's nearly three a.m. now, she's been missing for hours.

Taking a few moments to collect myself, I go back to what I was working on. There won't be any need for me to go back and collect her phone in the morning since I can get into her email and messages easily from here. Going through her private life makes me feel sick, but given the situation, I think she'll understand why I have to do it. Besides, she loves her privacy and would hate it if I let anyone else go through her things.

Opening her camera roll gives me the chance to see the world as she sees it, and it's beautiful. She finds beauty in all the small things around her; a single drop of rain on a leaf, a snail filling its belly. She doesn't seem to miss a thing. Among the pictures of the natural world around her are a bunch of selfies with Hayden and me, candid shots of us, and pictures of herself and Nyasia. Half of the pictures of me I didn't even know she took. One look at the rows of images tells you the kind of person my girl is and what's most important to her.

I'm glancing through the most recent ones to see if there's anything unusual when I see a picture she'd taken of the three of us a couple of weeks ago. I click on it to expand the photo when my sister calls. She's letting me know everyone's top priority is finding Tatum, but all I can focus on is her saying there's no progress.

Growing more frustrated after hitting yet another dead end, I search for something to break but I don't keep anything on my desk other than the monitors, mouse, and keypad. It takes everything in me not to smash them to bits just to see if it will make me feel better. Instead, I rake my fingers through my hair and tug harshly at the roots, bellowing in frustration.

"Get some rest, Anthony," she suggests from her end of the line. "Start the search again in a few hours."

"No, I can't stop."

"*Yes.* I'll keep looking, so will everyone else, but you need sleep so you can keep a clear head. Besides, it wouldn't hurt to see how Hayden's handling everything. You've been at this for hours. Check on our boy for me."

She and Hayden have bonded over the past month since she's been coming around more with Kiara. I wish I could say it was because of me and the fact that I've made my house more guest friendly since Tatum woke up, but I can't. She comes for Tatum. The only time I had a problem with that was when I saw Zara hug Hayden. It was then that I fully realized the impact our father's actions has had on us. She initiated the friendly hug, and in that moment, I saw her the way I did when we were little, and our mom was still alive. It hurt because I know we're still years away from having a moment like that ourselves.

After the line disconnects, I sit in the silence surrounding me for a solid minute before I get up to find Hayden. The bedroom is closest, so I search for him there first. Finding only Lenny, I'm about to leave the space and look somewhere else when I hear the shatter of glass. Pulling a gun from the dresser, I raise it and step quietly down the hall. When I reach the main room, I quickly scan the open space, finding nothing. That's when I hear shards of glass clinking together in the kitchen. Whipping toward the noise, I walk silently toward it. At first, I see nothing. But then there's a sliver of movement on the other end of the island. Maneuvering around it, I whip around the island in front of the figure kneeling on the ground, ready to shoot.

"Fucking hell!" Hayden shouts, jerking his hands into the air and dropping the pieces of glass he was holding. "It's me, Jesus!" His eyes are wide and bloodshot. His shaggy brown hair is a mess with strands lying every which way on top of his head. To top off his miserable appearance, a line of blood runs over his wrist and makes its way down his arm. Glass likely sliced his skin in the heat of the moment.

"What happened?" I question him, lowering my gun and looking at the pile of broken glass that was once a cup.

Hayden drops his bleeding palm onto his leg. "I'm sorry man, I just...I lost control for a second."

He means he threw it. I almost want to tell him this kitchen has seen its fair share of emotional breakdowns. They don't always lead to broken glasses, though. Sometimes it's just me looking pathetic and mentally cursing my dad out for the life he's made me live. Hell, he missed the emotional breakdown I had in my office right before I came looking for him.

Hayden starts picking up the sharp shards of glass again. Blood traces are left behind on each piece he touches. Setting the gun on the counter, I crouch in order to be eye level with him.

"Don't worry about this. It's my mess. I got it." His voice is quiet yet rough and accompanied by a small shake of his head, telling me to leave.

Instead of the glass, I reach for his hands. "I'm not worried about the mess. I'm worried about you. *You* are the mess I care about." Like the glass that was shattered, he suddenly breaks in my hands. Hayden's eyes squeeze shut, and his breaths increase in pace. His hands are shaking in mine. "We'll get her back."

"What if we don't?"

I cup his red cheek. "We *will*. I promise. I'm just as devastated," — *devastated seems too weak of a word to cover how I feel* — "but I know we'll find her. I'll do whatever it takes to make that happen."

I should have told her I love her sooner. Because I do. God, I am completely in love with that woman. It's such a cliche to say that love is a powerful thing, but now that I've experienced it in a way I never have before, I realize how true that statement is. I've seen people do crazy things, both good and bad, in the name of love. It drives people to their limits and they will fly past the boundaries they thought they'd never cross without thought because of it. They test themselves, break themselves, make themselves new, all for the four letter word that's written everywhere. You find it on couch pillows, t-shirts, coffee mugs, and whatever else you can fit a label on. It's said both too often and not nearly enough.

When we love someone, we give them a part of ourselves. I resisted at first, but I opened up for her to see me as I am. She saw the me no one else was allowed to witness before. Tatum saw all my faults and stayed. That's love. In return, I saw her. Not the person her parents or ex boyfriends wanted her to be, but *her*. And I am in love with every damn thing about her. Giving up the search, no matter how long, will never be an option. Not even death could stop me because even in death, my soul would search for hers.

I suddenly get reminded of the night of the crash when

Tatum was in the hospital and Hayden and I had to return here for the night.

'One of us always seems to be hurt. Then there's the stalking and near abduction....'

That's what he said. He then went on to say he's *'just a logger. Not the kind of guy who has ties with this stuff on the regular.'*

Now, here we are again, months later, in my house. He's bleeding, and Tatum has been abducted.

The difference between now and then is that he's still a logger. But now he's a logger who has ties with this stuff on the regular. Who's fault is that? Mine.

Far too familiar feelings of shame seep their way into every part of my body and the weight of failure sits heavily on my shoulders. It feels like the world is crumbling around me and I don't know what to do to stop it. All I know is I need to try and protect Hayden — the only person I have left I can try with — from feeling the same deep sense of emptiness I feel.

Bringing comfort to others is an area where I fall short. It isn't something I've had much experience with since my mom passed. My dad was too busy blaming me and making me wish I was the one who died to realize that I was just a kid who lost his mom and needed the only parent he had left. I tried to be there for Zara, but there was nothing I could do after my dad sent her away, forcing me to have no contact with her for years. But Hayden is right here in front of me. I can help him. It's not that he's weak. Not at all. He's *normal*, and reacting like any normal human being would in this situation.

"Come on," I quietly urge him, pulling on his hands a little to signify that I want him to stand with me. Taking him into the bathroom, I wet a washcloth and grab some tweezers. While I pull a lingering bit of glass from his skin and stop the bleeding, I softly speak words of comfort for the both of us.

'You are not alone in this.'
'She will make it through this.'

'We will make it through this.'
'She's a strong girl. She'll be okay.'

Chapter Forty-Two

TATUM

"Tatum?" a hesitant voice asks. It's the last voice I expect to hear. Opening my eyes, I blink against the light and confusion. Every part of my body aches. When my vision clears, I see that I'm in some sort of concrete room the size of my bedroom. To make matters more unnerving, bars run halfway through the space, creating a cell. One I'm on the wrong side of judging by the closed door on the other side.

"Are you okay?" Nick is on the other side of me, on the wrong side of the bars like I am. He's bruised and dried blood that comes from his hairline has crusted on his face.

"What the hell is this?" I demand of him as I sit myself up from the concrete floor beneath me. "Wait, what are you even doing here? I thought you sold your business and left Maple Crest a week ago."

"Tatum, there are things—"

I squeeze my eyes shut and shake my head, focused only on the dozens of questions running through my mind. "Where are we? How did we get here?"

"*Listen to me.*" Nick comes closer and holds onto my arms in an attempt to ground me. When I stare into his pale blue eyes, I can clearly see his fear in them. I've never heard Nick's voice to be anything but friendly. Never knew him not to be warm and smiling. Then again, I've never woken up and been stuck in a prison cell with him before. "Okay. You okay? I need you to know that I tried to stop this."

"Stop what? I don't even know what *this* is."

"Them taking you, I tried to stop it."

Retreating from him, my body continues to shake. "How did you know they were going to? And who are *they*? Only one man took me."

Nick's face melts into a look of guilt and shame. "Clay wanted the coffee shop and was going to screw me over completely. He was fabricating false claims and 'evidence,' using them to blackmail into a terrible deal. I didn't want to sell, though. That coffee shop was my life and I've never done anything wrong. The townspeople know that, and more than that, they know me. I trusted them to have my back. I was so mad about what he was trying to do that when Benjamin came to me and—"

"You know Benjamin?" I question loudly.

He shushes me and looks nervously at the door. "Yes, I know Benjamin. Tatum, listen, I knew he was leaving you those...gifts. But I swear to you, I didn't know what he was going to do to you." Boiling anger runs through me and intensifies my shaking. Still, I continue listening. "We had different agendas. I thought he was going to help me get back at Clay and that was it. When I asked him why he'd help me, he told me about being fired and screwed over himself, so it made sense. I didn't know he had his own plans for revenge as well. Especially that those plans included harming you. When I learned he was leaving stuff for you, it wasn't until a couple of days before your attack. When I confronted him about it, he said he thought you were pretty. The guy is a little messed up in the head, so I figured that was his way of trying to flirt with you. Had I known about the stalking and stuff, too, I would have told you."

"Would you?" I demand to know. "Because if that was the case, why didn't you tell me all of this after the attack?"

"I couldn't," he shouts, and it sounds like a plea for innocence. Nick glances at the door again before he starts speaking quieter this time. "I couldn't tell you. My life was on the line. They said they'd shoot me if I said anything to you. Plus, I thought it was over. You kicked Benjamin's ass. He was pissed, but he was shot. You proved you could take him in a fight, so I figured we would just carry on with my revenge on Clay after he healed some. Then I overheard them talking about a new plan to abduct you and I was done. I was going to warn you, even if it cost me my life. It nearly did, and I didn't even get to stop it." He gestures at his blood-crusted head.

I don't know what to think. Nick. Sunny Nick. Happy, sun-bringing, best-friends-with-my-boyfriend Nick is involved in some really shady stuff. Remembering the time I literally ran into Clay at the coffee shop, I think back to how defensive and mad Nick looked when they started talking. When I asked him about it later, he said it wasn't a big deal. But Nick was different after my attack. I could tell that much. Though sunny, it was like a cloud was muting his light. Once I got back to my daily routine, which included grabbing a drink from his shop, his beautiful, pale blue eyes didn't stay on me as long as they used to when we'd talk. Then he began to feign business when I lingered for a conversation as I did before. I remember thinking it was like he was ashamed of something. Now I know what it was.

"So, that's why you up and left? Hayden has been concerned." There's a bite to my tone. Though there's a reason behind his actions, Nick should have told me all of this sooner. Surely Anthony, or even the police, could have protected him from being shot.

"Just concerned?" He chuckles weakly. "I've been down here for...I don't know how long and my best friend is just *concerned*."

"Well, it bothered him that you never wanted to call anymore, but you were texting him." Once I finish my sentence, I realize that part doesn't add up to the situation we're in.

"No, I wasn't." He sighs, confirming my previous thoughts. "They were probably texting him from my phone to keep up some sort of illusion. I did not 'up and leave.' They intercepted me from getting to you and I've been here ever since."

"You keep saying *they*, who is doing this with Benjamin?"

As if on cue, the door opens and Benjamin walks in. Hobbles in, really. He's limping alongside a cane, looking far from pleased with me. His hardened stare spells misery for me, but I don't shrink from it.

"*You*. You took my cat." Those weren't the first words I was expecting to say to him, especially since I just regained consciousness from a successful abduction. Mostly because I thought he was dead, but yet, here he stands. Benjamin doesn't reply to me. Instead, he adjusts his stance with the cane, presumably to make himself more comfortable, and puts a hand in his pocket. He tilts his chin up to look down his nose at me. I should be scared. Anyone else in this situation would be. But I'm incredibly pissed off. We glare at each other for nearly a minute before I talk again, unable to stop myself from rubbing salt in his still-healing wound. "You needed a month off to lick your wounds before coming back to try again, huh? Second times a charm for you when it comes to kidnapping, is it? Where are we?"

"Don't you recognize it?" he finally speaks. His voice is low and easy. Almost lazy. "This is home."

"That's helpful," I lie. "Where. Is. Home?"

He cocks his head in that predatory way of his. I hate that it makes my heart jump and am thankful he can't sense that sort of thing. "You mean to tell me you don't know your own address?"

Now I'm really confused. This isn't my house. I've never been here before in my life. Benjamin pulls a small remote from his pocket and points it over his shoulder before clicking one of the buttons. A second later, a woman's voice begins to sing. Her voice echoes with whispering in the background of the soundtrack, and what sounds like a heartbeat amongst the eerie music. The song is a remix of a popular children's song I remember my mom singing to me; '*Down By The Bay*.' Except this is a horror version of the song with lyrics about rotting watermelons, liars, and not getting caught. It chills my skin.

But not as much as when I realize why this song is so familiar. I'd heard it in my house on multiple occasions during his countdown. It was always quiet, and I could never figure out where it was coming from. Half the time, I couldn't even tell if it was ever really paying.

"You didn't know this place had a basement, did you?" Benjamin chuckles once he notes the expression on my face.

"My basement," I whisper in shock. "We're in my basement?" Still, this does nothing to ease my confusion. My house is only one level.

"Yep. I found a covered-up entry to it one day while you were out and I was taking a look around. Someone was trying really hard to keep this place a secret. The things I found down here..." He clicks his tongue with a slight jerk of his chin. "I mean, you should see the things we found down here. Let's just say one of the last owners of this residence was a bit of a psychopath. Which is really saying something coming from me. Anyways, there's no better place to keep eyes on your target than right under their nose. Literally. Which is exactly why I moved in. It was a little annoying always having to fight Anthony's cyber blockades to clear footage of me, but nevertheless, I persisted. And now that we have you, we won't have to do that anymore."

"You keep saying *we*, if either of you ignore my question one more time, I'll—"

"You'll what?" a new voice chimes in. It's another voice I recognize except, this time, it really is the last voice I expect to hear. Footsteps sound behind Benjamin, and a moment later, a body emerges.

"*Lucas?*"

My ex-boyfriend lifts his arm and I find myself looking down the barrel of a gun.

"What are you doing?" Nick demands, his voice full of panic. Lucas adjusts his gun slightly and pulls the trigger. I scream out and cover my head even though there's no way I'll be able to stop the bullet. Only, I never feel its burn. Beside me, Nick's body crumples to the floor. I can feel his blood on my face.

"Miss me?" Lucas asks.

Chapter Forty-Three

HAYDEN

"So please, give her back to us. We want our daughter back." I watch on Anthony's TV as Tatum's mom pleads for her safe return in front of half a dozen microphones and television cameras. Even though she was taken from a small town, Tatum's abduction has already made national news in less than twenty-four hours. It helps that her parents are part of the upper class and for that, I'm thankful. The more eyes we have looking for her, the better our chances are of finding her. I just hope Benjamin doesn't freak and do something even more irrational under the pressure.

Standing beside her parents is Tatum's sister, Grace. She looks so much like Tatum. The only major difference is that Grace is more tanned. In fact, Grace looks so much like her sister that I have to turn the TV off. I wanted to watch what the reporters had to say, but there's no point. When something new comes up, we're going to be the first ones to know, anyway. I guess I can sum up my news watching to wishful thinking. Every second that passes by, I'm hoping and praying for some sort of development.

It's a small town so I know everyone on the police force. Half of the officers are friends I went to school with. The other half are people I've known pretty much my whole life. But all of our history aside, I think I burnt some bridges last night. I was in their faces yelling like I never have before. They didn't deserve the full force of my fury, I know that, but I wasn't thinking about that in the moment. I'm pretty sure Anthony is the only reason why I wasn't taken to jail and put in a cell to 'cool down.' Because of that and the fact Anthony and I aren't related to Tate, it's a gamble as to whether or not they'll keep us in the loop anymore. That's fine. We don't need them anyway because Anthony has people watching and listening in to all police systems for any new input.

Bracing myself against the doorframe of Anthony's office, I find him clicking through stuff I can't make out from here on his computer monitor.

"I don't get it," Anthony mutters. He uses a tone that makes it difficult to determine whether he's talking to me or if he even knows I'm here at all. "Every camera in the city and the ones around it shows nothing so far. There's not a single sign of them or even something to show the footage was even tampered with. There's no loop or inconsistent timestamp. No sort of footprint to show someone else was in these networks. Nothing."

"How can he just disappear?"

"He can't," Anthony states simply. "The cockroach probably memorized where all the cameras are and avoided them somehow. Benjamin is going to show up somewhere. All we have to do is find the right camera and time."

I think about how he could be getting around undetected as Anthony continues clicking his mouse. When an answer comes to me, I realize how accustomed I've gotten to my surroundings and I mentally curse at my ignorance.

"The forest," I say, straightening. This is the first time I've ever used such a bitter tone while talking about my home away from home. Anthony turns in his chair to face me, two fingers pressed to his lips. "It's fucking obvious. We were thinking he drove out of there to move her, but what if he didn't? The forest is literally at the house's doorstep. Benjamin could've easily transported her somewhere else while avoiding the cameras that way. Not to mention there's abandoned cabins and other shelters scattered throughout the mountains. He probably found one and holed up there."

A SEARCH PARTY was quickly organized, made up of police officials and volunteers who scoured the forest for hours, finding no trace of either Benjamin or Tatum. I joined the search while Anthony stayed behind. I don't even know if I'm looking for *her* or her corpse, and not knowing if she's still alive or not is a fear unlike anything I've ever experienced before in my life.

Leaving the forest only when it's too dark to effectively search anymore, I discover Nyasia has already made posters that are set up in front of Tatum's house, up and down the street, and likely all over the rest of town. Though, I haven't been on Main Street yet to confirm it. It's eerie to see a picture of my beautiful girlfriend smiling with the word *missing* above it in big, bold, red letters. It's even more eerie to be standing in her last known location.

"I found them," Anthony informs me as he walks out of Tatum's bedroom, lifting up the medicine bottle containing Lenny's pills. They rattle with the movement. Knowing Tatum, she'd be pissed if we slacked on the wellness of her cat. Even now, which is why we're currently in her cabin.

I've never really liked this place, to be honest. I can't explain why, but something about it doesn't feel right. It's not solely because I have pent up resentment about being drugged here or remaining bitterness from seeing her here petrified with fear. Though, those both definitely help support the uneasy feelings. No, even before all that, my wariness was there since I first came to this house. Now that she's disappeared from here on top of everything else, the feeling has intensified to a near unimaginable level. I can hardly breathe in this place.

Anthony walks past me on his way back to his Audi and I take one last look around the place from where I'm standing, just in case there's *something* that had been previously overlooked. Nothing stands out, so I begin making my way out with Anthony when I hear it.

"Hayden!"

I whip around. It was faint, but I heard it. It was Tatum, I know it was.

"Did you hear that?" My voice is quiet while I look around the room again, this time much more intensely than before.

"Hear what?" Anthony asks. There's no urgency or concern in his tone. *He didn't hear her.* Maybe it wasn't real after all. Is it that I'm so desperate to find her, for any sort of sign that she's still alive that my head is playing tricks on me now?

I don't answer him. Instead, I strain my ears listening for her again.

Nothing.

In fact, it's so quiet I swear I can hear the blood running through the vessels in my ears.

"Hayden?" It's Anthony saying my name this time.

"Nothing." I shake my head. Not as an answer to him, but to shake myself free from the illusion. "I thought I heard something." I continue for his car, but now Anthony stays in place by the door. He's listening now, too, but eventually he leaves the house behind like I did.

If I can't see her, I wish I could at least talk to her. I would remind Tatum she's *beyond* strong and that no matter how hard things are right now or how hard things will get, she will make it through, coming out of this stronger. I'd remind her that she's loved beyond measure. I'd give my last drop of strength to her if she needed it to help her through this. When this is all over and we have her back, because we *will* get her back, I'll do *anything* I can to help her heal.

But I can't tell Tate any of that. I just have to hope she already knows it all and that I did a good enough job of proving my love to her.

Chapter Forty-Four

TATUM

They made me sit and stare at Nick's body for hours before they took him away. I'm unsure how long it was since I don't have a clock or a window to help me keep track of time. It could have easily been at least an entire day.

Before they took him away, I hated him for not taking a risk and telling me what he knew sooner. Anthony could have provided protection for him. If he had come to us, to his best friend, with the truth, then none of this would have happened. I wouldn't be sitting in this cell and he wouldn't have died.

Then again, it's not fair to blame him because this isn't his fault. He's as much a victim as I am. Nick was being blackmailed and threatened. He was scared, and rightly so. For that reason, my heart aches for him. The ending he got was far from the one he deserved. Especially because he wasn't just Hayden's friend, but mine as well.

Especially since he was coming to do the right thing in the end.

Before they took Nick's body away, Lucas reunited me with his fists, and my ribs met his shoes several times. On top of sleep deprivation and dehydration starting to kick in, I feel like a corpse myself, sitting in the corner of this cell. The cell that's in the goddamn *basement* I didn't even know I had.

I didn't believe Benjamin at first. I thought there was no way this was underneath my nose the whole time. But then I heard *them*. My guys. Lucas knew when they'd pulled in front of my house and instructed Benjamin to keep me quiet. He clamped a hand over my mouth and threatened me before they even entered my house. It's incredible how much you can hear from the floor below. They were talking about where I might keep Lenny's medication and though they sounded nearly as mentally drained as I felt, I nearly sobbed with relief. The sound of their voices alone filled me with new strength.

Anthony remembered where I kept the pills, so I knew I didn't have long. Especially as I heard Anthony's footsteps retreating for the door to leave. If I was going to do something, I'd need to do it soon. I tried to thrash my head from side to side in the hopes of freeing my mouth from the confines of Benjamin's hand, but failed. By some miracle, though, Hayden hesitated, giving me a few extra seconds to fight. And it worked. Clamping down hard with my teeth on Benjamin's fingers, he released me long enough for me to shout Hayden's name. That one word was all I was able to get out before Lucas knocked me to the ground with a fist to the side of my head. I laid dizzy and weak on the floor, unable to speak but able to listen to Hayden walk out the door.

As quickly as hope walked in, it walked right back out. I would've cried, but the bastards down here have been keeping me dehydrated. My body is so desperate for water it barely produced any tears after I cried over Nick for so long.

It's all so crazy to think: my ex and my stalker murdered *my friend* and are holding me captive...in my basement. I'm sure everyone has heard stories where homeowners find out someone has been secretly living in their attic or something, but this feels like some next level shit.

I'm equally horrified and curious to know what else is down

here. Benjamin said there were things on the other side of that closed door which surprised even him. There are items that are so twisted, apparently, that rather than clearing it all out, someone just blocked the space off entirely.

Or maybe, the entrance was so well hidden because this space was still being used for whatever purpose.

Thinking my late uncle could have been as sick-minded as the men that abducted me makes me want to throw up.

The door opens, and Lucas walks into the celled space. The sight of him only intensifies my nausea.

"Good morning, sweetheart." I still remember sunny mornings in bed back in Dallas when he would say that to me. We had our troubles then, but things were still good. After he lashed out and hurt me, I kept trying to remember him as he was in that morning light. It gave me hope that even though I would never give him another chance, he might be better for the next girl. "My dick was so good it takes two men to fill the void now, huh?"

Just like that, the memories vanish. I let my head drop back against the wall and look at him with a hoarse laugh.

"Oh please. Either one of them could thoroughly satisfy me with a single finger and two minutes, more than you ever could. In fact, they already have." His smile from moments ago drops. "What are we doing here, Lucas? How did you get involved in Clay's business?"

"Oh, I'm not involved in his business, honey. Do you remember Drake? My buddy from school you always hated for some reason? As fate would have it, he's a friend of Ben's. Small world, isn't it?" He squats before me, dangling a bottle of water between his hands. "You want to know what we're doing here? Well. It turns out you were right."

More than anything else right now, I want the water. Even after they killed Nick, and after the beatings, they gave me nothing. But I'm not going to ask for it. I'm weak enough as it is. I'm not going to show mental weakness too.

"Right about what?"

"Once wasn't enough. When you were going around and telling everyone that I was going to hurt people again, slandering my name, I didn't believe it. You've got to understand that I didn't intend to hit you when I did. It just happened. After you left, I chased that feeling with other girls. The thing about them, though, is that they weren't..." Lucas puts a contemplative finger to his mouth and looks over my shoulder at the wall to think, likely on how to phrase the rest of the sentence. "I don't know what it is. It's just not the same with them as it was with you. There's something special about you. They weren't fun."

"They weren't *fun?* You're talking about hurting women. You find that entertaining?" Disgusted doesn't even begin to cover what his words make me feel.

Lucas twists the cap off the water bottle and takes a sip. "Maybe it's your fire. I hated it when we were together, but I think it's the missing factor. The other girls are too easy to break. Not you though. Not you. You fought back and remained unbroken." He holds out the bottle of water toward me. For several seconds, I stare at it and ridiculously hope it'll turn into a deadly snake and bite him. But it doesn't, and I'm only human, so I take it and swallow a careful sip even though I watched him crack the seal and taste it.

"You came all this way because you're hurting too many women too quickly?" He nudges the bottom of the bottle with a single finger, tilting it back so I drink again. Given the circumstances, I'm sure it isn't because he cares about my well being. After all, one of my eyes is almost swollen closed thanks to him. So, I take it as a sign I have to drink now because I won't be able to later and guzzle the bottle down.

"Atta girl. Yep. There you go, drink up," Lucas praises. When he goes to stroke my cheek with the back of a finger, the same cheek I'm sure he cracked a bone in earlier, I flinch. He continues the touch anyway and pets me like a scared dog. "No Tatum, that's not the only reason I came all this way. You really screwed up my life for a while. I have to make things right. I'm here for revenge."

I finish taking in the last drop from the bottle when he says that. My body stills with renewed fear brought on by the change of his voice. It's flooded with the promise of pain. When my worried eyes meet his, I see the pure satisfaction in them right before he moves his fingers from my cheek to my hair. He digs his hand roughly through the tangled mess and starts to pull me as I kick and scream out of the cell and into the main section of the basement.

Once we reach the center, he shoves me back to the ground. My arms shake as I push myself up and look around the room. I'm proven once again that Benjamin didn't lie to me. This truly is a room of horrors. It's the torture room of a serial killer based on the wall of newspaper articles declaring missing hikers and the polaroid photographs of the same missing hikers. Only, the polaroid photos show them here, in this room in my basement, covered in blood.

My whole body shakes now. Whipping my head to another part of the room, I spot Benjamin. He's leaning against some sort of...table with his arms crossed, cane beside his leg, and an evil smirk on his face. With Lucas around, I'd forgotten I'm not only a pawn for Lucas' revenge, but for Benjamin's against Anthony and his family as well.

"Let's get started," Lucas taunts behind me.

Chapter Forty-Five

ANTHONY

Zara:
Are you going to tell him?

Me:
No

My fingers are fast to send the two word reply. Faster than my brain, which has now caught up and scolds myself for the rashly sent answer.

I send another text.

Me:
I don't know.

Little bubbles pop up on my screen, indicating that my sister is typing out a reply. I already know it's going to make me feel worse than I already do.

The bubbles stop, then her message appears.

Zara:
He deserves to know. You tell him or I will.

The *him* to whom we've been referring to walks out of the forest, back into the parking lot where his dad's work truck waits for him. He still hasn't been able to buy his own vehicle since the crash and he refused to let Tatum and me buy one for him. I'm not sure why, though, since the vehicles he prefers would hardly be a noticeable amount of money taken out of either of our accounts.

Hayden is wearing hiking boots and jeans, with the hood of his hoodie sitting over his hat in an attempt to keep him dry longer since it's drizzling rain. When he spots my car, I step out.

"What are you doing here?" He eyes my clothes, my usual attire, then stops at the hood of his truck and unfurls a waterproof map of the mountains, placing it on the flat metal. "I take it you didn't come to join the search party."

There are posters and ribbons all over the place. Some have pictures of Tatum and describe her physical features in case anyone comes across her. Others thank volunteers for helping to look for her. The posters were all likely made by Nyasia. She talks to Hayden more than she does to me. Still, she sent me an aggressive text threatening to make me the next missing person if I don't keep her updated on everything I know. Tatum and Nyasia are like sisters, so because of that, I told her I already intended to.

Stopping beside him, I watch as Hayden traces a river on the map, then drags his finger some distance away from the water before making a mark. Knowing his system now, I know he found either a man-made shelter or some sort of cave. Whatever it was, it held no sign of our girl.

My shoulders deflate. It's stupid, but I got my hopes up that something would turn up today. Then again, something did turn up. Considering *who* it was, maybe I'm glad there's still no sign of her. Maybe that means she's still alive.

"You know my skills are of better use somewhere else." This morning as Hayden set out to search the forest again, I made myself busy sorting through some potential leads my father's people came up with. They all turned out to lead nowhere.

Hayden makes one more mark on the map before folding it up and tucking it away in his backpack. He's angry and tired, and I want to ask him if he's still in this, but I can't. And the reason why is purely selfish. I don't want to ask because I don't want to hear him say *no.* Maybe if I don't ask, he won't walk away from all of this pain.

It's hard picturing him leaving me — leaving *Tatum* when she needs him the most. Especially since I know the kind of man he is and that he truly loves Tate. But people leave. I've experienced it with every person I've ever cared about, so I'm waiting for the moment he leaves, too. The fact he hasn't yet makes me persistently anxious.

"Yeah, I suppose you're right. Did you find anything?" His tone is flat, and he's still not looking at me, proving he wasn't feeling as hopeful today as I was.

This is it. My opening to tell him what was found.

What if this is the final straw? This could be the very thing that makes him walk away.

But I can't keep this from him. It wouldn't be right for him to hear it from Zara, so I take a breath and lift my chin.

"Actually, that's why I'm here," I admit. The hope which fills his expression, the earnest look in his brown eyes...it destroys me. "Hayden."

He knows by the tender way I said his name that what I'm about to say isn't the good news he was wishing for. His expression slowly drops.

"Say it," he utters.

"The police found Nick's body. He's dead." A heavy breath whooshes out of his chest and he looks past me toward the exit of the dirt parking lot as if he's looking for his friend somewhere behind me.

"His body?" he breathes out. "That's...where? What happened to him?"

"A hiker found him off a trail on the other side of town outside the city border." I hesitate, hating what I have to admit next, but knowing I have to tell him because he's going to find out, anyway. "He was murdered. I'm sorry."

He curses as he tries to work through the information. I want to go to him but he took a couple of steps back the moment I said Nick was murdered as if I were the one who caused his best friend's death and he needed distance.

"No, that...that doesn't make any sense." Hayden's voice rises. "He isn't even here! He's with his girlfriend!"

That was a lie. No one thought to look into Nick before, but after Zara learned about the police's discovery from hacking into their database, she did her research. Phone records show he never left the county, but finding his exact location has been tricky. When it should show exactly where he's been, the location is scrambled. Knowing he has been in the county the whole time is the closest we can get.

Zara contacted his girlfriend after the discovery, and she claimed she hadn't seen Nick in months. Although his death raises suspicion and I plan to talk to my dad about it since I know he was aiming to acquire Nick's business, I don't admit any of this to Hayden. Though I never cared for Nick, I care deeply for Hayden. Nick was his best friend. I don't want to tarnish his image of him without having facts that can be supported with proof.

Hayden looks at me, his eyes filled with so much anguish. Then, he slams a fist on the hood of the truck and kicks one of the tires.

"God damn it!" he shouts loudly. "Fuck!" Hayden throws the hood off of his head and yanks his hat off, running a hand roughly through his slightly curly brown hair, tugging at the roots.

Going to him, I pull him into my body, wrapping him securely in my arms the way he did for me when I was hurting the first night in the hospital. He's slightly taller than I am, but he still buries his face in my neck as he finally releases the tears which had been brimming in his eyes. They're hot against my skin and when I feel his shoulders start to shake, I hold him tighter. However long he has to stand here and grieve, I will remain his steady shoulder to lean on. I'm not going to let him face his agony over his best friend's death alone on top of everything else.

"I'm so sorry," I whisper. If Nick was at all connected to Tatum's abduction, then his death is partly my fault. The list of things which will eventually make Hell my eternal home grows longer and longer every day. "I'm so sorry."

Two days later, I watch my father's arrival on the security camera screen in my office. Even as I watch him walk to my front door, I make no move to get up and meet him. He doesn't attempt to open the door, and he doesn't ring the bell. Instead, he looks up into the camera positioned above the door and stares through the lens as if he could see me. Not the other way around. The man already knows the door will be locked and that I'm watching. In order to enter through the front door, either a key or a passcode is required, and he has neither.

Talking to my dad is the absolute last thing I want to do right now because I know what it'll be about. I've been anticipating this visit since I've been screening his calls and am surprised it took him this long to show up. Still, it doesn't mean I'm any more mentally prepared for it.

Finally, I get up from my desk and walk leisurely to the door. When I get there, I pull it open and move aside for him to enter without saying a word. I barely even look at him. With eyes the same color as mine, he looks around what he can see of the house with veiled interest. I'm used to the type of power game that's at play now. We're both waiting for the other person to say something; the first one to speak loses. It's a game we've played hundreds of times so I'm quite familiar, but I'm anxious to get back to what I was doing. I might finally have some useful information. In order to confirm it, though, I need him gone. With him standing so close, my body is too tense to focus. Considering how riled up my nerves have been the past few days, I can't stand another distraction, so I open my mouth and lose the game.

"What do you want?" Facing me again, he crosses his arms, mirroring my position.

"I want to know why you think you have the right to pull all my people off of their current assignments for your own dealings?" *My own dealings.* As if all Tatum is is just another nobody tied to our business, making us more money we don't need. "Your insolence since that girl showed up has been intolerable. I shoul—"

"You can punish me however the hell you want when this is over. You can bring on your worst and I'll accept it with a smile on my face so long as we get *Tatum* back first." I snarl in his face since I closed much of the gap between us. My dad opens his mouth to say something, but I continue before he can start. "She's with Benjamin, Dad."

The use of that last word is strange to both of us, and I can see the flash of surprise on his face before it's gone. I'll call him *Dad* at events like I'm supposed to and mentally use the word. Perhaps that's for a reason which should be unpacked in therapy, I don't know. But in private, when it's just the two of us, or we're with Zara, I never call him that. As far as I'm concerned, he was stripped of the title and honor that should come with those three letters years ago. I don't know why I said it now. There's no audience or official reason to. *Pure desperation, maybe?*

I take things one step further in case my last words didn't have the same emotional effect on him as they did with me. "What if it was Mum? You'd do everything you could for her. Wouldn't you?"

Those eyes that are twin to mine eye me for a too-long, too-quiet moment before he finally nods. "They'll stay on assignment. But don't think your actions will go without punishment when it's over." The man doesn't even wait for a reply before he turns and walks away.

Chapter Forty-Six

HAYDEN

"Wait, wait, wait. I've seen that guy before. The night Tatum went missing, he was part of the crowd outside her house. Why do you have his picture pulled up?" I have one hand braced on the back of the desk chair Anthony is currently sitting in whilst I lean forward, pointing at his computer screen with my other hand. I got to the house right as Clay was leaving. My presence was obvious since we couldn't have been more than six feet from one another, but he didn't spare me glance. Not that I care. Anthony watched him leave from his front door before telling me to come inside. I received a text about half an hour ago saying he found something. Now, despite the light rain outside, I'm covered in a layer of sweat after cutting my latest search short and running back to the truck.

Anthony's teeth grind together and one of his hands clenches then flexes beside the keyboard. "Are you sure this is the same man?" Something about his voice is chilling.

I examine the picture again and take myself back to that night. The crowd of curious people who were drawn to Tatum's house by the flashing lights of police cars like moths to a flame pissed me off. I looked at people I've known forever with anger even though they weren't doing anything wrong. But, there was someone I didn't recognize. As I surveyed the crowd, I caught him staring at me. I figured it was because he'd witnessed me shouting in officer's faces, pinning the blame on them in a useless attempt to lighten the weight of guilt on my shoulders.

"Yeah, I'm sure. Who is he?"

Anthony inhales an angry breath through his nose. "This is the owner of the silver car we saw Benjamin with on the security camera in Colorado." He pauses and I use the time to recall the detail which had thrown us off. "Also known as Lucas Campbell."

My head whips around to look at him, gaping. "Lucas, as in Tatum's piece of shit ex-boyfriend from Texas?" Anthony pushes back in the seat to stand, grabs his wallet and keys, and storms out of the room without another word. "Where are you going?"

In a matter of seconds, Anthony is taking quick steps down the stairs that lead from his front door and continues hastily toward his car. "To Texas so I can pay Lucas a visit. Are you coming?"

This visit is going to be anything but friendly. That much is easy to tell from Anthony's murderous tone and the dangerous gleam in his eyes when he looks at me over the roof of his Audi. Whatever is going to happen in Texas is surely going to be unlike anything I've experienced before. I'm going to be part of Anthony's private world. Logically, I should say *no*. I should keep myself away from that sort of trouble. But there's no room for logical thinking right now. The things I would do to find Tatum, the levels I would stoop to...

"Fuck yeah, I am."

Less than an hour later, after shooting a couple of texts back and forth with Nyasia about taking care of Lenny while we're gone, I stare out the window of the Kensington family private jet. If someone would have told me six months ago that this would be my life, I'd think they were high as hell. Not a single part of this is even remotely close to what I had planned for my life. In fact, after I had to leave college, I wasn't interested in being in another relationship for a long, long time. I didn't care to be romantically involved. When I met Tate, though, damn. I'd never changed my mind about anything faster than I did with her. One look, one conversation, was all I needed to know I'd be hers forever if she'd have me.

As for Anthony? My younger self would have such mixed feelings about this. For years, he made me feel every emotion under the sun. But I never would have imagined we'd be *together*, supporting one another in our weakest moments and standing side by side through the hardest shit I've ever experienced in my life. Like I need Tatum, I need him.

Each day that passes without knowing whether she's okay, or even alive, feels like an eternity. This is the worst sort of punishment and it's like I've been sent to the very pits of Hell to live out this nightmare. Every second of every day is terrifying. The fear and hurt is constant since there has been no sort of inkling of reprieve until now.

My family has been trying their best to provide comfort while they tell me all we can do is pretty much wait for the police to do their job and hope for the best. They're only saying that because they don't know the whole truth, though. They know nothing about the horrors behind Benjamin's story and the real reason why Tatum was taken. Anthony is the only person who understands exactly what I feel. He and I are madly, truly, deeply in love with the same girl. Our brutal feelings of loss are matched. Shortly after she was taken, I pressed him to tell me everything he knew about Benjamin so I wouldn't be in the dark about anything. Anthony obliged my request, telling me details that churned my stomach. I know all the horrible things Benjamin's done to other people and what he could very well be doing to Tate.

So, yeah. I need him. When my thoughts become a jumbled disaster of the fear, regret, and sorrow running through my head *every single second*, Anthony is the one who can pull me out and steady me once again. Sometimes I feel like I'm going insane because the more I think about her, the less I know about what could be happening. I'm a mess. An absolute wreck but Anthony is always there, holding onto me. Always.

This lead is like a light in the dark. It's like sucking in my first real breath since we came back inside from searching the trees to find Tatum's car missing and that she'd left without a word. Rather than existing in torment, turning over every rock and branch and doing what I can to find her, I can finally do something *real* to help.

For the first time in days, there's tangible hope. It's almost too good to be true since things have only gotten impossibly worse since this started. When I saw Anthony in the muddy parking lot the other day, I knew he wasn't bringing good news with him. Still, I got caught up in a false sense of hope when I asked if he'd found anything. I never, ever would have expected it to be the body of my best friend.

Tatum's current fate is unknown, but Nick's is certain. He's gone forever. There's no getting him back, and the knowledge of that is gut-wrenching. He's been by my side since we were kids in school. We cheated off each other's papers in classes, played together on the same sports teams and always made sure the numbers on our jerseys were consecutive. For years, we gave each other equal parts shit for the decisions we made and loving support. Till the day he died, though the last few days were strictly from my end, his number was the busiest one in my phone. Calls, texts, you name it.

There's no doubt in my mind Nick was my platonic soulmate. He felt the same way, too. I'll never forget the night after our school team won a championship game and we were at an after party on the beach. There was a bonfire blazing brightly against the night, our classmates chatting all around us and music bumping through someone's speaker. Nick and I sat on the tail-gate of my truck drinking beers when he suddenly grabbed my shoulder and said, *"You're my twin flame, you know that? I love you."*

I didn't know what that term meant at the time, so I smiled and nodded. When I got home very early the next morning, I looked it up. Before falling asleep I sent him a text that said, '*Hey twin flame. You're mine too. BTW I got caught sneaking in way past curfew and it's ur fault so ur helping me with the makeup chores tomorrow.*'

After that, those two words became our contact names for each other in our phones. It was like an inside joke, but also, not at all. Some people gave us crap for it when they noticed, but we didn't care. Like I said, we were platonic soulmates. Minimizing the love I want to show for someone based on what other people think has never been something I cared about. Love is never something that should be hidden, no matter the type of love it is.

Knowing only one flame is lit now...it's devastating. All this time, I wanted him to answer one of my calls so I could hear him tell me things were going to be alright. Now I feel like a complete ass because while I was getting more upset every day thinking he was ignoring me in a time of need, he was...God, he...

So this lead, this fraction of hope, I will not let it go to waste. No matter what's going to happen in Texas, I'm going to make sure we get every bit of useful information we can out of it. And hopefully, fuck, *hopefully* today is the day Tatum comes home.

Chapter Forty-Seven

ANTHONY

Lots of men think they're tough. They talk a big game about what they'd do if someone ever broke into their house.

I hope someone would. I'd kill them.

If someone tried, I'd make sure that was the last thing they'd ever do.

It would be a mistake to come to my house.

I'm sure everyone has heard some sort of variation of those phrases. When the time comes, however, many often find out *fight* is not their trauma response after all. Most of the time, these people who thought themselves a force to be reckoned with experience freeze or flight in the heat of the moment. It's always so satisfying to me when they do.

A house this size provides plenty of space to run and hide, and a couple of Lucas' friends gave doing so their best shot, but Hayden proved to be able to throw quite the punch. I'd never seen fury or violence from Hayden like what I witnessed when we first burst through the front door.

Luckily, Lucas' closest friends all share the same house in

Highland Park. They're spoiled rich kids who think they can do whatever they want and get away with it thanks to their parents' money. That much is obvious by the way we found them all terrorizing a young maid, one of them running his hands all over her. Hayden darted up to them and that's when the violence started. When we got them bound and on their knees, I handed each of the three maids in total that we found in the house a stack of large bills in exchange for their silence. Then I wrote down a connection I have in the area where they can get work which will pay more and be far less handsy.

Now, four of Lucas' friends kneel bloody with their hands restrained behind their backs. The amount of blood they're covered in varies from person to person depending on how much trouble they gave us, but it didn't take long for them to cave and snitch on their friend. They say Lucas isn't here. As in, in the whole state of Texas and hasn't been for a while. If he's a part of Tatum's disappearance like I now suspect, then that tracks. He's likely been gone for at least a couple months, keeping surveillance on Tatum and aiding the healing of Benjamin's gunshot wound. That explains why he never showed up at any of the hospitals.

With a gun pointed at one man's head, I hold his phone to my ear and listen to the line ring.

"Hey, Drake. What's up, man?" Hearing Lucas' voice for the first time brings on a fresh wave of fury.

"Tell me where she is," I seethe through gritted teeth. *He's part of this. I know it.*

He pauses on the line, probably confused, trying to figure out why I don't sound like his buddy.

"Who is this?"

"Tell me. Where. She is."

Another pause. "Well, well, this is one of the boyfriends, isn't it? You've got an accent so let me guess, you're...Anthony?" He laughs and then what immediately follows is a sound I'll never be able to forget; Tatum screaming in pain.

Without blinking I empty the magazine of the gun into

Drake's head. The remaining three of his friends shout with terror and fear for their own lives.

"Give me your gun and reload this one," I instruct Hayden with an emotionless tone. He's shocked by what I did but he doesn't say anything about it. Had he heard what I just did, he wouldn't even be phased. I'm glad he didn't hear it, though. Because now all I can think about is the misery she's experiencing and the kind of fear that's come from being held captive by two violent men. "Tell me where she is," I repeat to Lucas, coming up to another one of his friends. This one immediately wets himself when I come to a stop beside him and press the barrel of Hayden's gun to his temple.

Having heard that there's multiple men here with us and not only Drake, the humor in Lucas' voice is gone now when he asks, "Who did you kill?"

I empty another magazine into the second man's skull. Without even having to ask, Hayden extends a freshly loaded gun my way. The only words I want to hear come out of Lucas is the answer to what I'm asking. Anything else will result in a body. When I run out of friends, we'll move on to his family. Old professors. Hell, the person who sold him his car. I will kill everyone he's ever come in contact with until I get my answer.

"Tell me where she is." I stop beside a third man who's crying like a child now, begging for his life.

"Okay, stop!" Lucas shouts. "Jesus. We're at—" but then there's a gunshot on his end and my blood stops. My first thought is that he just shot Tatum, but I can hear his phone clattering to the ground so that doesn't add up. There's some rustling, then a new voice is on the phone. One I recognize.

"Go ahead and pull the trigger, Anthony. You already killed the only person I cared about." *Benjamin.* "I'm enjoying making the process painful and slow for the girl you love. Who knows? Maybe Hayden will be next. Bye, bye now." The line disconnects and I'm left frozen with the phone to my ear.

"Kens?" Hayden questions when too much time passes where

I don't say or do anything. I can feel the anxiety creeping in. It slithers coldly up my spine and snakes down my arms into each of my fingers. The second my fingers start to shake I pull the trigger, splitting the rounds in the gun between the two remaining men.

"Let's go." My voice sounds hoarse and slightly out of breath for no reason. Except, there is a reason. A damn good one for my rising panic.

'I'm enjoying making the process painful and slow for the girl you love.'

As I start for the door, leaving the bodies in the middle of the floor, my head starts to spin. I'm on the verge of a panic attack and the difficulty to breathe has me pressing a hand to my chest.

'Who knows? Maybe Hayden will be next.'

"Kens, Kens, hey, what's going on? What did he say?" Hayden looks terrified as he grabs me by the shoulder and comes to a stop in front of me, blocking my path.

"She's alive," I say, and pain fills my chest at the knowledge.

A mixture of confusion and hope floods his face. "That's a good thing."

My mouth parts but words fail me. *Is it a good thing?* They're hurting her. Badly. God knows what she's been through with them. The endless possibilities and the knowledge of the things Benjamin used to do when he worked for my dad make me sick. Turning away from Hayden, I prepare myself for the possibility of throwing up by bracing my hands on my knees, but it doesn't come.

"She's being tortured." Saying the words out loud makes it more real and I know the sort of impact they're going to have on Hayden. Thinking of her pain and fear, and knowing I'm passing on my misery to Hayden increases my nausea until I throw up on the marble floor.

"She's..." Hayden whispers, shock in his voice. We both knew it was a likely possibility but didn't want to believe it. "No. No, that— Fuck!"

I spit the remaining vomit out then straighten. When I face

him again, I find that he's clenching the bridge of his nose like he does when he's stressed. Or in this case, completely freaking the hell out.

It's ripping us apart to know she's suffering and we're not there to stop it. We don't know where *there* even is. Anything we do isn't enough. We're hitting one dead end after another.

Clearly, this lead didn't pan out the way we hoped it would, either. While on the family plane, I tried to stop the thoughts since I know how blinding hope can be, but I couldn't help myself. I kept picturing us finding Tatum alive and untouched from any harm, then bringing her home with us. After, of course, I brutally slaughtered everyone that had the smallest thing to do with her abduction. Their bodies would have to be mopped up and carried out in buckets, not body bags.

Since that's not how things went, it's time we start over. All clues and any hints will be looked at again since the very beginning. Every route in and out of town will be explored again and if still nothing shows up, I'm going to send out my father's company to kick down every door and search every house, consequences be damned. After all, the law really has no power when it comes to the Kensington's.

Rules have already been broken, but I'm about to abuse the fuck out of my family name and the power it holds. I will have my dad's people search for days. Weeks. Years. They'll search every house in the country and then onto the next one if there's still no sign of her. I will never stop the search for Tatum. I will never give up. I will work myself and my father's people to the point of exhaustion. God help Benjamin when we find them because he's going to wish he was dead when I get my hands on him. Everything he's done to Tatum will be done to him and then so much more.

Chapter Forty-Eight

HAYDEN

Moonlight shines off the tips of the waves before they crash into silhouetted rocks and tumble into the Pacific NorthWest shore of my home state. Popping off the cap to another long-necked bottle, I barely taste the beer as I drink it down where I sit in the sand. The noise from the surf nearly drowns out the noise in my head. Nearly. But not quite, so I take another drink.

She's being tortured.

That's all I've been able to think about. My girl is being tortured.

What can I do to stop it? Absolutely nothing. I tried. I've hiked my ass off searching the surrounding mountains for a single sign. Shit, I just left a pile of bodies behind in Texas and it was all for nothing.

This isn't like some fantasy book, like the kinds she has on her bookshelf. Tatum wasn't taken by a rival kingdom I have to take a dangerous journey to, and I can't slaughter my way through the guards until I get to her. I would, if this was that type of story, but it's not. She was taken by a man who has no one. The only other man that was in this with him, he murdered himself in order to keep their location a secret. Unlike a castle in romantasy books, there's no massive landmark with a path that leads me right to where she is. We have no fucking clue where to go. Not. One.

The word *hopeless* keeps ringing in my head. It has been since Anthony and I sat on his plane to return home. My choices for the over four-hour plane ride were to either listen to that word on repeat, or replay the images of what we'd done since Anthony and I didn't speak a word to each other the entire time.

I'm conflicted about how to feel. The men he killed had nothing to do with Tatum's abduction, but they were killed for it, anyway. Yet, they weren't entirely innocent. There was fear in the maid's eyes when we got inside the young men's mansion and something I didn't like one bit on their faces. If they weren't going to do something to hurt her then, it was just a matter of time before they would have. Especially since they're friends with someone like Lucas, who clearly hurt Tatum, and they stood beside him regardless.

The way Anthony looked when he repeatedly pulled the trigger on those men is something I will never be able to forget. His flexed arm and his angry, red-rimmed eyes made him resemble a painting I'd learned about while at Stanford; *L'Ange déchu* by artist Alexandre Cabanel. In that moment of violence like I'd never seen before, Anthony resembled the fallen angel himself; Lucifer.

One day, back when we were still in school, Anthony and I ended up in a fistfight over something stupid, a prank, I think. I ended up sitting in the principal's office, holding an ice pack to my split lip and sporting a darkening bruise right below my eye. Anthony sat across from me sporting a nasty glare and held an ice pack to the ridge of his jaw. Clay walked in, made a hefty donation to the school as an 'apology' and then surprise, surprise, Anthony got to go back to class without any sort of repercussion. Meanwhile, I was on the verge of suspension. My dad is a kind man, though. He's always doing favors for the people in town and helps out as much as he can so has the respect of pretty much everyone. Because of that, not by flashing his money, I too was finally released without the fight affecting my school record. I remember that he stopped me in the hallway after the principal released me and admitted his disappointment, which is not something I was not accustomed to having in the least. I felt horrible because of it. He started to go on about how violence wasn't the answer like I'm sure most parents would.

"Do not lead by the Kensington's example," he'd told me. *"You'll only end up in trouble and become someone you'll one day look into the mirror and not like."*

What's my dad going to think when he finds out about Texas? Anthony said no one would since he had a team of people already on their way to 'take care of it' before we even left the house, but still. What if we get caught? His money and his name will surely keep him out of trouble like it did all those years ago in school. But what about me? I'll end up behind bars. Even if we don't get caught, can I keep a secret like this from my parents? At the same time, it's not like I can tell them about it.

I finish off the bottle in my hand and let it clink against the others when I drop it on the sand before grabbing another one.

Sure, as kids when we were fighting over something so minuscule, I don't even remember what started it, then I agree; violence isn't the answer. Right now, though...violence seems pretty damn deserving. After all, I can't escape it. It's all around me. Anthony has been hurt, Tatum has been hurt, I've been hurt, Nick has been fucking *murdered*. If everyone else is fighting, I should be too. Sometimes being gentle just won't cut it. I know that. I just have to get my dad's voice about it out of my head.

"There you are." Coincidentally, it's my dad's voice I hear over the sound of the surf. Shame forces my gaze down to the sand between my feet. I stay sitting and don't look behind me to greet him. His quiet steps can be heard as he approaches me and there's movement on the edges of my vision as he sits beside me with a quiet grunt.

We sit beside each other listening to the water for a couple of minutes before I speak up. "How did you know I was here?" I finally look at my dad and he braces his arms on his knees.

"Anthony came by the house looking for you. Said you took off after the two of you went through something pretty intense."

A lump builds in my throat and I look away from him, not wanting to see his face if he's about to look at me with disappointment. "Did he tell you what it was?" I sip from the bottle in my hand then turn it over, looking at the label I can barely see in the dark as if I've never seen it before. Anything to not look at him right now.

"No," he informs me, and I hold in my sigh of relief. "But whatever it was, I'm sure it had something to do with the specks of blood I noticed on his neck by the collar of his shirt." That sigh I was holding in completely disappears. I don't know what to say. What *can* I say?

"How did you know I was here?" I ask again.

He sighs quietly. Sadly. "You and Nick spent so much time in that water with your boards," he recalls, and I understand his tone now. Nick was almost like a second son to him due to how much time we spent together. "Getting you two out of the surf was like pulling teeth, sometimes. Whenever you boys didn't have practice you were always either hiking or surfing. It's too dark for the forest right now, so here we are."

"Here we are," I echo quietly. After the news broke about Nick, the whole town started grieving. I can hardly go anywhere now without seeing some sort of poster or something regarding Tatum or Nick. The city I love has become suffocating with the reminders of their loss. Two people I love with everything I've got have been reduced to posters. But this was my spot with Nick. We didn't want anyone spoiling our surf time by getting in the way, so we kept it private. Now, this is one of the only places untouched by ribbons and physical reminders of their loss. There're only memories here.

"You didn't tell Anthony about this place?"

"Nah." My dad picks up a stick from the sand and turns it over in his fingers. "I figured if you wanted to be with him, you would. But you're my son, I had to make sure you're alright. Do you want to talk about it? *Any* of it?"

My dad has always been someone I could talk to about anything but it's different this time. "No." *Yes. But I can't. Not to you.* "Can we just...sit here for a little bit without talking? You don't want to hear about what Anthony and I were doing and I don't want to talk about it. I don't want to talk about what it's like to lose your best friend, or to have a missing girlfriend, either. I want to sit." I swallow another gulp of beer. The effects of the already downed bottles are starting to take root. I drank them so quickly, one after another, the alcohol is finally starting to catch up.

"Why are you drinking right now, son?" My family doesn't care about drinking alcohol. They just didn't want us kids to drink it when we were too young to buy it ourselves, so his question confuses me for a second.

"Why does anyone drink?" *Maybe I'm thirsty and trying to quench the unshakable thirst only alcohol can fix. Or maybe I'm heartbroken and trying to forget. Maybe I'm trying to run from the ghost of regret like a damn coward.* It occurs to me then that that's the exact reason behind his question. No one in my family has ever turned to alcohol for comfort before. The family has always been all the support we needed. But they can't support me now. It's for their safety I'm keeping them in the dark.

Hopeless.

There's that word again. Coincidentally, it's also the reason for the drink in my hand. Or, *had* a drink in my hand. One moment, the bottle is dangling loosely in my fingertips. The next, it's being ripped away and dumped out into the sand by my dad.

"You quit that, now," he demands. I blink in surprise at him. I hardly ever hear my dad's voice when he's angry since it's not often he lets that particular emotion control him. "You've got a woman who needs you to keep your head clear and a man who's worried about you. I don't know what you two have been doing but I'm not ignorant enough to think it doesn't have something to do with your girl and that you're not breaking any laws. Am I right? Well? Am I?"

I clench my jaw and sigh through my nose. "Yeah. You're right," I admit with a small nod.

"I figured." My dad's tone has softened, but just a little. "He promised me you're safe, and you'll stay that way. That's all I care about. That, and Tatum's safe return, of course, but my childrens' safety will always be my top priority. Sober up and stay that way, son. Don't let alcohol be your crutch because you don't need one. Your family is here for you. Always. Don't keep us in the dark while your own light is fading."

The shake of my head is involuntary. I can't bring them into this. "I can't risk something happening to any of you." My voice is a whisper and when I look up at him, I feel as vulnerable as I did when I was a kid. Can he see the desperate plea in my eyes to stay out of this?

He holds my gaze, then his lips twitch into a frown. "Remember, no matter how hopeless it feels, you're not alone." It's like he read my mind and I feel emotion clog my throat again, preventing any words from coming out. Not that I could think of any to say right now. My dad puts a hand on my head and places a kiss in my hair. "Stay smart. Stay sober. Stay alive. I love you, Heyday." The use of my childhood nickname makes things hit even harder before he walks off. I turn to watch him go and am shocked to find Anthony standing nearby where the sand meets the treeline. My dad pats his shoulder lightly as he passes him and disappears in the dark, likely back to his vehicle to return home.

Anthony's hands are in his pockets as he stares at me with an emotionless expression, and he makes no move to come closer. Neither do I.

"You're here," I finally say. Hearing that he went to my parents' home to look for me was a shock, even considering how far our relationship with each other has evolved. Knowing he followed my dad here and is now standing in front of me makes it all the more surprising.

"You left," Anthony counters. Though his face shows no emotions, the tone of his voice displays it all. Anger. Worry. Relief.

I glance at the sand for a second then back up to him. "I know. I'm sorry."

"Are you...done?"

"Done?" I echo, confused.

"With us. This nightmare we're living. Are you stepping out?"

"What?" I ask, surprised he'd even ask that. "No, of course not. Fuck no, I'm not leaving. Especially while Tate is still out there somewhere. Jesus. I needed some time to...I don't know, think for a little bit, I guess. I'm not done. Just overwhelmed," I tell him quickly and honestly.

Anthony walks toward me now, stopping a foot away before grabbing the back of my head and bringing our foreheads together. His grip in my hair is tight.

"You *left* with no warning. No word. Nothing. You can't do that." And that's when I notice the pain in his voice. As soon as we landed in Maple Crest, we drove back to Anthony's place. Once his Audi was parked, I went straight for my dad's truck and drove off. I realize now how shitty of a move that was to just bail, but I couldn't think of anything else at the time. The way he said those words makes me realize not only was that a stupid move on my part, it was a big deal to him. One that scared him even though he won't admit it.

My hand moves to hold the back of his blonde hair, similar to how he's holding mine but in a softer grip. "I'm not leaving. Ever. Got it? No matter how hard things get, or how far we have to go, I'm in for it all. We're going to get Tatum back, *together*, and then the three of us are *staying* together. I'm not giving you up, Kens, I promise you that." His light eyes look from one of my irises to the other.

Chapter Forty-Nine

ANTHONY

I'm standing in front of the lit fireplace, staring at the painting which hangs above it when my cell phone rings. Glancing down at the screen, I see my sister's name. My fingers are quick to answer the call.

"Are you home?" Zara asks before I can even say anything.

"Yes," I respond with more bitterness than necessary. *She's trying to help you, you prick. It's okay to be mad. Just remember to be mad at the right people.* Scrubbing my face with my free hand, I take half a second to collect myself. I understand how Hayden felt on the beach yesterday. *I need this all to be over already.* "Did you find out anything useful?"

"Maybe. I'm coming over." She hangs up but I keep the device in my hand. Using my free hand, I undo a couple of buttons on my shirt. It feels like I'm being choked. The invisible hand of anxiety has had a tight grip on me since Tatum was taken and it won't let go.

Tapping the screen a couple of times, I hold my phone to my ear again and listen to the line ring. I expect it's about to go to voicemail, but Hayden answers the call before it does. Our conversation is short, less than a minute. He stays on only long enough to hear about my previous call with Zara and to tell me he's on his way.

Less than half an hour later, both he and Zara arrive within minutes of each other. Zara arrived first and made herself busy spreading papers all over the island in my kitchen. Hayden doesn't even knock when he enters the house, still dressed in his suit.

Today was Nick's funeral. I attended the burial, but Hayden went alone to Nick's parent's house afterward. Considering the sleepless nights, the constant level of business and stress we've had with Tatum, and now attending his best friend's funeral, Hayden looks awful. His face seems thinner. His eyes are muted brown and red-rimmed; almost haunted looking.

"Please tell me you have something that will help us find her," he nearly begs as he rushes into the kitchen like he doesn't want to waste another second before finding out what Zara knows. I feel the same way.

"*Maybe*," my sister starts, "it might be a long shot, but I think there's something worth checking out." She could have narrowed things down from anywhere in the world to a single country and I'd be shouting with joy. Just as long as I'm one step closer to getting my girl back.

"Well?" Hayden urges rather impatiently.

"You said to go back to the very beginning, right?" she addresses me. Although she wasn't seriously asking me to confirm, I nod anyway. "Well, I did, and I started thinking about the day I was with her during the camera set up. She'd briefly mentioned her house being only the one floor."

"And?" I question this time.

"You thought you heard something at her house a few days ago, right?" she asks Hayden who is standing with his arms crossed. He looks at me, probably because he wasn't aware I'd told Zara about the occurrence from when he and I went to pick up Lenny's medication, then nods. "What room did it sound like it came from?"

"I don't know." He shrugs lightly, and his eyebrows pull together with focus as he gives thought to her question. "I guess it didn't really sound like it came from one of the rooms. It sounded like it was far away."

Zara nods like his answer is both what she expected, and something that makes sense to her. The problem is that it makes sense to *only* her.

"Were you standing by a vent?"

Hayden cocks his head and I almost do the same thing. "Was I... what? I don't know."

"Think about it, Hayden!" Zara snaps. "Were you by a vent?"

Hayden sucks in his bottom lip a little and bites it as he thinks. Then, he nods again. "Yeah. Yeah, I was. Why?"

"When the sun sets tomorrow, meet me at home," my sister states flatly, looking from me, to Hayden, then back to me again.

I've read the note so many times I know exactly where that quote is from. "That's what Benjamin wrote to Tatum, but it doesn't help us. Hayden and I checked every inch of the place. So did the police, and so did our company. They were long gone by the time Hayden and I got there that night."

Zara points one of her emerald-green painted fingernails at a set of blueprints spread out on the countertop. "You didn't check every inch. Tatum's house isn't one level like she thought. There's a basement floor and according to these records right here, her uncle hired people to both expand and upgrade the space a few years ago."

My chest stills and a cold wave rushes through my body. "Meet me at home," I repeat precariously, the pieces finally coming together in my mind. I'm terrified and angry to think this is going where I think it's going. Yet at the same time, my heart has picked up its pace in the name of relief.

"Exactly," she confirms. Her eyes hold a whole new level of intensity, and I can tell that she sees me making the connections she uncovered.

"Holy shit," Hayden whispers, his arms falling to his sides.

His voice raises when he speaks again. "Are you saying she's at the house?"

Zara's gaze shifts to him. "You were likely standing by a vent that runs to the basement. I'm not saying it's absolute. But I'm saying you boys should grab your guns and come with me while I go check this out and hope your trigger fingers are faster than mine. If I'm right, Benjamin is going to die tonight."

Twenty seconds. That's the amount of time which passes from when Zara finishes speaking, to the three of us being armed and barreling out my front door. Zara runs to her motorcycle while Hayden and I get in the Audi. She finishes fastening her helmet right as my engine turns over and then we're taking off. My sister is on one tire when she first starts to move, then takes off like a bullet when her front tire touches the ground again. I pull out of the driveway fast enough to make Hayden fall further back into his seat and curse in surprise.

We're not going to call the police. Not yet. If Zara is right, then I want to make sure we're the first one's there. If she's right about what the presence of Tatum's secret basement could mean, then she's wrong about one thing, Benjamin will not die tonight. He'll wish he did, but I'll keep him alive the entire time I rid him of his fingernails, his teeth, each of his senses, and then finally his skin. Killing him will not be a fast process that happens in one night. I'll make it take weeks. Then when I finally do grant him the mercy of death, I'll make sure the pieces of him won't stop being recovered for a good long while.

HAYDEN

My heart is beating at a crazy pace and my leg is bouncing where I sit in Anthony's car. I've never wanted someone to be right about something more in my life while simultaneously never wanting someone to be more wrong at the same time. I want Zara to be right so Tatum doesn't have to live in that situation for one more second. But I want her to be wrong because that means she was right there within reach this whole time.

Tatum called out to me. I heard it, and I walked away. I had no idea. But how could I? Hearing her voice was something I wanted so badly I thought my mind was making it up, playing tricks on me.

My gun has a full magazine and a bullet in the chamber already, but I double-check it anyway. Then I reach over for Anthony's gun and check his too just to give myself something to do. What should have been a short drive feels like it takes an eternity even though Anthony is taking the many turns of the winding road from one end of the city to the other at a dangerous speed, and has the pedal plastered to the floor on the straight parts. Zara is barely in front of us, the brake lights of her Kawasaki like a laser leading the way in the dark of the night.

Coming to a screeching halt outside of the house, we're out of the vehicle with our weapons drawn and sprinting for the door within seconds. When the door is open, I flip the light switch beside the entrance with no result, so I pull two flashlights from my jacket pocket and hand one to Anthony. Zara has one as an add-on to her weapon which she switches on. One after another, we continue further into the house.

"Where's the entrance to the basement?" Anthony whispers to his sister. A second after his question we hear the clatter of several metal objects and a feminine shout. Sure enough, it sounds like it's coming from below our feet.

"Tate!" I shout into the dark, looking at the floorboards as if I could see right through them. The beam of my flashlight scans the main room looking for the damned entrance to the basement. It's a useless attempt, I know that, still I search anyway. Zara unfolds a paper she pulls from her back pocket and her brother shines his light on it.

"Over here," she directs, hurrying into Tatum's bedroom. Then she stops in the middle of it. Her flashlight looks around the area for a few seconds before she mutters something to herself that sounds like *here it is*. I can't be sure though since my blood pounds loudly in my ears. We don't know what's happening down there but whatever it is didn't sound good at all. Not to mention she's already spent too much time getting hurt by Benjamin already.

Zara heads for Tatum's dresser, pushing against it and then hisses for us to help her move it when it doesn't budge. Moving up to the massive piece of oak furniture, I push against it. As it starts to move, I notice faint scratch marks on the floor when our lights hit them at the right angle. With the dresser pushed aside, I realize it's from the previous times someone has moved it to reveal a hidden door that's only half the height of a normal sized one.

Tatum had mentioned once that everything remained in the

house after her uncle died. Since he was practically ostracized from the family, no one cared to help Tatum as she sorted through his belongings after she moved in. Most of it she gave away, but she still kept some things, including bits and pieces of the furniture he'd had. One of which was this very dresser.

Anthony is the first to burst through the newly revealed door, his gun raised. Bright light from the room below floods through the entryway, illuminating the way for Zara as she follows right behind her brother, then me. Each of us is ready to cause some serious pain and suffering to the shithead that took our girl. Yet when we reach the bottom of the short staircase leading down and take in the scene around us, we all stop.

"Oh my God," I mutter.

"Anthony," Zara whispers. A quick glance at him shows he's wide-eyed and gaping slightly. Together, the three of us stand frozen in the room that's covered with blood. None of us knows what to think of the gory scene before us. Unease and dread floods my body as I look around. It's as if we just stepped into a torture themed room of a haunted house.

Were we too late?

Articles of missing hikers — people I recognize — are taped on the wall. Beside them are photographs of the same people in various states of...fuck, I don't even know how to describe it. As my eyes scan the wall, it's abundantly obvious those people didn't get lost and die in the forest as previously thought. They were killed here, in this godforsaken basement. Peeling my eyes from the serial-killer wall of death and suffering, I make myself look at the rest of the room. There's a table and a chair with straps, knocked over trays of various instruments with the sole purpose of causing pain, and a device I assume is used for electrical shocking.

Across the large space, that I'm sure is the same size as the main floor, there's a half open door. Right as I spot a glimpse of someone's still foot lying on the ground in the room, there's a clatter off to the side of it. We all raise our guns again.

"I see movement." Anthony's voice is hard in a way I've never heard before. Then, rounding a corner, we see her.

"Tate?" I breathe. The relief of seeing her alive hits me like a freight train and fills me to the brim. However, I can't help but also feel a chill run down my spine at the same time. She doesn't look like the kind girl I know. She looks transformed into someone straight out of a nightmare. Not mine or Anthony's. But the nightmare of anyone who would ever try to harm her again. Our girl, the floor, everything — it's all painted red, in blood.

Tatum stares at us, tears brimming in her eyes. From where I stand, I can see her body trembling while she clutches a knife that's dripping with crimson. She looks relieved to see us, but at the same time, on edge, and I can't tell if she's holding the knife because she's mad at us for taking so long to get to her or if she thinks we might hurt her too.

Anthony lowers his gun and steps carefully toward her like she's a wild animal he doesn't want to spook. "It's okay, love. We're here now. You're safe." The tears stream silently down her face now, mixing with the blood that's already there, and her body shakes harder as she continues gripping the knife. Anthony keeps his accented voice soft, "Where's Benjamin?"

"He's dead. I killed him." Her voice breaks and she finally drops the blade. Anthony wraps her tightly in a hug and in a second, they're both on the floor. He's holding her in his arms in a way that makes it seem like he'll never let her go again. I don't blame him. Not one bit.

When I make it to them, he's kissing the top of her head and I see tears running down his face now too as I crash onto my knees so I can hold her as well. I have to touch her, so I know she's here. That she's alive. I want to keep her cocooned in our arms like this forever so no evil can ever touch her again.

But maybe that's not necessary. Zara moves around us to check Benjamin's body, ensuring he's dead. A quick check over my shoulder shows that she's standing over the body, not bothering to hold her weapon up,

"Holy shit, girl, you really made sure that guy wasn't going anywhere," I hear her say when I face Tatum again, putting my forehead against her tangled and blood-soaked hair. "Damn. Remind me never to get on your bad side."

If Zara is impressed by the level of brutality, then I should probably be concerned. But I'm not. I'm amazed by this woman. Proud, even, of her for saving herself. For fighting back. I'm in awe of her strength, courage, and bravery and I want to tell her how proud I am that she didn't need us to save her because she saved herself. Some other time, I will tell her all of that. Right now, though, I shower her with reassurance that it's over, Benjamin is dead, and that she's safe because that's what she needs to hear right now.

"Call 911," Anthony orders Zara when he's finally able to say something else other than telling Tatum how much he's sorry and that he loves her.

Zara removes her phone from her pocket, but our girl's head shoots up as she croaks out, "Wait." Zara stops. "Don't call. Not yet."

"What is it, gorgeous?" I ask gently in Tate's ear. My eyes close as I truly soak in the fact I'm this close to her, holding her again when I thought I never would.

She struggles to stand so Anthony and I help her onto her feet. She moves stiffly and I swallow down my questions demanding to know what happened to her down here. We'll have time for that later, thank God, but right now she's on a mission as she walks across the room. She doesn't look at any of the horrors on the wall, or the instruments which have been spilled on the floor. Likely because she's seen too much of them already. Instead, she goes straight up the stairs. Anthony and I follow close behind her, not ready to be further than an arm's length away. Reaching the top and stepping into her bedroom again, that's when she pauses and looks around. Only for a few seconds, though, before she's on the move again.

"Where are you going, love? Let us get whatever it is you want. You need to sit," Anthony urges gently.

Tatum shakes her head, reaching for something on her coffee table in the living room. "I needed these." There's the sound of a match being pulled against a striker and then a small flame sputters to life. The orange glow illuminates her face for a few seconds before she drops the match onto the couch where we used to lay kissing.

My mouth falls open as the small flame steadily grows into an impressive blaze. I almost ask her what she's doing but decide against it. Neither of the siblings ask either. Tatum is angry, and rightly so. She was terrorized here, then held against her will and experienced something unimaginable in a room she didn't know she had. Not to mention people — many people — were killed down there. Everything about her actions informs us she doesn't want anything to do with this place ever again. So, we watch.

Tatum moves around the house, striking one match after another to start a bundle of scattered fires until the house becomes an inferno, one we need to escape while we still can. Only when we're on the grass on the far side of her front yard, with the house completely engulfed in flames beyond the point of saving, does she give Zara the okay to call the police.

Tatum's legs give out underneath her likely due to physical and emotional exhaustion, but she doesn't fall. Anthony and I are on either side of her and won't let her. Instead, we slowly lower her to the cool ground. She clings tightly to us both with her face buried in our shoulders. I can't decide if I want to hold her tightly or hug her gently since we don't know where or how bad she's hurt.

That thought spurs me into action.

"I can't wait any longer, baby. I need to know where you're hurt." She nods, giving me permission to look her over, so with the bright light of the house fire, I do. Cuts, bruises, broken bones...I'm looking for anything at all to tell me what happened down there. I'm terrified of what I'll find since I know there will inevitably be injuries. I just don't know what kinds yet since she was running purely on adrenaline when we found her. Now that it's fading and she's content to just sit and wait for the emergency services to show up, I take my time looking over her body thoroughly. Anthony keeps rubbing her hands and pressing the occasional kiss to her temple, and I'm so thankful it's not just me with her right now giving her support.

It's long at all into my search when I spot the first injury. Zara finds water and a rag from somewhere which I pour carefully over Tatum's skin to clear the blood away. My world stops and there's a slight ringing in my ears. By the time I finish looking her over, I'm devastated. Cradling her body against mine again with one hand, I bury my face in my palm with the other to smother the fresh tears burning my eyes.

Zara stands nearby while Anthony and I hold our girl as sirens slowly become louder than the roar of the massive fire. Chaos surrounds us in seconds. Flashing lights from first responders mix with the light of the flames. There are people everywhere, their voices overlapping. Paramedics get her on a gurney and Anthony and I load up into the ambulance with her. Zara informs us she'll make the necessary calls to Tatum's loved ones and meet us at the hospital. When the back doors shut, the paramedic does what he can for Tatum as the ambulance speeds through the streets with its siren sounding and lights flashing.

She was the one to make it out alive. Not Benjamin. Not Lucas. Tatum. They thought they would be the ones to destroy her, and she proved them wrong. As much as Anthony and I would've loved to get revenge, I'm happy she did it herself. She made sure they never left the house again after taking her. Tatum is stronger than most people, especially her family, give her credit for. She fought for her life and won against two revenge-driven psychopaths. I can't say it enough, I'm so proud of her. *She's* alive while they're nothing more than charred bodies.

"My strong girl," I say in her ear before kissing her head once the paramedic moves away from her. My left hand is holding hers, while my right is holding Anthony's. His other hand is holding lightly onto Tatum's blanket-covered leg. For the first time in days, I can breathe easily and it's amazing how light my shoulders feel right now.

She's here, with us, alive.

We have all been through so much already, but I know Tatum's struggles aren't over yet. It's going to take time to recover from what she went through, and Anthony and I will be here to support her through everything. No matter what happens next, we will always be here for the woman we love. As well as for each other. This love we share is everything.

She is everything.

I respect her strength, her courage, and her ability to keep going. I admire her dedication and her persistence. Alongside her independence, which is something she once admitted to me was one of the reasons she came to Maple Crest in the first place. All of these reasons and more are why I fell in love with her.

As we ride in the ambulance toward the hospital, holding tightly onto her hand, a small smile appears on my face.

THREE(ISH) YEARS LATER

TATUM

We might still be in the same time zone as we were about three years ago, but nothing could be any more different. Instead of stepping out of Anthony's matte black Audi R8 with electric blue accents on the outside and an electric blue interior, he and I are stepping out of my own Audi R8. Except, the outside of this one is a shiny, cherry blossom pink. Nyasia needed a better car when she was moving to Portland for a brand-new career in makeup, so I gave her my Mercedes.

Instead of breathing in the cool, earthy, moist-filled air I loved about the Pacific Northwest, my lungs fill with the hot air of Stanford, California. As in, Stanford University where Hayden is a student again. He didn't get his scholarship back since he dropped out. Anthony just decided not to listen to him when he told him not to spend a penny on his tuition. Anthony said it's not a favor but rather an investment, but we all know the truth.

Even though Hayden hates it when people spend money on

him, probably because he never had the chance to get used to it growing up, he's thrilled to be back in school. He can really enjoy himself here now without having to worry about his family since finances won't be a problem for them for a long while. Apparently, they have had a string of random luck. I'm sure it is indeed random and has nothing to do with the handsome man leaning his lean body against the hood of my car in his fancy black suit.

"There he is," Anthony informs me after looking up from the familiar blue watch he was adjusting on his wrist. Following his gaze, I see Hayden descending the stone steps with a wide grin and wearing a neutral-toned dress suit.

"Hello, gorgeous." He plants a kiss on my lips when he's close enough to, then takes my hand and twirls me around so he can see the entirety of the gown I'm wearing. It's similar to the one I wore years ago to the fundraiser event with my guys and Nyasia, with only a few changes. What can I say? I'm a creature of comfort and familiarity. "You look stunning. And look at you Kens, all dressed up for once. What's the occasion?" Black is still Anthony's primary color, but he's toned it down on the suits a little bit. Now, he switches things up with more casual wear half the time. He might as well be wearing a suit still, though, since the price tags on his clothes are practically the same as a nice suit would have been. Apparently, Hayden thinks the same thing given his light-hearted jab.

Anthony tilts his head with a playful smirk. His gray eyes shine with something that makes me think he's about to say something inappropriate with potentially listening ears around, so I speak up before he has the chance to.

"Ready?" I ask Hayden.

"Absolutely. See you there." He gives me another swift kiss before walking away from my vehicle to his own. You know how I said Hayden doesn't like people spending money on him? Well, that's just something he's going to have to get used to since he's dating not one, but two people with money to spare and who love him dearly. So, the new orange Chevy Colorado he's currently getting into was my gift to him.

Hayden follows behind us as we drive to the gallery opening we'll be attending this evening. Only, this one is extra special because it's made up entirely of my own work. It was Anthony's idea to start the gallery, but I worked my ass off to make sure the pieces inside would be worth his effort. He told me a couple of weeks ago he was the one trying to make something worthy of my work.

Art is something extremely important to me and it means so much that this is something I get to share every single day with the two most important people in my life.

An art major.

An artist.

And a gallerist.

Together, we are perfect.

A little over an hour later, I'm standing in front of my building with Hayden and Anthony on either side of me and a crowd of people ready to go inside in front of me. From the front of the crowd, Maya and Grace both give me little wave, and I shoot a smile back at them as I lift up a pair of oversized scissors.

"My name is Tatum Davis. Welcome to the Nick Madden Memorial Gallery."

The End

Acknowledgments

To every reader who gave this book a chance: thank you. My passion for writing started when I was just a little kid with terrible handwriting, scribbling down stories in notebooks. Now I'm 24 and, although my handwriting still sucks, I get to share my stories with whoever will listen. Or in this case, read. So to you, the person reading this, thank YOU for making my lifelong dream of being a story-teller come true.

Thank you to my husband, who dealt with all my late-night writing sessions, answered all my random questions, and listened to me go back and forth a hundred times about this being the best/worst thing I ever decided to do. Your encouragement, hype, and love is what got me to this point. You have no idea how many times I replayed your pep talks in my head. This book would still be sitting in a document just for me if it wasn't for you.

Kaitryn, remember that time we happened to be watching the same TikTok live and then ended up becoming best friends? That still blows my mind sometimes. To think we sat in coffee shops dreaming about becoming authors...and now we're both authors!! You are another vital person I couldn't have done this without, so thank you for *everything*; being my friend when I needed one, for answering my 100+ questions about how to publish, and for sending me encouragement when I needed it.

To the moms in my life that supported me; my mom, and mother-in-law, your unwavering support and belief in me played such a big role in me getting to this point. I will forever be grateful for you both!

Renee, thank you for formatting my book and for answering all of our questions in the 'Help the baby authors' messenger group. I must have read through every screenshot and message you sent at least 5 times just to make sure I wasn't missing any steps. Your kindness towards me has been appreciated more than you know.

And finally, a big thank you to the incredible people I've met through Booktok who have been so supportive of me. (Some of you for years!!) You stuck with this project for so long and became its BETA readers, ARC readers, hype people, and most importantly, my friends. Thank you.

Alina Harper | TikTok, Facebook, Instagram, Goodreads, StoryGraph, Painted Red playlist |